BUTTERFLIES, PARATHAS
&
THE BHAGAVAD GITA

BUTTERFLIES, PARATHAS & THE BHAGAVAD GITA

A QUIRKY AND HEART-WARMING JOURNEY THROUGH GOD'S INSTRUCTION MANUAL FOR LIFE

S. HARI HARAN, M.D.

AMARYLLIS

AMARYLLIS

Copyright © S. Hari Haran 2017

All rights reserved. No part of this book may be used or reproduced, stored in or introduced into a retrieval system, or transmitted, in any form, or by any means (electronic, mechanical, photocopying, recording or otherwise) without the prior written permission of the Publisher. Any person who does any unauthorized act in relation to this publication may be liable to criminal prosecution and civil claims for damages.

The names, characters and incidents depicted in the story part of the book are fictitious. Any resemblance to actual persons, living or dead, or actual events is purely coincidental.

S. Hari Haran asserts the moral right to be identified as the author of this work

This edition first published in 2017

AMARYLLIS

An imprint of Manjul Publishing House Pvt. Ltd.
• 7/32, Ansari Road, Daryaganj, New Delhi 110 002
Website: www.manjulindia.com

Registered Office:
10, Nishat Colony, Bhopal 462 003 - India

Distribution Centres:
Ahmedabad, Bengaluru, Bhopal, Kolkata, Chennai, Hyderabad, Mumbai, New Delhi, Pune

ISBN 978-93-81506-93-6

Printed and bound in India by
Manipal Technologies Ltd., Manipal

CONTENTS

Author's Preface — vii
Acknowledgements — xi

VISHAADA YOGA
World — 3
Scripture — 47

SANKHYA YOGA
Life — 59
Mind — 94

THE YOGA OF KARMA AND DYAANA
Karma — 129
Karma II — 161
Dyaana — 218

THE YOGA OF BAKTHI AND JNAANA
Bakthi — 257
Jnaana — 269
Jnaani — 300

SARANAGATHI
World II — 323
Surrender — 347

Appendix — 394
References — 401
Further Reading — 406
About the Author — 409

AUTHOR'S PREFACE

Swami Vivekananda, returning from giving his renowned Chicago address at the Parliament of Religions, proclaimed the following words to a gathering in Chennai, 'Before flooding India with socialistic or political ideas, first deluge the land with spiritual ideas. The most wonderful truths confined in our scriptures... must be brought out from the books, brought out from the monasteries... and scattered broadcast all over the land, so that these truths may run like fire all over the country.'

The visionary monk saw that it was the knowledge of their spiritual roots and the right inspiration from it that can do more good to the people of our country than social and political revolutions.

This book is a bow to that call. A tribute of a scientifically trained mind to the Bhagavad Gita, and Hinduism. I, the author of the book, have been through a decade-long intellectual world tour – through various psychological, philosophical and spiritual theories of the West – only to come back and find it all articulated already, and quite well, in our own backyard; in the ancient teachings of Vedanta. Having got introduced to those sublime teachings, I felt that those treasure troves of spiritual knowledge of our country should be imparted to people who can benefit from it the most, our youngsters, in a way that connects with and appeals to them. And that feeling wouldn't leave me. Hence this book.

I have to concede here that I am no scholar of the Gita and its Vedanta philosophy. I have only attempted to reframe and present those principles from the viewpoint of a worldly man of our times, along with all the difficulties and challenges one would face when trying to follow the Gita. It is my experiences I have presented in this book in a fictional form.

Many great Gurus have written beautiful commentaries on the Gita. This one is by an inquisitive, rational-thinking student. After all, the well-meaning words of a parent to the child, say, to quit smoking, may not always be heeded. However, when a friend, an erstwhile smoker advises so, it has a greater impact. It is in such a spirit I wrote this book.

The book's intention is by no means to exhaustively cover all the truths the Gita puts forward. That would be like trying to put an oak tree inside a matchbox. All this book aims is to introduce its readers to certain key ideas shared in the Gita and perhaps inspire them.

There are many interpretations of the Gita. In this work, I have stuck to the classical Advaitic interpretation. The Gurus whose words I have mainly depended upon are Swami Vivekananda, Sri Ramakrishna, Sri Aurobindo and Sri Ramana Maharishi. I have drawn liberally from their works to explicate the principles outlaid in the Gita.

Though the book cover bears my name, to say 'I wrote it' would be like an envelope claiming ownership for the precious cheque it contains. All this author has done is string together in a pragmatic way the words of those spiritual masters, and course through the Gita's philosophy through that. Truly, it is to those great gurus all credit belongs.

This book doesn't follow the progression of ideas in the Gita. It courses through the philosophy taking up the existential questions about our world and life that are in our hearts, and discusses what the Gita, and the Upanishads, have to say on that. I hope the purists don't mind the liberty I have taken!

For the philosophy to be of maximum benefit to you, consider your first reading a starting point, a springboard. Mark the portions that appeal to your present state of mind and return to them later. Read the corresponding verses in the Gita and their commentaries. Don't accept anything at face value. Debate with what is said. Perhaps you can journal your thoughts side by side as you read the book. If it feels right for your heart, then contemplate on how you can translate it into your own specific situation. Think about specific steps you can take. Then do it. That is how mere book knowledge becomes wisdom; an integral part of your being.

Lastly, dear reader, whoever you are, to even pick and read such a book shows that you have a genuine quest for truth in you. A quest you have managed to keep alive despite all the pressing and swerving worldly forces. My salutations to that, for in that I see the Divine waiting to emerge. To that Divine spark in all I dedicate this work.

Writing this book was an inspiring and transformative journey for me. I sincerely hope reading it is too.

S Hari Haran

ACKNOWLEDGEMENTS

I owe a deep debt of gratitude to several people who were instrumental in me writing this book.

Imagine a boy after finishing his medical post-graduation and in the middle of his practice telling his parents that he wishes to do something else in life, and is planning to take a semi-break from his active medical practice. Many parents would have hesitated to agree. I thank my parents for saying yes (though not without a frown), and for the freedom and financial support they gave me. (A note about the protagonist's parents in the story: Those were characters brought in to serve as a foil for the philosophy. In no way is that a reference to my parents.)

I must thank my wife Viji for the unconditional love and support she gave me throughout the work, managing our kid on her own most of the times. Without that, this book wouldn't have been possible. And thanks to my father-in-law Sri Sankara Narayanan for introducing me to Vedanta.

Several people played crucial parts in the making of this book. My friend Krishna Raj gave me an honest assessment of the work and his invaluable suggestions have added quality to the work. My friend Dr Jim Jeba Kumar took pains to draw the illustrations for the book in the middle of his pressing commitments. My brother Vignesh helped me a lot with the technical work. My friends Dr Ganapathy and Dr Shraddha helped in fine-tuning the work, as much as their busy minds allowed. Shuchi Kalra helped with the editing of the book. Sidique helped me with the DTP work for the entire text. Thank you all. And thank you to the artists at Power Publishers, Kolkata for their drawings.

I am indebted to my uncle Sri Surya Narayanan for the generous help he did for the initial version of this book.

The illuminating treatises of the writers William Zinsser and Stephen King on the art and craft of writing, were of great assistance to a first-time author like me.

A special thanks to Vaijyanti Ghose, my impeccable editor, for making what was an unwieldy manuscript crisper and readable for a general reader.

Lastly all my friends, relatives and well-wishers spread across the globe who have wished me well. Thank you all. Your wishes matter.

Vishaada Yoga

WORLD

Whenever there is decline of dharma and a rise in adharma,
I manifest myself in the world.
And boy, do I have fun watching you humans mess it all up!

Like me, haven't you too thought that is how the renowned verse from the Gita should have gone; especially when you look at today's world with all its maddening conflicts and strife?

Now that I have got your attention with that bizarre opening, let me turn solemn. I first sat down to read the Gita, the supposedly God-sent scripture, many years back. All I was wondering then was whether with the hectic modern life whizzing past us at a frenzied pace, is it really feasible for us now to follow the wisdom of this ancient scripture?

Probably you too are thinking along those lines as you start reading this book. Or maybe you are wondering, 'Why bother to read the Bhagavad Gita? I do believe that there's a higher power controlling us all. But is it only through some ancient cryptic scripture it communicates with us? Has it stopped talking to us ever since?'

Or perhaps your thinking is a bit more radical, 'God and his holy word! The whole idea is for me a big time, major league mumbo jumbo. What can a scripture tell us that we do not already know?'

Fair enough. I am not going to answer them now. You will have to go through this book on the Vedantic philosophy of our country to arrive at the answers yourself – just like I did.

What is that 'Vedantic Philosophy'? The word Vedanta literally means 'culmination of knowledge,' and is considered to be the philosophical essence of Hinduism. Vedanta is concerned with answering questions like 'Who are we really?' 'What are we doing here?' 'Who is God?' and so on. And intriguingly enough, it is not so widely read or followed by Hindus, at least the ones I know. The philosophy is expounded in some lofty-sounding philosophical poems in the Upanishads.

It is this Vedantic philosophy the Gita gives an overview of in its seven hundred verses. If it were not for the Gita, we would have to go through the Upanishads and arrive at those truths ourselves. To fathom what a mighty task that would be, consider this: the Upanishads are more than two hundred in number, with the principal ones alone numbering around fifteen.

When compared with the wild garden of the Upanishads, the Gita is like a bouquet of the choicest flowers, with Vedantic truths beautifully arranged together in proper places, in Swami Vivekananda's words.

There is a Dyaana shloka about the Gita—

The Upanishads are like a cow.
Shri Krishna is the milker of that cow.
Arjuna is the young calf seeing which,
milk flows from its udders.
The nectar-like milk of these Upanishads
is the Bhagavad Gita. This the wise drink.

It is this Vedantic philosophy that we are about to get a taste of in this book as the narrator journeys through the Gita. Allow me to introduce you to him.

Have you seen a child play in the rain? I see one before me now; no, actually two. Our narrator is one of them. Some events are so vividly etched in our memory that each time we think of them, we see them happening right before our eyes. Those two little boys in the rain has been one such sight for me. It is those boys who are going to come to terms with the philosophy of the Gita and share it with us.

One is spinning under the raindrops, his head tipped back slightly and arms outstretched. *'Hey come . . . see if you can spin like this,'* he calls out the other boy. The other boy gestures *no*. He is content standing near the auto-rickshaw and watching the raindrops bouncing off his little hands.

'Venki, why don't you stay in the auto? I am coming with the umbrella,' comes the sudden loud voice of the maid from the house of one of the kids. She opens the tall wrought iron gate and comes running out towards the spinning kid.

'Okay, bye *da*. See you tomorrow,' the kid bids goodbye to his friend and merrily enters the house.

There he finds his parents arguing rather bitterly with each other in the drawing hall.

'I am not going to be mum anymore and keep listening to you telling me how impossible I am. Have you ever looked at yourself?' his dad yells at his mom.

'God! You are so unconcerned about me and my feelings. You exaggerate everything,' his mom retorts furiously.

They are in no mood to engage with their child. Venki had felt pretty frightened seeing them fight the first few times. But he had gotten accustomed to it now.

He goes and sits in the puja room opposite his grandpa, who is chanting aloud from the *Vishnu Sahasranama* in his hands. Starting to repeat those names along with his grandpa as he usually does, he turns and looks again at his parents quarrelling outside. A deep sigh escapes him.

His friend, the other boy was dealing with a much larger crisis. This boy had been born to a loving couple, and he was immensely fond of his mother. Every evening, as he returned from school, she would welcome him with a loving hug. However, only a week ago while giving birth to her second child, his mother had developed uncontrolled post-partum bleeding and had passed away tragically.

The auto-rickshaw next halted before the narrow, unpaved street in Ambedkar colony that day. The boy got down from it and entered his house. There, he saw his father seated in a corner of the hall, staring vacantly at the photo of his wife on the wall. He saw his newborn little brother sleeping in his father's arms. He walked slowly towards them. Sensing his presence, his father put the sleeping baby down on the bedding and got up. That was the day he had sent his son to school after a week-long leave.

'Perhaps this is all a dream, and we will wake up soon my dear Santosh, we will wake up soon,' he said embracing the boy. 'May God help us!'

Indeed pretty difficult situations for two five year olds to be in, right? Yet that's life. The Gita itself will tell us more about this. The timeline of this story isn't those boys' childhood though, so we fast-forward twenty-three years.

༄

Tuticorin, a scorching hot, heavily polluted coastal town in the southern corner of Tamil Nadu. It is a town known for its power stations, salt pans, shipping industries, and also for its *parottas* and bakery products. That is where this story takes place.

Almost all of the city should be sleeping at this hour, but we find the narrator, the first boy, sitting on the terrace and reading something in the cold of the night.

The guy's name is Venkat, named after Lord Venkateswara of Tirupathi, who his mother was an ardent devotee of at the time of his birth. Now, however, she has shifted her devotions to Dattu Baba, the new sensation in spirituality, who his devotees perceive as the incarnation of Lord Krishna. But the narrator considers it all bogus and hates the man's fanatical organisation.

With constantly quarrelling, unconcerned parents and a fat bank account, what would a boy become? Probably someone who takes to the pleasures of life and ends up a boozer, lecher or a drug addict, yes? However, Venki did not indulge in any of those and has become a straightforwardly pleasant man, a dermatologist to boot!

Venki, now a twenty-seven-year-old, completed his long-drawn-out studies just a few months ago and is presently looking to establish his practice in his hometown. How on Earth did he go on to become a doctor, you wonder? Well, he will tell us in a short while. The next pages of this book are about him coming to terms with the philosophy of the Gita and about the transformation it brought about in his life and in the life of Santosh, his friend.

Santosh, aka 'Sandy' as he likes being called, the other boy in the rain that day, is another young medical practitioner. 'A psychiatrist looking for my share of mad people in the world,' as he puts it. Venki and Sandy were classmates from preschool to college. And they did their post-graduation from the same institution too.

The two men are a study in contrast. Venki, at first glance, even at second or third glance, doesn't exactly fit the traditional image of a doctor. He is rather short, plump and looks like, well, the son of a rich father. His friends sometimes fondly call him 'Piggy,' after which they invariably have to run for their lives. Sandy is a tall, good-looking guy – an unfairly good-looking guy, I'd add – with coffee-brown eyes and a beckoning smile.

Venki is a quintessential small-towner. He loves his town, and gets edgy when he has to stay away from it for long. (Two other things that make him edgy: speaking in English and talking to girls, especially the fair-skinned, good-looking ones.) Gorging on good food, watching new-age Tamil films, and listening to Tamil *kuthu* songs are some of his chief interests. Thanks to his grandpa, he has a secret religious/philosophic streak in him, which he doesn't like showing to people. About Sandy... well there's too much for me to describe. Read and find out all about him and his lousy ways for yourself.

So let us return to Venki now, who is sitting on the terrace under the night sky – with the Bhagavad Gita in his hands.

ॐ

I looked at myself, sitting on the terrace under the night sky, without a tinge of sleep in my eyes holding the Bhagavad Gita in my hands. It felt strange! How the book has thrust itself into my life! I looked back at the day gone by. Man, what a hell of a day! Thank God I walked out of the bar midway without having my drink.

'It is fine when you have an occasional drink for recreation. But the moment you resort to it when you are a bit frustrated or dejected, take it from me, you take your first steps towards addiction,' Rajagopal Sir's words rang in my ears.

I looked around. It was a moonless, pitch-black night in the middle of August. The same darkness seemed to pervade my senses. How strange some days are! It is, in fact, funny that this chaotic day has ended with me putting my faith in a higher wisdom, and trying to connect with it through the Gita.

Vasudevah Sarvam Iti.

None of what the Gita says was feeling right. Sandy's words at the bar, his nasty philosophy of life, was still echoing in my ears, overpowering the Gita's verses. What a louse the guy has become! I have often accompanied people to bars to have an occasional drink, but this was my first visit to a bar in Tuticorin. I hope none of my prospective patients saw me. It all started when I asked him *that* question.

ॐ

'Do you come here alone every day, Sandy?'

Every table was occupied in the dimly-lit room of the bar. The lights alternately flickered a gaudy red and green. A loud percussion piece was blaring through the two-foot-high speaker beside us.

'Well, almost every day, and mostly alone. Sometimes Kumar comes along,' he said taking a sip from his glass. Kumar is our school friend who runs a browsing centre.

'And *why* do I come alone? That you have to ask other people, Venki boss. It's like . . . they hate me when I'm drunk! You know why?'

He drew his face closer to mine until I could clearly see the droplets of sweat punctuating his forehead. 'Because I express things that they harbour deep in their hearts, the fears, the unacknowledged truths . . . things they don't want to hear. And they just can't handle it.'

'Oh, is that it? And what are those truths they don't want to hear?' I asked matter-of-factly, with a hint of sarcasm.

I am not used to giving credence to anything Sandy says when he is drunk. But now, how I wish I hadn't asked that question! Looking back at how the day went since the beginning, it is no wonder I asked it though. There had been a series of events that made me accompany Sandy to the bar that day.

☙

When I glanced at my watch, I noticed that the enamel coating on its rim was wearing off. It was 9:30 in the morning and labourers were busy installing the aluminium partition and signboard for my new clinic.

SKIN CARE CENTRE
Dr Venkat Duraisingam MBBS, DD
Consultation timings: Mornings: 10 AM–1 PM
Evenings: 6 PM–9 PM

'Is it okay, Sir?' one of the men installing the signboard asked.

'Fine,' I answered.

I saw Sandy's signboard sitting outside, waiting to be installed next.

Dr Santosh Shanmugam MD (Psychiatry)

This was a nice feeling indeed, both of us returning together after a decade-long journey past school and settling in the familiarity of our hometown.

My eyes again fell on the name on his board. However, I wondered, are we the same people now, and is our relationship the same as it was when we had been in school?

The degree printed behind his name made me a bit jealous. I marvelled at the drastic manner in which the guy had improved in his studies since his first-year debacle.

'*Distance-la moonu moonu. Moonu colouru white-u . . .*'

The worker gave me a funny look. I took out my cell phone, silencing it with some embarrassment and muttering to myself, 'Uh-oh! I must change that holiday ringtone before I sit for practice!'

It was Dany, my junior colleague in post-graduation.

'Hi Dany, how're things?'

'Venki, have you heard the news? Sameer passed away this morning.'

'Is it . . . ?'

I was expecting the news, yet it came as a shock.

'He had respiratory failure. They kept him in M-III ICU. Rajagopal sir, it was his son's birthday, still he was with him all along! But to no avail. The boy died at 5 AM.'

'Oh?'

'How many sleepless nights we spent for the boy!' he sighed. 'When things like this occur, I don't know Venki, I doubt whether there is a God at all.'

'Oh, come on Dany. It all happens for a reason. We humans can't fathom everything with our minds.'

I said that to him. But as I put the phone back in my pocket, I saw my mind too wander in the direction of Dany's words.

Sameer was the young teenager in our ward I took care of in the last month of my post-graduation. When he was admitted under our dermatology department with generalised eczema and severe respiratory tract infection, I thought he was just another patient with atopic dermatitis, a fairly common disease of the skin. I was sure he would be okay and get discharged in a few days. I even reassured his parents rather presumptuously, seeing that they were eager to get him discharged soon so that he could return to college. His father was running a tea-stall in front of our hospital. He was popularly called *Muttakos bhai*.

'He is going to become the first graduate in our family, Sir,' his mother said to me, her hijab-covered face glowing with pride.

'Sure, we will try to discharge him before that. But only if you promise to invite us home for coming Ramzan,' I joked to his father.

However, life likes to land its mighty blows on us, when we least expect it perhaps. At his first glance at the boy, Rajagopal Sir had said, 'Get a peripheral blood smear and genetic study done. There is something syndromic about the boy's symptoms.'

The result of the genetic studies that arrived in a couple of days confirmed his suspicion. The boy had a severe type of Wiskott-Aldrich syndrome, a rare and debilitating hereditary immunodeficiency disorder. His blood smear showed that he had also developed cancer, a severe type of acute myeloid leukaemia. The seventeen-year-old had a year at the most to live.

'It is a surprise that he managed to survive this long,' Rajagopal Sir said, looking at the lean boy lying on the bed. 'It is more surprising that none of the doctors he consulted previously tested for this or even suspected it.'

The boy wasn't in a condition to talk as long as I was attending him. His vocal chords were immobile with pus accumulation.

It's not that I haven't seen such seriously ill young patients before, but what made me particularly remember Sameer and his parents was their faith!

'In the name of Allah the most beneficent and most merciful, when I am ill, it is He who heals me.'

Dany and I would be listening intently to such words coming from the vicinity of Sameer's bed. His parents often prayed to their god and one could feel the genuineness of their faith. They would sit near the boy's cot and read the Quran constantly except for the time when the doctors were to take their ward-rounds.

Sameer was their only child. He was born after nine years

of his parent's marriage, after his father returned from his first Haj pilgrimage, the mother informed us. The boy, too, was very pious for his age, we observed.

'Wherever he is, he does not miss one session of his *namaz*, Sir,' his parents proudly told us doctors. The family's faith seemed to comfort all the patients in the ward.

Sameer's condition seemed to improve slightly in the first few days, but it steadily declined thereafter, just as Rajagopal Sir had predicted.

By my last week at the hospital, even the strongest antibiotics were not working on Sameer. What good can external drugs do when the body has given up already? I handed over Sameer's case-sheet to Dany on my last day.

I vividly remember the last time I saw him and his family. Their faces were totally serene! They displayed a peace and composure that no words can capture. Despite all the hope they had pinned on their son, I felt they had accepted that his life was going to end soon, and they were at peace with it.

ॐ

Dnng . . . Dnng . . . Dnng. . . .

The workers were pounding the nails into the aluminium beading.

I have seen deaths before, of patients younger than Sameer. But somehow Sameer wasn't getting out of my mind.

Dnng . . . Dnng . . . Dnng. . . .

I walked out and called up Rajagopal Sir.

He sensed I was a bit upset. After all, I was in charge of Sameer for the entire last month of my post-graduation.

'These things happen, Venki,' he said. 'Poor Daniel. He too was very upset. Sometimes we feel so powerless, you know. You will get used to it with time. Oh, by the way, how's the new clinic work going? Preparing for the "butterfly period"?'

Sir calls the initial period of practice, 'butterfly period.' He used to tell us how he spent his free time as a young practitioner watching and tending to the butterflies that came to his clinic from the nearby nursery.

'My butterfly period lasted only six months, and I used to read many cookbooks during that time, trying out the recipes myself in my quarters. My wife still feels thankful to all the patients who went to other dermatologists in that time,' he would joke.

'But for you guys, times are tougher now. With the shady stuff and stray incidents in our field projected in a big way by the media, it seems people love to hate doctors these days. On the positive side, you can learn a lot more than what I learnt. Your wives could feel incredibly lucky,' he would add laughing.

Wondering how long I would have to wait for patients to trickle in I said, 'The Ganapathy Homa was conducted a week ago. I am planning to start my practice from tomorrow, Sir.'

'Okay, all the best.'

Well, Rajagopal Sir has seen enough to take things like these in a stride. But I was unable to get Sameer out of my mind.

What use was his faith to him or to his family? What effect did all his parent's prayers have? If there is a God, what the hell is he doing?

౧

'And what is that truth they don't want to hear?'

As I asked that question, Sandy, with great relish, started sharing his philosophy of life. 'This world and life in it, you know, Venki boss... *it just plain sucks.*' Leaning back on his chair, he continued, 'Even if no one wants to accept it honestly, the truth is that we are all trapped... terribly trapped inside this totally messed up, crappy world!' He raised his voice as the blaring speaker near us screeched to a high-pitched number.

'Whoa! Doesn't that sound a bit extreme?'

'Oh come on, don't fool yourself. What were we told as children? Study well, get a good job, marry, have kids, get old, retire, attend a few religious classes and... look forward to attaining *moksha,* right?'

The idiot was roaring drunk, still I asked, 'And what do you think is wrong with that?'

'What is *wrong*?' He had one more sip. 'Look at the

world . . . anyone in it. That same damn philosophy is what all are living by. You show me one person . . . just one person who is totally happy and satisfied. People . . . are . . . plain . . . stressed with this thing called life, Venki!' He spoke with long pauses.

'Life seems for most like . . . like a big, hostile demon holding them in a tight grip, from which they can't escape. Read any day's paper. Don't you see every single day, an unbearable dose of suffering and pain spread all over the pages? How does one respond to it all? All one can do is to forget the pain for a little while, seeking some sort of amusement. Did you read today's paper? A seventeen-year-old, his parents away, died, playing his video game nonstop for three days without any food!'

Sandy had one more sip and continued in a contemplative way, 'I often feel something has gone terribly wrong with the world's make, Venki boss. See what I mean?'

A music video was running on the 20-inch TV in the room's corner. A young actress was gyrating and stripping to a leering audience. Scant clothing remained on her body. A few men in the bar bawled excitedly, 'Come on, my girl, take it off, too!' Others turned to look at the TV.

After patiently listening to Sandy's lecture, I replied in return. 'Well. It is true that life is stressful for most. But isn't that the reason why you psychiatrists exist?'

'What? To help people lead a happy and productive life? You think so? My foot.' He took another sip. 'Venki boss, we just lower the volume of madness a bit. Do you know the first lesson a psychiatrist learns? *There is no normal person in the world.* Every single one of us here is mad in some way or another.

'Ask any psychiatrist and they will tell you. The people brought to my department are just those who have crossed the threshold. See the faces of people, at bus stands, in hospitals, religious shrines, wherever you want. The stressed out faces of worn out people . . . the burden, the confusion in them.'

He took a puff of his cigarette and continued, 'I tell you, Venki boss. This world we live in . . . bloody f***! It is one huge, mad, random, chaotic formation, and just facing it is plain stress.

There's no God, nothing. How do you explain tragic deaths like Sameer's, otherwise?'

ॐ

Vasudevah Sarvam Iti. All this world is divine.

The words of the Gita sounded so hollow. All that was echoing inside me loudly were Sandy's words. It was that which sounded more true. What kind of existence is this? Sandy seemed so right.

I had plenty of examples in my life as evidence of his philosophy. The prime one: the family I belong to; a deeply religious, rigidly traditional and totally dysfunctional one!

The patriarch of my family, my father, is a salt exporter and a well-known business figure in Tuticorin. Seeing me interact with him, you could easily mistake us for two unrelated people who bumped into each other on the road.

Mother is the type who gets up at five in the morning and does two hours of puja with the pictures, idols, and *yantras* her Guruji handed her. The day I remember seeing my parents happy together was last May when they were both getting ready for tours – to two separate destinations. My father was going with his business associates to Bangkok and my mother, with her Guruji and his other devotees to Manikarnika Ghat. 'It is the place where the Ganga river takes a turn in a new direction. It is a very auspicious place to visit before we die, our Guruji told us,' she beamed.

ॐ

I was driving my bike back home from the bar.

The crowd returning from a distant cinema hall was gathering momentum. Three emaciated, drunk men were lying unconscious on a platform near a temple. A lean bull, roaming the streets, was munching on a glossy film poster. Silence, a solid, blaring silence percolated the air.

All that Sandy told me echoed in my mind, 'messed up world, confused people, sleeping God.'

Maybe Sandy does have a point. The world *is* in chaos,

with no one up there to control it. Look at the world—the gory accidents, the horrible natural disasters, the grisly murders, the confusion, the pain.... If there were a God, with all his omniscience and omnipotence, couldn't he have done a better job?

And why blame people for their faults? The stress of facing such a 'huge, random, mad, chaotic' world does make everyone a bit mad with time. Mom's overt religiousness, dad's business-obsession and his pleasure-seeking ways, even Sandy's drinking and smoking were all symptoms of plain escapism from life, from facing the burden of real life as it is. All of us are escapists.

But then, what makes life so burdensome? How exactly does one face it the right way? Is there anyone I know who has approached it so, without resorting to such escapist ways?

Like a cool breeze on a hot summer day, the image of Big B came to my mind instantly. Not Amitabh Bachchan; for us, Big B means Barath Sir, our wonderful Barath Sir!

A good life begins with a good teacher, they say. Barath Sir was one such teacher for us. It was on the first day of our ninth grade that Sandy and I met him. I remember that day quite vividly.

CR

Santosh and I got down from the school bus and were entering through the school arch with the name *Sanskriti Hindu School for Boys* painted on it. Beneath the name there was a newly embossed India outline with the words *'India – my pride,'* at its middle.

'My pride? For what? All its corruption and overpopulation? Bulls**t!' I exclaimed. Then I turned to Sandy, 'By the way you know what? I heard that TK might be our class teacher this year.'

'TK? Oh my God!' Sandy was appalled.

We had done quite a few naughty things in his class the year before.

'Well, it's okay. When we have faith in ourselves, we are the all-powerful Hanumans, aren't we?' He repeated the lesson Rengarajan Sir taught in his class once, 'We can cross oceans.... This TK is just a small lake,' he guffawed, trying to conceal his dread.

As we walked towards our class, we heard the deafening horn of our doddering old school bus.

'What happened to our Benz today?' I asked aloud.

We turned around to find a little boy with braces on one of his legs trying to get down from the bus with his schoolbag and lunch box. Our driver, a pretty inconsiderate guy, kept blaring the horn impatiently.

Without a second thought, Santosh put his bag down, walked back swiftly toward the bus. He assisted that boy to get down, and offered to carry his bag to his class. All that happened in a flash, while I was still standing with the two school bags near me, watching.

Gayatri, the pretty face of Sanskriti Girls School, was in the bus looking at Sandy with great admiration. The boys' and girls' schools shared a bus until tenth grade.

Did I just say 'pretty'? Scratch that. She was a stunning beauty who would make every boy fervently wish for being born in her caste, as her close relative, and to get on the good side of her father—quite an authoritarian figure, from what I know—so that we get a chance to, ahem, become her life partner. One look at the girl, and I bet any boy of my age would find himself thinking like that. That is Gayatri.

I hated her looking at Santosh like that. I walked towards the bus, planning to offer to carry the boy's lunch box. She had turned away by then, though, and the bus had started to move towards her school.

The little boy smiled at both of us and walked ahead with Santosh as they struck up a conversation. Once again Santosh had taken the initiative to help someone in need, while most boys who got down from the bus hardly noticed it and were busy hurrying towards their respective classrooms.

'Man, I hate him when he does things like that' I mumbled within. Gayatri too was always looking at him admiringly. There is even a chance of her starting to love him soon, I felt.

'Rest assured, dear Santosh, I'll kill you if something like that happens.'

༄

'Get out of my class and stay there for the whole week you unruly brats,' TK Sir shouted at us with all his might.

He seemed so happy to get a chance to send us outside on the very first day of school. He caught us speaking in Tamil during class break. It was a punishable offence in our English medium school.

'All the rest, avoid moving around with those mischievous monkeys. Morons! Just get out of my sight.'

We came out and sat on the bench outside. Santosh was looking a bit jittery.

'What?' I asked him.

'I told you. See what you have done? Bloody Piggy!'

'Call me Piggy again . . . ' I said giving him with a dirty look, 'I'll kill you, I swear.'

'Ah, calm down. Didn't Rengarajan sir tell the story of Lord Vishnu incarnating as a boar to rescue the world?' he grinned. 'And how many times have I told you, to keep your mouth shut in TK's class?'

'*Maaps*,* how come your great sense of righteousness awakens only after you get caught? Where was this when you were reading that porn magazine last year in his class? Hey, look at us. We're just into the first day and we've already become outstanding students of the year. What a record!'

'Shut up, stupid.'

'And look at the hypocrisy of our people. We celebrate the day when the Englishmen left our country. Those guys tortured and murdered our people while they were here. They even treat us like s**t when we go to their country, but look at the pride we derive from talking their damn language fluently! Our people have an unbelievable complex about themselves, Santosh.'

---

*Maaps – short form of maapla, a Tamil slang with literal meaning 'Hi in-law,' but colloquially used to mean 'Hi dude.' Other versions of the word: maapi, maapu and so on.

'Well, don't try to rationalise your half-baked knowledge of the language in that way. Moreover, that doesn't mean you can voice obscene Tamil words loudly in class. Speaking of language, do you know what Kumar did last week, by the way?'

'What?'

'He joined a Prathmic class.'

'Really? Kumar wants to learn Hindi!'

'Hindi, my foot! He was hoping to meet some North Indian girls.'

'Ah, what noble intention! So what happened? Did our guy meet any?'

'Stupid! What North Indian girl would come to a class to learn Hindi?'

'Ah, ha ha ha . . .'

As Santosh and I sat outside the class guffawing loudly, we heard someone walk by. It was Barath Sir, our new assistant headmaster and physics teacher. That was his first year at our school. He was looking intently at us. He seemed quite surprised with the both of us laughing away sitting outside class on the very first day of the school year.

My heart was thudding in my chest. Santosh was squeezing his eyes shut in mortification.

ಙ

We got a good glimpse of him only later that day, on our way home in the bus. He seemed around fifty years old. He was tall, lean, and had a serene look about him. A self-assured half-smile seemed to play on his lips. We sat on the seat behind him, listening to his light voice and noticing his gentle demeanour.

'Quite soft, man, our new AHM seems to me,' I told Santosh, when we got off the bus. Barath Sir was a widower. His only child, a girl, worked in Chennai, we learned from one of our schoolmates.

'Wait and watch, he won't give us a hard time,' I added, with a forced hopefulness.

ಙ

It was true that Barath Sir did not make a big deal of our behaviour. But his arrival spelled doom on our old ways, in a manner we could not have expected.

I remember a particular incident even now. It happened during the fourth month of that school year. Every detail of that afternoon, including the green, broken paperweight lying on top of the staffroom steel table, remains vividly etched on my mind.

Barath Sir dropped the racy magazine on the table before us with a thud. He looked at us piercingly. Sandy, Kumar, and I—the culprits—were looking down at our feet. There was a moment of anxious silence. We darted stealthy glances at each other.

After having caught us red-handed in the middle of class, reading the magazine under our desks, he had asked us to come and meet him in the staffroom. All this was after we were the only ones to have fared badly in his monthly physics test.

'I wish to know what is in that magazine,' he said, calmly. 'Take the magazine and read a page for me, will you?'

'Sir . . . '

'I said, read it.'

Kumar read a portion from a page, as Sir had asked us to. He listened in silence.

'Now, tell me, in short, what you read.'

'Sir . . . ' we looked at him with dread.

'Come on.'

'It says actress Malini spends thirty-thousand rupees every month for her Chihuahua puppy, sir,' Kumar answered.

'That was all? I heard you read more.'

'Sir . . . '

'Come on. I want to hear you say it all.'

We spelled out all the tittle-tattle and the not-so-holy stuff that was printed on the page about Malini and her pet dog.

'Mmm, not bad.'

I still feel awful when I think of that day. What a ghastly thing to undergo! Getting caught by a respected teacher like Barath Sir with a magazine full of lewd stuff!

But the episode didn't go as we expected. That incident was, in a way, the turning point in both my life and Sandy's. Even Sandy would agree. It was the day when 'the two mischievous monkeys of the class,' as we were called back then, learned what it meant to do well in studies and actually started doing it.

Barath Sir gave us his copy of our ninth grade physics book and asked us to go through Newton's laws of motion, along with their mathematical statements.

'I give you people ten minutes,' he said and went to have his lunch. He was on a break, so he had time to deal with us at his leisure, much to our dismay.

Kumar heaved a sigh, coming out of the staffroom. 'Man, we are done for!' he said. 'At least we didn't get caught with the Debonair we read yesterday. That would have been even worse.'

He then grabbed the book from my hands. 'Newton boss, where are you? KKK LLL MMM Na Na Ne . . . Damn! Look at this index. The index itself needs an index, it seems. Yeah, got it . . . page 57. My God! You see this? It is one and half pages long, da. We are going to get killed today. We still don't know about this man, how he will beat people . . . with hands itself like our HM or with a cane like TK. We are going to be the first.'

'Shut up and give it to me,' said Santosh, snatching the book from Kumar's hands and starting to read what was on the page. 'I have told you guys so many times and what did you tell me? 'It's no thrill reading it at home. Doing it in the middle of the class gives a real kick!' Now you are going to know what 'real kick' means . . . and along with you, me too. Bloody Piggy!'

'And there goes our friend, blaming us!' I said. 'How is it, Santosh, that the moral compass inside you starts functioning only after we get caught?'

'Shut up and listen to what I read, "Every body persists in its state of . . ."' Santosh started reading what was on the page.

When we returned to the staffroom, Barath Sir was washing his hands. 'What did you learn?' he asked turning towards us.

We tried reproducing what the page said. He smiled softly

at us three, as he came back and sat before us. The words he spoke to us next, well, without them, Sandy and I would not have become what we are today.

'That is not the way one studies, guys' he said. 'You see how much interest you showed in what was in that magazine? You read it in the middle of the class with all the noise around, and yet you knew what it said. How different do you think reading a chapter of physics is? *You do it to know what is said in it.* It is as simple as that.

'I feel you let the exams, possible canings, scolding and all that stuff enter your mind when reading your physics book. I'm telling you, forget all that! There won't be any such thing in my class. Read only to know. I repeat, only to know. Regarding my subject, it is okay if you remember the concept alone without a single word in the book. I'll take care of the marks.'

We were standing there looking down, darting bemused glances at each other. I was surprised that he was not going to thrash us like our HM.

Barath Sir then asked us to read the portion on simple harmonic motion. 'Try and read it this time like you read about that dog of your heroine, and tell me what the page says.'

As we stepped out and tried to do as instructed Kumar muttered, 'What's up with this guy? I was limbering up my hands for receiving the caning and he gives a pretty innovative punishment.'

When we gave him the gist of what we had understood Barath Sir said, 'Good attempt, but do you know why it still appears difficult to you? It is because you have been trained this way. That's alright, though. You can train yourself in a new way when you are aware of it. No subject is interesting in itself, be it that actress and her dog, or these bodies in motion. Interest is what you bring to it, guys.'

He gave us an assignment for the following day and let us go.

'God, I think the caning would have been a much easier punishment da,' said an exasperated Kumar.

However, Santosh and I fared slightly better the next day.

'Good,' said Barath Sir with an acknowledging smile. 'As

I said, interest is what you bring to it. And you boys, at your age, should be careful where you focus your energies. The darned simple harmonic motion and Newton, if you bring your interest to them, will do you good. But Malini and all your actors and sportsmen won't! Distractions around us are so many, but it is your duty that you should bring your interest to, always. I feel happy that you are slowly getting a drift of the process.'

We were listening silently.

'When you try and connect to this joy in learning, then you will see a chain reaction starting to set in. You will relish knowing more and more about the subject. You will even read outside references with interest, in newspapers and magazine articles, when you come across them.'

'What da? What do you guys think? Some strange things our new teacher is telling us!' I said to my friends as we left the staffroom.

'Venki, without whacking us up, the man is asking us to do something constructive. Let us give it a try,' said Sandy.

'Okay, guys. Do whatever you want. But don't come to me hereafter for Debonair,' said Kumar. 'I have already bought this month's issue, and it features some really hot pictures.'

We never resorted to Debonair again. (Well, at least during the class.) Those words of Barath Sir connected deep enough for Sandy and me. That he didn't make an issue of our behaviour and spread the news of it around, the way TK sir would have done, gave us confidence in him and his words. In order to bolster our confidence, he gave us regular assignments, slowly acclimatising us to the new way. Our classmates noticed our improved performance in the exams and responded with awe. This gave us further incentive.

Kumar wasn't able to make the shift, somehow. His disinterest ran too deep perhaps. 'What, da? 89 and 91! Are those really you guys' marks in physics?' His mournful face as he asked that is still vivid in my mind.

However, for Sandy and me, that simple principle Sir shared that day was an invaluable treasure. We, the most unruly students of the class till then, saw ourselves slowly starting to perform well academically. It is like pure magic, when I think about it now.

He wasn't just a physics teacher for us students. He would talk about global warming in his class and our responsibility towards stemming it, about Krishna and Jesus, about Sun Tzu and Helen Keller, about world politics and India's role in that, about common themes in every religion, and whatnot! He relished his job to the core. The interest students were showing in his class and the unprecedented high averages in his subject inspired other teachers too, and that lifted our whole school to a new level. It even made a few people like our Head Master jealous of him.

ଔ

Apart from teaching, he had another passionate interest: spirituality. This appeared quite intriguing to us. Occasionally he would bring up topics such as Vedanta and Bhagavad Gita into his physics classes. He would often tell us, 'These are the philosophical treasures of India every young Indian should know about. It can do great good to your life.' And saying that, he would switch over to a metaphysical mode of sorts.

And yes, we would try listening too, but in no time would this begin to drive us nuts. Or was it me alone who felt this way? Sir would pause in the middle if he started feeling students were losing interest. Even if others showed interest, one half-asleep boy in the second bench would always make him pause, me. He would stop his lecture, smile and say, 'Someday I'll make you read it. Wait and watch.'

I felt he wanted to acclimatise us to those ancient teachings of our country fervently, but didn't know how. He would appear like a child to me at those times.

We didn't exactly adore all the stuff he talked about, even though he tried hard to make them interesting. Yet, all students deeply adored the man.

ଔ

The last time Sandy and I met Barath Sir was on the day we got our medical admissions. I drove my scooter to Sandy's house to pick him up. His father was outside, and was about to leave in order to drop Santosh's younger brother to school.

I could sense how happy he was. A peon at the district collector's office, he had brought up both his children single-handedly, since his wife had passed away. Quite a strict Dad he was, Santosh used to tell me.

There was a grand function going on at the Lord Siva Temple near their house, funded by all the residents in Santosh's colony.

'Are you not participating in it, Uncle?' I asked, while waiting for Santosh. However, I realised right away that I shouldn't have asked so.

'Participating in it?' he smiled with a heavy sarcasm. 'Dear young man, these deluded beings, their belief in God and spending lakhs on him. . . . Do you know the reason for it all? Plain fear and lack of self-belief! Their God is just a servant to their whims. Stay away from such things if you wish to remain sane.'

He started pedalling off on his cycle. Saravana, Santosh's brother, was sitting on the small carrier-seat, waving enthusiastically to me.

I wondered why religious functions angered uncle so much. The sticker with the picture of a hammer and sickle, at the back of his cycle said a lot. But how then did he name his two children after God? Maybe it was his wife's wish!

'*Dei*, get ready soon da. How much time are you going to take?' I called out to Santosh.

I checked the time in the watch that he had gifted me a day earlier.

'Hey stupid, what is this?' I had asked him, surprised.

Santosh replied, 'Venki, it was Barath Sir who made us both study, but without you around, and without all the resources you helped me with, I wouldn't have made it into medicine. You should accept it.'

He tied it around my hand as we were sitting on the beach. 'You and your sentimentality! Thanks, anyways' I replied as I beamed.

It was 10:30 AM now.

'I will drive' Santosh said as he came out of the house.

We were on our way to the school to meet our teachers. As the scooter was crossing North Agraharam Street, I asked 'Maapi, haven't you informed your girl Gayu of our plans? I thought she will be in the balcony and I have to go away for my tea to Raja's canteen as usual.'

He smiled, and glanced at her house. She wasn't in the balcony. Gayatri, that stunning beauty, and Santosh were in love. Love! In just twelfth grade! Girls always seemed to prefer such tall and good-looking boys. My dark skin, short and stout build and a face exactly like my father, didn't exactly enchant them. Anyhow, Santosh's and Gayatri's was not just the puppy love of adolescence; there was genuineness in their relationship.

'What is she planning to do next?' I asked Santosh.

'She wants to do BE in REC. She has got her free seat too, but her father is reluctant to send her out of town it seems' Santosh said.

'Why don't you advise your future father-in-law?'

He turned towards me, gave an unhurried, angry stare and said 'Maapi, say that a little louder. We will both get killed right here. Iyer will be roaming around in his cycle somewhere near, surely.'

'Oops! When are you people planning to disclose your love to your families, then?'

'Let us finish our education first.'

'Doctor weds engineer, huh?'

ॐ

We had reached our school and had finished meeting many of our old teachers. We chose to meet Barath Sir last so we could spend some time with him during lunch break. His class was going on inside. Knowing how involved he would be, we waited outside on the bench – the same bench we were quite used to sitting on during TK Sir's classes.

We heard a student's voice coming from the classroom. 'The usual Barath Sir stuff, Santosh!' I said.

Sir would select a student from the class, usually one who was weak at the subject, and ask him to prepare the theoretical topics for the following day. He would give the student a short outline of the topic and the necessary materials to prepare it. Once he has made the presentation, Barath Sir would add the missing links and finally conclude his lecture. That was his usual way of teaching in higher secondary. This way all the boys would be confident that they too could grasp the topic as their classmate had made the presentation.

He would often give Santosh and me tough topics to prepare together. We used to cherish the challenge. Not that we were very hard-working or bright compared to certain other subject-possessed devils from our class. But because it was our nature to ask questions to irritating limits, until our adamant minds grasped the subject, Sir believed we would do justice to the tough topics. He was sure that the once-average students taking on such topics would appeal to all students in the class.

He often said that there are three types of learners. The first type learn by reading, the second through listening, and the third by doing things. He categorised me as the first type and Santosh as the second. Therefore, it was his belief that we performed well when we studied together. 'Though Santosh is brighter among the two, it is he who benefits the more from the combined study with Venkat, given their studying styles. He should thank Venki for that,' I had heard him tell our class teacher. Perhaps, that was why Santosh presented me with the watch!

'What, Venki?' Santosh asked me. 'The bell has already rung and Barath Sir is yet to come out of his class? Has he found out the truth about the so-called research paper we won the prize for in junior scientist?'

He said it loud enough, not caring that it could reach Barath Sir's ears!

'Shut up, idiot. He might hear it.'

I had a funny feeling that the 'honesty-virus' has infected him again.

'Hello! my boys, how are you? What good news have you come to share?'

Barath Sir had finally come out. I noticed the smile on his face was a few millimetres wider than usual. We got up. Santosh told him why we had come.

'Both have got your seats in Tirunelveli Medical College! That's great . . . just great,' he said. 'Come, let's celebrate.'

ಙ

We were walking towards the canteen outside our school. Students were greeting Barath Sir as they passed by him and he made it a point to return each one of their wishes. He always did that.

We crossed a white Maruti van parked near the gate. On its side-door, I chanced upon the reflected image of Big B, with me and Santosh walking behind him.

Like a passing wind bringing out a chunk of trash from a garbage can, many images swarmed inside my mind; the carefully torn cigarette covers in my room, the self-signed progress cards, the low attendance notices to parents . . . and much more! I looked at Sir. This man has taken up two worst cases in the class and made doctors out of them. An internal conversation ensued: *'Let all that trash lie in the trash can. I promise I'll not resort to any of those things hereafter, Barath Sir,'* I took an oath.

'Relax, maaps. How is an occasional smoke going to interfere with your studies?' a part of me questioned.

I smiled and ignored it.

ಙ

When I placed the order across the counter and came back towards our table, I saw Santosh talking to Sir. He was still looking a bit too serious for my taste. We gave Barath Sir the plum-cake parcel we had especially bought for him.

'Come on guys, why such formalities?'

'No, Sir, just for our satisfaction.'

'Okay, if you insist.' He accepted it.

The lone waiter placed the three tumblers of orange juice that we had ordered on the table. Sipping the juice, Barath Sir spoke to us, 'You can relax and enjoy your learning more in college than school. After all, medicine doesn't have the painful grade systems. Even I hate pushing students so much towards these high grades, you know? Venki can be as enthusiastic in your studies and you Santosh can be as inquisitive as you were in school without worrying too much for the marks.'

'Yes, Sir. We too hope to do well. And, Sir, we heard you have been appointed the secretary for the magazine committee. We are really, really waiting to read it. Reserve a copy for both of us, please!'

The annual magazine was a big thing in our school. Copies would be given to all the students and would be sent to all the registered alumni. A hefty amount of money would be spent on the magazine annually, sponsored by many Hindu spiritual organisations. In return, a lot of their Hindu philosophy and thoughts would be written about, all over the pages of the magazine. As far as I know, no one read those things, but we knew if Barath Sir took on a job, he would do it amazingly well. He wouldn't allow such cursory things to be a part of the project. Besides that, we too would have a souvenir to his memory.

He smiled in acknowledgement and said, 'Yes, I'm fully occupied with the magazine these days.' He had a sip and continued. 'Instead of the ten-page-long prayers and invocations that our 'Hindu School' insists on printing at the beginning, I'm trying to write a short summary of the Gita, a very simple one for students to follow.'

'Here he goes again,' I thought.

'After all, the Gita has so much for you students standing on the verge of a sea change in your life. I feel you people miss out a lot, by not being acquainted with such a treasury of wisdom that our country has given to the world. Even men such as Emerson and Thoreau, who were instrumental in shaping the American psyche, were greatly influenced by the Gita, you know? However, much as I know it, I am just not able to write it at all. I am reluctant to write it all by myself.

'Our boys hardly listen to such things in the class. Who would read it? I am sure about this though, I don't want it to be something that people flip through cursorily. I really want to present it in an appealing way to the boys here so that they read it. It is a golden opportunity to introduce our students to it. It was then that I thought that maybe I can do it with the help of a student.'

Saying this, he abruptly stopped and looked at us.

I wondered whether he expected us to do it. I shook my head disapprovingly in a rather obvious way. Not bothering with my thoughtless gesture, he continued with his eyes fixed on the glass tumbler before him.

'No compulsions, but try going through the book if you can. It is available along with beautiful commentaries in every shop. Not the entire thing, I'll give you just a few important verses. Here.' He searched in his shirt-pocket, took out a folded paper from it and handed it to us.

'You know what? I was actually expecting both of you to come over, so I could give you this job. Just like your physics lessons, if you can give me a write-up as you understand it honestly, as you would share it with your friends, with all the questions that arise in you when you read it, it will be of great help to me, you know, to take it on from there. Of course, it would influence your life too in a good way.

'More than the cake you gave him, this Big B would consider such a write-up a greater gift from you. You two have always done that job better than other guys in your class.'

I was astounded to find that he knew our nickname for him.

And *Bhagavad Gita*? An assignment even after we finished school? That too, on a book like that?

We sat there exchanging uncertain glances with each other.

'We will try, Sir,' said Sandy.

'Lazy fellows,' he said, with a thoughtful smile sensing our reluctance. 'Do it only if you can, but know that you will make your Sir very happy if you do it. Alright guys, enjoy your college life. Do some good post-graduation that is not there in our town and then come back.'

He was about to finish his juice and was getting ready to leave. I felt like stretching the time we had with him little more.

'Santosh said he will be more than satisfied doing just

MBBS, Sir. He plans to come back and settle in his mom's village, which doesn't have any medical facility.'

'That is very nice of you Santosh. What about you then?' he asked me.

'Um, I am not yet sure, Sir.'

There was a brief moment of silence as we were both sipping on the juice.

Then Santosh began speaking . . . to my shock!

'Sir, before we go, I need to confess something I did in plus one.'

I turned and looked at him wide-eyed, apprehensive of what he was about to do.

'That junior scientist research paper I submitted on Foucalt, which you still speak so highly of . . . that was plagiarised, Sir,' he said looking down.

Barath Sir frowned in surprise as Santosh said that. Then he turned and looked at me. Sandy continued, 'I started out well, but in the end, due to time constraints and pressure, I took a similar thesis that was done in a university in North India, changed the names, numbers and submitted it as mine. Sorry Sir, extremely sorry, I wanted to confess this before I finished school.'

He looked down and apologised again. I was looking at Santosh in disbelief. *'Is this fellow out of his mind?'* The entire incident seemed so surreal.

'Is it?' Barath Sir kept the glass of juice in his hands on the table. 'Have yours,' he said and walked away.

༶

We were sitting in Santosh's room in his house. I didn't say a word to him during the twenty minutes it took to drive back. Once in his room, I went at him with all I had, 'Happy now? Are you happy? You . . . you . . . moron. What do you think of yourself? Are you some perfect being from heaven? From where did you get this flash of honesty? You stupid, sentimental, idiot! What will Barath Sir think of us now?'

Read that last question, 'What will he think of *me*?'

He appeared nonchalant, looking out of the window. I wasn't sure he was even listening to my rant. Why was I shouting at him anyway? Wasn't it he who had confessed?

But I was his partner in the project and Barath Sir knew that. It was I who had compelled him to cheat in that thesis, in order to cut his work short.

'Okay tell me . . . tell me one good reason you had to say that to him on the final day? Open your mouth you a*****e.'

He turned towards me and spoke unhurriedly, 'Venki, if I had told you earlier, would you have let me?'

Again turning to the window he said, 'You may not realise now, but what I have done is good for us, even if we don't meet Barath Sir in our lives again. We won't live with this small burden in our hearts every time we think of him. And why do *you* worry so much? I told him only about me. If you want, you tell him honestly that you were involved too. See how light you feel.'

I was fuming and didn't know how to respond.

'I know you are very angry but think it over. You'll go your way in life and I will go mine. I will have to live with myself, right? A plagiarised thesis winning me a competition and our Barath Sir holding high opinion of me for this reason; this is such a burden for my heart.'

'Aah, if you feel bad about it then don't do it in future. Why the hell did you tell Barath Sir now? Why all this drama; to impress on your honesty to that f*****g lover of yours?' I blurted out in an inconsiderate way.

Even as I realised I shouldn't have said that, Sandy rushed towards me and grabbed my collar, 'What did you say? Say it again . . .'

I didn't say a word. I gave him a patient look and then looked around the room. There was a photo frame on his table with 'Me and U!' embossed on it. Maybe Gayatri had given it to him, I mused.

He said, 'Sorry,' and loosened his grip on my collar. 'I have no need to impress Gayatri. When I told her that this thing was bothering me, she suggested I confess to Big B.'

'What?'

'Yes.'

'Great! Truth-filled spiritual partners! Long live your relationship! Alright Mahatma, a big goodbye to you and your high and mighty ways. Let's part ways here. I don't want to be friends with such a freak anymore.'

I didn't even say bye to him as I drove out of his colony.

Nothing significant happened after that in our relationship with Big B. That thesis of ours was really inconsequential to him, and though he was a bit disappointed at first, he was happy with Santosh's honesty, we heard later from our juniors.

However, that wasn't the case with our friendship.

ଓ

Three months went by quickly. We entered college.

At the end of the first week, we were well into our dissection sessions in Anatomy.

'We have to split open this dead guy before us? Man, I just saw him wink at me,' joked my frivolous classmate, Mano.

But some nerds didn't mind. They showed all their zeal in the task, as if it were an apple or orange, and they didn't mind talking about their findings over a meal either.

The first month of life in medical school was akin to facing an alien world for many of us. The nerves of the transition period between school and college, the occasional ragging we got caught in, people fainting in dissection sessions, the heavy and wordy textbooks, amidst all that, seeing the familiar face of Santosh gave me so much relief that I went and spoke to him myself even though his melodramatic apologising and the nasty little exchange between us was still lingering at the back of my mind.

'Did you prepare the Gita write-up Barath Sir asked us to?' I asked him.

'Of course not' he said. 'How is that even possible, Venki?'

I smiled with a sense of relief. 'Imagine, the two of us reading the Bhagavad Gita! Our Big B, despite being such a down-to-earth man, gets carried away sometimes, doesn't he?'

'True,' he agreed.

'Look at the stuff his Gita says, 'Do thy duty. Forsake the results.' Ha, how easy sounding!'

However, it was not that we didn't try at all. Santosh told me he had got on till the middle of the third chapter but found it too difficult to follow the book's course and language. I, for my part, read it once and even reached the end while trying to find a cohesive outline. However, I found it difficult to come to terms with most of the ideas shared in the book – the 'don't depend on the world for your happiness,' 'be without desire,' and the 'live without me and mine' ideas. It all seemed too abstruse and fanciful. The book's flow was not easy to grasp and the subject matter, too other-worldly.

'We will get into such things after retirement. Anyway, Sir didn't insist on us doing it.'

'Yeah, right. Sir won't like empty excuses.'

'Yes, yes. He sure doesn't like such things.'

We couldn't have known then that destiny had already put its first decisive knot tying the Bhagavad Gita into our lives.

୧

Days became months and months became years. College life had many surprises in store for us. Life, more often than not, keeps progressing on its course unchanged for most. But its course can also at times undergo a total turnaround when we least expect it. Joy becomes sorrow, confidence becomes fear, virtue becomes immorality.

With no one like TK to brand me 'lousy' in college, combined with the respect people around started giving me as a medico, and the oath I took in my heart to Barath Sir, I saw myself transforming gradually in a new direction, much to my surprise.

'Dei Venki, what's with you these days? Does becoming a doctor mean you won't even smoke? Come on, man. Have a puff.'

'No, Kumar. I don't feel like doing these things nowadays.'

'To hell with you, Piggy.'

The fellow would run off calling me that name, before I could catch hold of him.

On the other hand, I saw Santosh's life take a drastic downhill course in college.

Academic pressures make medical students go through many sleepless nights before internal and semester exams. I too went through all that. However, three sleepless nights that had no connection with those exams punctuated my medical life. The first one was when the first semester results were announced.

Eighty of eighty-four students in our class had passed the exams and entered into their first clinical posting.

'A very good result, guys, compared to your senior batches,' our anatomy tutor said to us.

Mano, my roommate, and I reached the college office and eagerly looked up the marks against our names on the noticeboard. We both had prepared well and didn't expect to fail in Anatomy and Physiology. But we had done our Biochemistry exams really well, even to our surprise. We were expecting at least a first class in the subject.

'129' the numbers against my name read in biochemistry. That was a wonderful feeling.

'How have you fared?' I asked Mano.

'Hmm, my roommate has beaten me by one mark,' he winked.

We were really excited. From racking our brains over dry theory in books, we were finally going to enter the hospital premises and work with patients. I was standing with a few of my classmates and browsing through the results on the noticeboard.

'Venki, did you see who have failed?' asked Mano.

I looked at the names typed separately in red ink. The first name was Santosh.

A gasp escaped me as I read that. He had failed by three marks in Biochemistry.

'Oh! My God!'

The four students would become an additional batch and

would finish six months later. They had to attend further classes with the juniors, while the rest of us entered our clinical postings.

A thousand thoughts assailed my mind. How could this happen? How is he going to take it? Was it my mistake? Maybe I should have included him in the combined study with Mano. He even asked for it once. But his hostel room was quite far away ... and the risk of getting caught in ragging and all that if we walked out of our rooms at night.... But the distance from his room wasn't the only reason. It was the distance I started feeling from him since that melodramatic last meeting with Barath Sir and the squabble between us. That incident never left my mind. Was it because of that trivial reluctance that Santosh was facing such a crisis?

My God! If only I had known, I would have surely welcomed him into our darned study-group. Maybe he wouldn't have failed if we had studied together like in plus two. I should have realised what was happening by his low score in the internal tests.

Big B's words to my class teacher and Sandy's own words of affection as he gifted me the watch crossed my mind.

I drove straight to his hostel. He wasn't there. 'Where is he?' I asked his roommate.

'I don't know. He told me he'll return in a week.'

'A week?'

I called up his house. He wasn't there either.

That night I tossed and turned in bed for more than four hours before I was able to sleep, but a terrible nightmare woke me up within a short time.

Santosh had climbed a steep cliff. I helped him climb it. On reaching the top, he slipped and started falling down. I walked towards him, and coldly pushed him down! Then I turned a blind eye towards him and walked away!

I woke up abruptly. It was 2.40 AM I saw that I was sweating profusely.

I went for a walk in the hostel corridor.

The night was pitch-black. A heavy silence pervaded the air.

Santosh's eyes in that dream – the helplessness in them, the sense of being let down – I could still see all of those vividly in my mind's eye. It felt like a thorn pricking my heart from the inside.

'No, I didn't push him down,' I heard myself saying out loud.

'Not helping him while he was falling down, comes down to that,' a voice within me retorted.

Not knowing what else to do, I prayed for him to get through the tough period soon.

The next day I called up Barath Sir as some of my juniors in school told me that he seemed a bit unwell of late. We didn't prepare the last assignment he gave us, but we hadn't even spoken to him after that. It was the guilt perhaps, at not having done the job he gave us with so much hope. But after what happened with the results, I decided to contact him and talk about Santosh's situation.

'These fellows... they give too much hype to trivial things,' he said in response to my enquiries about his health.

I told him about Santosh.

'Santosh failed in the semester exam!' he exclaimed

'And he has become an additional batch, Sir. It is a pretty traumatic thing to undergo, for a first year student,' I continued.

'Oh?'

After a brief pause, Sir said in an assured way, 'Don't worry. I know Santosh. He will be disturbed but he will bounce back... and do even better. I know about him. Just tell him it will all turn out well.'

He didn't ask me about the write-up on the Gita. He was a true gentleman. He sensed that we weren't interested and left it at that.

ଓ

My second sleepless night came a week from that day. Santosh's roommate told me during the morning OP class that he had returned. I left immediately to meet him.

Santosh was lying on the bed with an old cine-weekly in his hands as I opened the door of his room. I sat down in front of him. He looked away, seeming a bit tired and dishevelled.

'How are you, Santosh?'

'Yeah, good' he said, getting up.

Silence, a solid silence reigned in the room for the next few minutes.

'So, how are the 'clinicals'?' he asked next.

A shiver of guilt ran down my spine. I nodded mutely.

A minute went by. He then put a marriage invitation before me.

'Gayatri weds Sri Ram BE, MS.'

Gayatri was being made to marry an engineer in the UK. He was twelve years older than her. Her father arranged the wedding in a hurry, when he came to know of her feelings for Santosh. Her relatives had all objected to the sudden plan. Still her father had forced to discontinue her BCom – the degree course he had forced her to take – and tie the knot.

'Oh, my God! This isn't happening!'

Now I was frantic with worry for Santosh. First the results and now this! I glanced at him. The tender love between him and Gayatri came to mind. Their relationship had been sincere. Her father could at least have waited. After all, Santosh had joined medicine. To avoid giving her to a boy of different caste, he got his daughter married at seventeen! How stupid!

Santosh hadn't initiated the love affair, Gayatri did. He was reluctant from the beginning as he saw the practical difficulties. He knew both their castes were diametrically opposite and getting the nod from parents wouldn't be easy.

'Ambedkar and Agraharam can't get together boss. Some lucky nerd born in her caste will be waiting for her,' the words he spoke when returning from a tuition during our tenth grade crossed my mind.

And even in that instance, it was I who insisted and made him agree.

'A girl is proposing to you so boldly. Be a man, dude,' I had urged him.

There was a wry smile on Santosh's face. I could see he was devastated. What consolation could I offer?

'Did you try talking to her?' I asked.

'I called her up,' he said, letting out a weary sigh. 'What could she say? She cried a lot, said 'sorry' a hundred times, then said 'best of luck for your future' before her father came in and she had to disconnect the call.'

His tone was indifferent.

'Where did you go?' I prodded.

'Nowhere specific. Just like that. Leave it. Tell me how is your first medicine posting going?'

༺

After those few months of academic break, he became much better in his studies, even better than I was, to my surprise. However, things took a downturn in his personal life. Something snapped inside him. Just like seeing a flower in bloom wither away before one's eyes, I gradually saw his ways change.

As we both had our individual academic concerns, we couldn't meet often. But we happened to run across each other at least a couple of times a week. At those times, he didn't even smile back at me.

The academic pressures of medical life and the bad company he began keeping in the hostel made him a different person from the one I knew. He resorted to the bottle quite often, his roommate told me. I too frequently saw him on the terrace at night with certain regular boozers from the hostel.

The nightmare about Santosh began bothering me often. Those eyes, the helplessness, and the sense of betrayal they portrayed!

I prayed to god to help Santosh every time I woke up because of it.

Five months went by. Santosh entered clinicals with a distinction in Biochemistry (151 marks he had scored in it!). He had become quite lean by then.

During his clinical postings, I noticed him quite often with Reena Catherine, the gold-digger of our college. I didn't know whether Santosh really trusted her or not, but I frequently saw him around the girls' hostel, talking to Reena for hours and also helping her with all her record work. I also chanced upon them, chatting away at the bus stand every time she went to her hometown, Marthandam.

'Isn't he your friend? Why don't you warn him about her ways? She will soon ditch him too and keep going her way as if nothing happened,' warned Mano.

'You think I haven't already? He argued that it's the fault of the boys who previously went around with her and that she is a good person. Maybe it is true. How do we know?'

'You think so? Okay. Wait and watch.'

ಞ

The third sleepless night I went through was during the last month of our internship.

Reena did exactly what Mano had predicted. She dumped Santosh in a rather unceremonious manner and got engaged to a wealthy NRI from Kerala.

'How dare you talk to me like this? I would have never hung out with you if I had known,' she had snapped at Santosh when he proposed to her.

This incident created a buzz among the students in my last days of college. After that Santosh started resorting to alcohol even more, I came to know.

'Didn't I tell you? Your old friend is never going to come out of this,' piped Mano.

'Just shut up, will you?'

As an old schoolmate, I went to his room on an evening, before vacating the hostel.

'What, Maaps? Started your PG preparations?' he asked as I entered his room.

'Not yet, Santosh.'

The clock struck seven. I looked around his room in the dim light of its single electric bulb. Academic books lay scattered all around, along with many magazines. A vile smell assailed my senses even as I walked in, probably that of cigarette smoke mixed with that of unwashed clothes heaped on the chair in a corner. A few empty Old Monk bottles were piled up near it. The calendar on the wall had a picture of a nude girl.

His room in his house came to my mind. I used to go there for combined studies. I preferred the small room in his house to mine just for its soothing ambience.

I wondered at the way he had gone downhill as I sat staring at him. I felt like I was talking to some loser and not the Santosh I knew. All the dejections, betrayals and pressures of academic life had left his spirit barren.

'You have changed a lot,' I said in a solemn tone.

From lighting the cigarette in his hands, he looked up towards me and chuckled.

A wave of guilt washed over me as he did that.

I collected myself and said, 'I heard about Reena and, you know, about her engagement. Sorry da.'

He replied nonchalantly, almost as a reflex, 'To hell with your 'sorry' dude. First that f***ing Gayatri, then this b***h Reena. . . . This is all one can expect from girls. Opportunistic b*****s.'

He took a puff of his cigarette as he said that. I was sitting there, startled by his words. Was it Santosh who said that? More so, about Gayatri?

'By the way, have you heard about Barath Sir?' he asked.

'No. What happened?'

Santosh said in a toneless voice, 'He passed away last month.'

'What?'

'No one has been able to give a proper reason. Some say it was a haemorrhagic stroke, others surmised that it was the result of some heart problem. They took him to Madurai, kept him admitted in the ICU for four days . . . but to no avail.'

I was speechless.

'Poor man; I came to know of it only last week. I went to his house to see if his daughter or anyone else was there, but the house was locked.'

I left his room without another word.

'Barath Sir! You have passed away!'

I was riding back on my bike through the heavy silence of the night. All there was on my mind were fond memories of Barath Sir. I hardly slept that night. I kept talking to him in my heart. 'You have really left us all, Sir! You made us study hard, paved the way for us receiving this medical degree; we owe all of this to you, Sir. What could we give you in return? And how beastly of us! You made only one request to us all those years ago, that too for the sake of other students, and we haven't fulfilled even that.'

I didn't even remember where I had kept the slip he had given us back then.

☙

I got up the next morning finished my morning chores and went straight to the Ganesha Temple near the hostel.

'What, Venki? Looking very different today?' Mano asked.

I smiled back, started my bike and drove to the ward.

I had decided already – I would find time and complete the last project Barath Sir assigned to us. Rather than working on the few verses he had selected, I would dedicate myself to understanding and presenting the entire Gita to the students, no matter what it takes. In my heart I promised Sir that I would do it as a small token of gratitude for all that he did for us.

☙

Though days and nights seemed long, years flew by quickly. Santosh got an MD psychiatry seat at the renowned Chennai International Institute of Medical Education and Research (CIIMER). He got it the same year he finished his internship; indeed a fair result for his tenacity and hard work. The quota system too didn't hurt his chances.

I joined the Diploma in Dermatology course, a year later in the same institute. My father got the seat for me in management quota through his friend working there as even my second attempt at the PG entrance exam wasn't fruitful. My studies had taken a slump after that first semester.

During his nightmarish undergraduate years, Santosh kept himself isolated and determinedly neutral. I hardly saw him smiling. But after that incident with Reena he transformed in unexpected ways. The Santosh I saw during our years in post-graduation was way different from the one I used to know.

It was the first day of my joining CIIMER when I met him again. As I went to book my tickets at the railway station, I saw someone waving at me from the bike park. It was Santosh.

'Nice to meet you again, maaps' I said walking towards him.

He smiled at me, with a nod. He was counting the money in his hands.

I saw that he had a new CBZ bike, which was the trend among youngsters back then.

'Nice bike that. Yours?'

'Yup! Took a great deal to convince my old man.'

'So, how is college? How are your studies going?'

'Who respects our studies here, maapi? Serve the chief for three years, if possible his wife and children too; and he will give you a pass, that is the rule. It is totally messed up, but in a way it is easier to do when compared to mugging up all those wordy texts,' he winked.

He had come to the station to buy a ticket for his chief from his ward post-graduate fund. He said that the chief was headed for a family tour. When we returned to the bike park, I said, 'Alright, Santosh. Meet you later.'

He quickly turned towards me as he heard that and said, 'Hey, call me Sandy.'

ॐ

'This is how you perform suturing on the face, guys,' Rajagopal Sir was teaching us in the OP procedure room. The sacred ash on his forehead had become smudged due to heavy sweating, caused by the erratic power cuts in the hospital. He completed the procedure with us holding torches in our hands.

'Remember this, however minute and meticulous your suture is, a scar tissue always remains a scar tissue. It can never be as strong as the original skin,' he warned.

He did so to make sure we would not resort to unnecessary facial procedures on our patients. I began to smile, as it seemed a wistful reminder of my friendship with Santosh.

We had renewed our friendship now that we were in the

same institute again. I liked being in his company, and Sandy too seemed to enjoy hanging out with me, despite all that had happened between us. We went to the library, to hotels and movies together. But was it the same old honest relationship we had in school? It didn't feel that way. The guy I spent time with felt nothing like the Santosh I had gotten to know over the years.

The stiff upper lip of his undergraduate period had become a phoney smile now. He had so many girlfriends from among our juniors that I often saw him flirting around in hospital premises and occasionally outdoors too. From the grapevine I found that he had also become the pet student of his chief.

'Maaps, you know what type of man your chief is. Why are you still getting so close to him?'

'I didn't see you in your hostel room last night and Dany told me he saw you with that pre-final-year girl near Satyam. Where had you gone?'

For all the questions I kept prodding him with, a sly smile or wink was all that I got in reply. He often became unexpectedly hostile towards anyone who tried to advise him. People in college were disgusted with him and his ways; I alone felt guilty. After all, all his deviant ways had my behaviour at their base. The recurring nightmare never failed to remind me of it.

ଓ

This night as I am sitting on the terrace with the Gita in my hands, there were few more things, apart from the debt I owed to Barath Sir, that were pushing me to come to terms with the book's wisdom. I wanted to know if we really live in a chaotic universe, with no one in control. How else can one explain the miserable things that happened in Sandy's life in the past nine years? Or in Sameer's life in the last few months? What was God doing at those times?

And apart from this, today as I was listening to Sandy expound his philosophy of doom and hopelessness, a new fear got hold of me. With Sandy and me setting up clinics nearby, I have no other option than to hang out with him often, at least for the next year or so. Imagine a year of doing nothing and getting exposed daily to such a mind – such a stinking trench of a mind.

ଓ

The crowd in the bar was slowly starting to thin out as it was well past midnight.

'And this thing called God . . . ' Sandy continued, 'it is the stupidest invention of man, to fill his own emptiness. Oops! Sorry . . . You are a regular temple visitor, right? But I have to say this.'

'No, Sir. I feel God is indeed there . . . but seeing us and the world, he too has become an alcoholic I think, ditching us all to our own fate,' a man with a soiled dhoti from the neighbouring table deferred. I felt he had been eavesdropping on me and Sandy all throughout.

'Or maybe like this waiter, he is too dumbstruck having too many tables to attend to . . . ' Sandy guffawed, patting the man's back. 'Venki boss, see the real world and the way it is functioning, take for example your Sameer. He is the only son and the lone hope for his parents, who are quite pious people, and he dies at 17. Take my psychiatry department at CIIMER.'

'Yes I know. I've seen the pathetic living conditions of patients there when I came there for references,' I said quickly, to avoid him getting into it in full detail, but nothing helped.

'Is it? Let me tell you. *You have seen nothing.* I am not talking about their disease or their living conditions. That is something trivial. I am talking about what's happening there during the night, after the assistants and PGs leave. Do you know that? I bet you don't! Do you know what the attenders there do with those patients after night rounds? Do you know the reason behind all the menorrhagia references from the ward? You will doubt whether they are humans at all. No doubt there are good people there too but even they can do nothing. The inept dean and that f*****g self-obsessed chief has seen to that. It is a corrupt-to-the-core system.

'Sometimes in the ward, the female patients get an extra dosa for breakfast in the morning. If they do, you get to know what had happened to them the night before. You dermatologists come for references and often prescribe liquid paraffin, I have seen. Do you know where all that liquid paraffin is getting used?'

'Stop it, Sandy!' I screamed. A couple of people turned from the TV and looked at me. 'You are pushing me too much. I can't believe all that you are saying. How unbelievably pessimistic and cynical you are!' I said, easing away from him onto my chair. I felt my head aching. The heavy percussion from the two-feet high speaker nearby only added to it.

'*Pesssssimisssm*? Who is pessimistic here? Calling a donkey a donkey is pessimism? Come on, I am just mouthing the truths people have inside them. I am just saying that this is a crappy world and there's no God or a loving power up there controlling it. Or if there is one, the guy is a cruel sadist with a perverse sense of humour. Don't you see it? Chaos and disorder seem more natural to the system.'

'Yes, Sir. You are absolutely right,' said the man wearing the soiled dhoti.

'Thank you, boss. Leave out God, even humanity is dead here. It is like a vehicle running out of control towards the edge of a cliff, maaps. The sooner we match what is inside our head with the reality on the outside, the better for us. The world is dirty. What do you do? Take some dirt and apply it right on your face before you start your life. No stress, no conflict anymore.'

At exactly that moment, something intriguing that had happened earlier during the same day crossed my mind.

ఔ

'Venki, now that you have finished your studies, it is high time I started looking for a bride for you, da,' Mom started with her usual plea for marriage when serving me lunch. 'Why are you not agreeing to it? If you wait till you start earning and delay further, it'll be hard to find a suitable match.'

I didn't bother to reply and continued to eat. She became angry.

'Well, why should I worry? It's your life. All the pujas and *vrathas*, do you think I keep doing them all for myself?'

'Relax, mom. What is that bundle of books over there?'

She didn't reply and went into the kitchen with an angry face. I finished my lunch and had a look. I saw that they were the old books of her ashram given to her by her Swamiji. New editions must have been bought for all these, probably with my dad's money. Still, I was impressed by the huge bundle of books her Swamiji had given to her.

I went on and had a look. It felt as if some force was reminding me of the debt I owed to Barath Sir at exactly the right time of my life. An old book with a green calico binding sat atop the bundle. A painting of Arjuna kneeling with a distressed face and clasped hands before Lord Krishna, adorned its cover. It was the Bhagavad Gita!

It was as if Sir's favourite book had come in search of me straight to my living room! I hadn't realised it when I saw it, but on the way back from the bar I felt that the day's happenings were not random at all. There seemed to be a pattern in it, a reason for all that had happened throughout the gloomy day. The confusion was born, or rather the inherent confusions and doubts all of us have towards life were stirred up in me through various incidents – the morning phone call about the death of that young boy, Sandy's ranting in the bar – and as a way to solve those, the day also presented two paths. One was the path of escapism and hedonism that Sandy himself had put forward; and the less travelled one involved trying to find the reason behind all this and coming to terms with it. The latter offered an opportunity of living life from a new, profound level like Barath Sir.

I wondered whether I was capable of walking the latter path; of even understanding such a hefty philosophy, leave alone following it in real life. As I reflected on the day, with all the available free time in the year ahead and the book falling in my lap now, I couldn't help thinking that some mysterious force was directing the events. Maybe there really is a God somewhere!

I reached home, parked the bike, and climbed up to the terrace. And in my hands was a book I had taken out of the bundle, *The Bhagavad Gita*.

'Barath Sir, the time has come for fulfilling the promise I made to you.'

SCRIPTURE

I first informed Sandy that I was going to start the Gita assignment our Sir gave us, when we were eating at Vel Murugan Parotta stall.

We could get our seats only after a long waiting period that day. In front of us sat a man with a large *thiruman* on his forehead. He looked up toward the heavens, and prayerfully mumbled the name of Lord Krishna with closed eyes, as he got his seat.

There were two people standing nearby waiting to take our seat, when we hadn't even started eating!

'Didn't I tell you yesterday?' Sandy whispered into my ears. 'Look at these men and women standing all around rubbing their bums shamelessly against us. Do you hear what they are all saying with their actions?'

'Sandy, I am going to start reading the Gita,' I said, paying no heed to his words.

It didn't strike him at first.

'Boss,' he called the waiter. 'Little more gravy please, yeah, that's it. What did you say, maapi?'

'I am going to take up the Gita, the last assignment Barath Sir gave us. And tomorrow onwards, I will come over and share with you all that I read and understand from it, just like in school.'

'What?' Abandoning the parottas, he turned to look at me, and kept staring in disbelief.

ೞ

Before delving into the Gita let me state my biases. I am a man of faith! In addition, I have a fondness for Hinduism, just like most people have towards the religion they are born to. Sitting alongside my grandpa, reciting shlokas and assisting him in all the elaborate pujas for the various Hindu Gods was my favourite childhood pastime. Interests and sensibilities naturally changed as I grew up, but the fondness remained.

As an adult with a critical brain, I have approached the religion with a view to understand it. Whenever I had done that however, I had only ended up intrigued, puzzled and at times utterly baffled! Its unbelievable mythological stories and its staggeringly myriad practices would leave anyone so perhaps. I have wondered several times what this Hindu dharma is all about. When we approach it seeking the answers to life's imposing questions, it seemed only to confuse us further. Therefore when Barath Sir asked us to prepare the write-up, I did give it an honest try to see if the Gita clarified things for me.

However, verses like the one below, only added to my confusion.

Fix your mind on me, Be devoted to me, Offer service to me.
You shall certainly reach me. There is nothing higher than me.

And there are several verses like this in the Gita. They made me wonder whether God was some needy, narcissistic dictator perched up in the sky. The book's flow was too abstruse for me, and its ideas downright impractical.

Still, certain things in the book did intrigue me right in that first reading. When all the great spiritual masters of the world insist on love and brotherhood, the Gita boldly declares, 'When it comes to doing your duty, do not back away even if you have to take up weapons against your kith and kin.'

The book encourages this thought despite stressing on love elsewhere. In fact, not just love, it insists on seeing others as our self, as extended parts of our own body!

When you acquire Jnaana,
you shall see all beings in yourself 4.35

Therefore, according to the Gita you are me and I am you, even if you wage a war on me for the sake of Dharma! The Gita doesn't see a contradiction in that.

The sense of intrigue I felt at several such instances in my first reading was still there as I picked up the book after many years.

'Read the paper?' asked Sandy. 'The state minister is coming to distribute some freebies to my colony people today evening. You know what I think? Instead of all these free stuffs, our state politicians can give our people daily idly, dosa with chatni and sambar for five years.'

We were having a chat sitting in his new clinic the next day morning.

'And by the way, were you serious about that Gita thing yesterday?' he asked.

'Yes,' I nodded.

'Oh? Come on, man,' said Sandy. 'This spiritual living and all that, is it really possible to follow in our times, you think? What practical advice can a five-thousand-year-old religious book give for people today? This is an age where cut-throat competition and result-obsession are the norm. Moreover, psychology comes up with cutting-edge studies about the human mind every day. Look at this journal,' he put a Xeroxed magazine before me.

'"The psychologically stable and healthy are those who don't let conformity rule their lives, and discern and live by their own inner truth."' That is a latest Stanford study. Haven't you realised that these religious people only keep fooling themselves in the name of faith, slavishly aligning their life by some philosophy spouted by someone unknown to them a long time ago? I'm damn sick of the whole hypocrisy and dogmatism of these guys who clamour for *Shastras*, tradition and all that.'

I didn't respond and kept browsing through the magazine. I could see he was under his Communist father's sway.

'Okay, do what you wish. Read the Gita, become a monk, a Venki-anandha perhaps, whatever. Why include me, boss? This is not an assignment we are going to present before the school after all.'

'I need you as an opposing force, Sandy. Any truth's strength is revealed only when held up against an opposition you see?'

That finally calmed him down, but I really didn't need a separate opposing force from outside. There is a voice inside me – which I am not paying heed to – that is yelling incredulously right now, '*Reading the* Bhagavad Gita? *What the hell are you doing, dude?*'

The real reason I wanted to share the Gita with him was something else.

'The Gita, dear boys, tells us nothing new really,' Barath Sir often used to tell us. 'It just awakens the truth deep within us that lies obscured by all the worldly noise. That is why people adore it so much. It is not the book, but this inner truth about themselves that enthralls them, if one thinks about it.'

I often feel that Sandy, though he is far from the honest and somewhat eccentric creature he was in school, still has his core intact. Whatever others say, to me he was still a good person who had accumulated some dust in his mind. Maybe, just maybe, the book would appeal to his true self and help in his transformation too, as Barath Sir had said.

A derisive voice inside me kept insisting that my hope was far-fetched, but I decided to give it a shot anyhow. There was no harm in trying, and apart from this, there was no way I could see to try and bring him back to his old self.

In a way, more than my quest, more than the debt to Barath Sir, this was the strongest drive inside me. The darned nightmare was haunting me very much still.

'Oh! I see,' said Sandy, 'All I have to do is to play devil's advocate and not agree with you, huh? That's nice.'

'But don't mind if I give you a whack or two if you annoy me too much,' I said, before I got up to leave for my clinic.

೧

So, that is the story behind this Venki getting into reading the Gita. As I began with my preparations, I couldn't help feeling often how pleased Barath Sir would have been had I done it while he was around. But maybe it is true that there's a time for everything. Truly, I believed that it was he who gave rise to all those questions in my heart just at the right time, so I could work on it wholeheartedly in this free period.

In order to understand the Gita, I bought more than a dozen reference books: detailed commentaries on the Gita, those written by Sri Aurobindo, Swami Sithbavananda and Swami Ramsukdas; treatises on Hinduism, and works of many great Vedantic Gurus like Swami Vivekananda, Sri Adhi Shankara, Sri Ramakrishna and Sri Ramana Maharishi. In addition, a few mystical works of Christianity, Islam and Buddhism, were added to the pile, along with a few books dealing with scientific enquiries into the nature of God. (In case you are wondering reading that list as to what type of creature I am, here is the explanation: when one receives a medical degree, whether or not one becomes proficient in medicine, every student is forced to become adept at one skill: cross-referencing different books, racking one's brain to arrive at an understanding and then belching out one final product, with his name on the front cover!)

Why bring in works from other faiths, you ask? Well, Kurukshetra, Jerusalem, seventh century, 3000 BC, how does it matter where or when it was shared? The ultimate truth behind our existence can only be one. However, the expression of that truth will naturally vary among mystics, cultures, and ages. Thus having different viewpoints can only enrich our understanding in my view.* The basic path I will stick to is the Gita, Upanishads and the philosophy of Vedanta. However, in instances where I find similarities, I will bring in words from other religious traditions too, just like our Sir used to do in his class.

A note before you move further: if what you read till now was like travelling in a multi-axle vehicle along an express highway, from here on, you will have to park your vehicle in shade, get down, and stroll slowly and carefully by foot. The material will require patience, a willingness to think and a good

---

*A passage from the book on Sri Ramakrishna that expresses the same thought – 'A lake has many ghats. From one ghat the Hindus take water in jars and call it jal. From another ghat the Mussalmans take water in leather bags and call it pani. From a third the Christians take the same thing and call it water. Suppose someone says that the thing is not "jal" but "pani", or that it is not "pani" but "water", it would indeed be ridiculous. But this very thing is at the root of the friction among sects, their misunderstandings and quarrels.'[1] In this work we will concentrate on how to draw and drink water from the lake, not on what name or which vessel suits the liquid best.

amount of time to sink in. But if you are willing to make that investment, you will be rewarded enormously, I can tell you.

With that introduction, let's now enter into the philosophy section of this book. Seat belts on? Here we go!

༄

Sandy raised a doubt on the value and need of these ancient scriptures. We will take up that question before we get into the Gita philosophy: what is the relevance of faith, God and these ancient scriptures in our modern scientific era?

Not everything in the world can be brought under the umbrella of modern science. Science is primarily concerned about the exploration of the world with our mind. Spirituality is not against this pursuit of science, rather science is a child before spirituality.

Astronomers claim that the age of Earth is 4.5 billion years and humankind has been here since the last two-lakh years. That is, if the earth's lifetime is taken as one hour, we, Homo sapiens, have been here for less than the last one second! That is the age of the thinking part of the brain! Put it against the time our galaxy came into being, or the universe; it becomes awfully infinitesimal. Therefore, quite like a bacterium trying to understand the human world and arriving at definitive conclusions about us through its intelligence, aren't we just flattering ourselves making sweeping and gross over-generalisations about what lies beyond with such a mind? 'Every man takes the limits of his own field of vision for the limits of the world,' as Arthur Schopenhauer said.*

We can doubt, we can be curious, but when we embrace atheism, and assert with all certainty that it is a random and chaotic universe, we are closing ourselves prematurely to the possibility of it being otherwise. All we are really asserting, in doing that, is our own big-headedness!

However, does that mean we have no choice but to blindly accept everything the scriptures tell us? Of course, not. Such blind belief is only another way of shutting ourselves in and giving in to religious dogmatism and bigotry. We have only to be aware that there could be

---

*The spiritual masters encountered the reality that lies beyond our world not through the mind, but through a process of intuition and revelation, or in Sri Aurobindo's words, 'supra-mental perception.' We will get into this further in the chapter on Jnaana.

more to things than that meets the eye, and that some men through history could have got a glimpse of that. That openness alone is enough as we get into the Gita.

'Faith is not knowledge of what the mystery of the universe is, but the conviction that there is a mystery, and that it is greater than us,' as the Rabbi David Wolpe eloquently put it.

◈

Whoa! Is that this Venki speaking all that? As you can see, as I started my preparation, I found myself getting involved quite deeply in the job, much to my own astonishment. Perhaps my inner thirst for truth got kindled as I started going through the Gita.

In my opinion, this thirst is there inside everyone. But because the answers are locked inside the complex gates of religious texts, and because we don't find the time or interest to patiently unlock them, we push it to the back of our minds and smugly keep indulging in the usual. In my case, however, the thirst had met its river.

But neither when I began my preparations, nor when I brought in Sandy into it, could I have known that what we had caught hold of was the tail of a tiger. We would have hardly guessed that the book's wisdom was going to touch us deep and eventually bring about some radical and irrevocable changes in both our lives.

◈

Sandy commented on the disgraceful way religious people often ignore their inner wisdom and slavishly abide by what the Shastras insist. That is the thing we will take up next: what is the right way to approach and follow the Shastras? Though I arrived at the answer to this only at the end of my reading, it is important to share it here before we begin.

We are not called on to depend on Shastras like a crutch and blindly follow what they say. Then we confine our being inside the four corners of an external philosophy.

'They are asked to live upon words; can they do it? If they could, I should not have the least regard for human nature,' wrote Swami

Vivekananda. 'Man wants truth, wants to experience truth for himself; when he has grasped it, realised it, felt it within his heart of hearts, then alone, declare the Vedas, would all doubts vanish.'[2]

So if we ignore the alive truth in us and unthinkingly follow the rules set forth by Shastras, then we would only end up limiting ourselves. In Sri Aurobindo's words, we would be trying 'to create our spiritual life out of the men of the past, instead of building it out of our own being and potentialities.'[3]

Ergo, our intention should be to imbibe the spirit of the book and walk the path ourselves. A Shastra is not a crutch for our plant to lean on, but it should serve as the nourishing manure that helps in its natural growth. Take a look at Krishna's words in the Gita at the end of his exposition.

**Thus has knowledge, more secret than all other secrets,
been declared to you by me. Now reflect on it fully.
Then do as you think best. 18.63**

This is the spirit of the Gita. The scripture tells us, 'This is the teaching. You are free to hold it in regard, or disregard it. But consider it well before that. Reflect objectively on it. See if you can really come up with something better. Then do as you think best, as your inner being calls you to act.'

However, if we really do what Gita asks us to do in that verse, we can't help but end up transforming ourselves in a radical way. After all, the Gita is not about subscribing to a particular creed, or God. What the scripture looks to do is to awaken us to our forgotten glory, to our inner divinity.

So we read the Gita not to become Gita scholars, or to live by it. As Romain Rolland put it, 'No one ever reads a book. He reads himself through books.'

The purpose of knowing and contemplating on the Gita is to study and know ourselves, to know the highest truth of our being, and to reawaken to our own glory and grandeur. The Gita is a dependable truth-speaking mirror which sees the greatness in us that we ourselves don't see. The song of our inner celestial nature is the real Bhagavad Gita. The book is only a physical form of it, needed until we learn to hear that within.

'How long should one reason about the texts of the scriptures? So long as one does not have direct realisation of God. How long does the bee buzz about? As long as it is not sitting on a flower,' said Sri Ramakrishna.[4]

When so many sects and organisations are obsessive about bringing in more and more people under their umbrella, here is a book that declares at the very outset that there comes a stage when we will outgrow the need for it.

> **When your intellect completely pierces the veil of delusion,**
> **You will become indifferent to what has been heard**
> **And what is to be heard. 2.52**

'So offensive is all this to conventional religious sentiment,' Sri Aurobindo tells us, 'that attempts are naturally made to put a different sense on some of these verses, but the meaning is plain and hangs together from beginning to end.'[5]

The Gita tells us that it would be gladdened when we jettison the book out of our life one day, realising its truth in our core. It would happily accept our setting it aside, like a mother bird watches its fledgling stand up and fly.

Hence is the book held so high by many a wise man of the world. Hence do saints like Sri Adhi Shankara say of the Gita

> **Human beings must bathe in water every day**
> **to get rid of dirt of the body.**
> **But bathing in the water of the Gita once is enough**
> **to get rid of the dirt of the cycle of birth and death.**
> Gita Mahatmya (Verse 3)

Such is the power of inspiration from the book the Spiritual Masters assert. With that long drawn-out preamble, let's now take the plunge into the Gita's philosophy and learn what it holds for us.

Sankhya Yoga

LIFE

How comfortable are you with sentimental farewell messages? Our Big B is not the one to resort to such stuff with his students. Hence, when he gave us such a message on the occasion of our farewell, we sensed that something was amiss. But the real reason behind it, I learnt only much later. Before getting into the Gita, let me first share that speech he gave us.

Though it was a long awaited day of our school life, we could feel a vague sense of gloom in the air. That's because a few weeks before that day, a classmate's father had passed away in a road accident. The boy, despite being one among the toppers, couldn't take the final exams.

Our Head Master, TK and other teachers gave elaborate but boring speeches about being good students in college, good future citizens and so on.

'Maaps, did you notice TK using flowery words about the future looking at us in particular? I somehow sense a fear for his future from his words,' commented Kumar. He had come in a short and funky haircut, and in a baggy pant imitating his *thalaivar's* new avatar in his latest release.

Barath Sir had given us plenty of advice during his classes on choosing our career, college and all that. He would say things like, 'Don't look at "what works" boys, when choosing your branch of study. Look at what brings you alive. That will "work" more than you imagine. Don't be in a hurry to make money unless you really have pressing financial concerns. Learn more about the field you choose, dig deep till you gain expertise and until you feel you can do different or better than what is already being done. From there, take the world on.'

When he took the mike in his hands on that day, he delivered a short, eloquent speech on making the 'right choice'. We became absolutely silent as he began speaking.

'Dear Students,

I see you all standing at an important crossroad in life. Looking at you all assembled here, it feels like seeing little fledglings about to fly by themselves.
You are about to move from the safety and comfort of your nests to a world where you will find nothing easy any more. Thus, I thought of sharing a few words on Life, the real life you will be facing soon.
I know many of you will have questions about Pon Ganesh and his father's death.
I have a daughter working in Chennai. Every time she faces even a minor crisis, she becomes unsettled and calls me. As I think about it all, I feel like telling you a few things. Life, dear boys, is like taking a long voyage along a winding river.'

'What, maapi? Big B has gone into full flowery mode today,' sniggered Kumar.

'Shut up and listen,' I snapped.

'I already feel like crying you know? Boohoo,' he mocked.

I took no heed of Kumar and was all ears for Barath Sir.

'In this river, sometimes your ride will be smooth and all you will come across are beautiful gardens along the shore. But sometimes the ride might get real bumpy with baffling twists and turns. And all you will find along the shore is filth. See what I mean?
But all that is no cause for concern. The joy in the ride is not as we might believe, in the shore being beautiful or in the river being smooth; it is entirely dependent on what goes on inside us as we travel. Even a seemingly difficult journey for others can be a happy and fulfilling one for the one who knows how to respond well to life's challenges.
What do I mean by "responding well," you might ask! Every time you face an unexpected twist in the course, calm your nerves. There is a source of wisdom within all of us. In the core of our core, its voice always guides us to the right

choice in every situation. It is that choice that will make us freer, happier beings. Let me call that source the "heart." But there is a thing about this voice. The mind speaks to us through agitated thoughts and emotions. The heart, on the other hand, is very timid. It speaks to us in a silent voice. The one skill you have to develop in life is, silencing the mind and learning to listen to this voice of your heart. As the light from the moon is clearly reflected in motionless waters, the light of your heart shines in a quietened mind. Its guidance is available to you at every turn of life. Abide by that wisdom every time. Make it the guiding force of your life. You can't expect to receive a better counsel from any other source. Respond to all the challenges of life from your heart, from that space of peace in you, and not panic. Just this one skill you need to develop when facing life.'

Kumar whispered, 'Look at Gorilla, eyeing us all with contempt as we listen to Barath Sir.'

'Shut up and allow us to listen, Kumar,' Santosh protested.

Kumar laid his head comfortably on my shoulders and closed his eyes as Santosh said that. I stealthily extended my hands behind his back and pinched his buttocks hard. He got up with a jerk and looked behind him.

'Responding from the heart. What good does it do? When you do so each time, every decision you make will be something that enriches you. With time, you would realise that neither the course of the river nor what is on the shore are important; it is always about what goes on inside you. So my dear boys, don't ever become attached to any of the "stuff" life brings you; the possessions, power, recognitions, success and all of that. They are all like pretty gardens you pass along the shore, things that come and then go. Accept these gratefully when they come, but let your joy be in relishing the ride along this wild river, and in becoming good sailors of it.

If you do, you will realise some day that this was what the journey of life was about. When all the things leave you at the end — forgive me, I am getting too ahead here — what will stay with you is what you become as a person, the peace and wisdom you have gained inside.

I just shared my thoughts on life, which I thought might be useful to you. Contemplate on them when you find time and see if your heart resonates with them. If you find that they make sense, abide by them.

Wish you all the best on your ride.'

We all pounded a thunderous applause as he finished his speech. It barely mattered if we understood it wholly or not.

'Great message, Sir! Does the river have riverside bars and parotta stalls?' asked Kumar as he was clapping. This time I pinched his backside squarely. Everyone turned and looked at him yelling like an injured dog in response.

Quite a message that was, for a bunch of teenagers finishing school! It almost sums up all that we are going to see in the coming pages. When I watch the video recording of that day, I realise how our batch was slightly over-dependent on Barath Sir. He had hence tried to introduce to us the source of wisdom inside us.

Barath Sir was no doubt a 'good sailor' of the river he spoke about. As I began reading the Gita with those words of Barath Sir in mind, certain doubts niggled me. I wondered whether the river just 'twists and turns.' Doesn't the course of the river sometimes bring some 'unexpectedly huge boulders and whirlpools' so to speak, that capsize our being totally? It happened to Sameer's parents; in Santosh's life right before my eyes, and also in the lives of many more people I have come across.

☙

I met this teenager on the day I began reading the Gita. A butterfly with scarlet-red wings fluttered past me, as the boy entered my consultation room and sat in front.

'Saradhamma asked me to give this letter to you,' the boy said. He appeared familiar to me despite the fact that it was the first time I was meeting him.

Hi Venkat,

Hope you are doing well.
I am herewith referring this teenager who is suffering from patchy hair loss of his scalp since childhood. He also has recurrent respiratory tract infections with occasional attacks of bronchial asthma.
Please give your opinion on treating his hair loss and also rule out possibility of any syndrome.

Regards,
Saradha

Saradha – Dr Saradha Rajasekar, as I remember her name being called out from the attendance register – had been my classmate in under-graduation. She was an introverted, self-effacing girl I hardly had a chance to talk to. She was successfully running a five-bed hospital in Pasumaikudi, a village near Tuticorin.

'So how's Saradha?' I asked the boy.

'Saradhamma is fine, Sir.'

'Your name?' I asked, repeating what he said within myself, 'Saradhamma!'

'My name is Muthu Kumar, Doctor.'

'How long have you been suffering from this hair loss, Muthu?' I asked examining his scalp. It was clean-shaven. Most of the hair roots seemed atrophied.

'Since I left school years ago, Doctor.'

The lean teenager had a large band of sacred ash with a dot of red kumkum at the middle of his forehead. The red coloured dhoti and white shirt he was wearing, usually worn by devout Sakthi worshippers, made him look like a man who had taken sannyasa.

My dry-witted mind fancied him a Dattu Babu in the making.

'And when did you leave school?'

'I . . . ' he seemed a bit reluctant.

'Come on, young man. When it comes to a doctor, you don't hide anything.'

'What, dude?' my conscience taunted me, 'Just three days

into practice and you consider yourself a big doctor already, huh?' 'Oh! Cool down,' I shut it up, 'It feels grand to make such statements before patients, you know.'

'That is almost six, seven years ago, Sir. First there was just one patch here,' the boy pointed to an area above his left ear. 'Then it spread up to over here. That was when I decided to leave school. My classmates . . . would make a lot of fun of me. Some teachers would do so too! So I said to my father as he was entering our hut in the evening, 'Appa, I don't like school. Everyone there bullies me. I won't go there anymore.' As it is, bookish knowledge never seemed to penetrate my thick skull.'

'Patients like it when doctors listen,' Rajagopal Sir's words came to mind as the young man continued. There was an innocence in the way he related his story.

'It must have been quite a shock for your father!'

'Father was . . . ' A mosquito interrupted our conversation. He immediately got up, taking care to hold the arm with the mosquito quite still.

'One minute, Doctor Sir.'

Slowly walking to the window, he opened the blind and let the tiny creature out with a wave of his hand. Returning to his seat, he continued his story as I sat there wide-eyed. I noticed that he walked with a slight limp. As I continued listening, I wondered if he was a real spiritual Guru in the making!

'Father was working as a mason. He first thought I was joking. Then he realised that I had taken a decision he just couldn't digest. I was pretty adamant though. He hit me hard with a bamboo stick lying in front of our hut with all the neighbours watching.

'He was illiterate and my elder brother had also had to abandon his studies and become a mason as the family needed another earning member to make ends meet. So my father had pinned all his hopes on his younger son, me. He would often urge me to complete school, go to college and become the first educated man in the family.'

'So, what happened after that?'

My teenage period and its self-image obsessions came to my mind as he continued with his story.

'He asked me what I am going to do. I had no idea. All I liked was sitting with my mother and helping her with cooking. As he heard that, he gave my mother a good beating next. 'Is this the way you have brought him up?' he yelled and went off.

'All the people from the neighbouring huts were watching. It was embarrassing for Mother. She took me inside the hut, hugged me to give some solace, but the *palav* of her saree was wet with tears. She too had pinned all her hopes on me.'

Despite the obvious pathos of the story, the boy was sharing it with a smile, in a matter-of-fact tone as if it had all happened to someone else. It made me presume that he had come a long way in the years that followed since he left school.

'As we lay down to sleep that night, some questions arose inside me. Was it my fault that I was disinterested in studies? The disfiguring disease, and all the scoffing and beating . . . what did I do to deserve it all? I got lost in an ocean of self-pity that night.' He smiled broadly as he said that.

'The next day was Friday, when I would accompany my mother to the village temple. The local Goddess Muthumaari was her family deity. Mother was an ardent devotee of the Goddess. She would be jubilant every time we walked down to the temple. However, that day Mother didn't speak a word to me. She was shedding silent tears. As Mother walked into the temple, I went to the grove nearby as usual, but with a heavy heart. Would you believe, Sir? I had decided the previous night that I would end my life that day, by jumping into the well. And I was all of seven years old then!'

꩜

DESPAIR DIVINE

What does one do in such moments: devastating moments that make one feel that some sinister force, and not a benevolent God, is in control of it all? How does Barath Sir's 'relish the ride' apply when our boat crashes totally? This is the first question I had in mind when I began reading the Gita.

The Gita owes its origin to such a moment of crisis that occurred in a warrior's life. Arjuna was a Kshatriya. His duty was to fight injustice. War was an inevitable part of human life back then, more than it is now. Such fighting for the sake of Dharma, was the defining aspect of the Kshatriya clan. It was in their blood. They were trained for it from birth. The Gita declares,

> **There is nothing more meritorious to a Kshatriya**
> **than a war for Dharma 2.31**

Arjuna had led his men to victory in many circumstances until then, but this was the greatest of them all. A great number of kings and soldiers were waiting for their most able warrior to lead them in the colossal war against *adharma*.

However, Arjuna couldn't. His eyes saw the opposing army. For the first time, the people standing there appeared to his eyes, not as representatives of adharma that he had to fight against, but as kinsmen – *his* brothers and relatives. It blinded the warrior's senses, and bred weakness in his kshatriya blood. He kept his bow and arrow down and surrendered totally to Krishna.

> **My heart is overpowered by weakness.**
> **My mind is confused about Dharma.**
> **I'm your disciple. I have taken refuge in you.**
> **Teach me what's good for me. 2.7**

The first chapter of the Gita, which describes Arjuna's predicament in detail, is called *Vishaada Yoga*. The term *vishaada* means despair and yoga refers to oneness with the Divine, with the eternal truth within us. In Sri Aurobindo's words, yoga* is 'a union of the human individual with the universal and transcendent existence.'[1] By giving a seemingly paradoxical name *Vishaada Yoga* to its first chapter, the Gita seems to tell us that even despair is divine and can lead to such an oneness.

ଔ

---

*Yoga is not just about twisting our bodies into fascinating shapes if you are as ignorant as I was. The yoga of Gita is an inner one. The outer aspect serves as a preparation for this inner yoga.

'Whoa! Whoa!!' Sandy raised his eyes from the write-up. He was staring at me incredulously. 'Venkiananda, you seem to have gone in too deep with this.'

'Well, if something is worth doing, then it is worth doing well, maaps. Our Sir used to say that to us, remember?'

'Hmm, whatever! So Arjuna went into distress, and Krishna shared some esoteric truths and brought him back to his senses! But there's a question I have here. In medicine, to handle a crisis you need knowledge . . . but to face the tough spots in life, do you think knowing these 'mystic truths' is the only way? No other go? Something doesn't gel for me.'

Fair question! I gave the answer to this the next day in my subsequent write-up. 'Writing is a form of thinking,' Barath Sir used to tell us. I was using the write-up as a means to get a good grasp of the Gita's message. Once I finish with it, I had planned to give copies of the abridged version of it to the principal of the school and request him to give it as an annexure with the school magazine.

This was what I had promised to Barath Sir in my heart, and I knew that if done well, it could influence not just me, but thousands of men and women.

ଊ

Stress is inevitable in life. There is the daily work pressure, differences with loved ones, and sometimes there are the great, unexpected tragedies as well that life presents us with. We do need a stable and dependable way to handle stress, and of course, such spiritual knowledge is not the only way to do it. Different people adopt different methods that suit them.

Many just avoid facing the inner pain and steer clear of it mentally. They resort to some form of escapism like shopping, eating out, watching movies, boozing and so on. Such things can be a means of occasional recreation, but when that becomes a consistent lifestyle, where we keep the mind soaked in one sensual pleasure after another not wanting to face the tough questions looming behind, then it is not much unlike keeping an air-filled ball forcibly under water. We only keep ourselves fooled.

'Maaps, is there anything to be read between the lines here?' Sandy asked in the middle of his reading.

'Still have doubts? Of course, it is about you, Sandy.'

At times the stress appears colossal to some that they take such escapism to an extreme. They try to end their lives like Muthu, or wish to become ascetics as Arjuna did.

However, some people manage to perk themselves up and meet the grim side of life head on. A stoic acceptance of everything as a part of life and bravely fighting on is their answer to the challenges that life throws at them. A stoic's way of living life is like a passionate wrestler's delight in his game despite its hardships.

Trust is another way people cope with stress. They believe that the Divine would take care of their wellbeing, and that they are absolutely safe. They unwaveringly hold on to this belief no matter what happens in their life. Faith is their shock-absorber.

However, the reality about all such approaches is, life's power is such that even the tenacious courage and the deepest trust can be shaken. Running away, physically or mentally, isn't the right choice obviously; one's inner turmoil would only keep growing. It isn't living at all.

So is there a better way? What is our Creator's take on it in the Gita? He is the one most qualified to answer the question, and it was in such a moment of crisis that the Gita was born.

'Too much build-up, dude. Hope what follows justifies it,' Sandy remarked.

'Read on, read on.'

When we search for the answer we find that, Gita in its flow of ideas does touch upon such stoicism – when it advises Arjuna on *titiksha* (forbearance) in verse 2.14. It also insists on rootedness in faith in its later chapters. However, the ultimate solution it offers for all our worldly problems is none of these, but something quite radical.

Do not depend on the world for your happiness.
Who you are is larger than it!

That is the ultimate solution the Gita offers for facing stress the right way. Forbearance and trust are important and valid only when we see ourselves belonging to the world. The Gita goes one step further and insists on **inner renunciation from the world** even as we continue to live here. That is the way to disentangle ourselves from the world and all its problems.

☙

'Don't depend on the world! That's the solution, huh?' Sandy stared at me for some time, a sardonic grin on his face. Then he put down my write-up and reclined in his snug chair.

'Alright, dude, you know what? I always had this idea about these religious scriptures and how they are only fit for fakirs cut off from life, to sit alone in ashrams and resorts, and experience some freaky inner state. Else they are for people who have earned enough already and don't have anything else to do. You have just confirmed it. You keep continuing . . . renounce daily life, go for meditation camps, attain enlightenment, and all that. Let's end our discussion here. I thought your analysis of the Gita was going to give us better ways to live in the world. But the first thing the book says is 'renounce everything.' Imagine, that is the first step. I've had enough already.'

I waited for him to finish.

'Done with your blabbering, are you? It's the first principle shared in the Gita, but it is not the first step to take. In a way, it's the essence of the book. All the rest of the book is about ways to reach there and live from there.'

'Reach where; this 'renouncing' thing? No. I've had enough.'

'Are you sure?'

'A hundred percent sure! Farewell to you and your Gita.' He got up to leave.

'All right. Where are you going now, past OP time?' I asked looking at my watch. 'That new staff nurse girlfriend of yours, will she still be waiting for you in Mars hospital?'

He turned towards me with a big frown of surprise. He was oozing incredulity.

'A skin doctor too gets calls from hospitals boss. By the way, does she know about your colourful past, all your affairs in UG and PG?'

He sat down almost as a reflex response. 'Maaps, is this what we have come to? . . . All that you want is I should listen to what you wrote and give my opinion, right? Consider it done.'

He moved himself forward and rested his arms on the table. It seemed that what I had heard on the grapevine was true. He himself confirmed it inadvertently. Quite a Casanova he has become these days. I knew Sandy had no intention of marrying her or anything. I felt sorry for the girl. I decided to drop a hint about him someday. But the affair had given me a good leash for controlling the fellow.

A part of me was condemning my sharing of the Gita and its eternal wisdom with a person like him. I felt as though I was debasing the scripture. The scripture itself advises against it.

> This should never be spoken by you to one
> Who is devoid of austerity, who is without devotion,
> Who does not desire to listen, or who speaks ill of me. 18.67

Such people will only degrade themselves more by twisting and using the principles to their convenience. However, in sharing the scripture with him I took my cue from another verse of the Gita.

> Even if one is the most sinful of all sinners,
> He can cross all his sins in the raft of knowledge. 4.36

I remember vividly the Santosh from our school days. And I see this as my only hope to redeem myself for my mistakes that are at the base of all his present ways.

'So even if I incur sin by sharing it, it is okay dear Krishna. Let me do it,' I had already decided.

ॐ

RENOUNCE, REALISE

'Renunciation, that is the flag, the banner of India, floating over the world, the one undying thought which India sends again and again as a warning to dying races, as a warning to all tyranny, as a warning to wickedness in the world,' Swami Vivekananda had proclaimed.[2]

The Gita stresses exquisitely on this *be larger than the world* attitude, an inner transcendence from life even as we live here. However, we see the same conveyed in every religion one way or the other. The Bible says, 'And the world passeth away, and the lust thereof. But he that doeth the will of God abideth forever.' (John 2:17) Prophet Muhammad insisted his followers visit the sick and attend funeral processions.

The first noble truth taught formally to a Buddhist is, 'Life is suffering.' It is the 'Noble truth' according to Buddhism. This is also the first teaching of the Gita. It is the foundation on which the subsequent parts of its philosophy rest.

> **It is the contact of the senses with sensual objects**
> **That gives rise to the feelings of heat and cold,**
> **pain and pleasure.**
> **They are transitory and impermanent.**
> **Endure them, O Arjuna. 2.14**

For the Gita, the mind too is a 'sense-organ' to perceive the world. Heat and cold metaphorically indicate all the favourable and unfavourable circumstances we face in life. Thus, sensual objects don't denote the material stuff alone, but power, prestige, recognition; anything extrinsic that we depend upon for a high.

> **The calm person who is not afflicted by these,**
> **and who is steady in pain and pleasure,**
> **He is fit for realising his immortal nature. 2.15**

That means if you are basking in your worldly success and possessions, don't do that. You are bigger than that. And if you are distressed by your worldly failures and hardships, there is no need for that either. You are bigger than that too. 'Stop fluctuating between happiness and sadness and arrive at tranquillity,' is the Gita's advice.

'Dude, I don't know. I thought when you started to share the Gita, you are going to tell me fluffy things like, 'Trust in the Lord. He will relieve you of all suffering' and all that. But 'Be larger than the world'? Pretty intriguing, right?' said Sandy.

Yes, I too was starting to sense what the Gita puts forward isn't some frothy philosophy. Its wisdom isn't for people looking for a convenient type of spirituality to hold on to. What is in my hands is a philosophy that is going to take guts to understand. And following it is sure to bring about immense changes in our psyche, I realised at this point. Let me see where it is going to take me and its readers.

֎

Life has a grimmer side – composed of the deaths, the disappointments, the pains, the failures and so on. The Gita asks us to look at life as it is, in its totality, and to do it with an inner calm. If we do not do so, we will only live as weak, insecure creatures hankering for the good side of life.

When we are truly able to embrace the darker side, then our mental energies are freed from the stubborn grip of the world. Once that happens, we are able to get a taste of *that* within us which is beyond the world; that which is a part of eternity! 'The calm person who is not afflicted by these, he is fit for realising his immortal nature!' the Gita has told us already. In its very next verses the Gita appropriately introduces the qualities of the eternal self within us.

> **That, by which all this is pervaded,**
> **Know it to be indestructible. 2.17**

What 'That' refers to is the nameless, formless Atman – the Great Ground of Being – the spiritual foundation on which the world stands.

> **That is never born when a body arises**
> **and never dies with the body 2.20**

It is the infinite being at the root of our limited being, the Great Cosmic Self, that is at the core of our little individual self.

> **Bodies have an end. But that in the body is eternal,**
> **Indestructible and incomprehensible. 2.18**

Whether it is a delectable dish or our Divine Cosmic Self, trying to understand it *mentally* is not the way. If we try, it would forever remain incomprehensible.

This immortal reality is called 'the Self' in Vedantic terms. Our Father in Heaven, Allah, the Tao, the *Shunyata* or Emptiness of Buddhists, the Gods of Hinduism with their various names and forms, Atman, Brahman, are all various terms that refer to this Supreme Universal Spirit. It is this that is the origin and support of the material universe and our individual existence.

> **This Self by weapons is cut not. By fire it is burnt not.**
> **By water it is wet not. And by wind it is dried not. 2.23**

It is a step beyond the physical realm we are in. The Great Cosmic Self doesn't refer to some ghostly ethereal entity that lives inside our body. It is our original identity. It is who we are! Our body is just a temporary carrier for it.

> **Even as a man casts off his worn-out clothes**
> **And then clothes himself in new ones,**
> **So the embodied casts off worn-out bodies**
> **And then enters into others which are new. 2.22**

The Gita says we are beings belonging to Eternity. Our body is just an attire. Like the spacesuit of an astronaut, this body is an 'earth-suit' for us, so to speak. Quite like a spacesuit, our body is needed for where we are, but it is not us. And we are not our mind either. Our mind is just the software to operate our earth-suit and interact with other beings. We are spiritual beings clothed in a human body, or to put it in Epictetus's vigorous words, 'You are a little soul carrying a corpse.'

The Gita says when we live at that level we will come to know that nothing is worth grieving for in life or in death (2. 11). Even death would become a mere undressing of ourselves from our cramped outfits.

ॐ

Sandy seemed lost in thought after reading it all.

'So it is like that, huh? As an answer to the proverbial question "Is the cup half-empty or half-full," our Big boss Krishna says "Take your eyes off the glass you birdbrains. You have an ocean inside you."'

'Exactly, Sandy.' Not bad. The guy had finally started absorbing it!

'You know what, I think I can become a spiritual spokesman in my free-time hearing it all from you. Look at the amount of money clueless people shower on you if you grow a fluffy beard, put on some exotic robes and spout such fanciful stuff with a solemn face, "You are not who you think you are. You are the Eternal and Pure Self... untainted, unblemished," whatever that means.'

'I can't believe my ears, Sandy,' I said staring at him, repulsed. 'Listen, dude, Vedanta is the world's ancient spiritual tradition and has helped many genuine seekers across the world. Don't keep disrespecting the teachings like this with your lame comedy.'

'Hello,' he said waving his hands in front of my face, 'don't get carried away with it all, boss. All these high-handed talks, "You are the soul. Don't worry about your worldly affairs," and all that.... Do you think it is really possible for us to follow these in this day and age?'

The question made me pause and think for a moment. 'Dei, everything is a matter of choice, da. The Gita tells us the truths of our existence here and shows us a way to live life from that level. Whether you follow that or your same old lousy lifestyle is a matter of your choice and yours alone.'

He gave me a glare. My honest answer to his question should have been, 'I don't know and I didn't even give a thought to whether it is practical or not. I had the drive, a strong one, to go through and complete the Gita, whatever it takes. That's all.'

If I replied any other way, I would be giving a chance to that vermin to repeat his usual philosophy about life and rope me in for his visit to the bar. I think I have also started experiencing a guilty pleasure in demeaning the guy's ways with the Gita by my side.

'Ouch, that really hurts, boss. Someone is going to 'walk' the Gita here, hmm? All the best. For me, this 'lousy' lifestyle serves the purpose. By the way, as you say, if we take impermanence to be the quality of this world, then why will we even continue being here? Won't we lose all our drive and desire to live? It only disheartens us and makes asceticism a sane choice in my view as Arjuna decided... or perhaps even suicide.'

'Dei, you think you can understand everything in such an eternal philosophy upfront? Didn't it take us one and a half years to complete a *Grey's Anatomy* for this little body of ours? Let's take it slow da. Anyway, we can be sure no patient is going to come in our direction for another one year or so.'

'*Vanakkam*, Doctor Sir,' the next patient opened the swing door and entered Sandy's cabin, as I was saying that.

ಲ

So that is the Gita's opening message for us, 'Don't live attached to the goodies of life. Then you really live insecurely in control of its grim side. Realise your Self, and accept life in its totality.' It is, in a way, the foundation for all it is going to tell us next.

I came home after the OP, had my dinner, watched some Tamil songs in a music channel and lay down on the bed. As I mulled over all that I read on that day, I realised that the doubt raised by Santosh had started taking root in my mind.

If we embrace the impermanence of the world, won't we lose all our drive and desire to live? Only asceticism and doing away with life seem like sane choices. Why should one look to serve the world, love people and all that? Won't we become oblivious and indifferent to it all?

I thought and thought for a long time. I couldn't answer the question. The first truth Krishna tells Arjuna in the Gita shakes the very foundation of our existence here. Is this what an eternal scripture advises humans?

'How weird!'

'Hope your book doesn't want to make its readers ascetics, Sir, like in the Vedic times,' I said to Barath Sir in my mind.

I continued with the Gita for the next few days, but my doubt wasn't resolved. Even if we recognise ourselves as eternal beings, where is the drive to act? What is the motivation to live a good life here in the physical realm? Won't we become indifferent to it all?

'Maybe as Sandy believes, the Gita is not for us worldly people. Maybe there is a good reason it is not widely read and followed,' argued my skeptic side.

Much as I kept telling myself not to act in haste, my skeptic side continued, 'Perhaps it is a book for reading after having finished leading our life. Then we can accept what it says and follow its path more easily.'

I got up the next morning and looked at the Gita on the table. It was as if an argument had gone on within me all night and had finally ended the moment I opened my eyes and saw the Gita.

'What was I doing reading the Bhagavad Gita; that too all by myself? Barath Sir, you were something else. This life, with its mad conventions interspersed with bouts of escapism . . . the daily monotonous work, weekly cinema, the junk foods, cricket, TV shows, the occasional drink . . . this is what we are destined for, it seems. I thought you overestimated us once, but somehow you were proved right in your expectation. Yet, this time, sorry Sir, it seems you are wrong about us!'

'Mom, where is that book bundle your Swamiji gave you?' I asked aloud.

'In the puja room, Venkat,' she replied from the kitchen.

Mother obviously thought that the bundle too is for worshipping daily! I placed the Gita back on top of the bundle. My eyes fell on the image of Lord Krishna on the cover as I was about to step out of the room. It seemed as if he was scoffing at me, *'What, dear boy? You too are going to adopt your friend's lousy lifestyle?'*

I decided not to spare it another look. I called up Kumar and said, 'We will plan the trip to our Kumbavuruti falls this weekend.' He had been asking me to decide on the dates for quite some time now, and I too needed a break.

Well, my decision didn't last and I returned to the Gita soon enough. But what I hadn't expected was that the weekend tour would make me change my decision!

ଔ

On Saturday morning Sandy, Kumar and I set off in my father's car to Kumbavuruti, the beautiful, secluded falls about an hour and a half from Tuticorin.

'So boss, what happened to Venkiananda?' Sandy asked while bathing in the falls. 'He has renounced the Gita itself, huh?'

'Will you please shut up?'

'This is what happens when people become too big for their boots! Didn't I tell you? This Gita stuff is not practical in this day and age. We live in interesting times, maaps,' he said applying soap over his potbelly.

'Just shut up and finish your bath.'

After spending a good two hours there, we reached home quite late that day. Before settling down for the night I switched on my PC, opened the social networking website and uploaded the photos of our trip.

I did so largely to tease Narein, my school batchmate. A hard-nosed skeptic and an atheist, he had begun scoffing at India a great deal since he settled in Nottingham, UK a few years back. His last email had something to the effect, 'Thank God I escaped from the country. With all its sickening religious hypocrisy and long-running political conflicts, you can only keep dreaming about development. You should come and see here – the clean streets, the infrastructure, the facilities . . . '

I titled the album, *'A tour near Tuticorin'* and sent a message to Narein, 'Not exactly the best, but a fair-enough place to spend time near our town.'

Then I saw the posts few school friends had posted on the site and as I was reading them, Barath Sir came to mind again. After spending quite some time browsing the web, to stop thinking about Barath Sir and the Gita, I went to sleep.

It was funny. The person I wanted to ruffle up by putting up the photos gave me the much needed answer to the nagging block I had reached. When I woke up the next morning I saw his message, 'Nice photos, dude. The place seems quite impressive! I can see you guys having a great time. But such a beautiful waterfall, and you guys spent just half a day?'

'Not bad. The message I sent seems to be working,' I muttered to myself, smiling triumphantly.

But then I wondered, 'Just half a day! What else? Did the show-off think we would settle there? Imagine what would happen if we were to stay there forever!'

My thoughts idled, 'Maybe we would start thinking about acquiring a portion of the waterfall for ourselves, put a fence around it, collect money to let others in, create an income, provide more facilities and finally . . . '

'and finally . . . .'

The epiphany was like a lightning bolt. Yes, we spent just half a day there . . . few hours really. We knew that the tour was going to end that evening. **But did that stop us from having all the fun?** Maybe that is why we had real unadulterated fun there without getting attached to stuff like we do in real life.

'Wow! That is just . . . WOW!!'

'Dei show-off, thanks da,' I typed in reply to his post. Keep scratching your head about that, Nottingham Narein!

'So, the impermanence of the world is no reason for despair,' exclaimed my inner voice, and I was back with the Gita from the next day. 'Alright Krishna, I promise! No more flaunting, no more debasing people with what I read in it.'

ଓ

'The Vedanta system begins with tremendous pessimism and ends with real optimism,' said Swami Vivekananda.[3] What it denies is the sense and stuff-optimism, so to speak, that many people largely remain stuck in. The reason for denying us this is not to make us ascetics, but because we are larger than those material things!

Vedanta looks to take us from the false sense of security we are basking in, towards the ultimate security that is beyond all worldly securities and insecurities. The world is like a tourist place we have come to. When we start building castles in it, we start becoming too attached to it, forgetting that it is a tour.

Did we spend our days in school or college worrying that it will all end in a few years? Or do we give a thought during a tour that it will end in a few days? On the other hand, when we acknowledge this truth, we will start living in the present even more, we will 'get real' and not look to hold onto things. That will become burdensome for us. This wisdom is what the Gita looks to illuminate us with.

The question arises in our minds because we equate happiness with permanently possessing a thing. If we recognise that happiness is in the 'ride' itself as Barath Sir said, it vanishes. Even if Kumbavuruti dries out tomorrow, we are still going to exist and that doesn't take away the fun we had in it yesterday. 'What you have become . . . that alone will ever stay with you,' in our Big B's words. I had attained a better understanding of the concept now.

Few things need to be clarified regarding this renunciation the Gita calls for. First, **the impermanence of the world is not a license for hedonism**. Minds like Sandy's might go, 'Anyway, the world is temporary, why not just go on a binge as long as we're here?'

Well, that is falling into the world's clutches again. When we acknowledge truly this truth about the world, rather than becoming hedonists, we would start living life in a certain way. That is what the Gita way of life is all about, which we will explore in the following chapters. The principle doesn't mean, 'life is short, so go nuts!'

Second, **renunciation isn't about negating the world**. What the Gita calls for is not a cold, impersonal or melancholic detachment. Only by renouncing the lower do we move to the higher. To go to college, you renounce school life. College doesn't make school 'bad.' Living centred on our Original Cosmic Self is not negating our little human self. It is the next evolutionary stage. A spiritual life would also beautify our material life.

ଓ

THE GHASTLY GOD

There are many gods and goddesses in the Hindu pantheon. Some of them are depicted in a separate, terrible, destroying form as well, for example, the Rudra form of Siva, Kalki for Vishnu and Kaali for Gauri. In the Gita when Krishna shows his cosmic form to Arjuna, it too encompasses such a terrifying, destroying aspect that makes Arjuna tremble in fear. He described it in the following manner,

> Just as swarms of moths precipitately rush into
> a blazing fire, although only to perish,
> So do these creatures rush into your jaws of doom.
>
> Swallowing all the worlds on every side
> With your flaming mouths, you are licking your lips. 11.29-30

All this stands evidence to the great importance Hinduism places on acknowledging the world's impermanence. Destruction always alternates with creation. They are two sides of the same coin.

Let us take the image of Goddess Kaali. It is a bold and striking figurative form the Rishis use to depict the evanescence of the world. The same Rishis who personified knowledge in the form of Saraswathi, and prosperity, progeny, and success in the form of Lakshmi, also gave us Kaali, an aspect of the fierce Goddess Durga.

Kaali is portrayed as a Goddess clad only in a garland made of human heads dancing in a cremation ground with her blood-tinged tongue sticking out! Corpses, jackals and terrible female spirits surround her. Surely, her image appears quite shocking when we come across it for the first time.

The Divine Mother who is the embodiment of knowledge and love, the embodiment of all the good things in life, also has this Kaali aspect to her. What truth can such a figure represent?

The image of Kaali points to the same truth that the Gita shares as its first principle. Kaali denotes the spirit of destruction inherent in nature.

I am the mighty destroyer of the world 11.32

God declares in the Gita, the same God who elsewhere affirms us,

I am the friend to all beings. 5.29

Both aspects of the Eternal are real. Even as we cultivate knowledge in us, and enjoy the good things that life has to offer, if the Kaali aspect of existence is not there in the back of our mind, wanton indulgence in the world and bondage to it are bound to be the results.

The intellectually-oriented religion of Buddhism, conveys this as its first noble truth, 'life is suffering'. Hinduism has always conveyed its teachings in forms that appeal directly to the heart, through songs, stories and such images.

Kaali is the symbolic representation of time. Time is all-devouring; constant change and death are undeniable truths woven into its fabric. That is the bare, unembellished truth of life Kaali represents with her nakedness. If we can accept this truth from our core, then there is nothing further to fear in life.

Kaali won't appear horrific to us. A deep understanding and unconditional acceptance of what she stands for, will give us the necessary thrust to realise our True Self. Kaali would liberate us! Just as a child knows her parents' love for her even when she is rebuked by them, when we too learn to look beyond the outward form of Kaali, we would feel a Divine presence in our hearts with infinite and unchanging compassion for us humans.

A policeman is a fearful figure only to a thief. Likewise it is the part of our mind basking in worldliness that flees away from this aspect of the Divine.

All the worldly men who live caught up in the materialistic side of life are really like children who keep clinging to their toys; they need their stuffs to feel secure. Whatever position of power and authority they enjoy on the outside, they feel weak and fearful within.

> **It is the childish among men**
> **who follow after desire and pleasure,**
> **And walk into the snare of death**
> **which gapeth wide for them.**
> Katha Upanishad 2:1:2

It is the strong among men who are able enough to see and accept the Kaali side of the world bravely and take their first firm steps along the path of truth. Swami Vivekananda described the Gita as, 'a wonderful poem without one note in it of weakness or unmanliness.' The Gita wishes to make us such strong, brave beings. That is its first call to us, 'Be brave – *a dheera*.' (2.15)

What happens when we don't do this? Well, our dependence would entirely be upon the world then. As long as it is so, we are really like chickens relaxing in a slowly boiling bowl of water. With our muscles getting flaccid and too used to it with every passing moment, it is going to get too late to try jumping out.

'Rather than running away from it, embrace the terrible side of the world!' Surely, that is a bitter medicine at first, but we would realise it strengthens us with time, because we would start living life in a wholesome manner, embracing it in its true magnificence. We wouldn't hanker after a romanticised version of it with our eyes half-closed to reality.

'What is life? It is the flash of a firefly in the night' said a wise man, contemplating on the evanescent and fleeting nature of our life. And his words are quite true too. Still a delightful and extraordinary thing to come across this life is – like the beautiful flash of the firefly in the night!

It was a sunny Monday morning.

'Boss, two teas, two *vadais*, one Kings,' Sandy ordered in the tea-stall.

A person wished Sandy as he passed by our table. Wishing him back, Sandy said turning towards me and pulling in a puff with concern, 'Oh my God, I think our privacy is at stake as practice picks up.'

He then asked me, 'What boss? Looking fairer nowadays, are you using some new cream your reps gave you as a sample?'

I told him that I had started reading the Gita again, not caring about his sarcasm.

He took two contemplative puffs of his cigarette.

'Venki, you have really got into the assignment Barath Sir once gave us, huh?' Sandy asked with a solemnness I hadn't seen him display for a long time. 'Very rarely do I think about Barath Sir and all our school days, you know? Hmm, good old days. Sometimes I feel as if a part of me died along with him. Okay, boss. I didn't think you were this serious. I am glad you are pursuing our Sir's last assignment. Do it well. I'll do whatever I can to help,' he said between puffs of smoke.

I was pleasantly surprised. Did I really hear him say all that, I wondered.

'That's really nice of you, Sandy.'

'How's work by the way? You haven't spoken about it for quite some time?'

'Only now have I gained some clarity in the work, Sandy. I will bring it again from tomorrow.'

A wolf whistle was in order. My journey with the Gita took on a renewed vigour from that moment. I had started seeing glimpses of the old Santosh I knew and envied.

During a break next morning I asked, 'How many filters do you smoke per day, Sandy?'

'Umm, five I think!'

'Just five? Oh! You mean five packets?'

'Yup,' he nodded, putting on a proud face.

I looked at him exasperated, 'And then the daily late night

drinking! Why don't you think about gradually setting these aside, maaps?'

'Boss, please don't intrude into that part of me. Your work will have my cooperation, but that doesn't mean I am going to change. This is one track and that is another.'

'Do as you please,' I said, sighing.

'I will be who I am. You follow the Gita if you like.'

☙

A few days had gone by. Sandy's words often resonated within me, 'You follow the Gita if you like.'

Barath Sir would often say, 'If you wish to start practising something, do it when the inspiration is fresh, or it fizzles out.'

So apart from trying to understand it, why not try following it as well? After all, it is an age-old and highly-valued scriptural wisdom. If I don't try living according to it, and just keep covering it as a 'philosophy,' there is a chance of it becoming just intellectual knowledge and fizzling out. What is my intention? Just to 'understand' our Big B and his composure? If this is the philosophy he was living by, why not try following it as well?

I decided that I would try and take baby steps along the Gita's path, as I read it.

The Gita says when one Self-realises, one would find nothing is worth grieving for in this world (2.11). Thus Self-realisation is the way to perfect equanimity towards the world the Gita calls for. But it also says

> A calm person who is not afflicted by these,
> And who is steady in pain and pleasure,
> He is fit for realising his immortal nature. 2.15

Thus practising it beforehand too can be an effective *sadhana* towards that Self-realisation. Equanimity is *the result of* and also the *path towards* Self-realisation.

As I contemplated on how I could practise it, I came up with an idea – I would make this contemplation a regular ritual.

☙

RENDEZVOUS WITH KAALI

At regular weekly intervals (or monthly intervals if that suits us) we can take an off-period from our routine. It could be an hour or even a day to begin with. We could take this break not just to unwind, but to contemplate and imbibe this principle of the Gita in silence.

Remind yourself that impermanence is inescapably linked to everything on earth. Embrace this truth of the world from your heart. Whatever we hold as ours – our house, vehicles, gadgets, friends, partners, close relationships, the special skills and talents we possess, everything is bound to depart from us one day. Remind yourself of all that not in a gloomy or pessimistic way, but as a truth of life. You can even watch a tragic movie/drama, or a read a tragic novel in order to kick-start the process. By constant practice, let this awareness become a part of your thought process at all times.

This line of thought can be depressing at first. However, if sincerely pursued, the same thought process can take us to a real and honest relationship with life. 'Have earnestness for death. You will have life,' said the saint Abu Bakr.

When we train and disentangle the mind gradually from its world-dependence, we would come to a place where we start realising the preciousness of things. That can lead to amazing changes in our daily life. The husband would realise he has never taken the time to express his love to his wife and children. The boss could realise that instead of using his employees as machines to work towards his inflexible goals, he could use his power to take care of their real needs and nurture their creativity. A youngster could realise what he really wants to do with his life. The ritual could awaken us to what is really important.*

Not only in our relationship with life, the same thought process can take us to a real and honest relationship with Eternity as well. In embracing the seeming dark side of the world, we would find something opening up within us, some inner tightness loosening down. When we pursue this

---

*Words of Steve Jobs in his Stanford University address that reflect the same wisdom: 'Remembering that I'll be dead soon is the most important tool I've ever encountered to help me make the big choices in life. Almost everything—all external expectations, all pride, all fear of embarrassment or failure—these things just fall away in the face of death, leaving only what is truly important.'

thought process sincerely, we could indeed get a taste of the peace and composure of our True Self at our core.

Seen from this perspective, people who face sorrows and difficulties in life are nearer to God, so to speak. The energy of sorrow in them could give them the impetus to perform this exercise with an earnestness that an ordinary man might not be able to attain. 'The Lord is closer to those whose hearts are broken,' the Bible tells us (Psalm 34:18).

We started this section with the question, 'How does the philosophy of 'relish the ride' apply even after our vessel crashes totally?' When our business suffers a huge, unexpected loss, when people close to us become victims of terrorist acts, when our blood report shows that what we feared is true – what do we do in such moments?

The answer to all those is in this principle of the Gita. When our boat capsizes totally, if we can let go of all our preconceived expectations and ideas of how things should be, and let go of the resultant struggle, if we can calmly surrender to existence and let the river take us where it will, we would see our entire being revived and gathered up in a whole new way. We would see that we are not just travellers, but one with this great river. * We would realise the truth behind the Gita's teaching, 'The calm person who is steady in pain and pleasure, is fit for realising his immortal nature.'

It is in expanding to accommodate the challenges that life throws at us that we expand towards the fullness of our deepest nature. Only the caterpillar that gives up being itself becomes a butterfly!

ॐ

It has been three weeks since I started contemplating on the impermanent side of the world, as a regular ritual. What changes have occurred as a result, you ask? It is too soon to judge, but it did seem to give me some inner composure. I became aware of the wild wandering and craving thoughts of my mind. A new voice seemed to keep warning me, *'It is a world of Kaali, little fellow. Beware of your petty attachments and aversions.'*

Let me wait and watch where it takes me, whether I'll, ahem, attain the immortality the Gita verse talks about.

---

*We will get more into this in the later chapters on Jnaana.

When I told Sandy about it the next day, he gave his characteristic response, 'So you are trying to follow the Bhagavad Gita and become a real Venkiananda? Great soul!'

'You were the one who urged me on, psycho. I was only trying to write about it.'

'By the way, maapi,' Sandy said looking at me curiously in the middle of his reading, 'it doesn't seem like you are doing it for Barath Sir at all. The vigorous way you are writing it seems as if, I don't know, you are motivated by some deep personal quest.'

I didn't tell him that I really wanted to bring out the old Santosh in him and hoped that this would do it.

'Well, I am following only what Barath Sir told us once, Sandy.'

'What?'

'Never do anything for the sake of something else.'

'Oh yeah, I remember.'

'When you study, don't do it for getting a pass or getting marks . . . '

'But just to study, to know the subject,' Sandy finished the sentence for me.

'Let the study *study!*'

Sandy smiled as I said that. 'Okay, Boss. Let me do my job here and throw some questions at you. I too am getting involved in this. I can understand what your Gita is upto, till now.

'It says, 'live in the physical world, but with your roots in eternity,' though I don't know how much we can follow all that. But . . . ' he continued looking downwards with a thoughtful frown, 'something isn't clear. If we are this 'tranquil, eternal self' supporting the mind and body, why didn't we stay as such, Boss? Why the hell did we get into this place, acquiring the body, mind and all other stuff?'

Or in simple terms, 'Why is there a world? Why was such an 'evanescent' world created at all?'

It took me six days and nights of racking my brain through the Gita and other philosophical texts of Hinduism to answer that question.

'Dear Krishna, that is a reward for that petty joke on my part a page back, right? Pretty mean you are. Okay, no more jokes with the Gita. Get serious, Venki!' I told myself.

ॐ

WHY IN THE WORLD?

If we are this tranquil Cosmic Self beyond the mind and body, why didn't we stay as such? Why get into this world of Kaali? Why in the world is there a world? Why is there anything at all rather than nothing?

In the Gita, there are pointers that answer our question, when Krishna describes the relationship between him and us. We come across a verse in the tenth chapter, where Arjuna expresses his respect and veneration to the Lord seated before him.

> O Lord of the universe, no one can fully comprehend You.
> You alone know Yourself by Yourself. 10.14-15

Next Arjuna asks Krishna a very practical question.

> O Blessed Lord, in what various aspects
> Are You to be meditated upon by me? 10.17

He says, 'I understand that I won't be able to comprehend your transcendent form with the puny, little mind of mine. But please tell me how you are manifested in the world, so that I can perceive you in it.'

In reply, Krishna first says

> O Arjuna, I shall explain to you my prominent manifestations
> As there is no end to the ways I am manifested here. 10.19

He begins with the aspect of the Divine closest to us.

> I am the Self abiding in the heart of all beings.
> I am the beginning, the middle, and the end of all. 10.20

He then proceeds to the natural world

> Among luminous objects, I'm the Sun.
> Among bodies of water, I'm the Ocean.
> Among trees, I'm the Peepal.

> Among animals, I'm the Lion. 10.21-30

In the world of men, he says

> Among generals, I am Skanda.
> Among the great sages, I'm Bhrigu.
> Among warriors, I'm Rama 10.24-31

The answer we are searching for is indirectly conveyed in those verses. There are age-old theories behind the purpose of creation which go something like this, 'Consciousness chose to express itself, to manifest itself; hence it became the world. The world is a field of expression, a canvas God created, to paint himself. We are portions of God that have come here for self-expression.'

Asking God why you created the world is no different from asking a talented singer why she sings, or asking a mother why she loves her child. What can be the answer to that? Where there is a potential, it invariably seeks an expression.

The Divine power behind the universe is the reserve of every and all kinds of potential we see in the world. The world was the stage it created to express itself.

> **The one power of the universe thought,**
> 'I am one. Let me become many.'
> Taittriya Upanishad 6-2

For the Gita, the world is a *Dharmakshetra*, a field for doing our Dharma. It is a place for us to act out the truth of our being. The fulfilment of any potential is only in its expression in a suitable field. The world is, as it were, *a field of expression of Divine potential*. That is the reason for its creation. The water of life is a free flowing profusion that keeps expressing itself through a zillion forms.

> **O Arjuna,**
> There's no end to divine glories manifested in the world
> Whatever that is glorious, brilliant or powerful in any being,
> Know that to be a manifestation of a spark of my splendour.
> 10.40-41

I handed the above write-up to Sandy only for him to scoff at it, 'Oh? So what the fans say is true, huh? Tendulkar, Federer are all Gods, then?'

'Well, they are not Gods in the way you mean. But their talent is a spark of the Divine manifested. It is true for any talent.'

'Spark of the divine . . . ' he repeated after me. 'But I think there are exceptions. I bet Thalaivar Rajini is the most consummate manifestation of God in the world, as his fans would assert. Not a spark, but a big blazing flame.'

'Will you please stick to the topic?'

He thought for a moment. 'Hmm, interesting theory, Boss. Our Big Boss felt like expressing himself, and split himself into a billion life-forms, like electricity becoming heat and light in various instruments. But something doesn't gel for me.'

'Your Gita said, "Don't get into the clutches of the world." But if you think about it, Venki, the argument you gave continues to push us into the clutches of the world. If a hedonist is dependent on the sensual pleasures of the world, don't you think such an "expression-centred person" is still dependent on the world; on acting and expressing in it? Is it not still world-dependence?'

Yes. As he said, the reason I have arrived at seems too action-oriented. A few more days went by grappling with the question he had asked.

When I gave my next write-up to Sandy a few days later, I felt that this time I had chanced upon the real reason behind it for sure. This reason I arrived at was even more basic than what I discussed earlier.

ଓ

The world is a field for action as per the Gita. Though it seems valid, that alone can't be the sole reason for creation. If it were, then where does it culminate? When does the game end for an individual soul? The reason, though it seems to have truth in it, is too action-centred and world-dependent as Sandy said. What is the real reason then? We find the answer in a verse from the third chapter of the Gita.

> For the one who is content in the Self, satisfied in the Self,
> And who is pleased only in the Self,
> For him there is no further work to be done. 3.17

The same idea is conveyed in a later chapter too.

> **Having known me in essence, one forthwith merges in me....**
> **And he attains my eternal imperishable abode. 18.55-56**

So that is where the journey culminates. The Spiritual Masters of every religion, convey us the same message: humankind was created not by chance but for a legitimate purpose; for this great end.

As the Sufi mystic Jalaludeen Rumi put it in his poem *'Be Lost In the Call.'*

> *Why did you create these two worlds?*
> *Reality replied: O prisoner of time, I was a secret treasure of kindness and generosity, and I wished this treasure to be known, so I created a mirror.*

Sri Ramakrishna puts it in his characteristic plain-spoken style, 'The only purpose of life is to realise God.'[4]

So then, God-realisation or Self-realisation is what our life is basically about. That is the purpose life in the world was created to fulfil. Let us explore this idea further.

Imagine you are the nameless and formless universal spirit of serenity, wisdom and oneness; the reserve of unlimited potential and all the power that exists. Assume you have been that for Eternity. Now you plan to create a realm to express yourself in various forms. So you go on and create a world for yourself.

The world you have created is a place of great beauty and yours is a life of wonderful sensuous pleasures, with beautiful landscapes, sumptuous food, cool gadgets and so on. You would be the master of this world. The past, present, future are all according to your design. Having split yourself into a zillion beings, you would keep joyfully expressing all your latent potentials in this world through those forms.

Then, after a period of time, you might start feeling that the world you have created is cloying and insipid. Fed up with everything being normal and right, bored with knowing everything upfront, you might wish for an element of surprise and thrill. So you bring in some unexpected twists and turns in your life; situations with a bit of adventure in them, still fully knowing you are much more powerful than those situations and very much in control. This goes on for a period of time. Then the old boredom creeps in again.

Again you try to think of a way to make this adventure even more exciting and worthwhile and you wonder, 'What if I forget my all-powerfulness for a while, so that by calling forth the latent inner power in me while facing the adventure, I might wake up to the glory and greatness of who I am. How great would that be!'

The joy in such rediscovery of yourself is immense and beyond words, you realise. So you decide that that is the best way to put your created world to use. In order to do so you find a way to hide your true identity from yourself–through the self-imposed veil called Maya.

That is how this world and our lives in it in the present form came into being. Sri Aurobindo wrote that, *'Nature is a progressive self-manifestation of an eternal and secret existence.'* That is the truth that should guide the outer aspect of our life: progressive self-manifestation! He then goes on to say, *'The characteristic law of Spirit is self-existent perfection and immutable infinity.'*[5]

That is even more important for us to understand. Such self-existent perfection is the real nature of our Self. And to arrive at this real nature of ours is what the game is about, primarily. What happens after that? We make the entire outer mechanism a tool in the hands of the Spirit. When the bud is connected with its source, it blossoms spontaneously.

'Whoa! That was deep man,' Sandy started, 'I think I will have to read it again after two rounds of . . .'

'Dude, will you please shut up and complete reading the whole part?' I snapped.

ॐ

THE GAME OF LIFE

The statement, 'God created all beings to express himself,' makes it sound as though the process is need-based or narcissistic. Well, it sure isn't. The Divine needs nothing outside it to satisfy itself. The Divine is called *sarva kaaman*, one whose natural state is a supreme contentment.

Then what impelled the One to become many? It is just a game, a *leela*, asserts Hinduism.

> **Brahman's creative activity is not undertaken by any need,
> But simply by way of sport.**
> Brahma Sutra (2.1. 32–33)

In the words of Swami Vivekananda, 'There is no purpose in view with God, because if there were some purpose, He would be nothing better than a man. Why should He need any purpose? If He had any, He would be bound by it.'[6]

Now, if you can get that confused look off your face, we can try and understand what that means. Imagine you are a guitar player. An opportunity for a concert comes by. You cherish the challenge, train hard, and play a beautiful composition before a packed auditorium. Your performance is greeted with thunderous applause and you receive a standing ovation. That completes the action-reaction circle, but the question is, what does the whole thing *'mean'*?

What is the 'meaning' of a sunflower, a jellyfish, or a Fibonacci sequence? What is the 'meaning' of India winning the cricket World Cup? Or that of you attaining great success at work? What is the meaning of anything at all in the universe? If you think they are all wonderful patterns, things of beauty, joy and relish, they are! And if you want to consider them absolute nonsense, they are that too! They are both simultaneously, to borrow the words of the philosopher Alan Watts.[7] And that is true of anything in life.

At one level, life is about expression – something with a purpose. However, at its deepest level, at the level of Ultimate Reality, nothing means anything. It is all a game, *leela*. The world is 'an art and ingenuity without sense,' as Sri Aurobindo describes in his Savitri. (Book 2, Canto 5)

But wouldn't that philosophy – it all ultimately means nothing – dishearten us from getting involved in our worldly affairs? Not at all. It is a truth that liberates! Once we realise this for ourselves, we would then return to the game with a new, buoyant spirit. We would be done with all seriousness in life once and for all and start playing our roles in it gleefully. Because that is what it is after all, a game! Nothing would disturb our composure henceforth. But seeing it for ourselves is the key. And that is what the Gita aims to take us towards.

Sandy read it all silently sitting in front of me. He nodded his head contemplatively a few times while reading it. There was utter silence in the room for quite some time. I thought the material was starting to have some impact on him. I waited patiently for him to finish while browsing a Tamil weekly on his table.

'So, Boss,' Sandy said, 'Kaali, Brahman's leela, realising our True Cosmic self... I can see what it all points to, your skin practice is much worse than my psychiatry practice, isn't it?'

'Shut up, you nasty pig. Stick to the discussion.'

'Ha ha, just kidding. Guess I need to reread and think patiently about it all a bit. But one doubt I have. We are beings of Eternity you said. Then how do we keep doing so much wrong stuff in our lives? And what is the Divine impulse in us doing at those times?'

'...'

'What?' he asked.

'Nothing.'

I knew those questions are going to take some answering. I kept glaring at him, exasperated. The pig-head, without showing an iota of intent in following it or helping me, how easily he sits in the clinic and keeps effortlessly asking such pertinent questions!

Krishna deals with the question quite elaborately in the Gita when Arjuna asks it on our behalf. The answer to this question is at the very core of Vedantic teachings, and forms the second principle of the Gita we are about to get into.

> **O Krishna, by what is man impelled to do sinful acts,**
> **As if by force, even beyond his will? 3.36**

How indeed!

MIND

The Chinese philosopher Sun Tzu tells us in his book *The Art of War*, 'Know your enemy and know yourselves; in a hundred battles you will never be in peril.'

Quite true! Defeating an enemy requires that we understand him and his ways fully first. That is what we will try to do in this chapter, understand the enemy who has led us into the bondage we are in. But who is that enemy? A verse from the Upanishad answers us –

**Mind alone is for mankind
the cause of its bondage and liberation.
The cause of bondage when it is bound to objects.
And the means to liberation
When it is pure and divested of them.**
Maitri Upanishad 3:34

༺

I had taken my father's car to the morning OP. When I parked it in front of my clinic, an audio CD slid off the dashboard. Dattu's image graced the front cover, his hands raised up towards the heavens and a condescending smile on his face. It was the CD of the speech Dattu delivered at a Hawaiian resort. The blurb read, 'You are all caught up in ego. Give it off. Become egoless. It is this Baba's responsibility to guide you from there on.' The alarming statement immediately made me put it back and get down.

Kumar was waiting for me in the clinic.

'What's up, maaps?' I asked him as I entered my cabin.

'Saw the trailer of my thalaivar's new film? He sports a new handlebar moustache and rockets his Audi through the streets of Bangkok. Man, it's mesmerising! I am killing the replay button on YouTube. This film is definitely going to cross the 100 crore mark in our state, just wait and watch.'

I walked to the window, pulled open the chain of the vinyl

blinds, and then went and sat in my chair. Seeing me not showing interest in his words, he changed the topic.

'What type of weather is this, maaps? All saltpan owners of our town pray for the climate to be like this, I guess.'

'True, Kumar... this scorching heat!'

'Man, keep a bowl of corn in the open. It'd become popcorn by itself. Imagine, how great it would be if I were in Kodaikanal now? By the way, maaps, can you get us your father's car next week?'

'Yes, yes, good idea. Would be nice to take a small break,' I said excitedly.

All the philosophical stuff I was into over the past one month or so was indeed making me feel a tad heavy in the head.

'When are we going?' I asked him.

With a roguish twinkle in his eyes he said, 'Well, Sandy told me yesterday... I, he and a few of my friends will go to Kodaikanal, in the first week of October, during the Puja holidays. There won't be any patients at that time for Sandy anyhow. We are five people already, you know. We need a car. So if you can ask your father and get it...' he said half-hesitantly.

I understood what he was up to. 'Mmm, so everything is already planned, huh? Fine. My father will give his car if I ask. But I need to know something. What makes you guys believe that I will get it and give it to you?'

'Dei, maaps, is this what things have come to? Please da. Just this one time. You won't find our company enjoyable, you know. All these people are not to your taste. Next tour we will plan together for sure.'

'To hell with your friendship. When do you want the car?'

When they waved goodbye to me that Friday morning in my dad's car, what I was musing was, with Sandy and his lame remarks not going to be around for some time, I shall concentrate as far as possible on the book's philosophy and finish off the next portion before he returns. However, I had not realised at the time that with the tour Sandy would drift far away from the Gita.

THE CELLULAR UNIVERSE

A saying in Ayurveda goes

> As is the human body, so is the cosmic body.
> As is the human mind, so is the cosmic mind.
> As is the microcosm, so is the macrocosm.
> As is the atom, so is the universe.

Medical research comes up with new findings from time to time to help human beings regain and maintain optimal health. However, every medical researcher agrees that the body's natural tendency is to be healthy. It is enough that humans do not disturb this equilibrium. All medical interventions only complement this natural tendency.

Such an amazing machine this body of ours is! A staggering number of cells, hundred trillion of them almost, woven into a dozen systems approximately. Yet all the cells function interdependently in an amazingly immaculate way.

All these cells owe their origin to a single cell. At the moment of conception, every human being spent about half an hour of his life as a zygote, a cell the size of one-millionth of an inch. But now each of the hundred trillion cells that constitute our body is distinctive and well developed. The bond that holds together all these cells is the body's innate intelligence. That is the conductor of the orchestra. It is in abidance with this that every cell functions.

This intelligence is quite a remarkable entity. It is this which cures us of all diseases, and it never falls sick even when the body gets sick. Like a loving mother waiting to embrace its child, this intelligence is ever ready and willing to deliver health to its offspring. It is eager to set right whatever and whenever things go wrong in a cell or an organ. It is this ever-perfect and nourishing intelligence that every cell in our body is subordinate to.

In the body's cellular community guided skilfully with this innate intelligence, no cell considers its role separate from the scheme of things. Contributing to the body is all that matters to a cell. As the significance of the contribution increases, a cell gets more resources from the body to function better.

The system is close-knit and mutually benefitting. Suppose there is a disease affecting the skin cells, say an exfoliative reaction where the skin peels off from large areas of the body. In such case, the heart, in abidance with the innate intelligence, reflexly pumps more blood to the skin to cope up for the fluid loss through it and to provide extra nourishment to the remaining skin cells.

However, it is not like this way always. A few cells can become mischievous at times. They can undergo a genetic mutation, a change in their basic way of functioning, and start acting autonomously. If we could record the cell's thoughts, they would probably be, 'Why keep listening to the body's intelligence? I am going to function and acquire for myself.'

The body's intelligence wards off such cells at initial stages, but when the cells become too persistent and their number crosses a threshold, the intelligence withdraws and watches from a distance, so to say.

With time, these stray cells give rise to a new generation of cells, all functioning the same way. This abnormal behaviour is called anaplasia, or in layman's terms, cancer. These cancer cells proliferate in a rapid and uncontrolled way. They infiltrate and wantonly destroy the normally functioning adjacent tissues. They excrete enzymes and other chemicals that adversely affect the whole body. They greedily consume more vital nutrients of the body than they need, undermining the body's long-term viability. The result of it all is serious distress to the body and thereby to the progeny of the cancer cells as well. What is happening in the macrocosmic world of humans, as you might have guessed, is not something different from this.

ॐ

GOD AND THE LITTLE BIRD

One Pure Undivided Consciousness. That was all that existed at the beginning of time.

> In the beginning all this truly was the absolute Self alone.
> One without a second.
> There was nothing else whatsoever that winked.
> That thought, 'Let Me create the worlds.'
> Aitareya Upanishad 1-1-1

We saw in the last chapter the 'why' for the world; that it is a Divine game of hide-and-seek and what does the concealing job is the power called Maya. Let us explore this further.

Imagine a world where this Maya doesn't exist. What would we have then? All beings that evolved would have retained the memory that they are the 'One all-powerful Universal Spirit now clad in these interesting suits.' However, if it had been so, the play would lose its relish. There would remain no interest or joy in it.

Take a bird at this stage, say a little bulbul seated on the branch of a banyan. Ask it 'Who are you?' The bulbul would turn towards us and tell us in its gravelly voice: 'I am the One Great Universal Self, sustaining the cosmos. I am the origin as well as the dissolution of the entire universe. Tweet, tweet.'

Difficult to stomach, right? If the person who is hiding and the one who is seeking already know their whereabouts, where is the joy in the game? The very reason for the One Spirit individuating itself is not fulfilled. It is like you reading a mystery novel after having known every twist and turn in the plot beforehand.

This is how 'Maya' came into the picture. It hid who we are from us. It is this power that makes us identify with the body we are in. If I believe I am Venki, a small-time doctor in a coastal city in South India, it is because of this. Or else, right now, I would realise I am God.

> **Veiled by my divine Maya, I am not known by all.**
> **Therefore, the ignorant one does not know me,**
> **The unborn and eternal Spirit. 7.25**

Maya is not evil; it is a divine illusion. It is the expression of the creative joy of life. It is Maya and the ignorance that arises from it that confers on us the joy of living life here as a human; and it is Maya that bestows on us the joy of discovery of who we are – the very purpose of our existence in the world. How would we know light, if we don't experience what is dark?

So through Maya, one comes to believe that one is limited to a physical body. This individual identification that has arisen through the power of Maya is the ego – the sense of being 'you.' It is the body's intelligence in a cell identifying itself with that cell, and becoming the 'cell's intelligence' as it were, so that it can function in the body as the liver and kidney and heart cell. Absent this ego, you won't be able to feel or function as this 'you.'

The ego that has come into being remains in its original and pure form. Though now identified with the body, at its core the ego is still connected to the Great Cosmic Self. It is ever in an embrace of Eternity. It is from this level of the pure ego that the great Self-realised Masters functioned in the world. 'The ego continues to rise up in its pure form even in the Jivanmukta,' said Sri Ramana.

Thus, being a spiritual person or a saint doesn't mean that you give up your individuality and become egoless. That is not possible till the time you are in a body in this world. What you can do however, is recognise your ego to be an instrument of the spirit within.

Think of the great sages and saints of the past from any religion: Sri Adhi Shankara, Swami Vivekananda, Buddha, Rumi or Lao Tse. They were not docile or timid beings. They fiercely shook the minds of people to their very foundation. With deep love and an iron resolve they pulled people out of their smug worldliness. The powerful ripples they set forth in time by their life and teachings continue to reverberate in the minds of men and women through centuries. These feats were not accomplished without an ego, but the point is: *they didn't consider the ego as themselves.*

When Sri Adhi Shankara met his Guru for the first time, his Guru asked him who he was. The seven-year-old instantly responded,

Neither am I mind, nor intelligence. Nor ego, nor thought . . .
Nor am I earth or sky or air or the light.
Siva I am! Siva I am!! Of the nature of wisdom and bliss.
Nirvana Shatkam. Stanza One

That is what we too are, the Supreme Cosmic Self. The moral of the story: Transcending the ego doesn't mean getting rid of the small ego, but being centred in something higher within us, and using our ego as a mere instrument to Spirit's cause. I inhabit the identity of 'Venki' with vitality, vigour and wisdom! It is not about doing away with my sense of being 'Venki' and becoming egoless.

So Dattu Baba, what you said in your speech in that Hawaiian resort is inaccurate. Muahahaha!

It has been four days since those guys, wearing gaudy

T-shirts, waved me a gleeful goodbye sitting in my Dad's car. Not wanting to intrude into their fun, I hadn't called them up since then. However, I was curious to find out what they were up to and thus called Sandy that evening.

'Tour is going great, Boss, except that we are finding it quite difficult to control this Kumar when he is drunk. So, how's the Gita going?' asked Sandy.

'Well, I am trying to understand even more intriguing concepts now. How do your psychiatry textbooks define ego?'

'Aargh! Dude, why on earth did you have to remind me of my subject here? Ego! Well, it is the sense of 'I' we all have.'

'But do you know what Vedanta says? This 'I' is a prison, and we have willingly got ourselves into it.'

'Whoa! So the Gita is not going to say a single thing that we can accept easily, huh?'

'Hmm, if the scripture was a man, I think it would be one tough, hard-nosed task master,' I said half-jokingly. Even as I blurted that out, a part of me wondered if any punishment was in store for me for joking like this.

'Sandy darling, why are you behaving so politely with that guy these days? Come on, give the phone to me,' intruded Kumar.

'So, Piggy doctor, how is your business going?' he asked. After a pause I heard him sobbing!

'What is it, maaps?' I heard Sandy ask him.

'Sandy, this bloody pig Venki . . . he used to roam around with us till yesterday, sit and read all the books and magazines we gave him, smoke, drink and . . . and today suddenly he considers himself a big doctor! The pig thinks himself above us. He doesn't even talk properly to us. What are we to him then? Remember, Piggy . . . You are just a diploma. But my Sandy, a *Medicinae Doctore* . . . in the great branch of "pissichatry."'

'Dei moron, it is his car!' I heard Sandy shouting in the background.

'Shut up. Hear my final words before I hang up the phone, you, Piggy. Oh, you don't like that name, right? Piggy, Piggy, Piggy! It was so boring to sit inside the four walls and keep boozing, Piggy. So we are taking a tour of Kodaikanal. What should we call it, Sandy darling? Our whirlwind city safari?'

I listened patiently to all Kumar's blabbering, knowing it was no use talking any sense into him right then. I had had this behaviour from Kumar earlier as well.

'Give me the phone you fool,' Sandy hollered, right before the call got disconnected.

'Your friend eagerly awaits your arrival jackass,' I messaged Kumar, before I opened my Gita notebook.

ॐ

MAN AND HIS MAKE

Unlike a simple cell or a bird, man's internal make is a bit more complex. It is compared to a chariot in the *Katha Upanishad*.

> **Know the Atman to be the master of the chariot.**
> **The body is the chariot.**
> **The intellect, the charioteer. And the mind, the reins. 1.3.3**

The wisdom of the Infinite in our hearts* is said to be the master, the guiding force of our chariot. The intellect is the charioteer which is to be ever subordinate to that wisdom, and in control of the reins.

> **The senses are the horses. The (worldly) objects, the roads.**
> **The Atman, united with the body, senses and mind,**
> **is the enjoyer. 1.3.4**

Atman – Buddhi – Mind – Senses, that is the hierarchical model of our internal system. The senses are the horses by which the chariot meets the road, the world. So if we wish to bring the chariot under control, harnessing the wild horses can be a very effective first step.

That is, by the way, the basis of all the pujas in Hinduism. A visual form of God, the clanging of the bell, the lighting of incense, the *prasad*, the sandalwood paste or the sacred ash smeared on the skin are all

---

*'God resides in our heart,' it is said in the Gita. By 'heart' is not meant a place in our body, but the heart of one's being, the pure essence of ourselves. ('This is the abode of Brahman, the small lotus flower of the heart. What exists within that small space, that is to be sought after, that is to be understood.' *Chandogya Upanishad* 8.1.1)

regular parts of any puja. It is not God who requires all that. All those are methodical ways to turn the energy of the mind, ever frittering itself away through the five sense organs, inward and Godward.

To get a good grasp of that inner division within us, let us try an experiment. Try bringing to your mind someone who has hurt you in the past, someone whose very thought gets you pretty hot under the collar. Next, try visualising in detail the incident, the behaviour that infuriated you so much. Done? Are you seething with anger yet? Are you feeling like giving the moron a good hard punch? Excellent.

Now observe how the above said mechanisms functioned to produce that result. It was your sense organ, your eye, that conveyed the words from this page to your brain and made you *think* of the person. The entity that took over from there was your mind. In a flash of a second, it called up all the buried hurts and pains that person inflicted on you and caused your anger to well up.

And as you read that last paragraph, that part of you which took a neutral look at you from an outsider's perspective and perhaps smiled a bit, is your *buddhi*, the discriminating intellect.

Now let's take this just one step further, to the way in which things should be perceived. Try imagining the childhood of that person. No child begins its life on an evil note. That person too must have started off in the world as a sweet little child. Imagine the child looking at the world with eyes of innocence and wonder. What type of people must the child have met, what incidents could have pushed its heart to such meanness?

Think of the person as that child now. Imagine the child peeping out from the adult with confused eyes, through the mirror of murky beliefs laid over it by the world. We all are that after all – sweet, innocent beings transformed in various ways by our environment. If you are not blinded by emotion, transcending your personal anger, you might have felt a tinge of pity and compassion for what the person has become.

If you felt it, congrats, you just got a taste of the Divine Self in your heart. 'The holiest of all the spots on earth is where an ancient hatred has become a present love,' as the book *A Course in Miracles* puts it.

The body's intelligence connects and coordinates all the cells. Likewise, it is through the wisdom of our hearts our Greater Cosmic Self connects and coordinates all its individual portions.

> All creation is strung on me
> like jewels on a thread of a necklace. 7.7

Beyond the intellect, in our heart, where our Real Self resides, we are all not only connected but *we are all one*! That silent voice of the heart within, when listened and heeded to, is the compass that takes us towards the greatest glory of our being. Even while we lead separate existences, our true identity is shining in all its glory within our hearts, though not everyone is aware of it.

> **There is a light that shines beyond all things on earth,**
> **Beyond the highest, the very highest heavens.**
> **This is the light that shines in your heart.**
> Chandogya Upanishad 3.13.7

When we see pictures of two and three year old kids of distant nations who become casualties of war and terrorist acts, it is not without reason do we describe it 'heart-wrenching.' At the level of the heart, those children and we are connected. *We are one with them.* The heart is our end of the connecting thread to the Divine. The *buddhi* that heeds the silent voice of the heart can never sway from right judgement. We are always supposed to function in accordance with that discriminating wisdom of the heart.

> **If the mind is restrained**
> **and the buddhi possesses discrimination,**
> **And therefore always remains pure,**
> **Then the embodied soul attains that goal**
> **from which he is not born again.**
> Katha Upanishad 1.3.8

So that is the way Vedanta divides our internal being. The division is subtle. For, the functioning of it all is so seamless that it appears as one organic unit. However, it exists. What went wrong then? The Gita gives us the answer directly and indirectly in several of its verses.

> **It is desire and anger born of man's active nature**
> **That is the greatest enemy of man.**
> **It is insatiable and is of sinful nature. 3.37**

> He who abandons all desires,
> And becomes free from the feeling of I and mine
> attains tranquility. 2.71

That advice of the Gita could be easy enough for a person to follow in our times if he is comatose perhaps. How else can the others follow it? Let us analyse.

ॐ

'His name is Arumai Selvan. He belongs to your community only Sir. An important name in the ruling party's youth wing. Our Sir knows him quite well. He wanted to consult you since he heard you started practice here,' said Zab, my father's new P. A. (Zabdiel Finton – his peculiar full name). 'He will come today evening or tomorrow.'

'Okay, Zab.'

I was starting to get plenty of such 'community patients' referred by that particular guy.

The man came to the clinic the next day, clad in a sparkling white shirt and dhoti. The chunky gold chain that hung over his shirt had his leader's photo embossed on its pendant. Two similarly dressed minions came in along with him and stood behind as he sat in front of me at leisure.

'Wait outside,' he gestured to those minions.

After introducing himself, he started giving a lengthy, unhurried speech in his booming voice – about the long friendship between him and my father, about his pleasure in coming across a doctor from his community, about my community people being the original inhabitants of Tuticorin and how all others who are rich and famous now in the town were the ones who came in from Andhra and other Northern states and settled here. He also ranted how it is the duty of every person of my community to keep their growth under check.

'Oh! Our country needs more people like you, Sir' I replied.

As I was wondering when he would get up and leave, he said, 'Okay Sir, I will let you know when we plan our next regional meet. You should attend such events. Knowing our people would be hugely beneficial for you.'

'I'll try.'

He said before leaving, 'This building belongs to a Fernando, isn't it? If there's any trouble you face from those people, or any kind of problem you face in your practice, do let me know. I shall take care.'

'Sure.'

He left after forty minutes or so, as I let out a huge sigh of relief.

'So dear Krishna, the encounter with that slacker is a punishment of sorts for the tiny joke on my part a few pages back, isn't it? I get it' I said looking at Lord Krishna's drawing in the Gita's cover. 'Alright, no more frivolousness in my reading, I promise. Please don't subject me to such tortures again.'

There were even a couple of murder charges on him, I learnt from Zab. That guy has demonstrated for us exactly what we are about to discuss next.

ᴄ♋

Each of our minds is a unique and glorious instrument of spirit. In order for it to remain so we need to keep our individuality, the 'I' feeling in each of us, centred in the heart! Then it would always be in touch with, and be at one with the Divine intelligence. The wisdom from the Atman would be the master of the chariot.

However, since free will is inherent in humans, the 'I' can be centred anywhere we train it, depending on which thoughts we allow and nourish in us. Unfortunately the misuse of that free will lies at the root of all our problems.

ᴄ♋

THE SLIP INTO THE EGO

The mind and the senses are the parts of our consciousness that are in constant touch with the world. It is the rubber through which the vehicle of our inner being meets the world road. Just like a child at times forgets its mother and gets involved with its toys totally, in some people this new entity that has come into existence – the 'mind-child' – keeps chewing idle thoughts of worldliness straying away from the peaceful composure and wisdom of the heart. This is where it all starts.

The mind, when it keeps mulling on materialistic things disregarding the heart's wisdom, lays its first foundations of worldliness. The mind can't help but develop an attachment towards what it continuously dwells upon.

> **As much as a man thinks of objects,**
> **Attachment for them arises 2.62**

Hence do spiritual masters say we must maintain our mind like a garden keeping the weeds of unhealthy and unwanted thoughts away. Such stray thoughts are where it all begins.

> **When one can completely withdraw the senses**
> **from the sense objects, as a tortoise withdraws its limbs,**
> **Then the (inner) consciousness of such a person**
> **is considered a stable one. 2.58**

After work, man returns home. Likewise, the mind when idle, should be kept focused on its origin rather than remaining turned towards the world. Like a tortoise withdraws its head, neck and limbs into its shell, we should be able to withdraw from the world whenever needed. The Gita considers the one who has such ability, the man of stable and well-grounded inner consciousness, *prathista buddhi*. If a mind is repeatedly allowed to entertain materialistic thoughts, then it can't help but develop a strong attachment to the stuff it keeps thinking about. Like a cancerous cell, the mind would soon start flirting with the idea of living for itself ignoring the world. The dynamics are already set in motion. It gradually becomes stronger and out of control.

> **From attachment, desire comes.**
> **From desire (unfulfilled) originates anger.**
> **From anger arises delusion. 2.62-63**

Repeatedly thinking of something leads to an attachment towards that. Attachment transforms into desire. When a desire is satisfied, it gives birth to greed – the pattern becomes stronger. When it is not, it gives birth to frustration and anger. Anger is really the energy of desire expressed towards the obstacle that is blocking us from getting the object of our desire. When turned towards oneself the same energy of anger can transform into melancholy and depression.

The result: man, an eternal being whose nature is untainted bliss, becomes a deluded being of the world. The ego in man, instead of staying connected to the heart where the Lord resides, gets caught up in the tangled web of the mind, senses and their desires.

This delusion leads to loss of memory. 2.63

The memory being referred to here is the memory of what is right and what is wrong, of who we really are and why we came here. We become deluded creatures afflicted with the disease of worldliness.

It leads to destruction of discrimination.
By this man ruins himself. 2.63

Our discriminating power isn't just ignored or overpowered but *can be totally destroyed* as a result!

This is of course a simplified overview of things. But it is such small and simple things we miss in life that often get us into many a great trouble.

Watch your mind the next time it thinks, 'How nice it'd be if I get it', looking at a new gadget, for example. Observe how easily that thought transforms into, 'I have to get it,' ending up making you more edgy.

So it all starts with the constant worldly thoughts. That is the first mutation that occurs in our consciousness. The mind doesn't know that such a 'free' existence cut off from the heart's intelligence, is something that will imprison it in the world.

As this continues, something untoward happens; a new ego is formed – the mind's ego. Like a military dictator taking control, this ego – intoxicated with the whims and fancies of the mind – starts functioning autonomously. It turns a deaf ear to the wisdom and discrimination from the heart. Its style of thinking is exactly akin to a cancer cell.

Our sense of 'I' can be trained anywhere we want to – *Atman*, *buddhi*, mind or the senses. What happens now is, from being centred in its original Unity Consciousness and using the mind as its instrument, this new 'I," pitiably, *identifies itself with the mind.* It is like you identifying yourself with the vehicle you drive or the pen you write with. The 'I' loses its inner connection and a sense of its origin. It constrains itself to the impressions in the mind.

But how could the Divine in our heart allow such a thing to happen? What is he doing while all this is happening? This is where the 'freedom of will' that is inherent in the system, comes into play. What a good mother wants for the child is not dependence on or obedience to her, but the child becoming independent. God too doesn't want subordination, but willing adherence to truth. True love is always patient and kind. It doesn't howl like untruth. Its language is silence. As Rabindranath Tagore put it, 'God seeks comrades and claims love. The Devil seeks slaves and claims obedience.'

So that is the first problem that occurred in man – getting imprisoned in this new sense of 'I' that is deaf to the wisdom of the heart.

THIS IS 'I'

In a later chapter the Gita describes a man of divine nature. His first quality, it says is *abhaya* meaning fearlessness (16.1). Its corollary: the first quality of the mind's ego is *bhaya*, fear. This new ego is a very edgy creature. 'An empty, dull, stupid, ugly, guilty and anxious, petty, shoddy, second-hand entity,' in the striking words of philosopher J Krishnamurti.[1] A constant agitation and fear, *jvara and bhaya* according to the Gita, is its basic state.

Why should it be fearful? Let us try a thought experiment to understand it. Suppose you enter your room by twilight after a tired day. There, you happen to see a stranger – not directly, but as a shadow on the window curtain. What would be your first reaction? You would become alert and look to protect yourself. Then you would go near him carefully, enquire who he is and ask what he is up to in your room. You might look to drive him off as soon as possible to establish your monopoly again.

So you gather courage and start walking towards him. 'Who the hell is that?' you keep wondering as you take your steps slowly.

You then notice his reflection growing bigger and bigger as you approach him. A sliver of a doubt enters your mind and as you turn back you see the new knee-level bulb that has been put up in the house outside your room. That stranger behind the curtain was not a real person, but your own shadow cast on it. 'Ah,' you sigh in relief, 'that was nothing but myself.'

When we acquire ultimate knowledge of who we really are, we heave a similar sigh of relief.

> **By knowledge you will behold
> the entire creation in your own Self. 4.35**

We would live in a marvellous oneness with all there is. There would be nothing outside us to feel insecure or edgy about.

> 'There is nothing else but my Self, What am I afraid of?'
> he thought; Thereupon his fears were gone.
> It is from the presence of a second [entity]
> that fear arises verily.
> Brihadaranyaka Upanishad 1:4:2

However, for the 'I' disconnected from the heart, suddenly it becomes 'my body', 'my mind' and 'my beliefs' versus things outside that are not me. It feels frightful. And to allay this fear, the ego constantly looks to preserve its own identity.

When the ego becomes imprisoned in the mind, we become identified with the mind. We are nothing more than a bundle of beliefs, habits, judgements, opinions and imaginations we have acquired from the past that we always hold on to by all means. What I call 'I', is the prison I have imprisoned myself in and 'you' – the prison you are talking from. It is these dead past impressions living a life through us in an alive and dynamic world. We become pawns in the hands of our past. *When the ego reigns, it is virtually a world of walking corpses we live in!*

This pattern too is not stable or fixed entity. We don't think the same thoughts or have the same beliefs as we did a few years ago. Fifteen years ago I used to be a fan of Madhuri Dixit. Now another heroine, Samantha, has replaced her. (For the uninitiated, she is the heroine of that housefly movie.) Tomorrow it could be someone else!

Even our deeply held preferences change through life, thereby changing our sense of 'I' too. Like a chameleon, the 'I' periodically gets coloured by different entities it comes into contact with. For some their religious dogma colours it. For some, a fanatic affinity towards their caste colours it, and for others it is a movie star. Our language, our state, our political ideology, or for that matter a toothache, a respiratory infection, a traffic jam, a casual comment, a stare, all have an amazingly free hand in colouring the inner walls of this ego prison.

Having imprisoned ourselves inside it, there is no way we can feel real intimacy with anyone and anything – though we may delude ourselves into believing so. The ego's love is at best a sense of camaraderie between confused souls. The ego always looks to preserve its identity intact. And it always wants to be surrounded by people supportive of its pattern. When someone disrupts the pattern, it feels threatened, chagrined. A man whose pattern is disturbed would turn all the energy of his inner fever and conflict towards the factor threatening it. All the squabbles, disputes and heated arguments we come across in daily life are two ego selves interacting. An ego always tries to prove itself right and the other wrong. Our Real Self, on the other hand, never feels insecure or threatened.

Equanimity of the mind is indeed Yoga. 2.48

Samatvam Yoga uchyathe' in the Gita's words. When you live in Yoga with your Divine Self, you are totally equanimous. All the serious things in life seem playful. The frightening things become interesting. This loving presence – the fundamental 'I' of ours – is a plane quite different from the ego-plane we live in.

'The pure impersonal self which supports the universe has no egoism and makes no demand on a thing or person; it is calm and luminously impassive. (It) silently regards all things and persons with an equal and impartial eye of self-knowledge' wrote Sri Aurobindo.[2]

However, when I am just an ego, I can't help judging things as it relates to my model. I do it continually. When this inner dynamic translates itself into the real world, the results can be horrendous! Personal enmities, racism, communal riots, religious wars, all owe their origin to this: someone out there threatens 'our' pattern. And we need to reassert our pattern by vanquishing the 'other.' We have come to strongly and fundamentally believe that we are that pattern, and when the other demeans it, it seems to us like he is threatening our very existence. And the ego will go to any extent to establish its rightness and reaffirm its pattern again – even terminating the other one's life in a brutal way!

ଔ

THIS IS MINE

All that we saw – sticking to and defending the 'me-ness' at any cost – is just one way the insecurity of the ego looks to balm its pain. If that is all there is to our bondage here, then getting out of it would be as easy as turning our heads and having a look at what is behind us. But the cancer of the mind that is quite well-established now progresses to its next dreadful stage. Let us travel back in time to see what it is.

Humans arrived on Earth. A few among them got infected with the 'I' disease and started defending their 'me-ness'. They admonished, punished and killed those who didn't comply with them and established their authority every time. However, the ego inside them, now well-established in its own pattern, still felt edgy.

The ego then sought counsel from the mind, 'No one is around to threaten my pattern. Still why am I feeling this edgy within?'

And what the sagacious mind came up with was this, 'Yeah true, I still feel the edginess. Let me suggest a solution. See that beautiful hut over there by the riverside? You see how happy the guy residing in it is?'

'Well, yes.'

'We will make it ours. When we do that, this feeling will go off. Then see how happy you are going to feel.'

'Is it? Are you sure?' the ego asked.

'That is to the best of my knowledge,' the mind replied. This mind only has worldly temptations as its foundation. That is all it knows.

That is the second part of the mad solution the mind comes up with: to keep acquiring and hoarding more and more worldly stuff as 'mine.' It brings in a worldly desire as a solution for the itch. From the ever-alive oneness in its heart it can securely be rooted in always, the ego turns to external stuff for security. The energy of deficiency gets transformed into the energy of desire.

So the ego now starts spending all its energy and resources to acquire such a hut for itself. If the heart-centred people ask, 'What are you doing? What will you gain by acquiring that hut?,' the ego answers circumspectly, 'What will I gain? Well, happiness.' In other words, 'I think the hut will solve my internal itch.'

However, the disconnected ego doesn't know that as it works to acquire the hut, all it is doing is keeping itself busy so that the itch doesn't surface.

Even after years, when the hut is built, it has only scratched the itch a little without addressing its cause. Even the most sensuous pleasure in the world has but a short reign. The ego finds that once it finally gets the hut it dreamt of for years, the mind wants a villa. The itch always returns and remains. And the ego keeps trying to fulfil its every desire in order to get rid of the itch.

> **Those who are ignorant of the Self have no choice**
> **but to keep depending on outer objects and experience.**
> Chandogya Upanishad 8.1:5

When desire is what controls our life, it is like, 'trying to extinguish fire with petrol,' in the words of Ramana Maharishi. Each such materialistic chase only makes the pattern stronger. It not only doesn't solve the problem, but also leads to more and more desire and separation. A terrible and vicious cycle ensues. To use Swami Vivekananda's words, we end up becoming like the bull used for grinding oil seed. We just keep going round and round without getting anywhere.

An oft-quoted incident from Mulla Nasrudeen's life demonstrates this truth quite vividly. Mulla was a mystic of the Sufi sect of Islam. He was once searching for a lost coin near oil lamps in the dark of the night. His neighbour, a materialistic person to the core, who passed by the scene, saw Mulla and accompanied the search. He had respect for Mulla, though he never understood what Mulla taught.

After some time, he asked Mulla, 'Sir, there's no coin here. Where did you lose it?'

Mulla pointed to a place far away and said nonchalantly, 'Over there, Sir . . . near that well.'

'There? Then why are you searching here?' the neighbour was puzzled.

'Because it's bright here,' Mulla replied.

The neighbour thought he was mad and went off. He didn't realise that it was his materialistic ways the monk was compassionately making fun of with his allegorical action: man losing his connection within and searching it outside to fix the incompleteness.

ଓ

I was watching my mom as she sat near me and started making a long list in her notepad.

'What, Venki, looking very calm these days?' she asked even as she was busy with her list.

'Nothing, mom.'

'I don't know, but something seems out of place with you. I have been noticing you for some time. You don't look alright at all.'

'Mom, won't you leave me alone?'

Even when I talk to her, I either mock her ways or scold her for it. Still she can't put up with my silence. My sweet, stupid mom!

'I have to go to the textile shop to buy certain things for our ashram. Can you drive the car for me?' she asked me next.

'There's been a devastating flood in Ambai. Our ashram people are going to distribute clothes and food to the people there.'

'Oh, is it?'

I couldn't believe that Dattu's people were doing such things. It didn't sound plausible. There had to be something more to it.

'Kautilya Maharaj, our Swamiji's chief disciple is going to give free Deeksha to all the suffering people there, so that they gain the inner strength to come out of what happened to them,' she continued. 'And if they want to continue with their spiritual journey, they will be offered further courses at a much discounted price.'

Now that was more like Dattu. Not missing the slightest chance to bring in more people into his organisation. And mom wants me to help her with this? No way.

'Dei Venkat, please da,' her request had become a plea now.

ॐ

I was taking her to the shop in dad's Santro. Sitting in the front seat, she was still busy checking the list in her hands.

I could see that Dattu and his whole organisation exemplified the principle of the Gita I was studying now, trying to bring in more and more people under their umbrella to alleviate the fever of their egos, to make themselves feel better.

Musing along those lines, I lost concentration and almost bumped into the two-wheeler that stopped before us at the traffic signal.

'Venki...' mom screamed in fear, at last raising her head in a frenzy from the list.

I stepped on the brakes in a flash and stopped the car.

'Sorry, amma. I was lost in thoughts.'

The two-wheeler guy glared at me.

'Stop playing this ego game dude. Be equanimous,' I felt like retorting angrily.

But something within me told me to be careful. I was getting punished whenever I think like this.

So I decided to accept my mistake and apologised to the man. He turned away, shaking his head in frustration.

'Venki, are you alright da? You really don't seem normal at all to me these days,' mom started talking with real anxiety.

There she goes again! I felt like telling her that I was trying to become normal but that would only have made her more anxious, so I desisted.

ॐ

To continue with our topic, though totally identified with the mind and what is in it, there are moments when streaks of light from our true identity shine through the ego-mind. Orthodox psychology, ironically, calls them 'peak experiences.' 'Peak experiences are sudden feelings of intense happiness and well-being, possibly the awareness of an "ultimate truth" and the unity of all things... the experience fills the individual with wonder and awe... he feels at one with the world, and is pleased with it,' Abraham Maslow said.[3]

People in peak experiences are closest to their true identities, their real selves, said Maslow. Freud describes something similar in his works under the name *religious experience*. According to him religious experience is something primitive, archaic and lower than the experience of daily life!

Psychology sees us as minds and egos. Then, the experience of our True Self is indeed a 'peak experience.' But Vedanta tells us, 'You are the Eternal Light of the Brahman. Your nature is untainted, Infinite Bliss.'

It is our separated ego that is a perversion according to it. It isn't satisfied with momentary glimpses into our real nature. It wants us to get out of the pit we are in and always live there. What we are undergoing is a *trough experience* according to it. As long as we don't realise this, we would continue to undergo all the weariness of life, longing for such occasional 'mind-blowing,' 'out of the world,' 'peak' experiences.

ଓ

VASANAS

When Krishna speaks about the importance of taming the ego-mind, Arjuna expresses his anguish on how he feels about it.

> O Krishna, the mind is very unsteady, turbulent,
> powerful and obstinate.
> I feel restraining the mind is as difficult
> as restraining the wind. 6.34

That is a pretty accurate summing up of all the qualities of our mind. The 'mind' doesn't refer to a mechanism for conscious thinking alone. It also has a deeper part. Freud's psychoanalysis calls it the unconscious mind – that deeper part of the mind outside our awareness that contains forces that are directing our behaviour. It is composed of feelings, urges, and memories that are outside our conscious awareness. According to Freud, the unconscious is the underlying influence of all our thoughts and actions, even though we are unaware of it.

Vedanta calls those impressions in the unconscious, *'vasanas.'* Vasanas are the deep imprints left in the mind by our past actions. All actions, good or bad, leave these footprints in the mind. The 'me' and 'mine' thoughts too, when repeated over a period of time, become deep seated vasanas in us.

The mind first creates its vasanas, and then in turn is controlled by those. When we get inspired to change our negative habits, it is the attracting force and familiarity of these vasanas that pull us back to our status quo the next moment. These vasanas are the imprints which an individual soul carries with it when it separates itself from the physical body upon death. Vasanas are the very cause of rebirth.

The bad vasanas can be annihilated only by gradually creating good vasanas to counter them. They cannot be plucked out and thrown away just like that. We have to give the devil its due. And that is what Karma Yoga and Dyaana Yoga are all about.

ଓ

THE TWO BIRDS

One of the sages who composed the Upanishads saw this whole human predicament with a poetic eye. He compared the untainted Self in our hearts and our puny ego to two birds seated on a tree, the latter formed from the former – akin to the moon illuminated by the rays of the sun.

> Two birds, united always and known by the same name,
> Closely cling to the same tree.
> One of them eats the sweet and bitter fruit.
> The other looks on without eating.

One bird excitedly hops between branches on the lowest part of the tree eating the sweet and bitter fruits. 'Oh, how pleasurable life is!' it thinks while nibbling at the sweet fruits. Coming across a bitter fruit, it feels miserable. The other bird, seated with a serene composure on the top, doesn't get into this game. It sits and watches everything peacefully.

Soon the excited, hopping, bird is fed up with the fleeting and impermanent pleasure it experiences, accompanied by periods of misery. Utterly disgusted, it flies up and loses itself in the first bird from which it had arisen to begin with.

The two birds are inside us right now. The bird on the top of the tree is our Greater Cosmic Self, and the bird below – our puny ego self; the mind's 'I.'

> The individual self, bewildered by his ego, grieves and is sad.
> But when he recognises the worshipful Lord
> as his own true Self,
> and beholds his glory, he grieves no more.
> He, the wise, transcending both good and evil,
> And freed from impurities, unites himself with him.
> Mundaka Upanishad 3.1.1–3

To be the mind's 'I' is discomfort, frustration and pain. To save ourselves from the discomfort, we have no choice but to keep amusing ourselves. We virtually amuse ourselves to death! All the daily power struggles at home and workplace, the potpourri movies and tabloids, shopping sprees and fashion obsession – all of those are attempts at psychic numbing of that discomfort. It is our version of the excited hopping of the bird.

That then is the second principle of the Vedantic philosophy: **Be wary of the mind and its 'I' and 'mine' games.**

'In thinking 'this is I' and 'that is mine,' man traps himself, as does a bird in a snare,' goes a verse in Maitri Upanishad (3.2). Like a silkworm getting caught in its own cocoon, man is caught in his own self-created web of 'me and mine.'

ॐ

Sandy and Kumar had finally returned from their trip – my father's car standing in the car parking told me. The guys had come to my house by early morning, parked stealthily and slipped away. The driver they had taken with them had already informed me elaborately of their adventures in Kodaikanal.

'I asked them to go to your room. They were in some hurry and went off,' my mom, the only early riser of the house, told me.

I took a look at the car. For all that it had been through – Kumar carrying a street-dog to Coaker's Walk in Kodaikanal, ('Poor little creature, never has been beyond the lodge premises you know!') an attempt at his driving it like his thalaivar and dashing against a two-wheeler parked on the pavement, and the puking he did in the car on the last day – it looked quite okay, except for some food stains in the back seat and a dent in the front bumper.

An internal conversation ensued:

'How dare they do all that to the car?'

'Relax, maaps, it is father's car after all. Let the man spend a bit for your friends.'

'But how dare Kumar talk like that to me over the phone?'

'Now that is what I call a legitimate concern. We will fix that.'

ॐ

I took the write-up and went to Sandy's house in the afternoon. I was wondering how he would react to it. Certain things I read in the Gita while preparing this topic were so awe-inspiring that I had to close the book and take a break for the concepts to sink in. And I couldn't control my amazement at such a startling concept: living outside the ego, which is a prison in itself! What a great release and freedom that would be!

I approached Sandy's house. My eyes saw what they were eagerly waiting for, Kumar's bike parked outside the compound wall.

'So, little rat, you are here, huh?'

As I entered Sandy's room, Kumar was laughing away at something. He turned and looked at me standing near the door. Before he could move, I quickly went and sat next to him, and caught hold of his hands.

'What, Sandy? Forgot that you have a clinic?'

'I just see two or three patients per day now, boss. Can't move once practice picks up, you see . . . and sorry about the car. We will share the repair charges,' he said.

'Don't bother. So, my friend . . . ' I turned towards Kumar, 'How was the trip? And how was your, what was that, whirlwind city safari?' I asked him. His hands were still in my tight grasp, and they had started trembling by now.

'Trip? Oh, it was good . . . good. Thanks, maaps. Okay, you continue,' he said turning towards Sandy, 'I have a purchase waiting at my computer centre.'

He took out his phone with one hand, dialled a number and kept it over his ears. 'Hello, has it been delivered? I am . . . I am on my way . . . '

He tried to get up and leave. All the time he was talking, I could hear the busy tone at the other end. I snatched the phone from him and said, 'He will talk to you later, dear busy tone. Now a friend has come to pay back a debt. So Kumar boss, tell me more about the safari. What happened to the dog you took with you to Coaker's Walk in the car?'

'Dei, I really have a purchase waiting.'

'Come on, man. First sit down. By the way Sandy, here is the next part of the write-up. Read it soon and tell me when you are finished. We will discuss.'

'Dei, my purchase da . . . '

'Purchase, huh? You know what? That is really wonderful, Kumar. How responsible and sincere some people are towards their duty . . . even when they know they are going to have a brush with death, shortly!'

Kumar's face was turning white.

'By the way, you said Venkat DD. You know what the other part of my name is?'

'Venkat, please da. I didn't really mean it, you know?'
'And can you please expand DD for me?'
'Maaps . . . '
'I said, expand it.'
'Diploma in . . . Dermatology.'
'No, no. That second D in your case stands for . . . ' I said getting up, ' . . . Demolition!'

Sandy got up, switched off the TV and started talking to a medical representative on his phone, not minding a bit the funny sounds Kumar was making as I gave him his due. After a short while, I turned back and said as I was about to leave, 'Kumar, it's been almost a decade since we finished our schooling. Today, after a long time, I really felt like a child yet again, you know? It felt like a release for me really. Thank you, dear.'

'I told you, dude. Did you listen?' Keeping his phone down, Sandy asked Kumar who was lying flat on the floor, staring vacantly at the fan.

ॐ

A day went by. 'Did you read?' I asked Sandy.
'Sorry, I will read it today for sure.'
Two days later, 'Oh I totally forgot. Today hundred percent.'
Three days, then four, till an entire week passed by. 'Just started' he said when I called him.

He seemed to be in the hangover of the tour. Anyway I was determined to make him read. More than anything, I had faith in Barath Sir's words. I believed that Sandy would transform gradually as he read it, all his present ways notwithstanding.

After a while I got fed up with his lethargy and went straight to his clinic.

'Ha, here comes Venkiananda! Just now I finished it. So boss? My field treats various disorders of the mind. But your Gita, I don't know, it is pretty bizarre sounding for me . . . portraying our ego-mind as some megalomaniacal villain. I don't understand this living in some stillness beyond the mind! The mind with all its impressions is what we "are" according to my branch. It is our centre of existence. But when that seems to be the centre of all our problems, man, it sounds freakish.'

Well, to answer him, the Gita doesn't demean the mind.

I am the mind among the senses 10.22

says our Big Boss when describing the glorious things in the world. The mind with all the past impressions in it is sure needed to function in the world. If one is to live ignoring that, a Gandhiji wouldn't have bothered fighting the British, or a Tagore couldn't have written his poems at all. All these impressions are there in a Self-realised Master too. But how he differs from us is, *he doesn't consider himself as that*. He doesn't get caught up in it.

Hinduism presents before us so many Gods to worship. That doesn't mean there are numerous gods. Each god represents a power, a personality of the one Divine Self.

> **God is truly one.**
> **The knowers of Brahman**
> **do not admit the existence of a second.**
> **He alone rules all the worlds by His (various) powers.**
> Svetasvatara Upanishad 3.2

And all those powers, those facets, are alive in our being right now to be invoked by us. When we study the images of those gods, each of them is shown to be sporting a *vahana* or a vehicle, which is an animal. Lord Muruga, who represents the charming aspect of the Divine, has a peacock as his vehicle, which reflects the qualities of the God. The creative god Brahma is depicted with a swan, denoting sensitivity and beauty. Durga, the goddess of valour, is represented seated over a lion, denoting power, will and determination.

When we invoke each aspect of the Divine in us, it is the mind that assumes the form of the vehicle. The mind is indeed like a powerful animal. It is there to serve as a vehicle for our inner spirit. Discipline it and it will do wonders. The mighty monster will put all its power and potential at our feet. Like the snake around the neck of Siva, it would serve as an adornment for one's spirit.

However, the mind as a master? We are doomed then. Because when it crowns itself as the master, the mind doesn't realise that it would only become a servant to its own wanton worldly desires.

I met Sandy next in a doctor's meet that was arranged in banquet hall of a three star hotel. I saw him from a distance with a plate in his hands and having a lengthy discussion with Dr Prakash Periyasamy (PP, as we refer to him) – one of the senior-most physicians in Tuticorin. Sandy was always fond of talking about his exploits: his mesmerising manners with patients, how he extracts till last drop, the perks and stuff from the medical reps and lab people, and so on. Quite a repulsive caricature the man was!

Sandy noticed me standing in a corner and came near me.

'Hmm, Venkiananda, it's what you shared that is occupying my head mostly these days. And you are starting to make me feel very guilty da. Why don't you leave me out and carry on by yourself? You are doing very well without me,' he said.

'Ha! That's great. Just what I wanted.'

'Don't say that, Sandy. It is, after all, the last assignment our Sir gave us. For his sake at least we will do it together one last time.'

'All your nasty philosophies about life have at last met their right match, my dear! Doomed are your ways. Ha ha!' I laughed within.

'I am still not convinced of one thing though. Our Big Boss, didn't he know before giving this faculty called mind to us that it has its side effects? That it could go wrong like this? Why doesn't he withdraw it from the market then?'

'Of course, he knew, just like our mother knew when we were babies that we'd fall down a few times before we start walking on our own.'

'Oh! You have learnt to handle questions rather well. It is his farsightedness and patience that is mistaken for indifference, huh? Fair enough. But even then, this falling down and getting up, and the pain associated with it . . . it seems to be lasting a long time . . . since the birth of humanity, isn't it? Doesn't it appear like a mother who has become callous towards the child?'

GOD AND US

Why does the Divine let us fall down and get up time and again? *It is because we are not falling down at all in reality!* We can never fall down because we are eternal portions of the Divine.

We have just become *identified with the part of us that falls down*. And that is the cause of our misery. It is the sunlight now identified with the moon believing that it undergoes all the waxing and waning. We would see the truth of this statement for ourselves only when we wake up to the Ultimate Reality. That was the reason Masters like Sri Ramana were never interested in giving any other solution to the problems their disciples brought to them. The one ultimate solution of Self-realisation was all they put forth to everyone every time.

'When someone sleeping next to you shouts seeing a tiger in his dream, what will you do? Go into his dream and fight with the tiger or wake him up?' Sri Ramana asked his disciples.

ॐ

'Whatever, Boss! Something isn't sitting well with me still. We are now identified with the part falling down, and feeling the pain hard, isn't it? The mother, at least she can send us some message or maybe some guidance, right? "Children, you are doing this wrong. Do like this. You won't have to suffer anymore . . ." something of that sort. How can she just sit and watch her children falling down and getting up repeatedly? She still appears callous to me . . . . Hey wait.' he stopped abruptly, 'I am getting the answer to that question myself. She does send us her guidance, right?'

Exactly! This is what the Lord declares emphatically in the Gita in one of its renowned verses

> Whenever there is a decline in Dharma
> and the rise of adharma,
> I manifest myself (in the world) O Arjuna. 4.7

> He who thus knows in its true light, my divine birth and action,
> Leaving the body, is not born again. He attains to Me. 4.9

Whenever materialistic energy dominates the world, the spiritual energy, though it may seem to be at low ebb, always resurges. 'Whenever on earth you see an extraordinary holy man trying to uplift humanity, know that He (God) is in him,' said Swami Vivekananda.⁴ Every God-realised man is in truth God himself. He has died to his little self and allowed the Divine birth to take place in him.

It is the Divine who came as Krishna and Jesus and Mohammed, as Ramakrishna Paramhamsa and Ramana Maharishi, as Saint Francis, Meister Eckhart and Jalaludeen Rumi, Buddha and Mahaveera, Guru Govind Singh and Swami Vivekananada. All those are various eponyms of the same author; different adaptations of the same story. We disregard him and his message at our own peril.

> **The ignorant ones, not knowing my supreme nature**
> **As the great lord of all beings,**
> **Disregard me when I assume human form. 9.11**

Leave out religion and spirituality. When was the last time you heard a song that totally calmed your mind and touched your heart; read poetry that connected deep within you? All that too comes from the Divine. Any creator of a good work will tell us that it is from their heart that they did the work. And who else is seated there?

There are so many ways in which the Divine Mother says to the child, 'It's alright. I'm here. Come to Me.'

The child listens, and it experiences a gleam of its lost connection too, but submits to the ways of the ego-mind at the next instant. The curse of familiarity! It has got so used to the ego-mind that it sees such moments of genuine connection as fortuitous *peak-experiences.*

The Divine doesn't impose its will on us. We have come into this realm as free souls. The Divine respects our freedom, wants us to walk by ourselves, and keeps sending messages knowing that one day we would hear it and heed it. We can't stray permanently from who we really are.

Jalaludeen Rumi expresses this thought in one of his poems this way, 'Come, come, whoever you are. Wanderer, worshipper, lover of leaving. It doesn't matter. Ours is not a caravan of despair. Come, even if you have broken your vows a thousand times. Come, yet again, come, come.'⁵

'Oh? That is nice to hear. So I can roam around for some more time before deciding to come back, huh?'

'Well, if a patient insists on coming to a doctor only in the terminal stage of his disease, what can the doctor do? Our Big Boss will cure it for sure, I guess. Only that the patient will find the treatment a bit gruelling.'

'Hmm! Dude, there's another thing I'm interested in knowing. How does God look at us when we are busy in our mental pursuits ignoring our true identity totally – as stupid fools? Or, 'What a mess these idiots have made of their lives and the world?' What does he think? Does the Gita say anything about that?'

It of course does. The Gita answers that question in one of its most poignant verses.

> **The Lord doesn't consider the demerits and merits of any.**
> **Wisdom is enveloped by ignorance,**
> **Thereby beings are deluded. 5.15**

A vacuum is not a demonic entity. It is not the opposite of air. It is just the absence of air. The darkness in our minds too is not the opposite of light, but an absence of light, our ignorance of our true nature. The grey clouds across the sky can obscure the sun temporarily. But what harm can they do to the sun? When we understand the darkness of our minds for what it is – an absence – then the dynamics of our approach towards it changes. We don't have to fight with the darkness. We only have to let in the light.

> **Therefore with the sword of knowledge,**
> **Cut asunder all doubts born of ignorance.**
> **Resort to Yoga and arise O Bharatha! 4.42**

Swami Vivekananda proclaimed in a similar spirit to the people of the world at the Parliament of Religions, 'Ye are the Children of God, the sharers of immortal bliss, holy and perfect beings. Ye divinities on earth. . . . Come up, O lions, and shake off the delusion that you are sheep . . .'[6]

Getting out of the set ways of our mind we have imprisoned ourselves within, to the freedom and bliss of our True Cosmic Self is the exciting journey we are about to take. The Gita elaborately discusses the various ways towards that knowledge. It integrates all the teachings of the Upanishads and gives us an orderly route back home.

'The next chapter has come finally, huh?' asked Sandy.

'Yup.'

'So we are going to become lions reading it. That'd be great. But one thing is sure, I will keep a shaving razor handy and keep myself well-trimmed if I become a lion,' Sandy went on, stroking his short stubble. 'Or maybe I'll keep a hipster beard.'

'I wish I had a scalpel that can cut through flesh now,' I said glaring at him.

'Ooh!'

☙

ON PRACTISING THE WISDOM

Be wary of the mind and its 'I' and 'mine' games! That is the second principle of the Gita we discussed so far. Practising this principle means this: *becoming aware of it all happening within ourselves.* Not just intellectually knowing it. Intellectual knowledge is just a starting point. If we feel content with that, it only adds to the pomposity of our ego. The way is not to intellectually know, *but to look at the matter from our heart!* That is how we put what we read till now into practice.

Hinduism calls this *Saakshi bhaava* – the attitude of remaining as a witness to one's mind and feelings without getting carried away by them. This 'seeing' is not a function of the mind. It is not about seeing 'with our mind' all those dynamics happening inside it. Then our 'I', at the most, only shifts to a different location inside the mind prison. *The witnessing process belongs to our Higher Self.*

I am the witness and the substratum. 9.18

Says the Lord when describing himself. As we cultivate this witness attitude in us, we grow more and more in oneness with Him. Like the Upanishadic bird, we become more and more united with the part of us that is detached and unaffected by it all: our Greater Cosmic Self.

We can begin by watching the roguish part of our mind from our good part. Then gradually, we can train ourselves to watch both our good and bad sides from the stillness of the heart.

Witnessing is not something to do once and be done with. It requires continual practice. If we can train ourselves to see the mind and its ways with compassion and understanding, if we can see and smile at it, then that witnessing itself can elevate us to that mystical experience saints have had – the experience that we are the Untainted Self beyond the mind.

I am Pure Consciousness, the Aware Witness,
Forever Sacred, and independent of all experiences.
Kaivalya Upanishad 18

We then practise engaging with the mind more and more as an 'aware witness', and not as a helpless creature caught up within it. This is a practice that is a bit difficult, yes, but not impossible for a beginner. A centring practice like meditation could help us. As we witness, we awaken more and more.

Our earnestness is the only criteria for such witnessing. Karma Yoga and Dyaana Yoga are all about purifying our being and giving enough strength to this witnessing aspect inside us.

The Yoga of Karma and Dyaana

KARMA

'Adraadra naakku mukka naakku mukka naakku mukka...'

The *kuthu* song blared through my room from the audio system. I was singing along as I was getting ready for the day's work.

'Dei Venki, what kind of song is this? Lower the volume! Sheik uncle has come from Qatar, and your father is finalizing an important business deal with him,' mom yelled standing outside the room.

'Oh is it?' I said to her and kept continuing. 'Adra adra nakku mukka nakku mukka...'

'You are one stubborn mule, Venki,' she lashed out and went away.

Not bad, I was progressing quite well with Big B's last assignment. *'Good work dear boy. Keep going,'* I could feel that he was telling me from somewhere. I also felt triumphant that I made Sandy read till this point and that the write-up had made him feel a little guilty about himself.

'Last days for your unscrupulous ways dear friend! Let me see how you counter this. And hopefully last days for the burden of guilt weighing me down too. Nakku mukka, nakku mukka...'

ଓ

I entered Sandy's clinic with the initial write-up on Karma Yoga. Opening his cabin door I sat in front of him.

In the corner of the floor, I saw a large, new AC lying in an unopened box bearing a strange red sticker.

'What, dude? You never told me you are getting an AC. Which company is it? Never heard such a name?' I was trying to read what was printed on the sticker.

Looking downwards, he was typing something in his cell phone. 'That is a psychiatric drug company boss. They gifted it. I am taking it home' Sandy said continuing with his typing.

I was taken aback by his words to say the least.

'The rep told he will give it a few weeks back. See when he has finally brought it,' he continued.

I felt he was putting on that serious expression as he did when making jokes. I didn't speak. I sat there holding the write-up in my hands staring at him. *'Should I keep giving the write-up to him further? What's the use if he is able to do such a thing even while reading it all?'*

'Hey, come on, maaps,' Santosh raised his head and looked at me with a frown. 'Did you by any chance think I am going to follow the Gita, simply because you are sharing it?'

ॐ

The next morning I saw a missed call from Sandy. I called him back.

'Venki, can you come to pick me up on your way to the clinic? My bike has gone for servicing,' he said.

'Okay,' I replied curtly.

As I drove into the colony where his house was, his brother Saravana stood outside, siphoning water from the submerged lawn. Saravana was doing his PhD in computer science.

'How are you, anna?' he asked smiling.

'Yeah, doing fine, Saravana. Long time since I saw you. Like your brother, you too are going to become a doctor soon, huh?'

The cordial smile on his face vanished as I asked that. 'Anna, please don't compare me with Santosh. What a piece of filth he has become these days! He drinks daily. 'Just a little bit to ease tension in practice,' he replies if we ask him. He barely lends an ear to me or appa. . . . Since the day he became a psychiatrist he has really gone mad!'

I was listening to his words silently.

'You know something, anna? Before he joined medicine, he was the one I used to depend on and trust for everything, more than I depended on appa. Appa used to be too strict. It is repulsive seeing him degrade himself like this, anna. I feel as though he has become some other person.' There was real regret in his voice.

'Don't worry, Saravana. He'll surely change one day,' I patted his shoulder. What Barath Sir said once rang in my ears, 'I know our Santosh. He will be disturbed, but it will all turn out well.'

'But when is it going to happen, Sir?'

ॐ

I kept asking myself whether or not to continue sharing the Gita's wisdom with Sandy. The Gita itself insists that its wisdom is not to be shared with such unscrupulous men. The nightmarish image of him falling down into the abyss with me looking indifferently, the shiver of guilt I feel even now looking at him, his brother's regretful tone as he spoke to me about him; all those passed through my mind.

I kept pondering over what I would do if I stood in his shoes. After all, I come from a reasonably well-off background. Such temptations have never crossed my mind. Suppose my father too were a peon with a lean, four digit income, and suppose my life too had been as unfair to me as Sandy's, what would have I done? Add to that, the nature of the times we are living in. There are many people in this profession for whom such things are commonplace. If I were him, what reason would I have not to do it?

ॐ

'It is okay, doctor Sir. I will get the change tomorrow,' the shopkeeper was saying to Sandy, flashing his betel-stained teeth.

We were having our evening tea. Sandy sensed that I was still angry with him.

'Don't be put off by such trivial things, Venki boss,' he said, 'These medical companies, they have the money. They have a big budget allocated annually for 'doctor's hospitality.' And they are ready to shower it on you if you give them the nod. If I don't accept, it is going to go to someone else. I don't write the company's drugs to every patient . . . only for those who can afford it.'

'How considerate!'

'Oh man! Come on. See our PP . . . smuggling every inpatient from GH to his private clinic, going for a yearly foreign tour through those reps. And you make such a fuss for a small one and half ton AC?'

'He too would have begun it all like this.'

'Aah! So you don't accept any of the gifts your reps give you or what?'

'Well, accepting the books and clocks they give isn't the same as demanding ACs and foreign tours from them and thrusting the load upon patients.'

'Man, you and your silly utopian ideals. By the way what happened to your Gita? Stopped again?'

'No, I will bring the next topic I prepared, tomorrow,' I said looking away.

'Dude, you are mad to expect such a person to change by making him learn a few things from the Gita,' the voice within me mocked.

'I know, but I have started it. I will finish it off and leave the rest to God, as the Gita says.'

'And our next topic in the Gita is?' Sandy asked puffing on his cigarette.

꽃

KARMA YOGA

That is the next topic we will take up. If our previous discussions were about correcting our wrong notions about life and disentangling ourselves from the world, the following section is going to be about the right way to function in the world.

From modern day psychologists to the sages of yore, all agree on one truth: man is a pleasure-seeking organism. It is the drive to seek pleasure and avoid pain that is the motive behind any human action. When we become mature individuals, we can at the most defer this gratification, if necessary. For example, when we work out, we postpone the immediate pleasure of rest and laziness for health and fitness. Still we need some kind of pleasure as the drive behind our actions. We can give up a small *rasgulla* today only when we believe that we would get a larger and tastier one the day after. But a rasgulla there should be!

The Gita emphatically tells us, however, 'If you wish to get out of your mind's half-baked ways to real communion with your True Self, Karma Yoga is the means.'

> **For the one who wishes to attune to Yoga,**
> **Action is the means. 6.3**

That is the starting point of our spiritual journey. And the essence of Karma Yoga is –

> **You have the right to act. But no claim over its results.**
> **The fruits of the work should not be your motive.**
> **Neither should you ever become inactive. 2.47**

That is, 'Do thy actions, relinquish the results.' So then, taking into account our basic human nature, what kind of advice is that? And how on earth do we practise that in our times? That is what we will try to figure out in this chapter and the next.

Gita enumerates certain qualities a Karma Yogi possesses: He is sincere to his *Swadharma* and *Swabhava*; He does his work as a *Yajna*; He is aware of his *Varna*; He is a *sattwic* in temperament. And lastly, the most important quality: he does his actions for God! We will take up those one by one. The first quality of a Karma Yogi is . . .

గు

HE RECOGNISES HIS DHARMA

There is no confusion in him regarding why he is here for and what his role is in the scheme of things. He goes about his life, playing his role with tranquillity.

If someone asked us what constitutes a happy life, what would we tell him? In the early part of the last century, Abraham Maslow, the American psychologist, conducted elaborate studies on the happy and fulfilled people he came across in life – like Albert Einstein, Eleanor Roosevelt and many others – to arrive at an answer to this question.

The common denominator Maslow identified among those people was *self-actualisation*. Maslow defines it as, 'the tendency for a man to become actualised in reality, what he is potentially. The desire to become . . . everything that one is capable of becoming.'[1]

Expression of one's unique potential in the world, actualization of all that one is, was that common denominator. The difference between such a man and the so called 'ordinary' man is, in Maslow's words, 'The average man is a full human being with dampened and inhibited powers and capacities.'

Though some still criticise it as lacking in formal, structured research, Maslow's theory had a major impact in the field of psychology and human achievement.

The Greek philosopher Aristotle took up a similar question, 'What constitutes real human happiness?'

And he came up with a similar conclusion; a happy, flourishing life is one of 'virtuous activity in accordance with reason.' By 'virtue' (*arête*, his word) he meant the strength or quality unique to a particular individual. A life of happiness is a life of arête according to him.

When we look at our Vedantic teachings that predate all recorded history, we see that it is the same thing they too tell us. That according to the Gita is the starting point of a worldly man's journey towards his Divinity.

ೞ

MAN AND HIS DHARMA

If we take a look at the world and at the way people live, we would see most men living under the hypnotic spell of conformity. The beaten path is what they take, or many times, are pushed to take. Most men are *'other's people'*, and their lives, *a mimicry* as Oscar Wilde put it.

The time we spend on earth can feel meaningful and worthwhile only when our life is made the unique expression of our deepest truth; an expression of the beautifully unique, authentic beings we really are. Only the work that is deeply meaningful to us can give us any lasting satisfaction. When we are well-grounded in that deepest unchanging truth of ourselves and make our life an ongoing expression of that, it is then that we truly live. *Dharma is the name the Gita gives to such a living.*

Dharma is inherent in every element in nature. Today's rain never pours down the same way as yesterday's. The wave that touches your feet now isn't the same that touched you a moment before. Each and every child of existence too, likewise, is created with its own stamp of individuality. Every soul has its own gifts to give to the world and enrich it.

As a cell in the body has its function encoded in its DNA, every man too has a unique make of his own. He has a 'spiritual DNA' at his core so to speak. *Swabhava* is the name the Gita gives it. That is, 'the seed for self-expression,'[2] a soul brings forth with it when it is born. And it is its 'law of self-becoming' in the world. 'The law of action determined by this Swabhava is our right law of function (and) working, our *Swadharma*,' Sri Aurobindo tells us.[3]

Our task in life is to discover and fulfil that deep, innate potential in our core. When we are connected with our deepest nature, and make our life a process of ongoing expression of that, then we live our Dharma in the world.

'Everyone has been made for some particular work, and the desire for that work has been put in every heart,' wrote Rumi. The work of a man who is true to his Swabhava is marked by a naturalness, efficiency and grace – like the free flow of a river or the blossoming of a flower. When a man is true to his Swabhava, he does his precise part in the scheme of things. Life in our world is an adventure in which the Swabhava and Swadharma – our innate nature and the karma governed by that – should be the chief driving powers.

ॐ

DHARMA AND TAPAS

To say that a child is born with an innate potential does not mean that there is a world-class talent sleeping inside every child awaiting an awakening, that can be put to use right away. No! For the seed of the potential to blossom into such real talent, man has to train himself in his field of work. He has to first train the unsteady and powerful monster called 'mind', actively in his field. He has to cast his mind along the mould of his inner Swabhava, before he can cast his life and world along it. And doing that requires, what our scriptures call, *tapas*.

'Those who really want to be Yogis must give up, once and for all, this nibbling at things,' Swami Vivekananda tells us. 'Take up one idea. Make that one idea your life — think of it, dream of it, live on that idea. Let the brain, muscles, nerves, every part of your body, be full of that idea, and just leave every other idea alone. This is the way to success.'[4]

Tapas is a process of self-discipline undergone willingly in pursuit of a higher goal. It not only refers to religious and spiritual tapas, but is true for any field or context. Only the man who has trained himself well in his field, who has concrete knowledge of his field, who is able enough to know and handle the intricacies of it can contribute well through it and succeed in it. To put it in modern Harvard terms, our core talent x 10,000 hours deliberate practice = world-class expertise.[5]

This should be the function of the first quarter of man's life, the Brahmacharya ashrama. The academic training of a child should focus on identifying this inner truth of a child and help it blossom. Sri Aurobindo tells us that, 'The child's education ought to be an outbringing of all that is best, most powerful, most intimate and living in his nature. The individual who develops freely in this manner will be a living soul and mind, and will have a much greater power for the service of the race.'[6]

Thus the right nurturing from parents and the education system is crucial if every soul is to walk the path of its Dharma. If they do, there is no need to force education upon any child. A plant grows by itself when the right soil, water and sunlight are provided. Every child too would blossom in the same way. That is the greatest gift we can give to a child; and through the child, to the world.

So that is the first step along the spiritual path for a man of action as per the Gita: *Find, and take delight in doing your Dharma.*

One who delights in his Swadharma attains perfection. 18.45

ॐ

This inner truth of our being, our Swabhava, seeks expression from within like a shooting geyser. When it is blocked, the place ends up a stinking swamp! When one's Swabhava is unrecognised and not expressed fruitfully, one remains an unfulfilled being, the 'average man' of Maslow.

That action which through delusion you do not want to do,
You will end up helplessly doing
impelled by your own Swabhava. 18.60

Such blocked Swabhava can lead people to many a perversion. The man who could have been a high-minded soldier for his country could end up an unscrupulous terrorist! The woman with intellectual temperament can keep passing her life in petty arguments. The unexpressed Swabhava goes through 'many lower forms, endless imperfections, perversions, self-losings, self-findings, seekings before it arrives at self-discovery and perfection' states Sri Aurobindo, 'It is always the Swabhava that is looking for self-expression through all these things.'[7] In Gita's words, *Swabhavastu pravartate*. Whether they recognise it or not, people always act from their Swabhava. It can't be otherwise.

The Dharma foreign to one's calling is called *para-dharma*. If one pursues another's Swabhava and Dharma ignoring one's own, it would only make one an anxious creature with a nagging sense of incompleteness.

> **Better is one's own Dharma though devoid of merit,**
> **Than the Dharma of another, well performed.**
> **For it is fraught with fear. 3.35**

So then, when a man of action starts travelling the spiritual path the Gita puts forward, this is the first thing he has to do: *understand the vehicle in his hands*. That is the initial step. It is worth taking some time to explore to arrive at it.

Then it requires us spending time to develop our expertise in it. When we do, we would see that the path we have to take in life has always been there, waiting for our arrival! As the mythologist Joseph Campbell famously put it, 'I say, follow your bliss and don't be afraid. Doors will open where you didn't know they were going to be. Doors will open for you that wouldn't have opened for anyone else.'

That is what Krishna told the grieving Arjuna, when he decided to desert the war and resort to something against his Swabhava.

> **Get up and attain glory.**
> **All these (men) have already been slain by me.**
> **Be merely an apparent cause, O Arjuna. 11.33**

ॐ

DO THY DUTY

All that we saw is just one aspect of Dharma. Dharma is a multifaceted term with many more dimensions to it. It also means being sincere in our duty towards our parents, spouse, children, relatives, profession, the society and the world at large. I had decided to skip this part, not wanting to sound condescending. But then, a patient walked in!

'Doctor,' the lady addressed me in a rather unfriendly tone looking away from my eyes.

'I've been to more than ten doctors till now and no one has been able to treat my condition. I met Dr Saradha last week when I had gone to my village to see my brother, and it was she who referred me to you.'

She was in her fifties. ('Fifty-four!' she sighed.) She was fair, tall and quite thin for her age. I knew it must take her quite some effort to maintain her body like that. Her face bore a bleak expression, beyond the eyeliner and the cosmetic cream that were adorning it.

She put a big bunch of prescription slips on my table. 'Look at all of this . . . absolutely no use.' She said.

'Tell me your problem, ma'am.'

'See this, and this too . . . ' she said in a way that made it seem as though I was the one who gave her all those prescriptions!

She pointed to the skin on her cheeks and forehead. I wondered what was wrong as I looked closely at the areas.

'You see this? It falls on my eyes whenever I look at my face.'

'What falls on your eyes, ma'am?'.

She stopped and gave me an almost furious glare. 'You can't see it? See how lustreless, how ugly the skin is. See the wrinkles on it.'

'Oh?'

'Dei, nice patient you have got here. That is a few thousand bucks pleading to get into your pocket. Suggest microdermabrasion, come on! And after few weeks regular peeling . . . '

My mind had already travelled quite some distance along the path of temptation; and was trying hard to pull me along.

'Yeah. Looks like she will agree to it easily too. But wait. Where is the indication for it?'

I looked at her face. All it showed for me was some age-related elastotic change and a few fine wrinkles that were not worth treating.

'I have big fights with my husband because of this,' she added.

'Your husband fights with you for this?'

'He doesn't understand my problem. He thinks it's nothing.'

'Oh!'

I understood what the issue was. I've seen quite a few patients like this who go 'doctor-shopping.' What they have is a sense of nagging incompleteness. Like Mulla demonstrated, they keep searching for the solution in places where they are never going to find it. This lady thinks curing the 'problem' on her face will fix it.

I explained to her that it was nothing to worry about.

'No! You doctors don't understand. I have come to you for treatment because Dr Saradha referred your name. I have heard enough of this 'it is nothing' stuff. 'It is nothing!' How easily you say that!'

I was so irritated that I stopped explaining further, prescribed a cream and said, 'Ma'am, as I have explained, it is an age-related change and is quite normal. Try this cream for two months. Let us see.'

'Thousand bucks, dude!'

'Shut up.'

A derisive smile appeared on the lady's face as I said that.

'Try, huh? So you are not sure?' she smirked.

'Ma'am, you are looking to make the clock run backwards. We are not gods. This is the maximum we can do,' I told her quite sternly.

She got up and walked out placing a hundred rupee note on my table.

'Oof, what all we have to face when practising!' I sighed. I heard someone drive off. 'Should be her. A fortune is in the waiting for some beautician in the town who can toady to her.' The lady was sure to go there and try something next.

After some time I felt I should have done better. What was the use of talking like that to an already deluded soul? But what choice did I have with someone like that? How could I have done otherwise and yet been ethical?

This is where the second aspect of Dharma comes into play. As per Vedanta, it is our karma that invites every single person we meet and interact with, into our lives. Whatever problem they have, however tough they seem, it is one's duty, one's Dharma to be sincere to them. The exhortation 'Be sincere to your duty!' means, when the recipient of your action has problems, it is not the reason to get piqued and put out. Just stick to what is within your zone of control – doing your duty – and be satisfied with it.

So ideally how should have the scenario transpired?

'Apply this cream. Let us see how it works in two months.'

'So you are not sure, huh?'

I lift my head and look at her rather surprised, and I tell her with a serene, compassionate smile, like Lord Rama in the tele-serial, 'I see that you are quite upset with it ma'am. But this is all this doctor can do.'

The lady gives me a *what's-up-with-this-doc* look.

After a moment of silence I continue, 'You see, ma'am, you can't keep wrinkles at bay forever. They are inevitable. But you can keep your inner being wrinkle-free, always. That is optional. If ageing puts wrinkles on the skin, it is such undue concerns that put wrinkles on the soul. Find out what is really important in life, ma'am. Concentrate on that. Then you will find all these minor issues fall away.'

'Then will I be forever young, doctor?' the lady asks. She has let her guard down now.

'Not just young, ma'am. You will feel Eternal!'

She gives me a stunned look.

'May God save the family of the dermatologists who are naive enough to say such things to their patients,' my inner voice butted in as I was imagining the scene.

'You think so? Watch the next part.'

'Thanks doctor,' she says, places a five-hundred-rupee note on my table and walks away.

'No, ma'am, my consultation fee is just . . .'

'No, doctor. Your words have stirred up something immense

within me. I owe you this much at least. Consider it a token of my gratitude.'

Let me see if it really goes that well the next time. Moving on to the second quality of a karma yogi....

HE DOES HIS ACTIONS AS YAJNA

Sant Tukaram, the great Marathi saint was once given a bundle of sugarcane by a landlord. On his way home, he gave them away to the poor children in the lane, saving just one for his family. When he arrived home and told his wife the truth, his wife beat him up with that sugarcane!

If we read about the life of any God-realised saint, we would find that, despite all such odds and hardships, they lived their lives in this way, as Yajna! Yajna roughly translates into heartfelt offering, sacrifice or contribution. The Gita asks us to follow our inner truth and do our Dharma in the world, with a sense of contribution. The product or service we create through our Swabhava should enrich the world in some way. That completes the circle.

☙

'Slept?' Sandy messaged.

Almost a week had gone by since I had given him the Dharma and Yajna write-up. I hadn't bothered to ask him whether he had read it. Let him, if he wishes.

'What?' I messaged back.

'My reading has reached the "Yajna" stuff just now.'

'So?'

I looked at the time. 11:30 PM *'Not bad!'* I thought, and called him up.

'What? Reading the write-up at this time? Didn't go to the bar today?'

'Don't ask. Kumar screwed things up. And you know what? This is making me yawn already. Swadharma, Swabhava, and now Yajna! Why isn't it simply "duty, passion and contribution"?'

'Why? Would you have followed it all if it were written in English?' I snapped.

However, he had a valid point that is best explained now. Dharma, Swabhava, Yajna – they all are key words in the

Gita's philosophy which don't have an exact equivalent in English. Duty is too rough a translation for Dharma; as are the words 'passion' and 'contribution' for Swabhava and Yajna. Furthermore, these are pivotal words in the book's wisdom that have been uttered by the Divine Avatar himself. They are words that have a certain spiritual dignity about them. Knowing them has its value, we would realise, when we take our steps along the Gita's path.

ॐ

The next morning in the middle of his smoking session Sandy said, 'What you shared as the first part of your Swadharma, I have come across fairly often boss. Naturally, the key to workplace happiness is to do what we love. But something isn't gelling in its second aspect. It's okay for us to do our natural duties. But as you say, how can one keep doing one's duty no matter what? Then what does a subdued wife do? Or a tortured employee? Undergo it all as their karma and keep doing their duty? That doesn't sound like good advice to me.'

'That's true. Let me go through the Gita and try answering it. Read the Yajna write-up till then,' I said before I took my leave of him.

I puzzled over the question for a couple of days, but couldn't arrive at a satisfactory answer. So I decided to put this question on hold and proceed with the write-up on Yajna.

ॐ

A POWERFUL MANTRA

A learned westerner who was an earnest spiritual seeker came to an Indian Guru. 'Guruji, how do I raise my spiritual energy – my Kundalini?' he asked. What he was expecting was some secret inner teaching, some ancient mantra the Guru would give him and ask him to meditate on.

The Guru said instead, 'Serve food to everyone in the ashram.'

'Serve food?' he asked puzzled.

'Yes. Serve food and feed everyone.'

'Guruji, my Kundalini then?' the man asked looking at his Guru and the rice plate near him.

The story is told by the western psychologist Richard Alpert (Ram Dass) when describing his experiences with his Guru.[8] It was the same experience, disciples of Swami Sivananda of Hrishikesh, Swami Satyananda of Bihar, or any traditional Indian Guru underwent. The Gurus did teach a technique of meditation, Kundalini or others, to the seekers eventually. However, in addition, they insisted on this one thing: service to the ashram and its inmates like sweeping the floor, rendering service in the kitchen, serving food in the dining area and so on. They termed it *Seva*.

Seva is not for saving on paid labour. The Gurus knew that seva did more good to the person doing it, than to the ashram. They knew that it trains the mind to walk in a new direction. Having got used to doing things motivated only by self-interest so far, the mind now begins to give a thought to things outside its old ways. And that does great spiritual good to the doer.

'I don't know what your destiny will be,' the Nobel Peace prize-winning Dr Albert Schweitzer tells us, 'But one thing I do know: the only ones among you who will be really happy are those who have sought and found a way to serve.'

ॐ

THE JOY OF YAJNA

When coming across this concept of Yajna, the status quo-mind, sporting a self-satisfied smirk on its face, might tell us, 'I told you! All this is not possible in our times. Put another's pleasure before yours. Jump from the tower . . . '

Stop it at that. Yajna means sacrifice alright, but it is not about becoming martyrs, putting the world's good before our own. In its true sense, it is not really a sacrifice at all. The person walking the path of the Gita too is pleasure-driven. Even as you do your work as Yajna, pleasure is what the game is about still! The following examples illustrate our point.

Chen Shu-Chu, the owner of a small vegetable shop in the central market of Taiwan, won the 2010 Asian of the year award given by a private magazine. She got it because through her frugality, the sixty year old vegetable vendor had managed to donate in her career, over 1.5 crore rupees in Indian value to charitable causes, including helping orphanages and poor children. How could a mere vegetable vendor donate so much?

'Spend only what you need and you will be able to save a lot,' she answered. Her daily meals cost little, a vegetarian dish and a bowl of noodles. Except her food and a place to sleep, she considered everything else a luxury. When she was asked about the motivation behind her work, she replied without second thought, 'When I donate to help others, I feel at peace. I'm happy, and I can sleep well at night.'[9]

The next example involves Abraham Lincoln. When he was the president of United States, Lincoln once rescued a pig stuck in the mud. The pig was hopelessly stuck. The more it struggled to escape its doom, the more it sank into the mire. Lincoln was driving by in a wagon when he saw it. He stopped his wagon, tied up his horse, and worked some old rails into the mud. He used them to support himself and also wedged them under the pig, finally freeing it.

The surprised onlookers asked him why he, the president of such a vast country, should dirty himself just to save a common pig. He replied, 'I got involved in this action not so much to relieve the suffering of the pig, but to relieve myself from the suffering I experienced at the sight of the pig. It is for my own peace of mind I did it!'[10]

What Lincoln and Chen Shu-Chu say applies to any altruistic deed anyone does. Like the desire-centred materialists, it is this desire for self-gratification that is, at some level, the motive behind Yajna as well. Nothing sublime about that.

The difference then? The people who do their actions as Yajna know by their experience that the pleasure of such Yajnic actions is greater, in fact *much, much greater* than the pleasure of results and returns. Such people have a taste of both the rasgullas and know that this is the most exquisite variety. They have known enough to know the difference.

Except the love of the Self-realised person, all love is indeed selfish at some level. However, the narcissist lives at the lowest rung of such selfishness. The pleasure of Yajna, on the other hand, is something that can elevate us when pursued.

But don't get it wrong. We still do our action with the other's good in mind. Doing it with a narcissist intention, 'I am going to become happy doing this' will only make us greater narcissists. A self-interest guided gift can't set one free. It is in doing actions motivated by the other's good that we experience the real joy of Yajna.

'All those who are unhappy in the world are so as a result of their desire for their own happiness. All those who are happy in the world are so as a result of their desire for the happiness of others,' the Buddhist Saint Shantideva elegantly puts it.

֍

THE REWARDS OF YAJNA

Even as we pursue this pleasure of Yajna and keep doing our work, it confers some positive long term benefits on us. When the drive for our action arises from the mind's whims and fancies we allow the mind dictator to overthrow the heart's rule and take hold of us. The 'I' becomes a hapless servant of the mind. How does one liberate the 'I' from the mind? It is here that Yajna comes in.

Yajna is all about the attitude that illuminates our actions. An employee of a corporate company, looking at an impoverished old man lying on the pavement while waiting for his daily bus, may give a ten rupee note to him feeling a genuine compassion for his condition. His boss, sitting in an air-conditioned room ten floors above him, may sign a perfunctory cheque for a few lakhs to be given to 'charity.' As per Vedanta, it is the ten rupee note that would qualify as greater Yajna.

> **Whatever sacrifice that is done with knowledge, with faith and (in the spirit of the teaching of) the scripture, It becomes to him that much more effective.**
> Chandogya Upanishad 1.10

When we do our Dharma in the world with such an attitude behind it, the motivation for the action doesn't come from our mind, but arises *from our heart*. It is the heart that can put other's good before ours and take delight in it. The mind can never do that.

When we keep doing our actions with such an attitude, streaks of light from the heart start to illuminate the gloomy darkness of the mind. Just as the moon becomes less and less prominent with sunrise, the mind starts losing its power over us gradually. That is the greater good Yajna does for us.

When the mind's whims and fancies drive our actions, the external high we attain lasts but for a short time and fades off. It feels stimulating and exciting to experience when it is happening, but the pleasure evaporates pretty quickly. Even the greatest pleasure of the world has but a short reign.

However, when we do actions with an attitude of Yajna, it connects us to the purity of our heart, gradually and smoothly. It makes us more and more serene, and sane. We don't have to struggle to calm our mind with exotic spiritual practices. Through our action, we attune ourselves to yoga, as the Gita said.

Our actions are still motivated by pleasure, and such pleasure-seeking isn't bad. Pleasure is what drives people to do anything. However, the Gita exhorts us to know and acclimatise ourselves to such a greater pleasure. 'Know what imprisons you and what liberates you,' it tells us.

> Man becomes bound by actions
> other than those performed in Yajna spirit.
> Therefore do actions for that sake alone,
> without attachment. 3.9

Yajna is like taking the flowers that have blossomed in our garden and giving them to people around us. We do it because if we hoard the flowers, they will wither soon. If we keep it for ourselves, the joy of the 'thing of beauty' on our table can last for a day or so. But when we give it to people, we experience a great joy and delight in the act of giving. And we grow in that daily. We know that is the most permanent of all the joys the flower in our garden can give us. The joy never withers or wilts whereas flowers do.

Yajna is all about building this inner reserve of joy in us.

If Yajna becomes a way of life and if all our major endeavours are undertaken in this spirit, imagine what changes it can bring to our psyche! We would no longer be jittery beings full of our petty concerns caught up in the selfish ego mind. We would be inspired by a greater cause than ourselves. That would rearrange and harness our energies. Our life would blossom into a positive and an enormously productive one. A Gandhiji, a Martin Luther King Jr, or for that matter a Jamshedji Tata, a Verghese Kurien, a Akio Morita were all able to achieve so much in their lives because it was this will to contribute to the world that was driving them.

When Swami Vivekananda was enumerating to his disciples the great services he expected them to render to the country, one of them asked him, 'Swamiji, but where is that strength in us? I should have felt myself blessed if I had a hundredth part of your powers.'

They thought they didn't have his strength or power to accomplish such things. Swami Vivekananda instantly retorted, 'How foolish! Power and things like that will come by themselves. Put yourself to work, and you will find such tremendous power coming to you that you will feel it hard to bear. Even the least work done for others, awakens the power within; even thinking the least good of others gradually instills into the heart the strength of a lion.'[11]

Thus what the Indian Guru gave the westerner was quite a valid advice. 'Serve' is indeed a powerful mantra, and 'Serve boiled rice,' a great spiritual teaching!

ॐ

By the way, if we do things with the intention of contributing to the world, and when we derive joy from that alone, what happens to our personal needs? Well, the Gita assures 'The returns will be taken care of when you walk the path. Don't worry.' *It is a law of the world*, the scripture declares emphatically.

> **In the beginning the creator blessed mankind**
> **'With this Yajna may you shine and prosper**
> **And this will give you everything you wish for.' 3.10**

It is natural. As one contributes more to the world's real needs, the world gives more in return. That is the way cosmic laws operate. They bless the doer of Yajna with the good things in life.

We can see in that verse that the Gita doesn't prohibit our materialistic desires totally. It acknowledges our all-too-human concerns. 'Desiring for stuff is normal for worldly men and it is fine with me too,' our Big Boss seems to tell us. At the same time he gives us a way to rise beyond it. 'You can have desire for toys, but need not let that define you,' is his counsel for us.

Moreover, it is not just our personal good that is taken care of by the Divine. The world itself is in a running order still because of the people with the Yajna-spirit in them, declares the Gita.

> **The world is sustained by food. Food is produced by rain.**
> **And what brings forth rain is the Yajna man does. 3.14**

The ancient Tamil saint Avvaiyar puts the same idea this way, 'The stream that supplies water to the farm also helps the shrubs along the canal to grow. In this world likewise the good deed of an individual man brings rain to everyone!' Surely, if the cancer cells start dominating a body, the body would have met its end long back.

Summing it all up, Karma Yoga is not something separate from our daily life. It is the same prescription we write, same projects we work on and the same pudding we prepare. However, when done in a spirit of Yajna, along with the perks, it can give us a sense of inner peace and a pleasure which are real and more enduring. 'Why miss it?' the Gita asks us.

ॐ

THE LAW OF LIFE

Yajna in Vedic times referred to the oblatory ceremonies done for various deities by priests who had specialised training and education in them. The Gita brings Yajna to the daily life of a common man. *Yajna is the basic law of life,* the Gita emphatically declares. We forget this truth when we give in to the mind.

> **The Creator created beings
> with Yajna as their basic law of existence. 3.10**

Just like every cell in our body is created for the body's good. When not done as Yajna, 'our action becomes a violation of the true universal law of solidarity and interchange,' states Sri Aurobindo.[12]

The sun doesn't give us light expecting a return from us; the trees don't bear fruit with the view of getting their nourishment. It is the spirit of Yajna that enlivens every single element in nature. All humans too ought to live in a similar way as a part of this natural harmony.

> **He who does not follow this wheel thus set revolving,
> lives a sinful life. Rejoicing in the senses, he lives in vain. 3.16**

Swabhava and Yajna, both elements are crucial in our actions. Your action should be an expression of who you are in your core, and it should be done in a spirit of service. Only then is the circle complete. You can play a violin blissfully in the solitude of the night. It is happiness no doubt. However, doing it as a Yajna, for making someone else happy, is even more joyous. That humans are social beings, is no abstract concept. It is a neurological fact. Individualism alone won't fulfil us. We are neurologically hardwired to connect; to belong.

People who wear their rebellious attitude on their sleeve, who value individual freedom more than everything else, see only one side of the truth. Such a freedom would degenerate into mere self-absorption unless it is approched with a sense of responsibility. Even if you are a superman, it is in putting your talent to help people in some way, that your 'superness' finds its fulfilment.

And keeping in mind what we have discussed previously, it is worth remembering that we shouldn't become world-dependent even when performing such Yajnic actions. We do it because it is our nature and this is the law of the world. Our dependence and poise should be *within*.* It is there we should be centred. 'A bird doesn't sing because it has an answer. It sings because it has a song,' in the eloquent words of the American poet Maya Angelou. And in that, the world finds all its answers.

ॐ

YAJNA AND EDUCATION

We saw in the discussion on Dharma about the importance of consciously nurturing the natural talent in every child. Likewise, cultivating the spirit of Yajna in every youngster requires we create opportunities for them to interact deeply with the world.

The primary concern of our modern day education seems not to create free-thinking humans, but to satisfy the world's workforce needs. Universities keep producing swarms of tunnel-visioned clones who are driven by narrow, selfish goals, and who are barely aware of a world outside themselves and their needs. Though experts in their respective fields, they remain unfinished as human beings.

For the spirit of Yajna to take root, however, we need to depart from these conventional standards. We need to interact deeply with the world. The varied life experiences of people and their diverse cultures should expand our awareness. The pain and agony of the underprivileged should impinge upon our conscience. If we read the life-histories of the men and women who shaped the world, we would see that they didn't confine themselves to bookish knowledge. They saw the world as a wide-open book which they studied and got inspired from. It is when the world touches every youngster deeply in such a way, the willingness to become a part

---

*We'll discuss this point more in the next chapter.

of it and contribute to it blossoms naturally within.

࿇

Nambi Thalaivan Pattayam is a small village about fifty kilometers away from Tirunelveli. It came into news recently in all TV channels in the state through the shocking news of honour-killing of a young couple, whose bodies were found in a lake. The bodies showed signs of strangulation, according to forensic reports. The boy was a Dalit. The family of the girl, coming to know of the love affair, had restricted the girl and shut her up in their house. When the girl tried to elope with the boy, they had gotten killed. The police were engaged in their investigations, and it had become hot news in the media.

Sitting in front of me in my clinic, Sandy read the latest police reports of the case in a Tamil daily. He kept the paper down in a few minutes. Taking a deep breath, he said, 'You know what? The boy is actually a distant relative of mine.'

'Oh, is it?'

'Dad has gone to the village to visit their house,' he added. There was a wry smile on his face. 'These f***ing "upper" class Hindus. . . . Citing their scriptures, they can do the most atrocious things to their co-humans. And you know what? The girl's family doesn't even belong to such "upper" class. By the way, this caste division and all that . . . is it all mentioned in the Gita too?' Sandy asked. 'If so, tell me, I will stop reading it immed . . .'

His phone rang in the middle of his words; it was Kumar.

Picking it up, he told Kumar, 'Yeah, we are both ready. You come directly to the theatre.' Keeping the phone down, he told me next, 'Alright Venki boss, we can start.'

For once, I was happy with Kumar for interrupting an uneasy conversation.

Sandy, Kumar and I had planned to go for a movie that afternoon. It was the first day of his thalaivar's newest release, and Kumar was sponsoring the tickets. He had got a free pass for all of us as he had donated milk-pockets for his thalaivar's cut-out from his computer centre.

࿇

The sun was setting when I entered the house. Mom and Dad were seated in the verandah, red-faced and glaring furiously at me as I turned off the ignition of the bike.

That's when it struck me; I had totally forgotten that a distant relative from Bangalore was coming to meet me. His sister wanted her daughter to be married to me. Mom had hence asked me to return early from my morning OP. And I, totally unconcerned, had gone off to watch that horrible film with Sandy and Kumar.

'Look at your cellphone. How many times we called you, you know!' stormed Mom.

'Oh boy, too hot the situation is! Hope I don't get vaporised as I cross the front door!'

'He waited till three o'clock you know?' Dad got up and went inside teeming with rage. 'Be sure your son doesn't bring home some unknown girl from another caste as his lover. I'll shoot them both dead.'

His business-brain had come up with its own reason.

'Don't worry dad, your genes that I have acquired have made that a difficult proposition,' I mumbled within, as I walked towards the chair in the verandah. Sitting down on it slowly, I started reflecting on the next topic to prepare in the Gita – the much-maligned caste system.

What a huge and ugly role this entity has played in our country for centuries! The people who practise it do so quoting the words of the Hindu scriptures, the words of the Gita, to rationalise their actions. What does the Gita tell us about it? That is what we will take up next as we get into the third quality of a karma yogi.

ଓ

HE KNOWS HIS VARNA

The Gita gives more guidance on the actions one should perform here. It talks about something called Chatur Varnas – the four inner colours of man. It divides men into four types based on how their individual Swabhava fits into society, around which unfortunately, plenty of negative connotations and controversies prevail. Let us analyse what is the real import of the Gita's message.

A naughty question and answer I came across in our college magazine comes to mind here.

Ragging – Is it needed?

Definitely not; till we become seniors.

Certain ignorant souls born in the so-called aristocratic families have interpreted the Varna concept to their convenience in a similar opportunistic way. Perhaps the last resort to feel good when one has nothing else to! Added to that, the divide-and-conquer strategy of the exploitative colonial regimen in India too promoted such religious, ethnic and cultural divisions to keep its subjects under its control. The sad result of all that, is the petrified system we come across in our country, one that is totally unrelated to its original form. Even in this modern era, a section of people remain underprivileged and continue to be lethally exploited in the name of caste in our country.

What is the Gita's take on the caste system? The Lord says

**The four fold Varnas in man were created by me
According to one's guna and work. 4.13**

Not as per one's birth! Yes, birth was one of the factors used to decide it in the Vedic times. However, the Gita, a scripture considered the quintessence of the Vedas and Upanishads, by not mentioning birth at all seems to clearly tell us, 'It is the temperament dominant in you that should decide your life's work.'

The concept of family occupation existed in ancient India as a matter of convenience. That was a time, unlike today, when not many engineering, medical or art schools existed in every state for one to choose from and enrol, based on one's interest. One's family and its occupation was the best training ground for one's life's work. So in ancient India, there existed the concept of family-occupation where the son of a doctor became a doctor and the son of a soldier became a soldier. That was the way to pass on skills and knowledge, and to be of service to the society.*

---

*However, even in the Vedic times, birth wasn't the only determinant. 'I am a bard, my father is a physician, my mother's job is to grind the corn,' goes a verse in the Rig Veda (9.112.3). As if to exemplify this, Sage Vyaasa who compiled the Vedas and wrote the Mahabharatha was born to a fisherwoman!

This system, though could prove disadvantageous to certain section of the society, was not without its advantages too. When the skills and knowledge are passed on through generations, it can help people attain an incredible level of expertise in their respective fields. As an example, the Wootz steel that was manufactured in ancient India as early as 500 BC and which was exported worldwide, took centuries of research before modern metallurgy reproduced it in the twentieth century.

However, in the liberal society of present day, the old idea of Varna needs to be eschewed and the concept needs to be reinvented. We have to learn to discern and embrace the essential truth behind Varna. What is that essential truth? Sri Aurobindo answers us, '(The) emphasis on an inner quality and spirit which finds expression in work is the whole sense of the Gita's idea of Karma. Too much has been made of its connection with the outer social order. What the Gita is concerned with is the relation of a man's outward life to his inward being.'[13]

Knowing our Dharma and living our life as a Yajna is the first and crucial aspect of Karma Yoga. Along with that, knowing how our inborn nature fits in with society is what Varna is all about. Whatever skewed way this idea has got translated in real life since ancient times, this is the real essence of the Gita's Varna. (To further guide us, the Gita divides men into four groups based on how one's inner disposition fits in with the world. This is discussed in the appendix.)

The second aspect of Varna concerns the tribal nature of humans. Man is not only a social creature, he is a tribal creature too. He has been living in closely-knit bands and tribes for tens of thousands of years. 'The urge to embed oneself in a family – to hold an endeavour in common with others, to be part of a team, a band, a group that struggles together toward a common victory – is an indomitable aspect of the human mind and brain,' an eminent psychiatrist tells us.[14] Vedanta understands this need for belonging that exists at our core. A cell that develops from the zygote has to take its proper place in a particular organ with other similar cells. Likewise people too should know how they fit into society's scheme of things.

The concept of Varna, thus interpreted and translated into the societal scheme of things, would refer to a group of people connected to one another by their shared interest, not by their caste or birth. Knowing our proper place in the societal scheme empowers us mentally, enhances our creative strength and gives us a much-needed sense of belonging. The ancient Tamil Saint Thiruvalluvar explains it this way, 'Goodness of mind is a worthy treasure for a man. However, it is the goodness of his company that takes him to glory and greatness.' (Kural 457)

ॐ

We saw earlier that the term Dharma is multi-faceted and to simply translate it as 'duty' is reductionist. All that we discussed above too is an aspect of Dharma. 'Dharma in the Indian conception is not merely the right, morality and justice,' writes Sri Aurobindo. '... it is the whole government of all the relations of man with other beings, with Nature, with God, considered from the point of view of a divine principle working itself out in forms of the inner and the outer life.'[15]

Thus Dharma is the quintessence of our life – both its inner and outer aspects; the 'why', 'what' and 'how' of our living founded on our divine roots.

'The goal of life is to make your heartbeat match the beat of the universe,' said Joseph Campbell. *Rta* is the word the Vedas give to that natural order of the universe. (The English 'rhythm' is a close enough approximation.) Every individual Dharma is a subordinate component of this Rta. Each one of us is a single note in this marvellous *uni-verse*; a part of this vast and extraordinary symphony that is playing itself unceasingly since the beginning of time. When we do our Dharma, we fit in naturally and sing in perfect harmony with Rta, this universal rhythm.

Dharma is truth. There is nothing higher than Dharma.
Brihadaranyaka Upanishad 1.4.14

ॐ

It was well past OP time. The noise and hubbub of the night traffic was on the wane. I was watching the sodium-vapour-lamp-lit road through the open window in Sandy's clinic.

I had recently found out through a medical rep that Sandy has started demanding cash to be deposited in his account for prescribing the company's drugs.

'We can extend the same courtesy to you as we did for your friend, Sir,' the fawning rep had said to me. 'We have a separate hospitality-budget allocated in our company for doctors. Or if you wish, we can also sponsor a family tour, Sir. Our company has guesthouses in Coonoor and Ooty.'

I had refrained from asking Sandy anything about it.

Sandy, who was reading the write-up so far sitting in front of me, placed the papers back on his table. He asked me no questions once he finished reading it. Nowhere was I seeing in the guy the trace of interest he showed in the earlier sections.

'Sandy, I met your new love interest, that staff nurse Manisha. She has a lot of love and respect for you.'

'Love interest?' he grinned impishly hearing my words, 'Hmm, this evening she picked me apart,' he said putting on a mournful face.

A squabble with Manisha? So it has ended? That is great.

'What? At last she saw through your intention?'

'No, no. She blushed all over and told me that I am not being romantic enough! So I promised to take her out this weekend for dinner. What do I do? The lamb is willingly offering itself for slaughter. I don't know where it is all going to end. Oh, that girl Manisha George! The chick should have become a model really, you know?' He eased back into his chair and continued with his eyes closed.

'The way she wears that cap of hers, the pin that holds it. . . . Man, I am just intoxicated with her. I want to bite and eat her up when the time comes. By the way maaps, be tight-lipped on all these things, okay? Hey, what is that threatening look?'

Only now had he opened his eyes and noticed me gazing disapprovingly at him.

'Whoa! Look at you man. I might get burnt. . . . Alright maaps, I shouldn't have blurted out all that to you. What is that in your hands? The next portion of the write-up?'

'No!' I said quite firmly and left his cabin.

What I had in my hands was indeed the next part of the write-up.

Finally, at that moment when he was speaking those words, I decided to stop sharing my write-ups on the Gita with him.

'You don't seem alright at all for me, Sandy. For the unscrupulous person you are letting yourselves become these days, I definitely can't keep sharing the Gita with you.'

What the Gita advised about sharing its wisdom with others was quite right. The Gita isn't a magic wand to awaken our inner truth where there is no openness in us. It can show us the way. It is we who have to embrace its wisdom and walk the path. How can people who are basking in the glory of the dungeon be set free from it?

'Sorry Krishna, for disobeying your words. My daydreaming about redeeming myself and transforming my friend through sharing your words comes to an end right this moment. Maybe it is fated that I should commit such a mistake and be haunted by that for life. It is my karma perhaps. Even if he is disinterested in all this, there are many thousands of students of my school, present and old, whom the write-up is going to reach, and might positively influence. Many among them will be able to bring to the Gita such openness and honesty. Let it help them at least. That is enough for me. No more Gita for Sandy,' I decided as I walked out of his clinic that night.

And that answered the question he had raised earlier,

'How can one 'do his duty, whatever, and keep loving people'? Then what does a subdued wife do? Or a tortured employee? Keep undergoing it all as their karma and do their duty?'

No, they need not. Doing one's Dharma doesn't mean be a doormat to people. Then the very war of Kurukshetra wouldn't have happened at all. Our allegiance should be to Dharma, not those people. There is a limit to things. When we feel that a person while degrading himself or herself, is also degrading us and our values, that is when things reach a breaking point. That is the time to step away from the person — not out of disrespect for them, but out of self-respect.

'Barath Sir, I don't see our Santosh coming to his old self as you said once. He is only becoming more and more animal-like with every passing day. Sorry Sir, the Gita doesn't seem to be working in his case, as you said. And Sandy too doesn't seem the type of person you, and I, thought him to be. From here on, I am continuing with the Gita only for myself and our school.'

The Gita speaks next about a Karma Yogi . . .

HE IS OF SATTWIC TEMPERAMENT

A good photographer often captures an image from different angles. That way the viewer gets a better and complete idea of the object captured. Likewise, the Gita puts forward the ideas shared till now from another perspective, one based on gunas. This guna-based discussion occurs in the last chapters of the Gita when it speaks of how we are tied to the world. Since we are trying to look at the practical aspects of the Gita together under one heading, we will now explore the gunas as well.

Gunas are the qualities inherent in nature. They are the fabric out of which every being is woven into life. Like primary colours, there are three primary gunas – *rajas*, *tamas* and *sattwa*. All beings are formed from a varying combination of these three.

Rajas is the guna of action. A rajas-dominant individual is like a cat on a hot tin roof – always 'doing' something. Rajas binds human beings by attachment to action.

> **When this rajas is predominant in a person,**
> **There's greed for more, ever-busy activity,**
> **Constant undertaking of actions, unrest and craving. 14.12**

This is the guna that seems to dominate the minds of today's men and women. Rajas keeps people running.

On the other end, the dominance of tamasic guna makes one heedless and lethargic. If rajasic people hover on the tide of excitement and action, tamasic people are overwhelmed by it all. They are heedless and oblivious to the world. 'The world sucks,' is their byword.

> **This tamas is born of ignorance.**
> **It deludes beings by heedlessness, indolence and sleep. 14.8**

> **Ignorance, inactivity, negligence and delusion**
> **are predominant when tamas rises, O Arjuna. 14.13**

They are in a lower rung of consciousness than the rajasic person.

A sattwic existence, on the other hand, is the one centred serenely on the higher principles of life. Sattwa means purity or virtuosity. If Karma Yoga is like tending and nurturing a plant in our garden and offering its flowers to the world, the guna of sattwa is the fertile soil in which that plant grows the best. It is the temperament we have to nourish in our mind as we practise being Karma Yogis.

Sattwa is a quality of nature unfolded only in man. 'The nature of a man of sattwa guna is that he is equally calm in all situations in life – whether it be prosperity or adversity,' Swami Vivekananda tells us.[16] Not every man has this sattwa unfolded in him. It is a guna of an evolved intelligence. Only a man of awareness can develop it in him, not a worldliness-imprisoned one.

So how do we nourish this temperament in us? One way is through the right method of action we discussed till now.

The fruit of (such) pure action is sattwa. 14.16

When we do actions guided by rajasic desire it only leads to more and more desires, and a slowly escalating pain inside. The heedlessly done tamasic actions gradually root us in a gloomy ignorance. However, when done in a balanced and principle-centred way, our actions bring a happy tranquillity to our inner being. With every action performed as Yajna, we become more and more sattwic.

Happiness arises from sattwa. Desires arise from rajas.
And negligence, delusion and ignorance from tamas. 14.17

As the second way, the Gita gives a set of internal principles and external aids to adopt for us to grow in this noble guna. (Impatient rajasic readers can refer the second topic in the appendix.)

The Gita's message to us so far is, 'Enough of being controlled by the world and your lower impulses. Take control of your life with the right perspective!' For tamasic people, the first part of the advice is important: taking control. Their movement towards sattwa is through rajas. That is the order in which we evolve along the ladder: tamas → rajas → sattwa.

For rajasic people, the second part is important, bringing in the right perspective into their actions. They learn to slow down, to let go of the urge to rule the roost and settle tranquilly into sattwa.

ॐ

Once we become a sattwic person, what next?

Well, we can stay as sattwic beings – good, ethical men and women sincere to our dharma who keep performing our actions as yajna. It is, no doubt, a superior way to live compared to the dreary world-centred existence most people lead. However, there are some inherent problems in such a living.

> **Sattwa, because it is stainless,**
> **is a luminous and healthy (guna to imbibe) 14.6**

But the problem with it is

> **It binds by attachment to happiness and knowledge. 14.6**

A sattwic's ego might, with time, become too attached to righteousness and purity, making him stuck in the mind yet again. We won't realise that it is the mind-dictator gaining his re-entry through stealth, while we believe that we are walking the path of goodness and purity. As in the puranic stories, it is the new form the demonic tendencies in the mind assume, to defeat us. This results in bondage, again!

So we must understand that the point of the game is not just to be good and ethical, but to go beyond that – to become totally free.

༄

Well, it is worth mentioning here that all that is not to belittle sattwa. The Spiritual path always begins with sattwa guna and the steps in Karma Yoga we saw till now. They are the indispensable preliminary steps for a man of action. 'To develop sattwa till it becomes full of spiritual light and calm and happiness is the first condition,' explains Sri Aurobindo.[17] However, by that alone one can't reach one's Divine Self, which is beyond all such standards of good and bad. By sattwic living, one achieves the qualification for it, the *'adhikara.'*

It is said that the Gita is a guide to a good life and also a *Moksha-Shastra* – scripture of liberation. The first aspect was what we saw till now. The Gita next presents us with a way to move towards ultimate freedom; a freedom in which there is no need to abide by such sattwic rules or scriptural injunctions.

> **As the blazing fire reduces wood to ash,**
> **The fire of Self-knowledge reduces all karma to ash. 4.37**

The holy flame produced by burning camphor is an integral part of worship in Hindu temples. Camphor is obtained from the distillation process from the much cruder oil of turpentine. With its characteristic milky white colour, camphor is said to represent the purity-personified sattwic mind. The refined camphor, when it is lighted with fire, loses its form totally and sublimates to become one with air. Our mind too, now purified by walking the path of goodness, can be transcended with ease when lit with the light of the Divine. That is what the ritual serves to remind us. And the way the Gita shows us for that is the most important exhortation of Karma Yoga – *Do your actions for God!*

KARMA II

'So, how's your son Akil, Sir? Did you manage to take him out for his holidays?' I asked Rajagopal Sir over phone. He had called me after a long gap.

'Oh that? I managed to convince our chief to give me one week leave for Delhi conference. But at the last minute he had to cancel it for MCI visit. So Akil is now livid, as usual. He'll be alright in a couple of days, I hope. By the way, it should have been a few months since you started practice. How's your butterfly period going?'

'Well, I am getting no butterflies, but only lot of houseflies here, Sir.'

'Read or learn something new in this period. That would be a good idea,' Sir added.

'Sure, Sir,' I replied, not wanting to disclose that I was already into reading something quite important.

ଓଃ

Do your actions for God! That is the next aspect of Karma Yoga we are about to discuss. The Gita told us, 'One who delights in his Dharma attains perfection' (18.45). Here is how the verse continues,

> **How engaged in one's duty one attains perfection,**
> **That now hear from me. 18.45**
>
> **From whom all beings arise, by whom all this is pervaded,**
> **Worshipping him with one's Dharma, man attains perfection. 18.46**

That is, 'Do your Dharma as a worship of God.' Once a person keeps doing his Dharma as Yajna and starts leading a sattwic life, it's then the Divine enters the picture. This is quite a vital teaching of the Gita that we find repeated at several places in the scripture.

> **Perform action for my sake.**
> **By doing so you shall attain perfection. 12.10**

> Dedicating all actions to me,
> With the mind firmly fixed on the highest,
> Free from desire, attachment and mental fever,
> Do your duty. 3.30
>
> Those who always practice this teaching of mine
> With faith and free from cavil,
> are freed from the bondage of Karma. 3.31
>
> But those deluded ones who carp at this teaching
> Consider them doomed to destruction. 3.32

Whoa! Alright, we shall not carp at it. After all, our Big Boss himself has insisted on it. However, given the fact that we are no God-realised saints yet, how in the world can we do our actions for a God of whom we have no definite idea?

(Note: This chapter is all about the nuts and bolts of such God-centred action. I realise that there may be people with a strong faith in their hearts already, for whom it may sound a simple enough concept to follow. If you are among those and wonder why so many pages have been used to convey it, please feel free to bypass it. This chapter is for people like yours truly – members of the stubborn-minded, stiff-necked association.)

☙

I had gone to Pasumaikudi for an NGO-sponsored medical camp. Saradha, my classmate from undergraduation was the only doctor in the village. She chose not to do postgraduation and had settled in Pasumaikudi, her native village. She was running a five-bed hospital there. I had gone to her house to pay a courtesy visit. She had been referring quite a few patients over to me since I set up my practice.

Saradha's father invited me in. He appeared quite old – my grandpa came to mind as I saw him. '*Saradha must be a late child*,' I assumed. He asked me to wait in the drawing room. The house was on the first floor of her hospital.

'Saro will come in a few minutes,' he told me.

He was busy watering the plants on the terrace. Her mother, who came outside to welcome me, seemed to have quite severely deformed knee joints. She was walking with great difficulty. I was sitting there and looking at the photos of young Saradha getting trophies and shields from local bigwigs that decorated the wall of the room. Birds were chirping from the neem tree close by the house. Not a bit of the usual honking and roaring of vehicles I am quite used to hearing near my place was to be found there. Through the window of the room I saw the rose plants on the terrace. There were at least a dozen of them bearing many flowers. Many butterflies were fluttering over them, trying hard to stay on the flowers waving in the breeze.

The iron hinges of the room's door screeched open, jolting me out of my reverie. It was Saradha.

'Hi, Venkat. Nice to see you after a long time. Did I make you wait long?' she asked as she walked in.

'Not a problem, Saro.'

She was clad in a blue saree. A pungent smell of spirit accompanied her. And I couldn't help noticing that she still wrapped her saree above her ankles as she was famous for in college.

'Does it keep raining heavily in her place?' Mano used to ask during our UG days.

Saradha is one of those petite, timid and plain-looking girls who never get the attention of boys. It was pretty amazing to see her run a hospital in the village all by herself. And the patient inflow in the hospital too was quite good for a village.

'Come, I'll show you my great hospital,' she said, and took me downstairs.

We were walking amid the fully-occupied rooms. Patients and their attendants were saluting her as we passed by their rooms. There was genuine respect for Saro.

'Saro, I am really impressed to see you like this. Also this idea of starting a hospital in a village. Incredible to see the potential here,' I said looking around. 'I am surprised how not many think of it when finishing their degree. All that's on our mind is doing a PG, working in an urban multi-specialty set up and all that.'

'Here, Venkat, before I forget.'

She gave me a postcard-sized invitation.

'We are in the process of building an annexure to the hospital making it twelve-bedded. Sorry for inviting you like this. Please come for the hospital expansion, alright?'

'Hey, that's great Saro! Congrats!'

'So you had your lunch?'

'Mm, not yet. It got late at the camp. But it's okay. I will reach home in less than an hour,' I said, not wanting to be an uninvited guest in her house.

'Ah, don't worry. I won't ask you to have anything at my house. Come with me to the hotel there,' she said pointing to one on the street near the northern corner of her hospital.

'Our daily food comes from the hotel owner's house. Dad was cooking all these days as mom was finding it difficult to even get up from her chair. However, he too has become lazy nowadays. The man thinks he has become too old, especially in the last one year,' she went on.

Lady of Snow Parotta Stall, the board towards the hotel entrance read. It had a picture of Mother Mary holding Jesus as an infant.

'You have hotel food daily, Saradha?'

'No, no. The hotel owner asks his mother to prepare food for us too, along with their own. We come here and eat his homemade food. My lazy father, you know!'

൏

I was looking around the hotel while waiting for the food. It was single-roomed and it looked pretty small for a hotel; hardly more than twelve by twelve feet. The kitchen was at the back. The room had a roughly cemented floor with stubborn food stains here and there. There were ten to fifteen stools stacked over each other. The walls had wooden boards attached to them. These were used as tables where the food was served. Apart from that, the hotel had plenty of chairs on the outside too. However, the room looked pretty neat and well-maintained despite all the stains.

A thin, middle-aged lady chewing betel, came down the stairs to welcome us. She invited us upstairs since there was some cleaning going on around us.

The way she spoke to Saradha showed that they were well-acquainted with each other.

'How is your stomach, amma?' Saro asked as we climbed the stairs.

'Ah, that? Your injection made the pain vanish.'

Saradha introduced the lady as the mother of the hotel owner.

Their house took up the first floor of the hotel. We were sitting on the balcony. The thatched roof above the terrace kept the place refreshingly cool even at the middle of the afternoon. A twenty-watt CFL hung over my head. Much like the terrace of Saradha's house, this place also had a lot of flowering plants, especially jasmines and crossandras.

The lanky waiter who walked towards us had a minor limp. He placed the banana leaves on the table before us. He was clad in a red dhoti, white vest and a turban.

Saro looked at him and said, 'Hi.' He smiled cordially at her and me too.

'He is our guest today,' Saro introduced me. I smiled back at him.

When I first saw him that day, I couldn't have imagined that this very 'waiter' would clarify a vital aspect of the Gita's Karma Yoga for me within the next hour. Neither could I have known that he would cross my life in the near future in an unforeseen way, transform it irrevocably and make me, who is reading the Gita with a rather intellectual quest now, a heartfelt and a sincere follower of the book's wisdom.

'Did my father eat?' Saro asked him.

He nodded.

'What day is it? Oh, Friday? Okay, okay. That is why...' Saro was talking to herself.

'Friday is 'mouna day' for our Hibiscus,' she exclaimed with wide eyes.

'Hibiscus?'

'Yes, look at him, with his red dhoti, turban and all that. And that large vermillion band smeared on his forehead to top it all! Doesn't he look like one to you?' she asked.

Then she turned towards the waiter and said, 'Muthu, I

wish you would teach me how to be like you . . . in a high inner state always with a heavy insulation around, like those wires above. Hmm, your God never blesses others, it seems. What time did my father come today?'

'One,' he signalled.

'Yes, doctor amma. He comes by this time nowadays and takes food for him and your mom after you scolded him last week,' piped up the lady who had welcomed us. She had started serving us lunch. She kept the vessel filled with rice next to us and went in to bring *sambhar*.

'You have taken big decisions, Saro. It feels nice to see you like this, and all the respect people here have for you,' I said, spreading out the rice on the banana leaf before me. 'Look at that waiter. How lovingly he is serving you!'

'Waiter? He is the owner of this hotel!' she exclaimed. Then as an afterthought she said, 'Well, almost.'

The lady returned and placed the sambhar and the side-dishes on the table. She looked relatively young. She too had a big band of kumkum on her forehead.

'The weather today is rather dull, no? Let us spice it up a bit,' Saro told me with an impish grin and asked the lady, 'So, amma, have you convinced your son to vacate this place?'

'Convince him? How can I do that? He won't leave this place and this stupid hotel at any cost.'

Then she turned towards her son and said, 'You sit here and keep sending all your earnings to the old owner. That stupid man, and this boy's love for him! The old man has already earned a fortune from this hotel because of my boy. This place was virtually nothing before . . . and he still wants a share of money from it!'

The boy gestured her to keep quiet. Since the very beginning, I could sense some coldness in his mother's behaviour towards him. Saro smiled triumphantly as the woman shrugged and walked off. She then turned towards me and explained what was going on. 'The mother wants to vacate the place and go and stay with her elder son's family in Erode. He is married and has a child. But Muthu wants to stick around this place and the hotel. He will never leave this place.'

As Muthu served us some more curry, Saro asked, 'So how's your wheezing, Muthu?'

He gestured that he was better.

'He keeps getting admitted due to his asthma.'

This made me look more closely at the boy and suddenly he seemed familiar! He was that young, intriguing alopecia patient Saro had referred to me a few months ago. 'Hey, you are, mm... Muthu Kumar right? I didn't recognise you with that turban. How are you?'

The boy smiled to show he was fine. I think he had recognised me as soon as I walked in. 'Saro, it was through him I came to know that you are in Pasumaikudi. You had sent him to me for consultation, right? I advised him to go for a wig.'

As I said that, the boy turned towards me and smiled in a rather serene way, as if to say, *'Who cares for the hair?'*

'But why did he even bother to come to me then?'

'He wasn't interested at all, Venkat. It was I who compelled him. So, Muthu,' Saro turned towards him, 'Doctor here is saying you have no choice but to sport this villainous look forever.'

Mischievous creature! Will she stop making fun of the boy? However, in the way she was interacting with the boy I sensed a sisterly intimacy, and not sarcasm.

We started having the food.

'Whoa! The food is great Saro!' I exclaimed even as I placed the first bit of it into my mouth.

'Yeah, both of them are wonderful cooks.'

'The boy seems pretty religious, Saro. He was clad in a red dhoti even that day. He is only fifteen or so, right?'

'Fourteen and a half. If we take his blood sample it will test strongly positive for *bakthi*.'

I took a peep through the front door of their house from where I was sitting. The boy had started cleaning the puja room.

'Not just the boy but the mother too has such sepsis, but of a milder variety. Friday is a highly auspicious day for both of them. They would visit their deity's temple early morning and they would only wear red clothing... and also clean the entire house and the hotel that day,' she said, looking intently at the boy cleaning the articles for puja.

She continued in a subdued tone, 'Coming across this boy ... that was the single most important thing that happened in my life. It is only that which helped me sail through my tough times. It was he who inspired me with his clarity and wisdom, you know.'

'Beg your pardon!'

'I will tell you later,' said Saro. She was busy eating. I could see that she was quite hungry.

After we had finished with our meal the mother and son accompanied us till the gates to send us off. It was drizzling by then.

On our walk back to the hospital I brought up the topic again. 'What did you say, Saro? That boy inspired you?'

Turning back and looking at the hotel again, Saro began speaking. 'You know what? That boy is in one sense, a wise little brother to me. But in another way, he is my Guru too. His mother says she will send the food to the hospital daily. But I make it a point that I come here and have it, so that I get a chance to talk to him. It is he who keeps my inspiration alive and gives me the right perspective towards things. Talk to him for few minutes and you will know. But you were out of luck today.'

'A teenage boy in a hotel inspiring a doctor? Dear girl, please explain what exactly you are saying here.'

'Do you know the story of the boy?'

'Yes. He told me that day in the OP ... about his suicide attempt due to his disease, how he discontinued his education and all that.'

'Oh, he told you that! Then did he tell you about *Alangadu* and his relationship with it? I bet not.'

'Alangadu?'

Saro continued the boy's story from where he had left off.

Muthu used to accompany his mother every Friday to the temple of the Village Goddess, Muthumaari. It was situated in a grove at the outskirts of the village. The grove, named Alangadu, was the property of the temple. A private trust maintained it. It had many large trees; mostly banyans. The trees seemed ancient, with huge trunks and massive prop roots. A few neems, tamarinds and many smaller shrubs and bushes interspersed the banyans in places. The temple stood on a natural rise on the ground in the middle of the grove. Around the grove were fertile lands used for paddy cultivation. The grove and fields were situated on the banks of a small stream that fed them both.

The grove was a special place for Muthu. His mother was an ardent devotee of the goddess. Muthu however, seemed to actually feel the presence of his God in that grove! He believed that there was a live presence in the grove and that it communicated with him. For him this presence was the goddess Muthumaari! He saw himself as part of that family of trees and shrubs.

It is said that the essence of a spiritual life is how spiritual people perceive a presence of a power, a force that is higher than them. They live their life in abidance with that. Such people suffer from fewer stress-related problems, says science. Muthu felt that power in that particular place.

It all started when he was six. His father scolded him pretty harshly as he usually does, when the boy scored poorly in a class test. The next morning found him unwilling to go to school. Unsure of where to go, he walked straight into the grove. As he walked in, it started raining heavily.

He took shelter underneath one of the banyan trees. Tears rolled down his cheeks as he thought of school. His father's words bit into him and the rain wasn't kind on him either.

It was then that he noticed a single, large, leathery leaf of the banyan he was standing under, as it fell from the tree. It floated towards a secluded crevice in the main trunk of the tree. It was as if the tree was telling him something.

He followed the leaf and crept into the crevice. He felt secure and protected. He looked at the tree. It seemed as though it was consoling him. The rain could not touch him any longer. Sitting inside the crevice, he watched the rain pelting down for a long time.

From that day on, Muthu felt a strange closeness with the grove and the trees there. He started believing that the goddess in the temple was the one who communicated with him and protected him that day. He began to accompany his mother every time she went to the temple. When his mother went inside the temple, he would go to Alangadu – his beloved banyan grove. He told his 'goddess' how that week had been and believed that she listened to him. Whenever he felt confused with the world and the demands it placed on him, he went and asked questions in front of the huge banyans in the grove. As he listened in silence his mind received the answers. He believed it was the goddess who answered him.

The day Muthu decided to discontinue his education, his father beat him up furiously. He returned to the grove the day after. His mother too was terribly upset with him. He was standing before the mighty banyans, but his mind wasn't in listening mode; angst and frustration teemed inside him.

He didn't speak a word but inwardly he was lamenting with all his might to his goddess for creating him without any interest in studies and for all the pains he caused his parents because of that. However much he tried, the lessons in his book just didn't penetrate his thick skull. He didn't want his father and mother to die because of him as they had said they would!

'I don't want this life you have given me. Take it. I am coming to you. You take care of my parents,' he said to his goddess and started walking towards the well in the grove.

As he was approaching the well, he heard his father call him from the entrance. Wondering why his father was there at that time, he turned around.

'What are you doing here?' his father yelled. 'Come with me,' he said and dragged the boy away from the grove.

'I muster all my resources and send him to study. The stupid dog doesn't want it... but says he only likes cooking with his mother. Then cook! Let the family at least get some income from you,' his father fumed while riding the cycle, with the boy seated on the front-carrier.

Muthu turned and looked back at his grove. He resolved to return and finish what he had decided to do.

His father took him straight to the Lady of Snow Parotta Stall. It was the only hotel in Pasumaikudi at the time.

Muthu's father pleaded with Francis Arockiam, the aged owner of the stall, to give Muthu a job. He had done some masonry work for the hotel in the past and that helped his case. The old man was initially reluctant due to Muthu's tender age and limping gait. Finally he took Muthu on as a table cleaner at a salary of ₹600 a month as his stall was short on labour.

In the months that followed, Muthu's father started drinking a lot. He started beating Muthu up every time he got drunk. His mother cried and prayed a lot. To Muthu, home felt like hell. His father dropped him at the hotel at seven in the morning and left for his construction site. Francis, the owner of the hotel was a pretty strict person. He wouldn't tolerate any shoddiness at work. Muthu could not take leave for the first three months, unless there was an overriding reason. He couldn't go to his Alangadu. He didn't want to. He was angry, bitterly angry, with his goddess. He suffered it all without a murmur.

The only day in the first two months of the job that Muthu was spared a thrashing was when his parents went to the neighbouring village for the Kumhabhishek festival of their family deity. He was denied permission to attend the function and was made to sleep in the hotel.

Muthu was afraid to stay with his austere owner at first. It was only that day he realised that the owner, who was pretty strict towards his staff during the working hours, had an amiable side to him. He cooked all by himself for the two boys who were staying in the hotel along with Muthu. The owner also happened to be the parotta master of the hotel.

For the first time, Muthu got to taste the food of the hotel where he had been working. It was kind of the owner to cook for his staff. However, Muthu was revolted by the taste of the parottas. It was nowhere near his mother's cooking. It tasted awful, and he couldn't have one bit.

He wondered what he should do. He was terribly hungry since it was an hour past his usual dinner time.

'Better eat it all, Muthu. Your life will be in jeopardy if our boss sees the food left over,' warned the boy sitting next to him.

However, the man didn't feel like such a threatening figure to Muthu. And even if he beat Muthu up, Muthu was now well-trained in holding up, thanks to his father. So it was really not a big deal for him. He shored up his courage and walked towards the owner, who was still making parottas.

'*Ayya*,' he called.

The old man turned and looked at the boy.

'*Ayya*, shall I make those parottas for you?' he asked in a feeble voice.

The boys who were staying with Muthu feared the worst and looked on incredulously. The owner seemed amused, however. The voice of the boy was coming from below the level of the cooking pan.

'You know how to make these parottas?' he asked patronisingly.

When Muthu nodded, the man gave him a chance. He placed a wooden stool next to himself. He asked Muthu to stand on it and try his hand at making parottas.

'Would be nice if Jesus has sent someone to relieve me of this work,' he said as he sat down, and began to massage his swollen legs.

Muthu invoked his mother's blessings. He remembered how she made parottas for him and his brother.

'Knead the dough well. The parotta's softness is decided here,' he repeated her words as the old man watched curiously.

Muthu had boldly stepped up to the stall owner but he felt nervous as he started his preparations. He prayed as he worked. After kneading the dough well, he fried the parottas for some time in the oil kept for frying the chicken pieces. 'Frying is a way to make them crispier and tastier. You can do that once in a while,' his mother would tell him.

When he finally served the hot parottas to Arockiam, the other boys moved to the back of the room in anticipation of the old man's reaction. They were sure something would go wrong.

Arockiam didn't say a word as he ate. But he ate seven parottas that night!

After he had finished, he put his hands around Muthu's shoulders and asked, 'Muthu, can I ask you something?'

'Yes, ayya.'

'Can you make these for the shop?'

ॐ

Things took a dramatic turnaround in the next six months. The boy who had discontinued his education, and was a table-cleaner at the parotta stall, had become the 'main chef', at eight and a half years of age. He was the one who prepared all the dishes. A few workers winced at that, but most loved him. They did what he asked them to, sporting a warm smile. They treated him like their little brother. 'Parotta master on a stool,' or 'Little boss,' they called him.

Within a few months business picked up dramatically in the hotel. Muthu's way of preparing parottas and their taste was quite distinctive, so people came flocking in, even from adjacent towns. Arockiam had to move to a bigger shop, and buy additional benches and stools to keep out in the open.

At the end of six months, the owner gave a fair share of the income to Muthu.

His father was speechless when Muthu gave him the money. The same child who had shattered his hopes a few months back had earned double his income at the age of nine!

'Go and give this to your mother,' his father said impassively.

Muthu didn't understand. He was hoping that his father would become happy when he received the money.

That night after he and his brother lay down to sleep, Muthu heard his father's voice from outside the hut. His father was talking to his mother sitting in the open.

'It is hardly a few months since I put him in the shop, and look at what our boy has brought home. All these years neither I nor our elder one have earned so much in a month. Maybe this is what our boy is meant to do . . .'

They were talking, thinking that their children were asleep. But Muthu was wide awake and listening to everything in silence. That night was one of the happiest nights of his life. In the week that followed, his dad didn't beat him or scold him – not even once. Even his Mother didn't cry. Muthu hoped that things would always remain the same.

ଔ

At the end of another busy day at the hotel, Arockiam called Muthu as he was about to leave for his house. 'Muthu, is there anything else you want here?' he asked.

All these months the boy was carrying some guilt in his heart. Therefore, without a moment's hesitation the boy replied, 'Sir, I want your permission for doing something every Friday morning.'

When Muthu told the old man what he wanted to do, the latter was taken aback.

'You want to visit your Goddess Muthumaari!'

He approached the boy. 'Muthu, you see that guy standing near that grinder, Velu? I asked him the same question a few months ago. He told me that he wants an hour off every Saturday night. He said that it was to visit his sick grandmother in an old-age home in Tuticorin. I believed him. It was later that I came to know that he goes to a sleazy theatre in Tuticorin, sleeps on the pavement and returns by the morning bus. And you,' he put his hands around Muthu's shoulders. 'You kept the wish to visit your Goddess on hold for so many months? Go, my son. Take an extra hour if you want. Whoever our god is, our faith should always come first.'

That week Muthu accompanied his mother to Alangadu after a long time. He stood outside the temple and watched as his mother was performing *angapratakshana* to the Goddess Muthumaari. She felt that she owed that to the Goddess as her son was making his way in life. However, even she hadn't expected that she would have occasion to do it in a mere six months' time. She had become hopeful about her son's future.

The boy slowly walked down from the temple into his grove. Even as he looked at it from a distance, guilt and remorse overrode his heart.

'What, Muthu, it's been long since you came here?' asked Esakki, the bare-chested old man, the caretaker of the grove.

'Hey, what happened?'

Esakki noticed tears rolling down the boy's cheeks as he asked that question. 'Come on, my boy. Tell me what happened? Did your father scold you again?'

'No,' the boy shook his head vigorously.

'It is alright, dear boy. Whatever it is, leave it to her. Our Great Mother will take care of it all,' the old man said hugging the boy, who was crying incessantly.

ᛞ

Saradha winked as she finished telling me about Muthu. I wondered whether she was making fun of the boy or paying her tribute to him.

'The boy apologised to the goddess and swore to never demand anything from her from that instant. He took an oath to leave it all to his 'Divine Mother', which he had kept up until now. The relationship between a banyan grove and a boy! Sounds weird, doesn't it? But this boy believes in it quite sincerely and it works for him. He has no interest in going inside any temple. The grove is where he feels his connection with his Goddess . . . a sort of animistic religion. After UG, it was actually quite a difficult period in my life Venki . . .'

Saradha continued after a pause, 'My PG entrance results weren't upto my expectations. Father wanted me to get married. I agreed for him to start looking for a match for me. However, the guys who came to meet me didn't make any favourable response. Well, as our movies portray, even the worst looking boy wants his wife to look like Trisha. I soon got disinterested in the entire process. I didn't know what to do next. Call it coincidence or divine intervention . . . it was exactly at that time, that I came across Muthu.

'Look at the gamut of problems his body has. Yet when one looks at him, at the peace and serenity always etched on his face, one feels it is he who is feeling lucky and happy about life. The boy is able to accept it all as a part of some larger pattern that only he can fully see. That is what amazes me. He is always in some high state within. He sees his body, and cooking skills as things that are not his . . . but as things given to him by his "Mother." He is just being responsible, he says. He sees them like the flowers in his garden! It was this particular thing that got hold of me . . . that detachment, that perspective. Isn't that true for all of us in a way? I began aping him and I have come this far, you know!'

I was walking beside her, listening to all she was saying without a word. Anything I said to her in response would be superfluous, I felt.

Saradha continued, 'When Muthu turned thirteen, they moved to the owner's house on the first floor of the hotel, where we had our lunch now. His mother became the supervisor of the shop. The owner decided to go and stay with his only son in Coimbatore. He gave the shop to Muthu and his mother to take care of. They still send a portion of the profit to him.'

'Which is the cause of the problems between the boy and his mother, huh?' I asked.

'True. His mother says that keeping a minimal amount for their needs, Muthu sends most of the profit to the owner. He loves that old man so much. This, his mother is not able to accept. That is why she wants to leave this hotel, move to her elder son's place and open a hotel there. She keeps scolding the boy every day for that.'

'But what happened to his father?' I asked.

'Oh, I didn't tell you that? He died of stomach ulcer perforation a year since Muthu took over as the chef. There wasn't even any basic medical facility in our village at that time,' she added.

CR

Muthu's life showed me the exalted way of life open for us in those five simple sounding words, 'Do your actions for God.' If Saro's story was inspiring, this young boy's story felt, well, surreal to me. The boy again confirmed for me what Barath Sir used to say, 'We don't have to read the Gita to live it. Discern and live true to your deepest truth and you live the Gita.'

Muthu! It was only fitting he had such a disease in his hair. The bald fifteen year old boy now appeared like a monk to me.

ॐ

There is pleasurable life. There is meaningful life. But above it all, there is Yogic life! 'Do your actions for God'—the wisdom behind those five words is what can help us take our steps along such a life. That is what makes our altruistic deeds Karma Yoga. And that is how our routine daily actions can connect us with the Divine. The Bible calls this Christ-centred life. Buddhism insists that one take refuge in the Buddha at all times. And in the words of the Quran (22.77), 'O you who believe, you shall bow, prostrate, worship your Lord, and work with righteousness, that you may succeed.' Though each religion refers to God with a different name, adopts a distinctive set of rituals and approach him through a different messiah or saint, when we embrace this teaching in our daily life, the dynamics that operate within us are essentially the same.

When we do our Dharma and contribute to the world through that, we become good, responsible humans. Yet through this facet of Karma Yoga, we go one step higher; we regain our lost oneness with our Divine Self.

So then, how exactly do we make this most important step in Karma Yoga, practical? How do we 'do our actions for God'?

For that we need to first make a crucial discovery: How does our heart see God?

ॐ

GOD AND MAN

There are two schools of thought Hindu philosophy puts forward to explain the relation of a person, a *jiva*, to the Divine: the *Bakthi* school and the *Jnaana* school. They are not mutually exclusive. However, a beginner in the spiritual path has got to stick to one depending on one's predisposition.

Bakthi says, 'There's an Omnipotent Power controlling us all. I am ever subordinate to it.' Jnaana says 'In the light of wisdom I am that power! There is no separate God apart from it.'

The Gita sanctions both methods. Karma Yoga can be performed on a foundation of Bakthi, as Muthu did, or on a foundation of Jnaana, without bringing an outside God into the picture. Both the paths lead to the same destination. The Gita says about the Divine:

He is inside as well as outside all beings 13.5

The person walking the path of Jnaana Yoga sees his God within himself. The Baktha sees and develops love towards an outside form.* This 'outside viewing' of God, let us divide into two ways for the sake of clarity.
- Bakthi towards a manifested form of God.
- Feeling subordinate to a nameless, formless power that controls the world – the viewpoint that sits more comfortably with modern-day pragmatic minds.

To take firm steps along a path we have to choose one we are comfortable with. Bakthi or Jnaana, we have to first get our foundation right and strong, before we can do our actions for God. We will take up the discussion of these methods one by one.

※

THE BARREL AND THE RAIN

Astronauts often report during their spaceflight the experience of what is called the *Overview effect*. It is a transcendental, euphoric and visceral feeling of connectedness they experience when they view Earth from orbit or from the lunar surface. It is an understanding that all plants, animals, humans and the natural systems are part of a synergistic whole. The experience leaves the astronauts deeply humbled and often ends up changing the course of their lives forever.[1]

Several poets too have recorded such transcendent experiences. 'The deep truth is imageless. For what would it avail to bid thee gaze on the revolving world?' asks Shelley in one of his poems.

All these are instances of the experience of the ineffable mystery, 'the deep truth,' sustaining the changing phenomenal universe. This experience renders one a profoundly humble being.

---

*This division is not a rigid one. Even Bakthi can have Jnaana at its core.

Humility! That is the keyword. 'Faith is not knowledge of what the mystery of the universe is, but the conviction that there is a mystery, and that it is greater than us,' said Rabbi David Wolpe.

Hinduism offers many forms of God for us to worship which might not always sit well with the pragmatic minds of today. Such minds can build their foundations for Karma Yoga viewing that mystery as, well, 'the mystery.' It doesn't need to be named, given a form or quantified in any manner. If we are comfortable seeing it as an ineffable presence that illuminates the world, the Gita and Vedanta give us full liberty to view it as such.

**Know that to be imperishable
by which all this world is pervaded. 2.17**

**That from which all beings are born, that by which they live,
That into which they enter at death, crave to know that.**
Taittiriya Upanishad 3.1

An objective look at our own mind will show us that there is too much of an I-know-it-all-ness and a taken-for-granted-ness in it. A stubborn arrogance and a scarcity consciousness is how the ego and the mind keep the game going.

'Sell your cleverness and buy bewilderment,' Rumi advises us, 'Cleverness is mere opinion, bewilderment is intuition.'

The right starting point of faith is such a feeling of bewilderment and wonder at the mystery which upholds our universe; at the power that enlivens and orchestrates this massive universe with its breathtaking beauty, diversity and detail.

When we silence our mind even momentarily and take a fresher perspective at things from our heart, can't we feel there is an intelligence behind it all that has put together this 'you' or 'me'? Can't we feel the presence of a loving power in nature that nourishes us this very moment through the air we breathe, the water we drink and the food we procure from it? The flowers that blossom at the night are white while those that blossom in the morning are colourful. What is behind it all? What is the power that makes our hearts beat and lungs breathe in such an impeccable rhythm?

'Seek me with all your heart and you will find me' says the Bible (Jeremiah 29.13). If we look at it from our heart, we would feel the presence of a mysterious, loving intelligence right now that gives the maple leaf its shape and the water lily its colour; that nourishes us right this moment in the form of the sun and earth and water and air. We can 'sell our cleverness and buy wonder,' right this moment.

This experience of wonder at that mystery and feeling humble before it, is how a pragmatic mind can step into Yoga. When we cultivate and grow in that wonder and humility, we grow in Yoga with the Divine. Such humility is the key to an exalted state of being that we previously didn't know existed; a blissful state of consciousness within ourselves that is in close connection with nature.

Feeling humble before that power is not something fanciful. An individual cell in our body remains ever subordinate to the innate intelligence of the body. Every living thing that sprung forth from that power, likewise ought to have this humility naturally in its heart.

What happens when we get to that place of real humility? Well, grace starts flowing into our lives. A disciple once asked Sri Ramana, when he could experience God's grace. The saint smiled, and replied, 'Grace is ever present. All that is necessary is that you not obstruct its flow.'

Feeling humble before that power is like placing your barrel in the rain. The barrel need not know where rain comes from or about its chemical properties. It can never understand all that, however much it may try. Place it in the rain. It will get filled.

He is incomprehensible because of his subtlety.
He is very near as well as far away. 13.5

There is no way we can 'understand' that power with our minds. If we try, it appears very far. But when we get to that place of real humility before that power, we can feel its presence right where we are. Then it becomes very close to us. 'When man humbles himself, God cannot restrain His mercy. He must come down and pour his grace into the humble man,' said the German theologian Meister Eckhart.[2]

The worship of all images and idols of God is only to aid the mind in developing this attitude, to help it arrive at this place of humility. In Swami Vivekananda's words, 'Can't you understand that whatever a man has in his own heart is God – even if he worships a stone? What of that!'[3]

A TASTE FOR MANGOES

Viewing God as a mere 'mystery' without name or form, though a good starting place for pragmatic people, may not be the best way for everyone. It may be too abstract a concept for us and we may need a more definitive and tangible physical form to hold onto.

Well, our Big Boss doesn't mind at all. He tells us in the Gita,

> In whatever form men approach me,
> even so I bless them. 4.11

Because the essential form of the Divine will always remain beyond our grasp, and because he is an omnipotent power, he doesn't mind when we relate to him through the form we are comfortable seeing him in.

However, Bakthi is not just about having faith in the existence of God and going to a temple in our hour of need. Asking God before a crucial exam, 'Let them not ask questions from the seventh chapter alone. I had no time to read it,' can be called belief, not Bakthi. Though better than atheism, it is a weak foundation for the exalted Divine life that the Gita puts forward.

What is true Bakthi then? Sri Aurobindo defines it for us this way, 'Bakthi is not an experience, it is a state of the heart and soul. The nature of Bakthi is adoration, worship, (and) self-offering to what is greater than oneself.'[4] He adds elsewhere, '(The) delight of the heart in God is the whole constituent and essence of true Bakthi.'[5]

In Valmiki Ramayana, Ahalya prays to Lord Rama this way, 'O Rama, it doesn't matter if I am born as a pig or any other being. Only bless me that my mind may be filled with real devotion to Thee.'[6] Such is the power and delight of true Bakthi. Once we develop such a delight in God, we will consider nothing else our prized possession.

Well then, here I am, with some faith in my heart about the existence of God. My belief is strong enough to say, 'Even though the examiner seemed a great lover of the seventh chapter and asked virtually nothing outside it, I still somehow trust in God.' How do I make such a vague belief, Bakthi? How can I learn to experience delight in God?

Well, we develop a delight in God by getting to know him and nurturing a relationship with him. We develop a taste for mangoes by eating mangoes.

But that gives rise to the questions, 'Where do we get our mangoes? How can we get a taste of the Divine who is by definition beyond our mind's grasp?'

It is for this purpose the Spiritual Masters turned up on earth. Just as aspiring painters study master painters, aspiring yogis should study the great yogis and gurus of the past. The lives of those great beings are live demonstrations of how one would live when one has surrendered to the 'mystery' and let that take over one's being. And sometimes the Divine Self itself incarnated as such for us, the *avatars* of god.

The self-realised masters and those incarnations of the Divine are our windows to the transcendent mystery sustaining the universe. They are the bridge from here to Eternity. There is no difference between a god-realised man and god. Every god-realised man is god indeed. He has died to his little self and allowed the divine to take centre stage in him. As Sri Ramakrishna put it, 'Do you know why God incarnates himself as a man? It is because through a human body one can hear his words.'[7]

'Don't you see that it is he alone who dwells here in this way?' he asks.[8]

The life of those avatars and realised beings is a mirror for humanity. How would we see ourselves in it? How does that mirror reflect us? Studying them can give deeper roots to the practice of *saakshi bhava* we talked about earlier.

There are beautiful recordings of how the incarnations of God lived when they were among us, the *Bhagavata* for Krishna, the *Ramayana* for Rama being the prominent examples. We can approach those books in two ways: we can read them intellectually and get stuck within the convolutions of our mind. Or we can silence the mind and reflect on them with our hearts. If we do the latter we would see that all the incredible tales are not what those books are about at all.

'It is human nature to build round the real character of a great man, all sorts of imaginary superhuman attributes,' Swami Vivekananda explains.[9] What are they about, then? **The state of consciousness of those incarnations is what they try to inspire us with.** That is the very purpose they were written for.

People to whom these are just stories, can start by getting to know a self-realised person who lived among us in our times. There are records of the daily lives, compositions, beautiful biographies and poignant works of every spiritual master. They are the instruments through which the divine light shined forth unadulterated in all its brilliance.

'What is the relation between those incarnations and gurus who existed in the past, and us?' you may ask.

The truth that was born as Sri Krishna or Sri Ramana or Sri Ramakrishna didn't exist in a segment of space and time to disappear later. *That truth is alive in us right now.* Swami Vivekananda clarified, 'Christ and Buddha were the names of a state to be attained; Jesus and Gautama were the persons to manifest it.'[10]

Countless years and miles may separate us from those Masters; but when we summon them, their presence can be felt in our hearts. That is why the sage Sri Ramana often told the disciples who used to adore him greatly, 'The true Ramana is in your hearts as your Self. This is who I really am.' He never gave importance to his external form. He always insisted that people turn and look within themselves.

A guru or avatar is like a mirror that reflects the truth in us to ourselves. Their physical form is just an aid; a tangible means for our mind to catch hold of this internal god. It is for this very purpose the Divine takes a physical form at all. We disregard it at our own risk.

> **The ignorant ones, not knowing my supreme nature
> as the great lord of all beings,
> Disregard me when I assume human form. 9.11**
>
> **Men who lack understanding think of me, the unmanifest,
> as an ordinary human being, not knowing my supreme state as
> immutable and unexcelled. 7.24**

As we come across them, if we have a deep longing for truth in our hearts, it may be a love at first sight. But that is quite rare. So we can begin with knowing the person and slowly getting a grip of his being first.

Start with wonder, with *bewilderment,* as Rumi said. Try understanding his being. What at all differentiates the Self-realised man's inner being? After all, every Self-realised Master too began life as a normal human being. What was the quest in their heart? Immerse your being in the truth of them.

'Man's mind stretched to a new idea never goes back to its original dimension,' said Einstein. When we give our mind a taste of the ultimate truths of our existence through a life of such a Master, we stretch our minds to *the level of infinity*. Slowly, if we have an honest and alive quest in our heart, we will see that, from such inquisitiveness and wonder, we start developing a true reverence for him. And that is the early sprout of

Bakthi taking root in us. *'As much as a man thinks of objects, attachment for them arises,'* the Gita said when it talked of the story of our bondage. It is the same principle we use here to free ourselves.

The company of these children of light, Swami Vivekananda stresses greatly. 'Five minutes in their company will change a whole life . . . such is the glory of the children of the Lord. They are He and when they speak, their words are Scriptures.'[10]

A Master's life is the kiss of Eternal Love on earth. He is the philosopher's stone capable of alchemizing us into gold. He is a keyhole for us to peep through and get a look at the Ultimate Reality. It is such God-realised men the Lord in the Gita talks about when he says

> **Time after time I come to the world for my devotees
> To establish dharma. 4.8**
>
> **He who thus knows in its true light, my divine birth and action,
> Leaving the body, is not born again. He attains to me. 4.9**
>
> **Freed from attachment, fear, and anger,
> Fully absorbed in me, taking refuge in me,
> and purified by the fire of Self-knowledge,
> Many have attained my being. 4.10**

When we allow this reverence towards such a Master and the wisdom he embodied to take root in us, we are letting our little egos get immersed in some important truths of our existence.

Set aside a separate time of the day for this work. This is the most important work we can do ever in our life, even if at first we don't realise its significance. Develop a strong bond with that one self-realised man or the incarnation who you connect with.

'Absorb yourselves in me. Take refuge in me,' our Big Boss said. Gradually, through exposing our being more and more to the influence of 'our God', we will see that we develop a total openness and an attitude of surrender to him. Truth has that power. After all, the connection with our spiritual roots is already there in our hearts. It simply has to be awakened and brought to our conscious awareness. We will with time recognise this was what our 'I' in the mind was frantically searching for all along. The little ego is regaining the connection to its origin. *We will, with time, willingly get ourselves rooted in Bakthi.*

Once that has happened, once our mind has got a taste of the Divine, our needle has got aligned to true North. Then everything falls into place. As Sri Aurobindo puts it, 'He who chooses the Infinite has been chosen by the infinite. He has received the divine touch without which there is no awakening, no opening of the spirit; but once it is received, attainment is sure, whether conquered swiftly in the course of one human life or pursued patiently through many.'[11]

ॐ

SATSANG

The method elaborated above is called *satsang* meaning *association with truth*.*

The saint Ramana Maharishi wholeheartedly encouraged such satsang. For him the most important element of satsang was the inner connection one feels with one's guru. According to him, satsang takes place not only in the guru's presence but whenever one thinks earnestly about one's guru. It is only by having such an association with truth first, one can develop a real affinity, a Bakthi towards it.

And only when a higher reality genuinely interests us, can we renounce the lower fully. Hence does Sri Adhi Shankara tell us, 'In all the three worlds there is no boat like satsang to carry one safely across the ocean of births and deaths.'

Our minds can keep wondering and speculating about god and spirituality for years. However, a real inspiration can come to us only from the touch of such a god-realised person.

So then, what happens once we have developed a genuine connection in our hearts with such a guru or avatar?

The journey that begins with 'me – Bakthi towards – God/Guru', slowly devours the 'me' totally. In Swami Vivekananda's words, 'We all begin as dualists.... Man begins to approach God; and God also comes nearer and nearer to man.... And the last point of his progress is reached

---

*The word is also used to refer to being with people of same spiritual inclination like us and periodically discussing spiritual teachings with them to deepen our understanding. Keeping the company of such like-minded spiritual seekers can help keep our inspiration alive in the spiritual path, which can otherwise feel lonely at times. But there too, this meaning holds true: one associating with truth.

when he feels that he has become absolutely merged in the object of his worship.'[12] Hinduism stresses that each person should have a chosen deity, an *Ishta deivam* for himself. Ishta deivam doesn't mean there are many gods or that one of them is superior to all others. It is just the way we are comfortable perceiving god. Whoever 'connects' and feels right for us is our god.

༶

REVELLING IN BAKTHI

Once this Bakthi starts sprouting in us, there are various ways to revel in it and get our being more deeply rooted in it.* *Japa*, the heartfelt repetition or a silent contemplation of our chosen deity's name is one way.

When I was a child I remember asking my grandfather once, 'Grandpa, why do you keep repeating your deity's name all the time? Does god love only those who do that?'

He didn't reply, just smiled in return. I see the reason for that now. When the mind demon is left alone with nothing interesting to do, it starts ruminating about the world, slowly laying its foundations for a worldliness-centred existence. This happens quite unconsciously as it is a long-ingrained habit. At those times, japa is a powerful way to keep the mind's energies directed inward; and godward.

An unconscious japa is going on within every person already, whether they recognise it or not. Sandy's japa is, 'The world sucks. Life sucks.' My father's is, 'Next big venture! Next big profit!' And my mom's is, 'Without Dattu baba, I am awful, my life horrible.' Sometimes an object of one's hatred is what occupies one's mind most of the time. And no wonder, everyone's life gets aligned around his or her own unconscious japa. We can make that process conscious and direct it in the proper way.

'The name of God has great sanctity,' said Sri Ramakrishna.

'Praising God is pure. When the Pure name comes into your mouth, all filth packs its bags and leaves,' wrote Rumi.

---

*In the Bhagavata, the little boy Prahalad teaches nine fold ways to practise Bakthi: (1) Sravana – listening to the scriptural stories, (2) Kirtana – ecstatic group singing, (3) Smarana – remembering or fixing the mind on the Lord constantly, (4) Pada-sevana – rendering service to him, (5) Archana – worshipping an image, (6) Vandana – constant prayers, (7) Daasya – being a servant executing the Lord's orders, (8) Saakhya – considering the Lord a friend, and (9) Atma-nivedana – a total self-surrender. (Bhagavata Purana, 7.5.23–24)

Japa is thus a simple but wonderful practice to root ourselves in the Divine. The Gita gives a wholehearted consent to the practice. In describing the glorious things in the world, our Big Boss says

Among spiritual disciplines, I am japa 10.25

Singing *keertans*, songs composed from the summit of devotion by bakthas, is another way to revel in bakthi. There are keertans in every language. When heard, read or sung in a heartfelt manner, such songs serve as readymade channels to direct the ferocious and bubbling energy of our minds towards the divine in our hearts.

Another way to train the mind is *meditating* daily, something we will discuss in the next chapter.

In a nutshell, we find a being that resonates with our heart, expose our all-knowing, arrogant mind more and more to him, and through that we nurture a live connection with his presence in our hearts. Then we offer ourselves to him; we sing, we pray, we meditate. Slowly and surely that being takes us over, with just a happy emptiness and utter humility remaining in our being where previously the rigid ego used to reside.

ॐ

There were two missed calls from Sandy. I ignored them. Last I heard, he had insisted and got an Apple iMac from a drug company.

I switched on my laptop to check my e-mail. My India-scoffing, atheist friend Narein had forwarded an article from a blog. As I started reading it, it felt like an interesting challenge to all that I had written in the last few pages.

'Break out of your prison dear believers,' the tagline of the article read. 'If you think about why you believe in god, if you explore that belief critically, you would see you believe because you were taught to believe. Your parents believed, the people you know believed; so you too believe. That's it. Such faith you are holding onto is just a tradition that is passed on from generation to generation. Subject it to the slightest critical thinking – it can stand not. Imagine the state of mind of the god who demands bathing his idols with milk and ghee and honey when millions are starving in our country.'

True! That does seem to be the prevalent trend with many Hindu temples and devotees; spending a huge amount of money on elaborate rituals and ostentatious ceremonies for worship. However, our Big Boss has stated clearly in the Gita

Whoever with devotion offers a leaf, flower, fruit or water,
That I accept – the devout gift offered by pure-minded. 9.26

By the way, why does our Big Boss need that even? It's for our sake! It is through the *ritual of giving* we are used to showing our love to anyone after all – one more addition to the methods for growing in Bakthi we discussed before. But the Gita doesn't approve of spending a fortune on that. 'A child can go to the lap of its mother, without any formality,' says Swami Ramsukdas when explaining this verse in the commentary he has written on the Gita. However, I was sure that Narein, the guy who forwarded the article would be in no mood to listen to all this.

'Krishna is "God" who visited the earth you were told. He had thousands of wives and even more number of girlfriends, you read. And you accept it all without questioning – because he is "God." And understandably you get edgy when someone questions it all. . . . Rational thinking asks you to question things even if you can't find answers. Faith on the other hand gives you weird answers and demands you never question those!'

Hmm. It seems there are quite a few people like Sandy around. That's the next possibility we will take up. What if one is bestowed a mind that doesn't believe in an external god at all, physical or abstract? What advice does our Big Boss have for such creatures in the Gita? 'Damn you, you opinionated stiff-necks?' Nope, those are mine obviously. Krishna surprisingly seems to empathise with and accommodate such minds too in his scheme. He presents us with the highest and most direct path to the divine which doesn't need any such external dependence, the path of Jnaana Yoga. We are free to take it if we will.

I AM GOD

If we are not comfortable with an external god and developing bakthi for him, we need not. We can follow the Jnaana Yoga path to the Divine. The essence of this path in the Gita's words is:

> **Those who perceive all works to be done by nature alone,**
> **And that they are not the doer, it is they who truly understand.**
> **13.29**

The Jnaana Yogi sees that his entire being, made up of the five elements that make his body, the ego-mind and the three gunas controlling it, belong to the lower nature or *apara-prakriti*, in the Gita's words. Actions are really performed by them, not the real Still Self that is him. This entire lower nature is a tool in his hands. To identify himself with his lower nature is to constrain himself, he knows. Hence he stays totally unattached in his work.

> **O Arjuna, the one who knows the truth about**
> **the role of guna and action,**
> **Does not get attached to the work,**
> **Knowing that it is the gunas that work**
> **along with their instruments – the organs (of action). 3.28**

That is how Jnaana Yogis do their work. They have an inherent detachment from the world, and even themselves! By working with such detachment, they get their being rooted more and more in a transcendent space within them, in an effortless, open awareness that supports all their experiences. In the Gita's words, a jnaana yogi remains 'a witness to his own working'(14.23).

Swami Vivekananda put it this way, 'Here are the two ways of giving up all attachment; the one is for those who do not believe in God, or in any outside help. They are left to their own devices; they have simply to work with their own will, with the powers of their mind and discrimination, saying, "I must be non-attached." For those who believe in God there is another way, which is much less difficult. They give up the fruits of work unto the Lord.'[13]

Yes, Jnaana Yoga is not an easy path to take. The detachment it calls for doesn't come easily for all. However, if it can be practised, we would come to see that all other Yogas are duality-based, roundabout paths to the Divine and take time. Jnaana Yoga cuts through all images, symbols and external dependence and takes us to the Still Self that is the real 'us,' in one leap. A Jnaana Yogi doesn't do his actions *for the Divine*; but does them by being *centred in his Divinity*.

If depending on an incarnated being or a Master is like taking a pre-existing road through the woods, here we make our own roads. Even on this path satsang can help; a self-realised being's life and words can resonate with the truth in us and help awaken it. We can follow the directions from a previous traveller even when making our own roads. The adventure is still alive.

If it can be done, then too we grow in our divine self through our work. We grow in tranquillity and get rooted in the space in us untainted by all our talents, skills and follies. The integral philosopher Ken Wilber eloquently describes such resting in our core awareness this way, 'If I rest as the vast, open, empty consciousness it becomes obvious that I am not in the body, the body is in me; I am not in this house, the house is in me; I am not in the universe, the universe is in me. All of them are arising in the vast, empty.... luminous Space of primordial Consciousness, right now and right now and forever right now.'[14]

ॐ

SHRADDHA

Whether we see the Divine as the nameless, formless and ineffable mystery, or in the form of a Guru or a personal God, or as the silent, untainted Self within, the most important thing is to get a taste of it and develop a tangible connection with it. Only when a higher reality genuinely interests us, can we renounce the lower without much strain.

'Where your treasures are, there will your heart be also,' said Jesus (Mathew 6.21). As long as we consider our talents, our possessions and all our worldly stuff as our treasures, we will remain entangled in the world. For walking the path of Yoga, a higher reality should take that place.

Shraddha is the name the Gita gives to this taste of a higher reality. Shraddha can be loosely translated as belief or trust. However, the essence of shraddha is the implicit faith and genuine emotional commitment we feel in our hearts that leaves no space for any doubts whatsoever.

> O Arjuna, the shraddha of each
> is in accordance with his natural disposition.
> Man is of the nature of his shraddha.
> As a man's shraddha, so is he. 17.3

'Man is the nature of his shraddha,' what a profound statement that is! The truth that you believe from your heart – consciously or unconsciously – that which your inner being gives full assent to, determines who you are and what your life becomes. 'We are shaped and fashioned by what we love,' as Goethe said.

In a materialistic person, this shraddha remains stuck in the likes and dislikes of his lower nature. But when our heart develops a genuine taste in the higher realities of life, that very shraddha can elevate us. It can be directed towards an external form of the Divine or towards our inner, untainted Self, as we discussed. Developing this shraddha in us is imperative while taking our steps in the path of Jnaana or Bakthi.

> The one who gains ultimate knowledge and supreme peace
> is the one who has shraddha. 4.39

Shraddha is the glue that keeps a person rooted in the Divine. It is shraddha that makes the spiritual path positive and nourishing. A person fond of the healthy vibrancy he experiences from consuming nutritious food, develops aversion to junk food of his own accord. Similarly, the renunciation we spoke of at length in the previous chapters happens naturally without harshness or struggle when there is genuine shraddha in us towards a higher reality.

Developing shraddha is a gradual process. The flower of shraddha takes its time to blossom in our minds. And developing it is crucial whichever spiritual path we take. Once we develop shraddha, once the foundation is set, then the 'doing our actions as Yoga' part becomes easier than it otherwise would have been.

☙

'*Dude,*' my inner voice whined, '*I badly need a break here.*'

'Come on! The study is progressing pretty smoothly. Why break the continuity?'

'Oh, you come on! The Gita's philosophy is not a capsule to swallow in one gulp.'

'Mmm.'

I thought about it, and decided to keep the Gita aside for a few days to give myself some time for all I have read so far to sink in. It was then I realised how much the work had taken me over. Studying the Gita was developing into a kind of addiction. I did not know what to do when I kept it aside!

Sandy turned up at my clinic the day after I decided to take a break. It is I who usually go to his. I wondered whether that was because he had sensed that I was avoiding him.

'What, maaps? Not taking my calls at all? Angry with me? Long time since you dropped by with your Gita? Stopped studying it, did you?' he asked.

Rather than my old guilt, it is disgust that welled up inside me as I met him. 'Yes Sandy,' I said, 'I have dumped the assignment. It was getting too cryptic for me.'

'Is it? Didn't I tell you? All these are . . . '

'. . . not suited for our times. You were right.'

He looked at me with surprise. 'Really?'

'Yes, Sandy. The first chapters were fine, but as I progressed, the concepts got too over-the-top for me.'

'Ha, how many times did I warn you of that?'

'Yes, I realised only now. So how's the new iMac the rep gave you?'

'Yeah, yeah, it is quite nice.' After a pause, he next started speaking in a contemplative way, 'I feel strange when people say that medical field has lost its service mentality and all that, Venki boss. Give me an example of one occupation which is not run in a profit-based way. Take this book,' he picked up the mythological novel that was on my table, 'It is priced at ₹350. How much is the production cost of this, you think? Not more than 50 bucks, I assure you. In every other field people are just minting money, but they expect us alone to run our clinics like charity organisations, and take great pleasure in defaming doctors if they earn a bit. We too have our needs and desires, isn't it? Bloody hypocrites!'

Now, why did he have to say all that to me all of a sudden? Is he trying to defend his actions to me, rationalising them? Or to himself perhaps?

'Yes Sandy, you are right. Who can follow such ways these days?'

'Okay, Kumar told you were angry that we left you out of our previous tour. We have a night tour planned this weekend to Kutrallam. We can avoid the crowds that way. Would you like to come along? The weather is quite pleasant there at this time, I am told.'

'Just now you went for a tour, right? Another one, so soon?'

'Well, it is Kumar's plan. His thalaivar's film has bombed at the box-office. It seems the opposite group has started trolling it in social media. Our guy is very pissed off at the rude memes and said he needed a break.'

'Kumar and his thalaivar!' I shook my head.

I thought for a moment. Going for a tour would give me too the break that my mind was searching for. But it would also mean getting exposed to the stupid philosophy of Sandy when he would booze. Then again, it was Sandy sharing his cynical philosophy that had galvanised me into starting my work on the Gita. Why not test where I stand by exposing myself to his ideas again? It would be a test of my shraddha in the Gita.

'Maaps, why this unwarranted experiment?' my inner voice queried.

I silenced it with, '*No. I have decided.*'

'Yes. Count me in,' I said to Sandy.

ॐ

'Know what?' Sandy asked me at the top of his voice inside the floodlight-lit falls, 'I've got a government posting . . . under 10 A 1.'

'Hey, that is great, Sandy. You never told me . . .'

'But do you know where they have put me?'

'Where?'

'In CIIMER – our damn PG institute!'

'Oh!'

CIIMER! I wondered where that would take him, considering the conditions and the darned chief of his. However, he himself had decided against working there, he said next.

'I am going to Chennai in a month. If I pull a few strings, I can get a transfer here. Imagine going and working in that environment again! Aaargh!'

On the way back to the lodge, Kumar told me how much Sandy was going to spend to get the transfer. He had whispered in my ear but I was so shocked that I blurted out, 'Three lakhs? Are you mad?'

Kumar looked on poker-faced, as Sandy replied, 'Yup! Poor guys! From the office clerk to our honourable health minister, everyone has to share it, you know? Have already taken a loan da. No problem.'

'Why spend so much, Sandy? You can work there for some time, wait and get a mutual transfer somewhere near our town.'

'Go and work in that depressing environment? No way. Not even for a day. Few lakhs only, no? Can sort it out with a year's salary, but no more CIIMER in my life, maaps.'

ॐ

That night after having a few pegs, Sandy turned into his usual alcoholic self. After some cynical musings on our profession and also on the world as a whole, he turned towards Kumar.

'God, this is bliss! Mmm. . . . Oooohhh . . . ' an exhilarated Kumar, tasting the scotch Sandy had brought with him, along with the chicken he had bought from the renowned Rehmath hotel, was making some peculiar sounds.

'Stop that shrieking, dude. You are sounding like a bitch in heat.'

'Dog, huh? Yes, I am a dog. Just wait and watch. I am going to chew off the heads of those idiots behind those memes. They just don't know to appreciate good art,' said Kumar.

'By the way, you know what this Venki fellow was doing?'

'What?'

'Take a wild guess.'

Kumar turned and gave me a blank look. He obviously didn't want to reveal what his guesses were, as I was seated close to him.

'Okay, let me give you a clue. He was reading a book.'

'Book? What book?' asked Kumar.

'Our Venkiananda was reading the BHAGAVAD GITA!' Sandy said aloud.

'What?' Kumar looked at me like I were from an alien planet. 'You were reading the Gita?'

'Yes,' I nodded quietly.

'That thing old farts sit and listen to at the end of their lives, in temples? That is awesome, maaps,' he said putting on a solemn face. 'That is rather awesome. So what does the book say?'

I didn't reply.

Kumar slowly burst into laughter, his eyes on me. In a short while the guy was snorting so much that he fell down from his chair. He tried to contain his laughter and struggled to say something, but burst out uncontrollably again.

'The fellow who once quarrelled violently with me for having an extra sip from the brandy bottle, is now reading the Bhagavad Gita! Ho, ho! Imagine! Our Piggy becoming Piggy Baba . . .'

I kept looking calmly at him as he continued blabbering.

'Dei, Venki, you have become a goody-goody person. But for that. . . . Imagine, our Piggy offering his other cheek when I slap him hard. Ha ha ha ha . . .'

'That is the Bible da,' Sandy broke in.

I slowly moved close to Kumar.

'No, stay there,' he stuttered.

He lifted his chair swiftly, put it close to Sandy and sat there. 'Whatever you want to say, say from where you are. Do I look like a temple bell to you? Smacking me whenever you feel like it. By the way maaps, is it true you were reading the Bhagavad Gita? I mean, really?'

Again, I didn't reply.

Then he turned to Sandy and said, 'Sandy darling, why are you not showing much interest in making fun of our Piggy these days? I remember how much fun we used to have back in school times. Come on, maaps, join the party.' He shook Sandy vigorously to get a reaction.

After another leisurely sip, Sandy replied, 'Well, you yourself are doing a good job.'

Ten minutes went by. Then the fellow's taunting got even worse, into an outright rude mode. He sat at a safe distance from me and blustered, 'You filthy pig. You leave me behind and become a doctor. I forgave you. Then you left us both and became a goody-goody a*****e. I forgave that too. Now, you have progressed to reading the Gita! Soon you will become a saint, huh? How do we appear to you? Poor Sandy darling. I feel like . . . like stabbing you, you bloody betrayer!'

ଓ

After all the madness had winded down I went out for a walk on the road outside the resort. I first shook my head vigorously to drive all the filth out of my mind.

'Mindless idiot, Kumar! He will never move an inch from where he is, and if anyone tries, he will pull that person down too with all his might,' I fumed.

However, after a while I observed that all those emotions and thoughts were only on the surface. There was a deep calm in me that was unshaken by it all.

I took a walk on the rutted road that connected the resort to the highway. I saw many a roaring drunk soul on the way, tottering unsteadily with their friends as their crutch. The world seemed to have too many Kumars and Sandys.

When I re-entered the room, both of them had slept off with the open bottles, dirty plates and spilled chips around them.

'How can anything get into our barrel when it is already full with beer and whisky?' I wondered looking at them. 'When we have imprisoned ourselves in a jail and fool ourselves that we are happy and free being inside it, what escape is possible from it?'

I looked at Kumar. He seemed like a child to me.

ଓ

KARMA YOGA – OUR GAINS

Before getting into the practical side of Gita's Karma Yoga, we will discuss the gains that one would accrue from one's practice of this discipline. The inner dynamics when practising Karma Yoga are something quite subtle, yet very important to understand if we are to become Yogis.

> **Those who always practise this teaching of mine,**
> **With faith and free from cavil,**
> **are freed from the bondage of Karma. 3.31**
>
> **Those who are devoid of attachment,**
> **Whose mind is fixed in knowledge,**
> **who do work as a service to the Lord,**
> **All Karma of such a person dissolves away. 4.23**

The effect of Karma Yoga on the doer: with his every action he becomes free from the world. He doesn't have to renounce the world; the world withdraws its clutches from him. *A Karma Yogi moves towards God with his every action.* How come?

Let us first take a look at what happens within us when we act driven by results or returns. Suppose the newest model of an elite mobile phone brand has just arrived in the market, and I can't wait to get my hands on it. But then my monthly expenses, the loans I have taken, the EMIs waiting to be paid, all cross my mind.

'Hmm, maybe a few months later,' I console myself. 'There will always be some fat slacker somewhere who will discard this one and move to yet another shining gadget. God, help me find such a one,' I secretly pray.

And that evening I get a call from my boss regarding a special project that I will have to work on for a week, which will get me a fat bonus. 'Oh my God! Express service, that is!' Thanking God, I agree to take the offer.

What was going on in my mind all this time? Through my desire I created a state of subtle agitation in my mind. When I was finally handed over the cheque, and I procured the device, the agitation settled down momentarily, and I experienced happiness. For the next one or two weeks this happiness lasts, as I keep looking fondly at the new device with its breathtaking design and features. And then I return to being my old self.

Now here is a surprising truth: when I unboxed and took a glimpse at the device, in that moment, what I got a glimpse of within me is *my true Divine Self!* The nature of our True Self is untainted bliss. The happiness that springs forth whenever the mind gets silent belongs to the True Self. In fact, all the happiness we think we get from materialistic pleasures truly originates from our Divine Self. 'The thief when he steals gets the same happiness as the man who finds it in God,' in Swami Vivekananda's striking words.

However, the problem with being a thief and with all such 'thing-dependent' happiness is this: we get only a momentary glimpse of our True Self's joy as our mind gets silent. And the dreadful long term result is that *we get centred in the mind.*

It is a natural process. From where the drive for my action arises, there my being gets centred more and more. When our mind-level desires drive our actions, we get settled at that level within ourselves, getting only an occasional glimpse of our True Self. We lock ourselves in a dungeon in our own palace and are satisfied with the occasional streaks of light from the outside. Hence does Swami Vivekananda complete the comparison by saying, 'The thief when he steals gets the same happiness as the man who finds it in God; but the thief gets only a little spark with a mass of misery. The real happiness is God. Everything that is bondage is not God.'[15]

Now let us take up the second way of performing our actions, which was elaborately described in the last chapter. When our action is performed delightfully, driven by our sense of duty, it makes us sattwic beings. It makes our 'I' more and more subordinate to the heart. Though still locked inside the dungeon, we have made a large enough vent in it so that a fair amount of light from the outside enters and illuminates our room.

However, when an action is performed driven not just by our sense of duty, but **driven by a genuine Divine obligation** founded on our shraddha, then our delight is not just in the pay cheque we receive, not just in the duty well done, but in having done our part well in a work the Divine has given us. **Our happiness is in being sincere to the Divine.** As Karma Yogis, we return after every action to our connection with the Divine. When done in such a manner, action centres us in the Divine. We find a way to step out of the dungeon finally!

> **Attached action is selfish work
> that produces Karmic bondage.
> Detached action is unselfish work
> that leads to nirvana. 4.18**

This is a subtle but crucial internal dynamic to understand if we are to become Karma Yogis. Lincoln's happiness in saving the pig was the delight of doing some good with what one is. Such sattwic delight, the delight of

Yajna all are much higher ones than the mere materialistic delights that drive many a man's actions. However, **this is the highest of all drives that can motivate our work.** By a simple change in inner attitude when doing our work, action can centre us in the Divine.

> **The thoughtful person equipped with Karma Yoga**
> **Reaches God consciousness soon. 5.6**

ॐ

PRACTISING IT

Now then, 'work as worship', 'do it for God,' all those definitely sound like good ideas. What happens when we try to follow them? How does one take the initial steps along this lofty-sounding path?

The Gita helps us by giving some practical instructions for Karma yoga in its twelfth chapter. First it starts with the highest way to live:

> **Fix thy mind on me and fix thy intellect on me.**
> **Thereupon thou shalt live in me entirely.**
> **There is no doubt about it. 12.8**

Not just doing actions for god, we can, in every moment of the day, live with our mind and intellect centred in the divine consciousness within. This is living with our inner being always in Yoga with the divine. An exalted way to live! As we eat, sleep, even breathe, we feel our oneness with the divine. We revel in the connection. We live a divine life. Karma Yoga is the first step towards such a way of living.

'Too much!' our status quo-entangled mind may protest at that. The Gita, as an answer to such minds presents its next way –

> **If you are unable to fix thy mind steadily on me,**
> **Then seek to reach me by practice of spiritual discipline. 12.9**

Go slowly. Get your being rooted in Bakthi or Jnaana gradually following the steps we enumerated earlier – japa, keertans, satsang, pujas, meditation – or any other regular ritual that suits you. Even if you find a new method to feel your connection with the higher reality, like taking a walk in nature, it is fine. Analyse the various ways religions have used to keep man connected to the higher power; Hinduism has a huge array for you. Stick to the one that you find most suits you.

But what if the mind with its ways is way too strong for one's feeble will? Then use your actions in the world.

> **If you are unable to train your mind by practice,**
> **Then perform actions for my sake.**
> **Even through that you will attain perfection. 12.10**

Proceed from the gross to the subtle. The gross – our action – is easier to control and it is an extension of the subtle after all. By putting your reins around the gross, you can control the subtle too. If the previous method was about living every moment of our life in Yoga with the Divine, this is about doing our action as Yoga; a good starting point.

It is quite amazing to see how much the Gita tries to extend its helping hand to whichever part of the ego-pit we are caught up in.

Another scenario: I have faith in God, and this 'do it for God' advice does sound pretty cool to me. But maybe, because it is all so new to me, I get carried away in the heat of performing my actions. This is bound to occur because all actions require the quality of rajas, and can hence disturb our centeredness. In order to counter this, the Gita advises everyone to return to their source after performing every action, just like people return home after work.

> **If this too is difficult for you,**
> **then (after your action) take refuge in me,**
> **And renounce the fruits of all actions to me. 12.11**

'If you forget me in the heat of action, re-establish the connection once you finish it,' offers our Big Boss. That is, when it is over, I can return to my source and say, 'Dear Big Boss, I've done my best with what you have given me. I leave it to you now.' I do my duty and step back for the Divine to take control.

> **Peace immediately follows such renunciation. 12.12**

Naturally! We don't let the obsession about the results or returns spoil our peace. We know that when we have done our best, the compassionate cosmic forces will always see to it that the result will always be what is good for us and everyone.

TAKING BABY STEPS

Let us take those practical instructions of the Gita and try applying it to our lives. The Gita tells us,

Yoga is the real skill in actions. 2.50

It is the internal skill that has to be at the base of all the external skills we acquire in our selected fields. How do we develop this skill? That verse makes a crucial point. If it is a skill, then like all other skills, it takes practice to master; we develop it gradually with time. A pragmatic mind can't acquire this *Yoga buddhi* and become a Karma Yogi in one sweep, any more than we can jump off from the highest diving board in our first swimming class and become expert divers. Walking the Yogic path comes down to taking baby steps along it. That is why the Gita has given us progressive steps through which we can acquaint ourselves with Yoga.

From my attempt at applying this high-sounding, 'Do your work for Me' teaching of Gita, I can tell you this, it is quite a simple thing to put to practice. It is much simpler than the *'saakshi bhaava'* we discussed earlier, which requires the subtle ability to witness ourselves. This is why the Gita begins its spiritual path with Karma Yoga.

We can use one aspect of our life to take our baby steps and get a taste of it. That can be the training ground for us. Which aspect shall it be? Well, the choices are endless. If love for nature dominates your swabhava, you can plant seeds in a public place and maintain them; you can give your voice and helping hands for preserving forests, or for protecting animals that are being heartlessly exterminated by humans.

We can practise Karma Yoga in our relationships too. If you derive joy from connecting with people close to you, you can choose a friend or a member of your family with whom your relationship has become a bit troubled off late. You can look beyond the petty concerns of your ego-mind and let your actions come from your heart. It can take the form of an apology, a heartfelt appreciation which you have never taken the time to express, or an honest and non-judgemental expression of the feelings of hurt you experienced as a result of their action(s) in the past.

If yours is an intellectual swabhava, you can find a few underprivileged students poor in the subject you love and teach them in your free time. The world and our lives are full of valleys for our river to flow. Our actions need not be of great magnitude, but the intention behind it can be.

'Why this experiment? Your own concerns are a handful already dude. What if a hungry goat eats the sapling you plant?' The status quo-mind will try all such tricks to pull us back, have no doubt. When it does, remind it, *'Dear mind, I am not trying to become a martyr here. It is still pleasure I am after.'*

As you do your actions, do not mind the appreciation or acknowledgement you receive or don't receive for it. We do things because it feels nice to do them; to do some good with what we are. Be centred on this 'nice feeling' alone.

So far so good? Now let us try moving one step further.

When you have been with this 'feeling of having done something nice' and relished it enough, next see if you can move one step higher and arrive at a place of gratitude within yourself and through that at a place of complete detachment from your work. 'Why gratitude and detachment?' your mind asks.

Let me try explaining with the help of a popular joke.

> A group of scientists created a human being from sand, much similar to how God created Man. They succeeded in constructing the complex DNA molecule from the simple carbon atoms in sand. The leader of the project called up God and proclaimed, 'See, we have become your equals. We too have created humankind like you.'
> 'Is it?' God exclaimed. 'Can you please demonstrate it for me?'
> The scientist gathered up a handful of sand.
> 'Child,' God exclaimed, 'create your sand first.'

In the same vein, take the case of me teaching a school boy. How is it that I alone faced the life situations that gave me such knowledge and skill, and the boy whom I taught, didn't? Furthermore, the power I have, the talents I am given, can anything really be called mine?

A lens held in the sun may concentrate the sun's light and burn a paper. And the lens may think itself to be the doer. But all it really does is concentrate an energy that is all-pervasive in nature. It is the sun's light that really does the work. Likewise, all of us are the different entry points for that one Universal Power into the world. Hence does the Gita say,

You have right to act alone, and no claim over its results. 2.47

When I give it a honest thought, gratitude is the natural feeling that would well up in my heart towards Existence – for the wonderful chance it has given me. It has placed me on a high so that through me, it can flow to the low. The high and low exist to fulfill each other in our world of duality. God's helping hands are waiting to be extended towards everyone through me.

A morning Vedic prayer goes, 'At the tips of our fingers resides Goddess Lakshmi. In the middle resides Goddess Saraswathi. And at the base of our hands resides Goddess Gauri.' What the prayer intends to remind us every day is this magnificent truth – when we lift up and look at our hands in front of our eyes, what we are looking at are indeed the hands of God!

ॐ

BEHIND KARMA YOGA

A Karma Yogi realises that the best things in life aren't *things*. He sees that true wealth is *what we are and what we have become in life*, not what we acquire on the outside. 'When all the stuff leaves at the end, what you have become . . . that alone will ever be with you,' said our Barath Sir to us. The Karma Yogi lives by this truth.

'Do not lay up for yourselves treasures on earth, but lay up for yourselves treasures in heaven,' says the Bible (Matthew 6.19–24).

'When you leave this house at last, you will only be able to carry what weighs nothing,' said Rumi. A Karma Yogi knows this in his bones. It is out of that wisdom, he resorts to Karma Yoga.

The inner connection with Existence that one gradually cultivates through one's actions; the inner stillness one grows into, is one's real wealth. That is the wealth that won't leave us ever. Hence a yogi values that more than all the stuff he gains outside. He grows in divine bliss through his work. And when we feel great and blissful inside, what external riches can compare to that?

> From bliss all beings are born.
> By bliss they are sustained.
> And into bliss they enter after death.
> He who attains this wisdom wins glory.
> Taittiriya Upanishad 3.6

ॐ

A NATURAL LAW

The Gita's prescription of Karma Yoga is the natural law by which the universe was created, and abiding which every entity in nature is supposed to function. Krishna explains how it came into being this way:

> I taught this imperishable Yoga to the Sun God. 4.1

> This Yoga handed down in regular succession,
> came to the Royal Sages.
> But through long lapse of time,
> it was lost to the world, O Arjuna 4.2

Humanity ignored the sages who out of their wisdom and compassion, exhorted us to do our work in that spirit.

> It is the same ancient Yoga,
> that has been declared to thee today by me,
> For thou art my devotee and my friend.
> This Yoga is a supreme secret indeed. 4.3

The knowledge just imparted, the Gita calls *Uttama Rahasya*, Supreme Secret, a subtle, important and very precious thing to grasp.

༄

'Dei Venki,' mom started in a pleading mode as soon as I sat down for breakfast, 'this January, you will turn twenty-eight da. When will you agree to get married? Take a look at these girls. These are the ones we have shortlisted,' she placed before me a few photos and continued, 'Look at this first girl. She is from Bangalore. Your horoscope matches very well with hers. Her mother and uncle are very much willing to get her engaged to you.'

'See, amma. I have already told you. No wedding before the wherewithal.'

'Wherewithal? What do you suppose all the money your father has, is for then?'

I didn't reply to that.

'Dei, just think about us. Won't I wish to see a girl in our house? And dandle a child?'

'If you want it so much mom, why don't you talk to your husband about it and plan for one? I have no objection.'

'Stupid donkey. Look at the way you talk to your mother.'

Three idlis fell on my plate as she went back to watch her TV serial. I took a look at the three photos before me. All the girls looked fairly pretty. An internal conversation ensued.

'Dei Venki, say yes to your mother for marriage da. See those girls,' the voice within tempted me.

'Well, err, it would be nice if I marry. Take a look at that Bangalore girl. Man, isn't she gorgeous. . . . But no! Again going and standing before that businessman, my dad, for every need . . . imagine! First earning, and only then wedding.'

'Really?'

'I have been ambiguous about many things in life. But about this, I am damn sure. So enough with this temptation game.'

'Hmm. Look at that . . .'

'I said, enough!'

ଓ

The bedside clock showed 10 PM I was looking at the cover of the Gita for some time before I opened the book. I was grateful to have the Gita and this assignment to keep my mind occupied. This period of life would have been maddening, otherwise. I can sense something happening within me, and it feels good.

As I was immersed in these thoughts, Mom came in to give me my tumbler of milk. She stood near the table and gazed at the dozen or so spiritual books that lay scattered on it.

'What da? I have been noticing for quite some time. Bhagavad Gita, Ramana Maharishi, Rishi Aurobindo . . . at this time of your life, you are reading all these?'

I thought for a moment. 'Yes, amma. Look at life in our world. We study, grow up, marry, procreate and finally die . . . all for what, amma? Don't you feel we are all trapped here?'

Those words came out quite spontaneously from my mouth without any tinge of sarcasm in them. However, my mother's hyper-exaggerated reaction was something I hadn't expected. Strange expressions made their way across her sleepy face. She didn't even believe me when I tried to convince her that I was just joking. Me refusing to get married, and reading spiritual books, got connected in her mind.

I wondered what this would lead to as she turned and walked straight into her puja room without another word.

'I heard someone talk a few weeks back about being sincere in one's duty towards one's parents,' said my inner voice.

'Err, who might have expected such a reaction to a simple joke?'

I let out a sigh as I opened the Gita file on my table slowly.

ॐ

LIVE LIKE A LOTUS LEAF

All that we saw till now is what the philosophy of Karma Yoga practically translates into. We detach ourselves from the result of what we did, and from the action too. We come back completely to this place of emptiness and gratitude. With time, we grow in it. We begin every day with such a grateful heart, and end the day in it. This is what a Yogic life is all about.

It need not be through gratitude alone we arrive at this place of detachment. It can be a sense of wonder, stillness, reverence, humility – whatever feeling comes naturally to us when we feel our connection with that higher power. We should discern what emotion comes naturally to us. Anything that makes us feel detached from our egoistic 'highs' after the action and return to ground zero, will do the trick. One quality brings in the others too. At the beginning, we can even make use of some symbolic practice after such action, say, going to our favourite temple, or to nature, or even the terrace at night, so that we can establish ourselves back in the connection. We can make use of affirmations or self-suggestions to direct our mind's energies in the right way. Whatever be the way we use, coming to this place of real detachment is key.

A result-centred (rajasic) person is overjoyed and elated beyond measure when his action produces the desired result. A sattwic person calmly delights in having done something beneficial with his potential. But a Yogi goes one step further. He too might be elated at first – at least a practising Yogi – but he trains his inner being in such a way that it comes and settles every time in this feeling of calm detachment from the action.

This moving from sattwic delight to detachment becomes easier if we have already established a strong faith and connection with the Divine. It is wonderful to do our work in the spirit of Yajna. However, Karma Yoga is an even more foundational attitude that has to enliven the spirit of Yajna. We nourish a plant and give away its flowers; the happiness of the people receiving it, driving our action. In Karma Yoga, we do it all for the love of the one who presented us with the plant in the first place, the Divine.

This subtle delight born of detachment is a Yogic delight. Like a stick made of sugar disintegrates even as it does the job of stirring the juice, this delight, as we keep experiencing it, slowly dissolves the ego mechanism and centres us in our Divinity. We don't grow in goodness; we grow in Godliness.

You shall be liberated, and come to me. 9.28

As a sattwic, one delights in having put to use 'what one is,' for the benefit of the world. But a yogi knows 'what he is,' is not that potential at all. He is just the custodian of that potential. It is all the energy of god/life. Yogis realise that they are temporary curators of energy, moving it around from one place to another. They experience not just a creative fulfilment, but a deep spiritual fulfilment from their work. They live their life in a state of utter surrender.

Surrender is not saying, 'Take all these stuffs and use it for your purposes, God,' but seeing for ourselves that those stuffs are not ours at all. The Yogi lives at that place of real humility before the Divine. His barrel is always placed in the rain. And it is always filled with divine grace.

We don't need to take to sannyasa in order to experience God. Through practising such detachment in our actions, we can grow in proximity to him.

The sages call sannyasa, the renunciation of selfish work.
The wise define *tyaaga*, **the renunciation of attachment**
to the fruits of all work. 18.2

This inner renunciation, this ability to detach ourselves from our work is the kernel of the Gita's teaching. 'Without non-attachment, there cannot be any kind of Yoga. Non-attachment is the basis of all the Yogas,' as Swami Vivekananda put it.

A Karma Yogi attains supreme peace
By abandoning attachment to the fruits of work.

> While others who are attached to the fruits of work,
> Become bound by selfish work. 5.12

While a materialistic person becomes a grosser and grosser being with every action, a Yogi – with all the clutter in his mind progressively getting cleared up – grows lighter and lighter every day.

> One who does all work as an offering to the Lord,
> Abandoning attachment to the results is as untouched by sin
> As a lotus leaf is untouched by water. 5.10

A lotus leaf remains completely dry even when floating on water all the time. Such is the life of a yogi; totally untouched by the world. A yogi is, 'in the world but not of it.'

The Gita makes an interesting statement when explaining about the path of Yoga:

> Even a little effort along this Yogic path is never lost. 2.40

Why is that so? Because we have given our materialistically-basking mind a taste of a new kind of joy, a subtle and 'other-worldly' joy which feels more real and nicer than the world-dependent joys. As this is something the mind has not experienced before, the mind will start wanting more of it. Pleasure-addiction is its habit, after all. And when it is pursuing it, the mind wouldn't realise that it is on a path that would destroy its authority someday. 'Happiness is your nature. It is not wrong to desire it. What is wrong is seeking it outside when it is inside,' tells us Sri Ramana Maharishi.

ॐ

LIFE AS YOGA

It is the same dynamics we need to train our mind in, when we apply the Gita's teaching to any field of activity – our family, career, wherever. For example, suppose an earnest follower of the Gita starts or joins a business concern, how would he go about it? We will try discussing this from the Jnaana Yoga perspective, which, unlike the previous path, doesn't need any external dependence.

First of all he would choose a field according to his dharma and not based on 'whatever works.' That is the deepest truth of his being and he knows that it is along that direction he is meant to travel in life.

He would then decide his intention in his job; what kind of person he is going to be in it, what kind of consciousness he would bring to it. From there, like his colleagues, he too would set goals. Life is in constant flow after all. Goals are what give it direction and purpose.

However, his goal-setting would differ in certain aspects from others. Be it deciding on his intention or fixing the next goal, he makes a decision not with the desire-driven mind, not by what the world pushes him to do, *but with the truth in his heart.* He listens to the voice within to take his decisions. 'Whatever comes up in the pure mind is the voice of God,' in the words of Sri Ramakrishna.

His goals and intentions are not just profit-driven; they are conscientious and responsibility-driven – the effect of listening to one's inner truth. There is no constant second-guessing, no half-hearted attempts in him. He is always fully present and fully into his actions.

Many men who are responsible and conscientious in their jobs might be doing all this. The Karma Yogi's goals and actions, however, differ further in two respects from others.

Firstly, the goal for the Yogi is just a means of focused expression. He is happy when the expected result is achieved, and he corrects his actions when it is not. And he enjoys the returns it brings, too.* But, *a yogi is not dependent or attached to any of those for his happiness.* It is out of his joy he does his actions.

(He is) content with whatever gain that comes his way. 4.22

What happens to the result, to the returns, then? Well, it is the actions done from such an inner composure and joy that would be the most beautiful and skilful in the world. Such works will be infinitely better than the ego-driven actions of most men. And it is such works, the world reserves its highest fruits for.**

---

*A tailpiece worth mentioning: being a Karma Yogi doesn't mean you forgo the returns of your works. 'Don't do it for returns' doesn't mean 'Don't accept the returns.' The Yogi receives the returns of his work like a prasad in temples - with gratitude. He doesn't fight for more. He takes what is offered and he shares it freely with all.
**Of course, it may not be the case every time. There are times when the result or the recognition doesn't seem to come by easily, and the situation is seemingly frustrating. Even then the worst day for the Yogi who does his works in such a way would be much better and would feel more authentic than the best day of a result-centred person.

The next thing about such yogic action, the final twist in the tale is, **the yogi is not even attached to the action!** This is how Karma Yoga is different from Maslow's theory of self-expression or Aristotle's arête.

When you are a Karma Yogi, you live from the deepest stillness of your being, your heart. You do an action because that is what you are and that is what your heart asked you to do. Inwardly, you are totally free from the world of action and work in absolute freedom.

> **Having abandoned attachment to the fruits of work,**
> **Ever content, and dependent on no one,**
> **Though engaged in activity, one does nothing at all. 4.20**

> **Free from desires, mind and senses under control,**
> **Renouncing all proprietorship, doing mere bodily action,**
> **One do not incur sin. 4.21**

Your body and mind do their actions. You are ever still. You not only act from your heart, but live in it. A yogi always stays close to his Divine origin. There is no external dependence at all in such action. That is what Gita's *nishkaamya karma* and its oft-quoted exhortation, 'Do thy duty, don't expect the result,' means.

> 'Even after all this time, the sun never says to the earth 'You owe me.' Look what happens with a love like that. It lights up the whole sky.'
> Hafiz

೧೭

Krishna tells us as he begins his exposition on the intricacies of Karma Yoga,

> **The true (and right) nature of action**
> **is difficult to understand. 4.17**

> **Even the wise are confused regarding**
> **the true nature of action and inaction.**
> **Therefore, I shall explain to you what action is,**
> **by knowing which, you shall be liberated**
> **from its evil effect (of bondage) 4.16**

A musician or an artist trains himself diligently to hone his skill. Yoga too is a skill we train our mind in. It is the skill that has to be at the heart of all our external skills. *A Yogi is indeed an artist of the soul.*

What happens when a yogi keeps walking the path of Karma Yoga? Because he is not attached to his goals or worldly success, all his energy is freed to concentrate on the process alone. When his actions succeed, he keeps progressing towards progressively bigger goals. The world is a field of action and he respects that fact till he is here. Life is about flowing and growing he knows. Even God says, 'I continuously act.' Why shouldn't he then?

> **O Arjuna, there is nothing in the three worlds
> that should be done by me.
> Nor is there anything unobtained that I should obtain.
> Yet I engage unceasing in action. 3.22**
>
> **These worlds would perish if I do not work. 3.24**

Swami Vivekananda explains it this way, 'It is not that God came and created the world and since that time has been sleeping; for that cannot be. The creative energy is still going on. God is eternally creating — is never at rest.'[16] The Yogi too keeps acting likewise.

There is nothing to 'achieve' for him here. There is only surrender to a life of Karma Yoga. The map is nothing. Going along the direction of his inner compass is all. It is not about the pursuit of happiness, but the happiness of the pursuit.

If a Yogi's action fails, he can calmly reflect on the reason and proceed to correct it, because he is not attached to the action. Does such a man have desires? Yes, he might. But he is not addicted to them. He might have great aspirations and great visions, but no attachment to them. A Yogi knows that it is all Divine play. While others get overwhelmed by their failures and achievements, he always travels light. That is the complete path of the Gita's Karma Yoga.

ॐ

I met my lanky school-junior Abdul after quite some time in a medical association meet. Abdul was now a pulmonologist. The meet was called for by Dr PP to protest against a recent attack on a gynaecologist by the angry relatives of a patient.

The patient, while being operated on for an ovarian tumour, had unexpectedly passed away due to pulmonary embolism – which the doctor had no chance to predict or tackle. However, the relatives, who owned a popular bar in town, believed that it was the doctor's negligence that caused it and had assaulted her violently in her OP room, with all the other patients watching. The doctor was admitted in ICU and was recuperating from the injuries now.

'You read that article that Kerala doctor had written on why he would never allow his son to become a doctor?' Abdul asked me with a wry smile, 'Hmm, practising this profession is getting harder by the day Venkat. How I wish I had taken the engineering seat that I got! I pity the OG-cian. Thank God we are not practising such branches. I doubt if I have the strength to bear all that,' he joked looking at himself. 'Hereafter they should add a compulsory martial art course in our curriculum, I think . . . Karate, Taekwondo or something like that.'

'Quite true, Sir,' the young doctor seated on the other side of us chimed in. 'Nowadays going to a doctor has become like going to a corrupt police station for people. Whatever we write, many patients view it all with suspicion. However, I have stopped caring these days, and just tell them in Goundamani* style, 'This is the right treatment for your disease. Take it if you want."

Standing on the podium with his trademark band of sacred ash on his forehead, PP was thundering in the mike, 'TV channels, newspapers, film actors all seem to be jumping on this bandwagon of defaming and insulting our profession. All of it is behind such happenings. I just returned from Tirupathi this morning, and hearing the news, I was totally shocked. I immediately called for this meeting. . . . We should show people that we are not ready to be soft targets.'

---

*A popular Tamil comedian known for his irreverent humor.

'PP, what you say might be true. But first and foremost it is people like you and the things you do in your practice that are behind such happenings,' I thought looking at his sacred ash. 'Hope someone first teaches you what the Holy Scripture of your religion preaches about work.'

ॐ

EQUANIMITY

The equanimity towards the result we mentioned in passing is worth elaborating on. A Yogi has 'unfailing equanimity upon attainment of the desirable and the undesirable,' says the Gita (13.9).

> Content with whatever gain that comes his way,
> Unaffected by dualities,
> The same in success or failure, even though acting,
> He is not bound. 4.22

A Karma Yogi has equanimity towards the results of his actions and also towards the ups and downs of the world. The Gita lays great emphasis on this equanimity in the path of Yoga.

> Perform actions being steadfast in Yoga,
> Being balanced in success and failure.
> This evenness of mind is called Yoga 2.43

Why is it so important? It is because such **evenness of mind is the real test for our connection with the Divine,** the test for the strength of our Yoga. How is such equanimity possible at all? Sri Aurobindo explains a Yogi's pleasure in life despite ups and downs this way, 'The warrior does not feel physical pleasure in his wounds or find mental satisfaction in his defeats; but he has a complete delight in the godhead of battle which brings to him defeat and wounds as well as the joy of victory.... He accepts the chances of the former and the hope of the latter as part of the mingled weft of war.... So it is with the pleasure of the soul in the normal play of our life.'[17]

That is how we cultivate and grow in equanimity – like a warrior relishes battle.*

Slowly we will reach a point where the pain or pleasure is no longer ours. They are just there before us.

About the Yogis whose minds are rested in such equanimity, the Gita says

Even here, the whole world is conquered by them. 5.19

Endowed with equanimity, one frees himself in this life
From good and evil alike.
Therefore, devote yourself to this Yoga of equanimity. 2.50

Such a renunciation is hard to attain without Yoga. 5.6

'The three kinds of results; pleasant, unpleasant and mixed are for the slaves of desire and ego; these things do not cling to the free spirit,' wrote Sri Aurobindo.[18]

Swami Vivekananda expressed the same idea this way, 'Every man is a slave except the Yogi. He is a slave to food, to air, to his wife, to his children, to a dollar, slave to a nation, slave to name and fame, and to a thousand things in the world. The man who is not controlled by any one of these bondages is alone a real man, a real Yogi.'[19]

In a world dominated by such slaves, the yogi alone is a king!

ॐ

IS IT EASY?

It should be conceded that training our minds in this new way of acting, isn't always an easy thing to do. We will face plenty of resistance from within as we take our baby steps along the path. When we find a way to tackle our inner resistance, the world around us will try to pull us

---

*The Tennis player Novak Djokovic expressed a similar sentiment when he won the 2012 Australian open final against Rafael Nadal after an epic 5 hour and 53 minutes long encounter. Djokovic remarked about the match: 'You're going through so much suffering. Your toes are bleeding. Everything is just outrageous, but you're still enjoying that pain.' And Nadal commented this way, 'When you have passion for the game, when you are ready to compete, you are able to suffer and enjoy suffering.' So it is when we have passion for life – with the right spiritual perspective at its base.

down in various ways. When we take a look at popular magazines, and hoardings erected on roads, when we watch popular shows on television, we will find that the world itself is conspiring to maintain every one of its denizens in a sensual and egoistic trance. Our ego is only a subordinate dictator under this totalitarian regime.

When feeling bogged down, remember Sri Aurobindo's words, 'The seeking of the Infinite through a constantly enlarging sacrifice culminating in a perfect self-giving is that to which the experience of life is at last intended to lead.'[20] All else is aimless wandering.

Ultimately it is not our liberation alone we are working towards. If the world's present condition saddens our heart, its redemption too is dependent on our walking the path. Transformation of the world's consciousness won't occur in one sweep through the descent of some transcendent force from the sky. It has to occur by each one of its citizens living by a new consciousness and bringing it in to the world through their life and works. We owe it to the world, if we care about it.

ଓଃ

THE GITA DUET

In spiritual language, the whole process of making our ego compliant to the Divine Self is described as a return to our true femininity.

In spiritual terms, masculine and feminine are not considered genders, but two aspects of Existence. Masculine refers to the active and driven, 'solid' part. Feminine symbolises the submissive and supple part. Both are indispensable aspects of everyone's inner being, irrespective of the outer sex. If we observe nature, we would find that it is the dead things that are brittle and dry. Wherever there is life, there is always suppleness. The significant problems humanity faces today stem from the abundant masculine energy circulating in the world, unbalanced by the feminine, say spiritual masters.

Lord Krishna is called Purushottama in the Gita, meaning the 'supreme male being.' When we understand the only male-female relation possible in the world, we would see we are all the consorts of god; gopis of Krishna.*

---

*In a similar spirit, Christianity sees Jesus as the heavenly bridegroom and the Church community as the bride of Christ, who would be united with him in his Second Coming.

The Lord is our personal intimate lover, and our life is a magnificent, divine, romantic dance with him. A divine duet. *Raasa leela*.

The spiritual path delineated in the Gita is considered the return to our feminineness; an existence surrendered to the Divine. The controlling power is given to the original and only male principle of the universe – the Still, Silent Self within. The rigid outer active part, ever running counter to our heart's wisdom, is harnessed and made subordinate to it. Its all-knowingness is replaced by 'a wise and still passivity in the hands of the universal and eternal Power,' in Sri Aurobindo's words.[21]

It's written in the Tao te Ching, 'He who knows his manhood's strength yet still his female feebleness keeps and maintains, all come to him, all beneath the sky' (Verse 28). When the strength and will of our manhood has such suppleness and submissiveness at its core, then we live our life in harmony with the universe. 'Let us open ourselves to the one Divine Actor, and let Him act,' wrote Swami Vivekananda. When we do so, the Great Cosmic Self starts singing its song through us. *Our very life becomes a Bhagavad Gita!*

An anecdote from Meerabai's life exemplifies how deeply the bakthas of God live by this principle. Meerabai once expressed her wish to see Jiva Gosain, the head of the Vaishnavites in Brindavan. But the monk, being celibate, refused to meet a woman. Meera retorted, 'I thought Lord Krishna is the only *Purusha* (the male principle). But today I have come to know that there is another Purusha besides Krishna in Brindavan.'

Jiva Gosain was put to shame. He realised that Meera was indeed a supreme devotee of the Lord and at once went to pay due respects to her.

A Karma Yogi can be thus considered a study in contrasts. He is self-reliant outside; yet in a totally surrendered state within himself. He is goal driven and active; yet is tranquil and not dependent on any of those for his joy. A Yogi may be male or female, yet on the spirit level, he is always feminine before the One Divine Male principle of the universe, Purushottama.

Bhagavad Gita, when we start living it, is thus a duet we sing with the Divine. We sing it with our lives.

THE FLIGHT GEAR

So then, that is the third principle the Gita shares with us, 'Do your Dharma as a worship of the Divine.' With his every action, the Yogi grows lighter, tranquil and humble compared to the dreary heaviness a materialistic person grows into. Our bumpy journey becomes a smooth ride. All that is needed of us is that we do not lose this inner connection as we did once.

What next? Doesn't that sound like some kind of culmination point?

Well, if our worldly life is all there is to it, if that was all that our body-mind vehicle was capable of, the Gita would end here. What more do we need? We would be living not just a good life, but a divine life. But we cannot feel satisfied just by regaining our connection with the Divine. We are not just human beings, but divine beings, we were told at the outset. How do we regain that identity, that true nature of ours?

For that, in this vehicle of ours, after the top gear there is one more gear left, the flight gear. Knowing how to handle it would help us progress along the path even better and smoother. It can take us to the state of surrender that the Gita talks about, even quicker.

Let us now get to know that flight path to the Divine, *Dyaana Yoga*.

DYAANA

When I took a break, I realised that it had been quite a few weeks since I heard from Sandy. Probably after an uncertain start, he had gotten into a stride in his new-found ways and hence didn't wish to meet me.

My recurrent dream had acquired a different complexion. Sandy had fallen deep into a dismal abyss. I tried saving him a number of times, extending my hands towards him. But he wouldn't accept my help. He kept falling, with a wide, contemptuous grin lighting up his face. Gazing at him for some time, I let out a deep sigh, then turned back and walked away with calmness. I have the Gita in my hand. My mom watches me. She is crying. I console her and walk towards a grove at a distance.

Those were the bits and pieces of the dream I remembered when I woke up. I had no clue what that dream meant.

ఐ

My eyes fell on the Gita sitting on the table yet again. I had a weird feeling that Barath Sir was overseeing it all from somewhere and that he was feeling happy about me too. Within my heart I had a conversation with him.

'Barath Sir, your old student has at last got all engrossed in the last assignment you gave him. I am not sure how much my write-ups on the Gita will inspire the old and new students of Sanskriti. However, the Gita has been a journey of revelation to me so far. In that way I should really thank you, Sir.'

The present day Sandy came to mind again and I said, 'Sir, I don't see any light at the end of the tunnel, looking at Sandy and his ways.'

That weekend, Saradha's hospital expansion function was on the cards. When Sandy got in touch with me, he said he too was planning to come; she had invited him as well.

Mom and Dad had gone on a tour. Mom had gone with her ashram-mates to Murudeshwar, and Dad had gone with his business-colleagues to somewhere in Kerala.

The next topic waiting to be taken up in the Gita was meditation! Karma Yoga was about action after all and wasn't too hard to understand. But boy, I wonder how I am going to come to terms with the Gita's Dyaana Yoga.

Meditation! The term has bewildered me since I came across it. I remember a meditation class I attended once in my UG days, lured in by the heavy advertisements put up in and around the college. I was taught the 'ancient, powerful technique that can make anyone experience meditation', as those ads claimed. However, I dumped it after a week or so, feeling weird about myself sitting alone and breathing like a cycle pump! And here I am again with the same topic before me.

I decided to forget what I learnt there and give the Gita's way of meditation a shot. I would continue to the next portion of the write-up only if I succeeded in following it.

The Gita tells us after its exposition on Karma Yoga

**For the one who wishes to attune to Yoga,
Action is the means.
For the same person who has attuned to Yoga,
Quiescence is the means. 6.3**

That is, meditation is the next step we have to take. The Gita lays great emphasis on the practice, and also assures us that it is easily done.

**A sinless Yogi who constantly engages the mind in the Self,
Easily enjoys the infinite bliss of contact with Brahman. 6.28**

My mind seemed to have gained some calmness even with my baby steps along the path of Yoga. That it was not reacting in its usual angry way to Sandy's behaviour or Kumar's occasional outrageousness, and was able to accept it all calmly, seemed to bear testimony to it.

The reason might be that I was getting attuned to Yoga. Maybe I was regaining my, ahem, connection with my True

Self, as the Gita says! So I decided to try to enter the next stage along the Gita's path. I wanted to try it out before going deeper into the topic.

In its sixth chapter the Gita gives a detailed step-by-step guide on meditation.

> Let a Yogi, remaining in solitude,
> try constantly to keep the mind steady,
> With the mind and body controlled
> and free from expectations and ideas of possession. 6.10

Very simple sounding! But there are very profound ideas conveyed in that verse which I missed totally in my first hasty attempt to meditate. More on that later. Let me continue with my first attempt. The Gita continues in its next verse,

> Having in a clean spot, established a firm seat of his own (...)

I chose the room on the terrace where my mom doesn't usually go, so that I could avoid alarming her further. I cleaned it spotless, then chose a wooden bench with a blanket on it.

In the next few verses the Gita gives details on the inner dynamics of meditation.

> Having made the mind one-pointed,
> With the actions of the mind and the senses controlled,
> Let him be seated in asana,
> Practice Yoga for purification of the self. 6.12
>
> Let him firmly hold his body, head and neck erect and still,
> Gazing at the root of the nose, without looking around. 6.13
>
> Serene minded, fearless, firm in the vow of brahmacharya,
> Having controlled the mind, the Yogi should sit intent on me
> Having me alone, as the supreme goal. 6.14

Each aspect of those instructions is a priceless gem, I realised only later. In my first attempt I chose one corner of the room in which I had hung a picture of Krishna and Arjuna on the chariot. As I went and sat down there after finishing my morning chores, the clock rang seven. Sitting there in the padmaasana posture I had learnt in primary school, I got rid of my habitual stoop and got my back erect.

'*Dude, what are you up to, here?*' my unfailing inner voice asked instantly.

'*Alright, not so stiff!*' I relaxed a bit and it felt nice. All Yogic traditions insist on the practice of a methodical deep breathing after sitting in the lotus posture. Even the Gita mentions it in its chapter before meditation (Verse 5.27). Yogis declare that the mind calms down through deep breathing. So I tried the deep and slow abdominal breathing I had learnt in that meditation retreat, years ago. My thoughts ebbed and flowed even as I did this.

'Boy, I am already feeling a nice and light sensation in my head. Not bad. It seems I am starting to experience meditation this time. Gita, you are great!'

'Hey dumbo, that is just the increased oxygen supply to your brain that is bound to occur if you keep breathing like this.'

'Shut up. Concentrate.'

Once my mind seemed to calm down a bit I went to the next step, 'Control your mind and sit intent on God.' Alright! From here comes the important part of the practice. I sat 'intent' on God as the Gita directed.

So there began my meditation on the lines of the Gita. And it did seem to go well for a few minutes this time till that darned puppy in the neighbouring house went ballistic, barking incessantly.

Once that unforeseen, unfortunate incident took place, and the sound entered my keen ears, the mind triumphantly reclaimed the reins of the chariot. It first jumped to the thought of the neighbour, the owner of the dog. He was a middle-aged man working as a college lecturer in the chemistry department. Sandy and I had gone for tuitions to his house in our final year at school and then we stopped going midway through the year, unable to find time.

Next the mind jumped to the thought of his brother, a Tamil teacher in a boarding school in Ooty. Last time I met him, he said how Ooty too, like Tuticorin, was becoming more and more polluted because of the unregulated new constructions.

He had moved to Ooty after his doctor had advised him to go to a pollution-free area as his lung disease was getting aggravated in Tuticorin.

From there the mind proceeded to . . .

'He seemed like a nice guy; but how scornful the Tamil teacher at Sanskriti used to be, thrashing every boy at his will! And how sweet a person our biochemistry lecturer was to allow us to sleep in his lecture classes! . . . College life! That midnight bike tour to Kutrallam falls in pre-final year! Damn good one, that! And that Debonair magazine we read with Kumar in the class once. . . . Steamy hot one that!! I feel like reading it again, right now. . . . Damn! The lower part of my right leg is starting to get numb. Why does this meditation thing need to be so uncomfortable? I mean, can't it be done sitting in a snug cushion chair?'

Those are the few among the countless destinations my mind took me to in five minutes.

'Focus, dude. You are just supposed to sit doing nothing and you can't even do that,' growled my inner voice.

I stopped my attempt midway and opened my eyes.

Ever got held forcibly in an uneasy position by a thug before he hits you? Wish to experience it? Try sitting down briefly with the body and mind still. Try meditating!

That attempt at meditation along the lines of the Gita was a flop of course, followed by all the variations I tried in the next few days. I noticed that every time I sat down to meditate, I was only meditating on my inability to meditate. However, to consider the positive side of it, look at the energy lying latent in that body and mind of mine. Isn't it something to feel happy about?

Meditation is a flight path to God, alright. But my engine seemed to have some problem in its lift-off. *'Didn't the Wright brothers have to experiment for many decades before they came up with a plane that flies?'* I kept asking myself.

'So, our Gita journey ends with Karma Yoga then?' asked my inner voice.

'Yes, it seems so. How am I to write about something of which I have no clue? Maybe meditation is not for a mind as frivolous as mine. Maybe I should try a hand at it a little later in the path, after a few years perhaps?'

ॐ

'Will you give me a piece of that chocolate?' I asked the little girl. The mother had brought her for a consultation to my OP.

'No. It is for me,' so saying, she hid it from me.

The mother, smiling at her daughter, said it was Dr Santosh who had given it to her when they had gone to him for her father's check-up. Her father was suffering from alcoholism-induced liver cirrhosis, and the surgeon had referred him to Sandy to treat the addiction.

'What an irony!' I smiled within.

What she said next gave me a pleasant jolt.

'I said to Doctor Santosh that due to his problem, my husband is unable to go to work and I am finding it financially difficult to send this girl to school. He thought for a brief moment, and said he will sponsor her education from now on.'

'Oh really? That's great!'

Once they left, I started wondering about Sandy. The Santosh I knew seemed to still be part of this new 'Sandy.' When Velu Sir – one of the old teachers from our school – had come to my clinic a few days previously asking for donation for the alumni association, I filled in the dotted lines with, 'Two hundred and fifty rupees only.' While I was doing that, I saw Sandy's donation amount in the previous leaflet, two thousand rupees! Velu Sir had told me how Santosh had given it readily, without a second thought. He too seemed surprised.

'What has happened to this fellow?' I wondered. 'There is no way the stingy present day Sandy with his stinking attitude towards life is doing it all. Maybe he sensed that I have dropped him out of our Barath Sir's last assignment and that kindled a bit of guilt. Perhaps it also triggered the dormant good feelings all of us have in our hearts for Barath Sir.

'But considering all the unscrupulous things he is doing now, has he really so much goodness left in him to be affected by such a meagre thing?'

'Who can say what goes on inside people's minds? Maybe that forgotten inner goodness is looking to sprout out through all the filth on the surface. Maybe there still is a chance for me to assuage the guilt in my heart.'

I saw myself smiling with a sense of relief. The smile soon became a wry grin as the irony of the situation struck me. Having heard something like that, I would have definitely started sharing the Gita again with Sandy. However, now there is no way to do it. I myself have stopped it, after all. Maybe I will share the previous section with him, if he is interested.

I opened the new issue of the quarterly medical journal that lay on my table near the Gita and started browsing through it. My eyes fell on the words of a review article that was in large print, 'Five minutes of meditative silence can do to the ripening of the mind and reduction of stress, what years of an ordinary life can't accomplish.' A US doctor had mentioned this in his study on the effects of stress on physical diseases.

'Now, what was that Krishna? You having some fun flaring up my inner conflict?'

I put it back on the table, letting out a sigh.

The words Barath Sir once told us came to mind, 'Guys, if there is one skill I would like you all to develop, it is that of asking questions. Questions are more important than answers,' he said about his subject. 'Questioning means your mind is still open and that you are willing to learn. Questions help you grow.'

As I have experienced often, his every advice can be applied to real life too.

So I decided not to close myself just because I couldn't find the answer.

It was then that I thought I could ask Muthu. After all, if it is true that the Gita is just the wisdom inside us expressed in a book form, then the meditation mentioned in the Gita must be an unwitting part of his life, just like the other things in the philosophy are. I decided to find out if that was so.

The function celebrating the expansion of Saradha's hospital was attended by almost everyone in her village, Sandy and I noticed. The people of the village appeared happier than Saro. A well-equipped twelve-bedded hospital was being opened in a place that lacked even basic medical facilities a few years ago. And it was meant exclusively for them.

Pasumaikudi taluk had many smaller villages under it, and a few of them had medical clinics already with in-patient facilities. However, Saro's was the only hospital that had decent enough medical facilities to handle even difficult emergencies. It was love and responsibility that was driving her work. Hence, when others were hesitant, she didn't bother about financial feasibility when buying the 300 ma X-ray machine or ventilator for such a setup. I hoped that those other doctors would buy it in the near future, seeing the response Saro got.

Saradha was standing in a purple churidar with rather garish embroidery work. A fancy beaded necklace demanded further attention. Sandy was staring wide-eyed at her and was intently following all the praise she was receiving from the village people.

'Dei, look at that. Is that our Miss World?' he asked. That was the nickname few of our naughty batchmates had for her.

'Hold your tongue! See what she has achieved in a village, single-handedly.'

'Whoa!'

We met Saro's father at the function. He seemed to be proud of all the love and accolades being showered on his daughter.

'It is fantastic work that Saradha is doing here, Uncle,' Sandy said with real astonishment in his voice.

Her father smiled back in pride.

'Where is Aunty?' I asked.

'There,' her father pointed, 'sitting on the verandah with a big, broad smile.' Many people were standing around her too.

As it seemed difficult to even get near Saradha, we presented the stethoscope we had brought, to him.

'Thank you. You didn't bring your wives?' he asked.

'Wives? We are unmarried, Uncle.'

'Oh?'

When he received the gift, beneath all the smile and pride, I somehow felt he was a bit disturbed on the inside. Recollecting my mom's pestering, I assumed he had the same concerns about his daughter.

ଛ

The function was over by morning. As I had planned previously, I drove my bike to Alangadu, Muthu's grove. I had decided on visiting it even as Saradha had told me about it a month ago.

'Maaps, where are you going? Our city is in the other direction,' said Sandy.

'Sandy, if you can keep mum for an hour, I shall take you to a hotel for lunch. I assure you, the food there would be the most delicious you have ever tasted!'

'Oof! Thanks, maaps. Hope at least that is the saving grace of the day. By the way, did you see our Miss World blush while receiving all the accolades? She looked scary!'

'Psycho! Don't mock too much. You will end up with a wife who looks scary!'

'You mean Saro? As my wife? Man, what a terrifying thought! I'll kill myself if that happens. Hmm, I hardly spoke ten words with that girl in the entire UG period, and today you made me spend five-hundred rupees for that stethoscope. Okay. I am shutting up. Stop glaring . . . the rear view mirror might crack.' He laughed at his own joke.

Even if a sprout of goodness occasionally thrusts its head out from within him, Sandy seems to have acquired a vile outer shell that is not going to allow for its easy growth, I felt.

We parked the bike outside the grove near its large wrought iron gate. A bare-chested old man with a large white moustache and plenty of chest hair, was sitting outside reading a newspaper. He enquired about our antecedents before letting us in. He was Esakki, the caretaker of the grove. He requested us not to smoke or litter inside, as it would affect the trees and shrubs. There was warmth in the way he said that. From his words we could also sense that the grove and the temple meant a lot to the people of the village.

That old man also shared an additional bit of information about the temple. A great Siddha was buried in the place. Over his grave, a small temple with a Sivalinga had stood for centuries, and the Muthumaari temple was a recent construction.

We stepped in and strolled on the narrow, rutted footpath that ran through the grove. It felt nice and soothing, but somehow it didn't seem as special to me as I had expected it to. Maybe I had expected too much based on what Saradha told.

However, as the path took a right angled turn into the thick of the grove, I immediately realised I had stumbled upon something special. The place had the perfect sublimity of an early, pollution-free morning, except that it wasn't morning, but mid-afternoon. We could see the Devi temple on the far side of a small rise at the middle of the grove. Esakki had already told us that the temple would not be open at the time. So we were roaming around in the grove.

I was quite amazed to come across such a place just half an hour from Tuticorin, a city known for its searing heat. The trees there seemed many decades old. Sunlight was coming in only sparingly through the closely set, intermingling branches. The place was shady and pleasantly cool even at that time of the day.

'Dei, you keep walking,' said Sandy, 'I will stay here and have a smoke. No snakes or anything will be around, right?' He sat under a neem tree and took out his lighter as I gave him a disgusted look.

I walked away from him. The sun was spreading its dappled light over the shining bushes. A variety of birds were chirping in the trees. A few goats were bleating nearby. It was a reasonably small place – not covering more than an acre. But it felt other-worldly to me.

I closed my eyes and sat under one of the banyan trees.

ॐ

'Dei, how long have I been searching for you? Look at the time. It is already thirty minutes since we came to this jungle. Some thief might come here, seeing us both alone. Get up.'

'Thirty minutes have passed?'

It was half past two when we entered Muthu's hotel. The afternoon crowd had started thinning out. Muthu had started kneading the dough for the evening. He was sporting his usual look. He greeted me with a coy, reserved smile and a slight nod, and continued with his work. Walking past him, I went and sat on one of the wooden stools.

'Didn't you come for the hospital function, Muthu? I didn't see you there.'

'Mother and I went and returned quite early, Sir. Got work here, you see,' he replied.

As Sandy and I were having our lunch, I kept looking at the graceful way in which Muthu was kneading dough. There was a fluidity, a calm flowing quality to his action.

'Is this parotta boy going to show me the way out of the nagging block I am facing?' I wondered as I ate. Not just about meditation, I had planned to ask him quite a few questions. What I had been doing all these months was trying to 'understand' the age-old Vedanta philosophy. However, here was a simple boy who, without any acquaintance with all that, was living that philosophy perfectly.

I wondered if he would be able to answer my questions. In fact, a part of me was skeptical still, and scoffing at the prospect, *'He is a simple guy practising what feels right to him. And it coincides with the Gita's philosophy, alright. Does that mean he would have answers to all your teeming questions? Come to your senses, dude.'*

However, that day as I interacted with him, I realised I had stumbled upon someone special, someone who had gone even beyond the need for such daily meditation and was living in a very high state of being.

'Ooh! As you said amazing boss the food is.' Sandy had finished his lunch much earlier than me.

He went to wash his hands in the cement sink kept outside. Standing near the front door, he gestured to say that he would be back in few minutes. Two youngsters who had parked their bikes outside, walked in crossing Sandy. They looked like college students. They approached Muthu and asked him something.

I heard muffled voices. Muthu seemed to be making a stern refusal. The two seemed annoyed by that and even Muthu looked angry, for a change.

They argued with him for some time and then left looking furious, I noticed from a distance. Taking a deep breath, Muthu sprinkled a few drops of water on the dough and put it down on the table. Then he noticed three people sitting at lunch without curry in their bowls.

'Antony,' he called out angrily, 'I insisted that seven beetroots be used in the curry. Mother used five. Look now, customers are eating without the curry. Go and tell her that the curry is finished.'

Antony nodded obediently and went upstairs.

'Who were those men, Muthu? They seemed a bit angry when they left,' I asked him as he approached me.

'Oh, that? Those two want me to take an order for their college annual day. They asked me to give an overvalued quotation for it. I refused.'

He came and sat before me. I felt a jolt. It was time to start what I came for. I wondered how to begin. I took in the frail bodied boy sitting before me. There was a lightness about him, in his body, his words and in his movements.

He himself steered the conversation in that direction by asking, 'Are you back from Alangadu, Sir?'

'Yes, Muthu. Quite a place it was. Hey, but wait,' it was only then that it struck me, 'how did you know we had been there?'

I was taken aback. There was no way he could have known it. He looked at me with a quiet, child-like smile as I asked that. But somehow it was I who was feeling like a child who had asked him a foolish question.

I started to sense that I was with someone different even before I had started asking him my first question; someone seriously different. A brief moment passed. 'Muthu,' I then started, still a bit off balance, 'If you don't mind, can I ask you something?'

He looked me in the eyes and nodded.

'Saradha told me about the bond you share with that grove.

I have never been to a place as calm and peaceful as that in some time. Quite a place it was.... I would like to know if you still go to those woods every week? Do you still have the same bond with it, as in your childhood?'

I looked at him to see how he took the question. After all, it was a personal question. However, his face bore the same expression as he replied in a soft voice, 'Yes.'

'Why I asked is, you have grown up so much now. Does that childhood bond still exist?' I rephrased the question to incite a detailed reply.

'I do, Sir,' Muthu said softly, as if talking to himself. 'Every Friday whether or not my mother accompanies, I go to the temple, pray for a few minutes, and then go there.'

'Can I ask you something?'

I was a bit reluctant to keep prodding the boy about it. However, I wasn't asking out of mere inquisitiveness, but wonder, so I continued, 'I can see your shrewd business acumen, Muthu. Even the way you have arranged the stools and benches here shows that. How can your mind also entertain such ideas ... a grove, a living presence in it, and all that?'

'How do I answer this, Sir?' he asked with the same calm, childlike smile. A moment later, he added, 'Well, it is the same mind that also feels that.'

'Fair enough,' I laughed. 'Just for argument's sake let me ask you something. Our brains don't agree to things easily. How can you be sure your mind isn't imagining it all?'

'Imagining it all ... ,' he murmured after me, 'What you say is true, Sir. I often feel it is we who are imagining it all.'

I understood the import of those words, only after two months or so when I was reading the later portions of the Gita.

Somehow, I didn't feel like asking him any more questions. I felt like a person who was dissecting a flower to understand it. He had unwittingly clarified for me already the reason behind the block I was experiencing. I just let him talk after that, as I listened, mesmerised.

'After returning from there, I feel my core recharged, Sir. I get into my work with a new enthusiasm. That day alone, I observe the vow of silence for the Mother.'

'The world and my work here in this hotel . . . it gets really strenuous at times. We have to worry for things, we have to shout, we get frustrated . . . I feel like ending all this and returning to Her at times. Then when I think about it, I see the truth. This too is given to me by the Mother, I realise. So as long as I'm here, I will be sincere in doing the work, I promise her.'

'I see.'

The boy seems to be living in such oneness with his Divine Mother, I was intrigued by his need for such a big sacred vermillion band on his forehead, and his striking red dhoti. The boy answered that too as he continued.

'I feel that I'm one with Her even as I do my work here. All this *kumkum*, dhoti etc. are ways to tell myself that that there is an owner in hold of the leash,' he said, smiling.

I was sitting there dumbstruck. Muthu seemed like some Vedic time baktha, out of place in this century. I was feeling so light and blissful sitting near him that I saw why Saradha valued the boy and his company so much.

'Muthu, you are awesome. I have done with my skepticism totally. I see you don't belong here. Or maybe it is you who truly belong. . . . I am into an important assignment in my life Muthu. I wish, someday when I finish what I am into now, I come back to you and spend more time with you. I really feel I should.'

It is totally different to read something in theory and be with someone who is living it.

'All the best for what you are doing, Sir. May Goddess Muthumaari bless your endeavour with success.'

His brother's three-year-old son came running into the room with a wooden stick in his hands as I was about to leave.

'Hey Raju, say *vanakkam* to sir. He is a respected doctor who gives injections to naughty people like you,' Muthu said.

'Respected doctor? I feel like a worm before you dear boy,' I felt like saying to Muthu as I got up.

Sandy and I were riding back from Pasumaikudi along the ploughed paddy fields. The crops were glowing in the light of the setting sun. The gentle evening breeze was consistent. Muthu's grove was on a diversion from the main road; the top of a few trees was visible from the road.

What a beautiful relationship between a young boy and nature! Saradha even said that he reads the *Lalitha Sahasranama* (The Thousand names of the Goddess Lalitha) sitting in the grove.

Seeing the beautiful sunset and the paddy fields that day, I somehow felt that nature has her arms outstretched for every one of us. It is we who don't realise it, and ignore her. As I passed by the grove I felt that it was Mother Nature who would be feeling happier to have one of her children return and live in close connection with her.

But man, how did Muthu manage to tell that I had been to his place? That was breathtaking. Maybe with a well-honed intuitive connection developed by being close with a place for so many years, one can guess that.

'What is the time, boss?' asked Sandy.

'Five.'

Sandy peeped at my watch from behind. 'Dei, isn't that the watch I gave you a long time back? I didn't recognise it before. You are still wearing it? See, the enamel coating on the rim worn out totally!'

'A sign of our eternal friendship, maapi.'

'Ooh, so moving! Tears are jerking out from my eyes!'

'Stupid!'

The brief time I had spent with the boy still lingered in my thoughts. The boy has reached a sublime inner state with the help of a grove! Strange! I had read that the great saints of India had a special affinity for a particular place where they felt their deity's presence. Ramana Maharishi saw his God in the holy hill of Arunachala. Sri Ramakrishna would say that the closer one comes to the river Ganga, the more one experiences a transcendent peace.

Interestingly, the boy uses orthodox rituals and symbols of religion, like the vermillion band, red dhotis and weekly fasting as physical symbols to retain his connection. The boy has created his own fusion between animistic spirituality and orthodox Sakthi worship. After all, Yoga is not a paint-by-numbers path. It is about the living dynamic relationship we share with the Divine. It is a path of the heart. Not some outer prescribed way, but our own personal way of feeling the connection is what paves our path.

'Damn religious, the guy seems to be. That large red band on his forehead, his dress, even the curry he gives in his hotel is of the same colour,' Sandy said, breaking into my thoughts.

'True, quite funny,' I assented, hearing his father's ideals in Sandy's words.

'Hey, keep your eyes on the road and drive, man. What are you day-dreaming about?' asked Sandy as my bike deviated towards a haystack on the side of the road.

'Oops, sorry.'

'By the way, you were lying to me, right?' he asked next.

'What?'

'You are still into preparing Barath Sir's write-up on the Gita, aren't you?'

'Is it? How come you found out?'

'Then what were you talking to that boy for so long?'

I saw a spark of the school-time Santosh, as he asked me that question.

'Sandy, it is true that I have stopped it temporarily. But if I begin it, and I hope to do so shortly, I'll definitely share it with you again.'

'Oh man! They should make you the villain of the next terminator movie. What tenacity! Great maaps, great.'

I didn't respond.

Several agricultural lands on the side of the road had been converted into residential plots. The few paddy fields that remained, appeared golden yellow in the light of the setting sun. The evening breeze was sweeping through the neem trees on either side of the road. In front of us was a white Ambassador that was moving at snail's pace, totally blocking the path. Sandy waited for some time. Then, getting too impatient, he extended his hands sideways beneath my shoulder, and started blaring the bike's horn.

The car immediately went to its left and gave us way. As we overtook it, we saw that the driver was talking on his cellphone with a huge smile on his face, and he was still signalling to us with his hands, as if to say, 'Why bother with the horn so much bro? Want to overtake? Do it.'

'Freaky creature,' snapped Sandy.

'People seem so relaxed in this village, Sandy. And you know something? We keep saying it's all impractical now. But what that parotta boy Muthu is living by, exactly fits in with the Gita's wisdom.'

'His way of life fits in with the Gita?'

'Absolutely.'

'Well, he is in a village, maapi. Ask him to come and live the same amid the ratrace in cities. Let us see,' he said yawning widely.

He seemed to show nice improvement. In the beginning it was, 'One can't live like that at all, in these times.' Now it is just, 'It can't be lived in cities.'

'By the way, I am noticing you yawning like crazy since we started from Pasumaikudi. What happened?' I asked him.

'You ask why? I recall someone saying we will return by noon. Look at the time. I have to go without my two hours afternoon nap now.'

'Two hours? Then when will you sleep at night?'

'Sleep? Maybe around two or three at night. Big issue you know ... Wait, what are you grinning at?' he asked looking at my face in the rear-view mirror.

'Was I?'

'Listen, you big-head, just because you are reading the Gita, don't behave patronisingly as if you have become a Gandhi all of a sudden,' he snapped.

'Oh? I didn't know Gandhiji behaved in a patronising way!'

'Shut up and drive,' his tone got a notch higher.

Well, that is Sandy demonstrating for us the opposite end

of the spectrum. But after I visited Alangadu, met Muthu and got a glimpse of his inner being, I saw clearly for myself the reason I couldn't experience meditation. It was, *I was trying to meditate!* I was putting in too much effort into a process that should have been as natural as breathing.

ଊ

KARMA AND DYAANA

There is a proverb in Tamil which goes, 'The way to milk a wobbling cow is to wobble with it for some time.' The entire practice of Karma Yoga was like that.

> **For the one who wishes to attune to Yoga,**
> **Action is the means. 6.3**

Through Karma Yoga, we went along the ways of our ever-active mind and its pleasure-seeking ways, yet we established a tangible connection with the Divine in our hearts. We connected the mind to a deeper sublime stillness behind it. Once we have done that, why keep 'wobbling with the cow,' forever? Can't we nourish this stillness in us through just *'being still'*? That is what the Gita tells us next in the same verse.

> **For the person who has attuned to Yoga,**
> **Quiescence is the means. 6.3**

The path of quiescence is the royal path towards God-realisation we become qualified to take next.

Dyaana can of course be practised from the start too, simultaneously aligning our outer being to Karma Yoga. The Gita mentions that too in a later chapter. However, for an active man of the world following the path of the Gita, Karma Yoga smoothly transforms itself into Dyaana Yoga, like an aircraft taking off having reached its threshold velocity on ground. Our being would start seeking that silent communion with the Divine.

When do we know we have attuned to Yoga and have qualified for Dyaana Yoga?

> **When a man is not attached to sense objects or to actions,**
> **And when he has renounced selfish motives,**
> **Then he is said to have attuned to Yoga. 6.4**

That is the test. The essence of that verse is: *there is an unshakeable detached stillness in him*. He, of course, doesn't mind enjoying the sensual pleasures of the world, and of course follows his heart and acts in the world – but he is not attached to those sense objects or actions, and his actions are not guided by his personal selfish motives. That is when one has qualified for Dyaana. With that knowledge as the base, let us get into . . .

THE WAY TO PRACTISE

I reread the Gita's key verse on meditation. It took on an entirely different meaning now.

> **Let the Yogi remain in solitude**
> **and try constantly to keep the mind steady**
> **With the mind and body controlled,**
> **and free from expectations and ideas of possession. 6.10**

Meditation retreats and classes conducted in exotic locations abound in our times. Technological breakthroughs are entering the spiritual market too; there are auditory beat meditations that promise us that we can 'meditate at the touch of a button.'

And a lot of people, having not done the outer work of purification the Gita calls for first, try to force themselves into Dyaana through those. The achievement-obsessed approach of popular culture seems to be thrusting its head into every arena!

We may indeed manage to experience a relative sense of peace through it all. But return to normal life, and the turmoil in the mind resurges. This is because our outer active being isn't yet attuned to Yoga. When the mind is not yet set to work by its natural mechanism, the noises coming from our mind-vehicle would keep demanding the oil of our attention. However, when it is functioning smoothly as it is supposed to then it becomes that much easier to transcend it.

A forced restraining of the mind, through an old technique or new technology, will only make the sense-enslaved mind wait for the next opportunity to bounce back with full force and knock us down. A peace that is found through some outside means cannot last long. But when we live our life in the way it is meant to be lived – as Karma Yoga – we naturally experience this quietude within; and we would qualify to go deeper into this quietude effortlessly through Dyaana Yoga.

That is what the above verse says. It doesn't say 'let the man trying to gain a stillness sit in solitude.' No! It says 'Let the *Yogi* sit.'

Secondly, it says, 'let him be free from expectations.' 'So long as there is desire or want,' says Swami Vivekananda, 'it is a sure sign that there is imperfection. A perfect, free being cannot have any desire.'[1] 'Salvation never will come through hope of reward,' he adds.[2]

So then, we don't sit in the hope of trying to achieve something. If we do, we only allow the desire-mind to sneak into our spiritual practice as well. 'You can't polish a buffalo and make it a cow,' goes a Buddhist saying. As yogis, we just sit keeping the mind steady, relishing the stillness, the connection with the Divine we've gained. That is the essence of meditation.

Meditation isn't a, 'do-this-achieve-that' thing. It is not even about *doing* in its truest sense. Meditation is based on the principle of letting go. It is a pretty new idea for a mind untrained in it. C S Lewis said, 'Many things, such as loving, going to sleep, or behaving unaffectedly are done worst when we try hardest to do them.' That is true of meditation too.

Meditation is about 'being'. Being what? Nothing. Just 'being.' That may sound baffling to our minds so used to 'thinking and doing' things, always. But the dynamics and significance of a genuine meditative practice can be understood only when we have, through Karma Yoga, purified a bit, the grosser tendencies accumulated inside us. We would gradually feel a lightness, a stillness growing in us. Then there comes a threshold stage where we naturally feel like nourishing this connection and stillness in us by just *being still.*

In the Gita's path, meditation happens! As we get up in the morning, we feel like remaining still and relishing this connection before we get busy with our daily activities. It is like getting our foundation right and strong for the day. Just like recharging our electronic stuff we recharge ourselves with the peace of our True Self. Without that we look to derive our charge from the world; from our goals, achievements, our relationships, and so on. All those are temporary highs. With meditation, we derive it from within, from, you guessed right, *the Divine.*

Meditation is about rooting ourselves in a solid ground of stillness within. We get rooted deeper and deeper in it, with each day. It is not reaching some culmination point in consciousness in a distant future. It's about getting our base right before beginning the day's work.*

---

*The focus in our meditative practice should only be on this. But we do grow in this stillness too as we meditate regularly — coming up shortly.

The meditative path is not a horizontal one, but a vertical – *and inward* – one.

As we meditate regularly, this inner atmosphere of stillness will become a background to all our work. It will become our truest companion even as we live life as our limited selves; a companion who is calm, constant, and understanding. Often during the day we would feel like meditating. Before going to bed, like removing our day dress, we would feel like gently doing away with all external load accumulated in the mind during the day and lie down relishing that stillness we feel within, again.

Through Karma Yoga, we turned all our actions – our thinking, emoting and doing – Godward. Here, we turn our *silence* Godward; and that is the highest way to commune with the Divine. It is hence Dyaana Yoga is also termed *Raja Yoga*.

> **When the five senses cease,**
> **and are at rest along with the mind,**
> **When thought ceases from its workings,**
> That is the highest state, say thinkers.
> Katha Upanishad 3.3.10

All that is about the essence of meditation. How exactly does it get translated into daily life?

Sri Ramakrishna gives us a striking example to explain a meditative practice, 'Dyaana is catching hold of the fish, then allowing the bait to be swallowed by the fish.'[3] That is the guiding principle behind a meditative practice, *giving our little self to be consumed by the Divine one!*

༺༻

PREPARING THE BAIT

Proper meditation begins right when we wake up in the morning and sit up on our bed. That is the time to establish the connection in our heart. We can do it in a way that suits us. For me a morning prayer does it.

It could be a silent prayer without words, as you wake up. What is important is not saying or doing certain things cursorily, but feeling the connection in our heart and getting the mind into a humble and reverential mode before its inner arrogance and all-knowingness raises its head. Establishing this connection as soon as we wake up is crucial because that is the moment the mind puppy has opened its eyes from a long rest. So one finds it easy to catch hold of it and tie a leash around its neck.

This is the warm-up. Then we need to do our morning chores without engaging in or thinking of anything gross or materialistic. If we do so we will lose the connection, that nice feeling, in our heart. Next comes the part of...

INVITING IN THE BIG FISH

Next we go and sit relishing that stillness and connection. We meditate!

> **The Yogi should sit intent on me**
> **Having me alone as the supreme goal. 6.14**

We should be careful not to allow the mind to get engrossed in worldly affairs before we have established our foundation right and strong for the day. The practice can begin with a ritual that is personally meaningful for you, like lighting a candle, reading and contemplating on a few lines from a holy book, lighting an incense stick and so on. It helps in attuning our mind.

As we sit with this stillness and connection, we really sit catching hold of our end of the divine thread. We sit 'intent on God,' in the Gita's terms. The sublime peace we experience when we meditate has to be experienced to be believed. As the stillness grows in our heart during meditation, we can sense our body expressing that stillness naturally; it gets straighter without any slouching, and gets more and more relaxed. We can sense our breathing getting deep and smooth, sometimes even stopping temporarily!

Next you will see that when there is this tangible stillness established inside, there is no need to control the mind. Holding on to this inner connection, you see the mind's ramblings almost like the ocean sees its waves. When you are in this stillness, you become too big for the mind. 'You say that the mind is like a cork and does not sink. What does it matter if the mind is active? It is so only on the substratum of the Self. Hold on to the Self even during mental activities,' advises Sri Ramana Maharishi.[4]

The mind will always keep wandering – barking of neighbourhood dogs, the tours we went on long back with friends and family, the steamy sex scenes, the sizzling hot heroes and heroines, so on and so forth. But our attention is not on it. We are rooted in the stillness within and don't mind the mind. *'You want to ramble around? Do it,'* we say. To use Swami Vivekananda's words, 'Let the monkey jump as much as he can;

you simply wait and watch.'[5] That is the right way to tackle the mind; just don't mind it!

There is a story in the Bhagavatha about a housemaid who prepared food for a Rishi sitting outside her house. She saw her bangles clanging noisily as she was grinding the wheat flour. Realising that it might disturb the Rishi, she removed all but one. When she served food the Rishi asked her why she left that one bangle. She replied, 'Guruji, what noise can a single bangle make?'

The Rishi named Dattatreya thanked her for giving him a wonderful insight and saw *her* as his Guru, says the Bhagavatha.

The insight he gained was this: when we don't react to our mind's constant prattle, then like the single bangle, how can the mind produce any noise?

Meditation is not about making the mind thought-free. It is the mind's job after all, to generate thoughts. It is about becoming larger than the mind is, so as not to be bothered by it. So far, we were identifying with the clouds called thoughts. In meditation, we become the sky.

Alright, once the body, breath and mind are all brought under this stillness, what do we do next?

When the mind is still, no further 'doing' is necessary. When we can just sit in this stillness, this connection we feel within 'without expectations and ideas of possession' without wishing to achieve anything great, and content in that alone, that is enough. It is the peace of God we are experiencing.

> **Thus by always keeping the mind fixed on the Self,**
> **The Yogi whose mind is subdued**
> **Attains the everlasting peace abiding in me. 6.15**

ॐ

'Practise meditation with a serene, fearless mind' (6.14) says the Gita. When we sit holding that connection alone in our heart, there comes a stage in meditation where the 'me' and 'you' ceases to exist and only the Divine reality in us shines through.

> **As fire destitute of fuel becomes extinct in its own source,**
> **So does thought, by loss of activeness,**
> **become extinct in its own source.**
> Maitri Upanishad 3.34

This is the stage of Samadhi. This loss of the sense of our self, albeit temporary, may be a bit disconcerting. The process is like suicide in a way. Hence does the Gita mention that a Dyaana Yogi needs to be fearless.

Children are afraid of the dark. Paradoxically, we are afraid of the light in us. It is because before the divine light all our cherished beliefs, preferences, likes and dislikes vanish; and we are afraid we would be nothing.

However, getting outside the little entity we have identified ourselves with, is not something to be feared. It is the experience of freedom. That is what meditation is all about. It is not about *'you'* reaching God-consciousness through doing something. *It is about getting yourself out of the way!* You surrender to the stillness, you catch hold of the Divine and let that take over and do its work on the 'you.' It is about the fish swallowing the angler along with the bait.

> 'O Arunachala! I approached you for food.
> But you made me your food and gave me great peace.'
> Ramana Maharishi (Akshara mana malai, Verse 28)

◯ॐ

HOW LONG?

How often and how long should one meditate? Well, to put it simply, as often as we feel like and as long as we feel like.

Swami Adiswarananda, a monk of the Ramakrishna order, in his book *The Four Yogas*, gives some guidance regarding the duration of meditation. 'Focusing the mind on the same object for twelve seconds achieves one unit of concentration,' he says. What Swamiji means by 'focus' is really the total silencing of the mind and sitting with our awareness totally on the object of meditation – be it an external God or the inner connection we feel in our hearts. He then proceeds to say, 'Twelve such units of concentration make one unit of meditation; twelve such successive units of meditation make one unit of Samadhi.'[6]

That comes to around half an hour. If we are able to practice it twice daily, we would be laying our foundation pretty strong for an exalted way of living. We would be doing some serious good to ourselves.

We saw how to commence and carry out meditation. To practise such constant abidance in meditative state, it is important to know how we should *conclude* our meditative session too.

ENDING THE SESSION

When coming out of meditative practice, learn to remain rooted in this foundation of stillness you establish within. And as far as possible, learn to perform your daily actions without losing it. Learn to process the things you come across from the stillness you feel within, and not with the ego-mind. If lost, take a break and re-establish it again.

When you thwart all its efforts and find a way to meditate, the next card it plays to gain its authority is, *How nice, how peaceful this meditation feels*!

If you allow that thought process to take hold, the entire meditation session becomes an ego trip and a temporary feel-good trance – with you back in your ego prison. To have experienced such a freedom and again getting trapped inside the mind is, well, claustrophobic.

Put the mind in its place. There should be no, 'I meditated, I felt nice,' thoughts or feelings in us. Our only focus should be meditation! Dyaana is our essential nature. And the 'I,' the ego is ephemeral.

Secondly, talking about our practice too isn't beneficial for us. The connection we feel within in mediation is 'as delicate as spun glass' say spiritual masters. There is no better way to wreck it than speaking about it with people.

> **One should be vigilant (having acquired it).**
> **For Yoga is acquired and lost.**
> Katha Upanishad 3.3.11

Let that stillness alone be inside.*

---

*Relishing the inner connection, the way we saw till now, is the way to meditate that suits a pragmatic mind. Gita puts the essence of meditation this way: 'Sitting and concentrating the mind on a single object, controlling the thoughts and the activities of the senses, let the Yogi practise meditation for self-purification.' (6.12) That 'single object' can be anything that makes us feel connected to God: a sacred sound, an external form of God, religious symbols and so on. Even heartfelt prayers and pujas are a kind of meditation. A puja gives an external 'hold' for our body and mind by giving it something to do. It is a methodical way to turn all the energies of the body and the mind inward. One can adopt any method that helps one feel connected with the Divine.

Apart from this, Yogic science gives us advices on the right posture, right way of breathing, right time and right place for meditation, which interested people can approach appropriate books or teachers to find out about. However, all those – posture, time, place, breathing – are only useful aids to meditating. None of these are absolutely essential for meditation practice. It all comes down to this: you holding on to the earnestness in your heart and doing what feels right for you. Doing it in a sitting posture in a quiet place during early morning is the starting point. But it can be done anywhere, in any posture, at any time. Any boring waiting period can be turned into a time for meditation – waiting in your cabin for the arrival of your boss, standing at the bus stop, sitting in the doctor's waiting room (or sitting as the doctor and waiting for patients like someone is doing right now and so on). As the Sufi poet Hafiz put it, 'Just sit there right now. Don't do a thing. Just rest. For your separation from God is the hardest work in the world.'

ॐ

That, then, is the fourth principle Gita shares with us: Meditate regularly. The entire Yogic path we saw until now can be summarised thus: Follow your Swabhava and do your Dharma for the Divine. Once you thus attune to Yoga, practise silent communion with the Divine in your heart. Or to borrow the pithy words of Swami Sivananda, *'Serve. Love. Purify. Meditate. Realise.'*

Just one more thing we have left to cover in the practical side of the Gita's Yoga – Moderation and self-control in sensual enjoyments.

THE GOLDEN MIDDLE

'There are two paths in the world: the path of Viagra, and the path of Vairagya,' Swami Satyananda quips. As we walk the Yogic path, there is one precaution to not lose our inner connection that we grow in: *practice of moderation towards the sensual pleasures of the world*. For our barrel to be filled by the rain, its leaks have to be fixed first.

Toddlers do not know when walking down the street about the risk of accidents. The senses too do not know when they drag away man's discrimination, the dangers of getting into the clutches of the world. The senses aren't just toddlers in the case of man, but *wild horses* as described in the Katha Upanishad. Trying to control one such horse is tiring enough. Imagine a chariot pulled by five such wild horses: our five sensual organs.

> The restless senses forcibly carry away the mind of
> even a wise person striving for perfection, O Arjuna. 2.60

Keep the horses under your control is the Gita's message. What does 'control' mean, by the way? Gita doesn't call for forced repression.

> He who, restraining the organs of actions,
> Sits mulling over in his mind the sense objects,
> He, of deluded understanding, is a hypocrite. 3.6

Take sex, for example. People often think that being spiritual or religious equates with total abstinence from it. However, in temples like Khajuraho, we come across striking erotic sculptures in the outer edifices, which jolt people holding such ideas. It stands evidence to the fact that Hindu philosophy doesn't see sex as obscene or something to be guilty about. It sees sex too with an aesthetic eye and as an inevitable part of life. In fact, the philosophy of sexual frankness without guilt is a gift of Indian spirituality to the world. If love can commune at the emotional level, it can also commune at the body level. What can be wrong with that? However, it is only a part of life. The same applies to all the sensual pleasures. If our mind stays stuck there, then we remain stuck at the fringes of life without reaching its essential divine centre.

'Forced, feigned repression is hypocrisy,' Gita said. We come across many young spiritual masters – sometimes the old too – in various religions who get caught in various scandals; ones who, to borrow the quirky words of a comedian, need a board hanging around their necks, 'Approach with caution, Unenlightened!' And this is the mistake that they make.

Real renunciation of the sensual pleasures of the world should happen naturally like a ripe fruit falling off a tree. All we need is to keep strengthening our connection. Repression would never help. (Try not to think of a white elephant for the next two minutes.) The path of Yoga doesn't prescribe forced suppression; **just a progressive self-control**. The method the Gita puts forward to achieve it is moderation in sensual enjoyments. That is the fifth principle it shares with us.

> He who in moderation eats, and in moderation rests
> And who in moderation exerts himself in works
> Will achieve Yoga that destroys all his pains. 6.17

An interesting statement, 'Be moderate even in exertion during your actions!' Even the actions done in the spirit of Karma Yoga should be with moderation, says the Gita. Over enthusiasm, excitement and overindulgence can happen not only with the sensual enjoyments but with our Yogic actions too. Our naughty mind will do anything to regain its control. 'Let your Yoga be a natural and strain-free path,' the Gita insists.

Even as we keep walking the Yogic path and practise moderation,

There may be a taste (rasa) still for the sensual objects,
But as one keeps experiencing the Self,
That taste too leaves him. 2.59

'Who would like to take water sweetened with molasses, after having tasted water sweetened with sugar-candy?' asks Sri Ramakrishna.[7]

ଓଃ

Sandy, after having finished reading the write-up, kept looking at me for some time with raised eyebrows. 'Dei, I remember our Big B giving us just some ten verses or so to prepare in the Gita. And you got on with the entire book. But now, what is this? The way you are discussing about temples, the various practices of religion. . . . Your enthusiasm about this stuff seems to be touching on some kind of mania, maapi.'

'Well . . .'

'Ah, please don't kill me with that, "If it is worth doing well" thing.'

He was chewing betel along with smoking his usual cigarette sitting in his clinic after the morning OP time.

'Well, a discussion on the Gita can't be complete without a brief look into the various aspects of Hinduism, the religion that is itself built around the Gita's philosophy.'

'Ooh?' he continued with his chewing and puffing.

'What was that last thing you said in your write-up? Moderation! Well, that one thing is enough to prove that no one follows the Gita in our country. If they had, and had restrained themselves, then we wouldn't have made a world record in population. Ha . . . Ha!' he guffawed with a conceited air. 'By the way Venkiananda, all that is to say you have really started living by the Gita, huh?'

'Well, I am trying. It doesn't demand anything farfetched. So what is the harm?'

'And you have started meditating daily too?'

'Yes,' I nodded.

He looked curiously at me. 'How's your meditation session going, by the way? How long do you sit for it? Have you started experiencing that "Samadhi" thing?'

'I don't worry about the time. I sit as long as I feel like sitting. Sometimes it is ten minutes; sometimes it crosses half an hour. Samadhi... well, I don't know. A mind like mine needs some more time to experience it, I suppose. I try not to bother too much about such things.'

He kept looking at me curiously as I was speaking. 'Boss, I really still can't imagine you like this, becoming a "spiritual man" all of a sudden, practising yoga, meditation, all that stuff. Pretty funny when one thinks about it. Ha ha . . .' he again burst into laughter.

I didn't feel like retorting to Sandy's taunts. The guilt that used to overwhelm me when I would look at him, the strong drive I had to bring him to his old ways through sharing the wisdom, they all had somehow faded as I progressed with the Gita. And there was no disgust in me either, as I looked at him. I saw that I was calmly beginning to accept him and his present ways. In my mind I found myself saying, *'If this is how you prefer to be, dear Sandy, who am I to interfere? I only wish that you someday realise the value of this precious wisdom that has come into our lives through our teacher.'*

ॐ

THE SPIRITUAL LIFE

The Gita acknowledges this pitiable predicament we see many people in.

> Scarcely one out of thousand among men
> Strives for the perfection of Self-realisation. 7.3

Pretty sad state of affairs! It is because most see spirituality as a cut-off-from-reality path which doesn't sync with the pressures and demands of modern life.

However, I realised it is not so, even as I started reading the Gita; even as I got the taste of the first few principles of the book with their intense practical bent.

Wouldn't we love to live our days rooted securely in life's sacred depths instead of continually anaesthetising our pain and weariness with ephemeral pleasures? Wouldn't we love to take part in this adventure with wisdom and composure, rather than being rudderless boats in a turbulent sea? And wouldn't we, at the dusk of our days, love to return home gracefully and with serenity, rather than with fatigue and confusion? That is what 'spiritual path' is all about. That is the gift the Gita holds for us.

A spiritual life is not about subscribing to a particular system, scripture, or even a God as many people would have us believe. It is about waking up to the spirit behind ordinary life and living centred on it. It is about realising the constant spiritual essence behind the changing phenomenal world.

> **When man rolls up space as if it were a piece of hide,**
> **Then there would be an end to his sorrow**
> **without realising the luminous Divine within.**
> Svetasvatara Upanishad 6.20

– a Rishi of yore comments wryly on our condition. Spirituality is not meant for a select few who are 'spiritual seekers' and saints, any more than rice is meant only for the peasants who cultivate it. Spirit is what we are ultimately. Matter is just an evanescent cover over it. Asking 'Why should I take the spiritual path?' is no different from a bird asking 'Why should I learn to fly?' The spiritual is our home. In it lies our true roots. It is the very foundation of life.

> **Life is an Eternal Ashvattha tree,**
> **Having its origin above and its branches below. 15.1**

ॐ

THE YOGIC PATH

To continue with our discussion, we start walking the path of Yoga. We do our actions as Karma Yoga and we meditate regularly too. We grow in oneness with our spiritual self, using our activity and our silence. What happens with us as we progress along? Let us get into that next.

In the path of Yoga, it is not just the destination that is beautiful; the path is strewn with beautiful flowers as well.

Yoga makes our actions skilful and beautiful, for we act not from the outer half-baked motivations. Our actions arise from a deep inner stillness within us. Its beauty and depth reflects in what we do.

'The power of meditation gets us everything. If you want to get power over nature, you can have it through meditation. It is through the power of meditation all scientific facts are discovered today,' tells Swami Vivekananda.[8] The great scientific discoveries, technological innovations, the exceptional works of art, the musical melodies which enthral us, words of people which inspire us deeply, all have come from that deeper plane within man. The Gita shows us the way, to live centred in that plane always.

The health benefits of Yoga on our body and mind are well-known now. Studies have proven that Yoga and meditation lead to considerable changes in metabolism, heart rate, respiration and blood pressure. There are other health benefits as well.

The precursors of perfection in yoga, they say,
are lightness and healthiness of the body, clear complexion,
pleasantness of voice, sweet odour and slight excretions.
Svetaswatara Upanishad II. 13

Swami Vivekananda says when explaining the effects of yoga and pranayama on us, '(It leads to) a change of expression of one's face; harsh lines disappear; with calm thought, calmness comes over the face. Next comes beautiful voice. I never saw a Yogi with a croaking voice. These signs come after a few months' practice.'[9] On the contrary, as much as we live caught up in the ego, our face and body become more and more tight and anxious.

Scientific research says that with eight weeks of meditation, the parts of the brain that help to form positive emotions become increasingly active. The dreary left-brain domination is balanced by the intuition, and creativity of the right brain.

Further, meditation opens the door to the subconscious. It gives us the inner space and composure to see things neutrally. We see the lies we are telling ourselves; we become able to deal with our inner conflicts neutrally, without being hijacked by them. The character-defects we struggle with are surpassed easily, even to our surprise. We become the masters, and not servants, of our inner forces!

The Gita elsewhere tells us,

> **In this blessed path,**
> **The intellect is determinate and concentrated,**
> **Whereas the intellect of the irresolute**
> **is scattered in many directions,**
> **And is endlessly diverse. 2.41**

A yogi's inner being and his life are divinely integrated. All of a yogi's priorities are subordinated to a single goal. One's personal and professional lives align themselves without any confusion, around a spiritual core. The name the Gita gives to such an intellect is *Vyavasayatmika buddhi*. It is a determinate and one-pointed intellect.

> **Such determined intellect is not formed in the minds**
> **Carried away (by seeking other gains). 2.44**

When our mind is pure with its energies integrated in such a way, we gain what is called *sankalpa sakthi*, thought power. Our thoughts and words become powerful and determined. When you think of something, when you say a word, there is great life force behind it that it realises easily. It is for this reason getting blessings from such elders is valued greatly in our country.

Swami Vivekananda conveyed the same idea through these startling words, 'The highest men are calm, silent, and unknown. They are the men who really know the power of thought; they are sure that, even if they go into a cave and close the door and simply think five true thoughts and then pass away, these five thoughts of theirs will live through eternity. . . . They will enter deep into human hearts and brains and raise up men and women who will give them practical expression in the workings of human life.'[10]

In the Yajna way of life we saw before, 'This will give you all you desire' said Gita. For people who live their life in yoga with the Divine, our Big Boss gives a different assurance.

> **For those ever in Yoga, I take care of their Yogakshema. 9.22**

This means that the Divine takes care of all our concerns here. What a great promise that is! We come across a similar assurance from God in the Quran* and the Bible** too.

Thus, considering all those benefits, yoga does seem a rewarding path to take. However, the most important changes of the yogic path are not the above, but what follows.

> **When the mind is absolutely subjugated**
> **And is calmly established in the Self,**
> **Rid of all cravings and attachment,**
> **One is said to be integrated in Yoga. 6.18**

The yogi lives in the freedom of the soul even as he persistently keeps acting on the outside. An imperturbable stillness becomes his nature. He becomes a happy puppet in the hands of the Divine. Sri Ramana explains it this way, 'You realise that you are moved by the deeper Real Self within and are unaffected by what you do or say or think. You have no worries, anxieties or cares, for you realise... that everything is being done by something with which you are in conscious union.'[11]

> **Such a Yogi's mind is like an unflickering flame**
> **Placed in a windless spot. 6.19**

The consciousness, the whole internal mechanism of such a Yogi is one step beyond the world; in a space above all the 'winds of the world' that keep blowing in the mind.

If we look at the very image of the Gita-upadesa, it conveys exactly the same idea. In Swami Vivekananda's words, 'This is the central idea of the Gita, to be calm and steadfast in all circumstances, with one's body, mind, and soul centred at His hallowed feet!'[12] It was to exemplify this that the Gita was set at the beginning of a great battle.

> **When the Yogi comes to know**
> **the immeasurable bliss beyond the senses**
> **He becomes steadfast in it and doesn't move away,**

---

*'Allah may reward them according to the best of their deeds, and add even more for them out of His Grace: for Allah doth provide for those whom He will, without measure.' (Ch. 24)

**'Indeed your heavenly Father knows that you need all these things. But strive first for the kingdom of God and his righteousness, and all these things will be given to you as well' (Matthew 6.32–33). 'The kingdom of God is within you,' the Bible adds elsewhere.

> That state once found he considers it a great treasure
> And considers nothing else a greater achievement in life.
>
> He is not overpowered even by the mightiest grief,
> Such a severance from all pains (of the world) is Yoga.
> May you practise that Yoga slowly and resolutely. 6.21–23

That is what the yogic path is all about, really. A yogi increasingly gets rooted in his True Divine Self. The light of the True Self begins to glimmer through, with one's mind and the whole external mechanism losing their dominance. They become a bright, transparent window of the True Self. The more we meditate, the more the mind becomes nothing.

For such a person, Dyaana becomes a way of living; not something he does for a fixed time in the day. 'When Dyaana is well-established it cannot be given up. It will go on automatically even when you are engaged in work, play or enjoyment. It will persist in sleep too. Dyaana must become so deep-rooted that it will be natural to one,' says Sri Ramana.[13]

'All life is Yoga,' in Sri Aurobindo's pithy words. Just like breathing is for the outer body, living in Yoga is for our inner being.

> Earth meditates, as it were. Heaven meditates, as it were.
> The mountains meditate, as it were.
> The Gods meditate, as it were.
> He who, among men, attains greatness here on earth
> Obtains it too through the power of meditation.
> While small people are quarrelsome and slandering,
> Great men are those
> who have obtained a share of meditation.
> Chandogya Upanishad 7.6

What happens to the mind in such a 'meditative living'? The mind, of course has its role. Meditative living doesn't mean 'despise the mind.' That is not the point. After all, feelings without thoughts are raw, like a block of gold. It is the mind with its imagination and intelligence that processes it and gives it a beautiful shape; and it is the body that executes it. We would respect them. However, we would give the mind and body their rightful place and not more. They are just instruments for the Self.

If desire-centred successful living is pleasure, if a sattwic life of yajna is joy, living in yoga with the Divine is *absolute bliss*.

I was sitting in Sandy's OP and looking through the window at the night traffic. These days when I hang out with him at the beach, hotels, or even when I go to his clinic to have a chat with him, I have begun to feel that something is going wrong with him. Spending time with him started feeling like being caught up in a dark, seedy place.

'By the way, you heard the news about the clash between our PP and KL scans?' he asked.

'No, what happened?'

'Don't you know? That's the latest buzz in the medicine-circle right now. Okay, the story goes like this, PP referred a patient with gastric pain to KL scans for an MRI. The radiologist there went through the scan and informed the patient that his condition was nothing serious. That made PP furious, when he heard it. He called up the centre and had a big, nasty fight with the radiologist.'

'Why? What is wrong with that?'

'Well, maybe he had given a big build-up to the patient regarding his disease and was planning to conduct some major procedure on the hapless fellow. After the incident, what he had been doing till now through KL scans came to light. He usually calls the centre it seems, and says, "I am sending a patient now, he is quite important to me. Please do an MRI at a price of eight thousand." And then he tells the patient, "Don't worry. I have asked them to subsidise the price for you. Usually they charge ten thousand for it."'

'What is the big deal in that?'

'You are asking me that? They hardly charge five thousand bucks for MRI in our town, don't you know? The phone call virtually means, 'Collect and keep the extra few thousands for me.''

'Ha ha! The news has spread around the media circles too. However, the guy's practice won't be affected much. He has strong community backing in our town, you see. Lucky PP!' Sandy seemed delighted sharing the story.

Something was really starting to feel wrong about Sandy. Was it the air of conceit he seemed to have developed? Or was it that damn unbearable smugness? I couldn't put my finger on it but my mind remained uneasy on that account. And I felt something was going to give way soon. *'Inspite of reading it all, in spite of having such a good core inside you, what is it that makes you vehemently sink into your lower impulses, Sandy? From where you are now, what will ever be enough to change you?'*

'Maybe like Arjuna in the Gita, you too need to face a crash – a crisis that shatters your ways completely. Only then I see any possibility of change,' I mused looking at him.

After having read the benefits of Yoga, he said to me the next morning, 'Maaps, your Barath Sir will be very proud of you, I think. By the way, you promise so much about the Yogic path. When we progress along it, we will attain stillness, peace, composure and all that. And everything seems to be our effort in what you say. It's we who have to practise Karma Yoga, then meditate, and then ascend to our Big Boss step by step. Then what does he do at all up there? Just sit with a pack of popcorn in his hands and enjoy seeing us toil through every hardship to reach him? The guy seems pretty cold!'

'Hmm, your intellect is as sharp as ever dear friend. Alas it is so fixed on its own ways that you don't even feel the slightest need to move out of it.'

ॐ

GOD AND YOGA

'What does God do at all, if all of it is our effort?' Well, the relation between God and the Yogic path is compared to our breathing. When we breathe, we create a negative pressure, a vacuum in our lungs through expanding our chest and air flows in to fill it. It is something similar that happens here.

Divine Grace is ever present. The helping hand of the Divine is ever stretched out towards us. It is we who have to turn inward and hold it. It is we who created those obstructions after all, by going along our mind's ill-informed ways. Through Karma Yoga and Dyaana Yoga all we do is this: remove the self-created hitches and hindrances inside ourselves. Just as air flows in when there is emptiness in the lungs, when we remove the obstructions and clutter accumulated in us and purify our inner being, the Real Self in our heart shines through in all its glory.

We hear people sing in a heart-felt way, 'Krishna come to me soon and show me your face.' Krishna is always standing at the door knocking. It is we who are sitting inside our houses smugly and preferring not to open it.

Uplift thy self by thy self 6.5

Gita insists. That means the responsibility is ours. Whatever defects, shortcomings we might have, it is for us to reflect on it and tackle. Use a journal, take a holiday occasionally. Use whatever way suits you to take a neutral look at yourself often and decide which areas in you need work. Gita or any spiritual master we come across can only give us the path; the broad principles. It is *we* who should find out a way to translate it into our life.

ॐ

WHAT NEXT?

So we take the spiritual path of Yoga that Gita has put forward for us. We start doing our actions with the attitude of Karma Yoga. We practise Dyaana daily. What happens next? Where does this twin path of action and silence culminate? The Gita answers it this way:

> **Becoming absorbed in Brahman,**
> **and becoming serene in the Self,**
> **He neither grieves nor desires; and regards all beings alike.**
> **He (subsequently) obtains a supreme devotion for me. 18.54**

> **By devotion one truly understands**
> **what and who I am in essence.**
> **Having known me in essence,**
> **one forthwith merges into me. 18.55**

So far, we were discussing our part of the equation, what we do to get rid of the hindrances we have created in us and how we grow in the Divine. From here, we are entering the realm of the Divine. We are about to see what happens when we reach the other end of the Divine thread.

The Yoga of Bakthi and Jnaana

BAKTHI

'Every action has an equal and opposite reaction' goes Newton's law of motion. When there is a zenith there is bound to be a nadir too. When Yoga, the path of light, has such a Divine encounter as its culmination, the opposite path of darkness too must have such a point. That too the Gita mentions. And as I was preparing this part of the write-up, I saw Sandy slip into it.

Hinduism doesn't have a figure like Satan, the way Christianity does. However, a man totally cut off from his inner truth, who willingly lets the mind's worst temptations reign supreme in him is an *Asura*, says the Gita. If what we are about to discuss is the highest point of consciousness, the Gita also paints a grave picture of the lowest way of existence – an extreme and unethical form of rajasic person. He is a self-created Satan, as it were.

> There are two types of human beings in this world
> The divine and the demonic. 16.6

'If the rajasic qualities are given the upper hand, then the trend of karma and its results necessarily culminate in the highest exaggeration of the perversities of the lower nature. The man has eventually the Asura full-born in him,' in Sri Aurobindo's words.[1]

The materialistic consciousness in man, when pursued relentlessly and unscrupulously, can reach a tipping point and turn into what the Gita calls, Demonic consciousness. The Gita says of such persons,

> Considering sense gratification as their highest aim,
> Convinced that is everything ...
> Bound by hundreds of ties of desire,
> And enslaved by lust and anger ...
> Bewildered by many fancies,
> Entangled in the net of delusion ...
> They fall into a foul hell. 16.11–16

That 'foul hell' was where Sandy was headed I felt, when I heard of his egregious act in Mars hospital.

Since the time I examined the patient in the ward, I noticed that Sister Indhra looked sombre. Her replies to my questions were terse. She was a close friend of Sandy's latest love-interest, Manisha.

'How long has the patient been getting Clofazimine, sister?'

'Three weeks.'

'Fine. What, Sister? Has your head nurse come up with some new stifling rule?' I asked while writing the prescription.

There was a wry smile on her face as she looked at me. 'All those rules and regulations we can tolerate, Sir. But dishonesty and deceit, that's very difficult.'

I stopped writing and raised my head to face her.

'What happened, Sister?'

'Nothing,' she said, turning away from me.

I sensed that I was up against something serious. When I insisted on knowing further, she divulged everything. It was Sandy. He had gone by the way of his lustful animal impulses and done something appalling with Manisha in the hospital.

'Manisha and I were alone during the night shift, day before yesterday. I searched for Manisha to put in a venflon for a patient, then remembered that she had told me she will be with Santosh Sir in the OP. I went up there. They weren't there. I then opened the doctor's room. There ... I couldn't believe what I saw. Santosh Doctor ... how do I say this....' She cringed. 'He was drunk, and he was forcing Manisha to get intimate with him. Manisha was screaming and putting up a fight while he was trying to drag her to the bed. As I opened the door, he looked at me in shock. He then grinned sheepishly and left the room without a word. It was disgusting!'

Indhra's voice conveyed great angst.

'His face, that smile ... that told me what kind of person he really is ...' she paused briefly. 'I thought of taking the matter up with the chief first. Then realised a girl's life was at stake.... Dr Santosh! We put him on a high pedestal. Manisha has immense respect towards doctors, you know! She almost looks at them like Gods. No wonder she is taken advantage of, like this.'

She fell silent for a moment. 'They say nursing is a thankless job. I now see why. For people like him, we nurses are just whores, isn't it? Leave it, Sir. . . .'

'Can we stop Clofazimine for this patient today?' she asked after having read the prescription.

ॐ

I was consumed by rage as I drove straight to Sandy's clinic.

When I entered his cabin, there was a rep from a CT scan franchise who was giving him an envelope.

'Yeah, yeah sure. Thank you very much,' he was talking over the phone with the sheepish grin that had become his trademark now. Next, he passed the phone to the rep standing there.

'Okay, Sir. I will come and meet you next month. Do keep writing CTs, Sir.'

I waited for him to leave. As the door closed behind the rep, Sandy turned and looked at me.

'What's up, maaps?'

'You lousy a****le! Are you not ashamed of what you are letting yourself become?'

'Whoa, whoa! Man, what happened? Take a seat first.'

I told him of what I heard from Indhra. He looked a bit surprised, wondering how she could have related everything to me.

'Oh that?' he asked, trying to conceal his emotion.

'You b*****d, the poor girl respected you immensely and thought you would marry her one day and you . . .'

He gave me a long stern look. He listened patiently without responding to all the vitriol I scalded him with. For the first time my words made him angry too.

After I stopped, he started speaking in a rather unruffled voice, 'Okay you think all this is "wrong" and I am vehemently going along an unethical path beyond my control, in the way of my "animalistic impulses," huh?' He took out a cigarette and lit it.

The attender opened the door at that time and said, 'Sir, a patient is waiting.'

'Later,' he signaled swiftly with his hands.

'Sir, they said they have a bus to board. They have come from . . .'

'Didn't I say, "later"?' he yelled at the boy in rage. 'Bloody idiot!'

Saying so, he turned and started talking to me. 'Let me put a question before you, Venki boss. Let us both press the rewind button. You remember our first year of UG? I asked you and your friend Mano to let me join your group-study and you turned a deaf ear to that. I subsequently went on to flunk pathetically in the exams and you both passed onto clinics with flying colours. That was in a way the turning point of my life. Let me ask you now my dear friend, what made you leave me out?'

There was a sarcastic grin on his face as he asked that.

'. . . well, er, how does that matter here?' I was taken aback by that question.

'Let me come to it. Answer me first,' he said, still grinning.

'Okay, I did something wrong then, I agree. I didn't realise how much that damn group-study could have helped you then. That's why I am sharing the Gita with you, ignoring all that you are doing.'

He laughed aloud, almost manically.

'You are sharing the Gita with me . . . to seek self-redemption for your past sin? Ha ha ha, that is one of the funniest lines I have heard from you, Venki. Ha ha, I will have to ponder over that. But you know what . . . ?'

His tone got solemn, 'I don't see what you did then as wrong. Really. You were justified in doing that then. What you did was absolutely the right thing. I mean it. Idealistic theory, we all can happily speak maaps, from the Gita, Bible, Quran all that. Let the rubber meet the road . . . we have no choice but to do what serves us the best. This is the only law the world operates on, just like you had done then.'

He added taking another puff, 'You are concerned about a girl's future and all that? Let me tell you one thing. Never underestimate these girls. They will put up faces and make all these big scenes today. Only let a nice-looking wealthy man come, they will move on in a trice as if nothing happened. F***ing opportunistic b*****s! I have seen and learnt all that very early on in life, my dear friend. Alright, let us leave what I did, aside. Let me ask you another question. Tell me honestly, if you get such a chance won't you do it too?'

I kept looking at him without answering. I was teeming with sheer disbelief.

'What are you looking at? I am serious. Give me an answer. Let us say, tomorrow you get a chance like this. A hot chick. Perfect solitude . . . just like I got. No one has any chance to know about it in the future. Will you think about taking her to bed, or not? Would this thought never cross your mind? Come on, my friend. Be true to yourself.'

I didn't feel like answering. The words of that eccentric twelfth-grade Sandy with a half-grown moustache as he confessed a meagre mistake of his to Barath Sir came to my mind, 'Don't scold me. We won't live with this small burden in our hearts anymore every time we think of Barath Sir.'

My thoughts came back to the person sitting before me with his parotids enlarged, spewing all this nonsense in his cold and deep tone of voice.

'Okay, Sandy. You say that conscience is nothing. What do you think of people like our Barath Sir, then?' I asked calmly.

'Aah! Barath Sir . . . ' he said derisively, puffing away further at his cigarette. 'Exceptions don't disprove a rule, Venki boss. Moreover we were children then. We never knew what could have been inside that guy!' he said in a muffled voice, looking away from me.

I got up quickly, not willing to sit there anymore. As I walked out of his cabin my last words were, 'So you are not being wanton, but walking the path with awareness, with your great principles governing you, right? Good to hear that, Sandy. All the best, dear friend.'

I decided I would never meet him again. The Santosh I knew was dead and a beast seemed to have taken his place. I removed the watch he gave me as a gift once, and placed it on the reception desk outside. As I recounted what he had said I realized what an absolute waste it had been, sharing the wonderful philosophy of the Gita with such a guy.

I picked up the watch I had placed on the table, and as the attendant and the patient sitting there watched astonished, I threw it with all my strength against the wall in a fit of apoplexy. It smashed to pieces as I walked out of his clinic.

'The sensual tendencies can carry away the mind like a turbulent wind,' says the Gita. That day I saw how powerful that pull could be if we are not careful and discerning. *'Oh, how much have you let yourself get imprisoned in your crude impulses, Santosh!... To the extent of even debasing our Sir who had given so much to us!'*

The question he asked me came to my mind. Will I do it? I don't know. Maybe there is such a beast inside everyone's mind. Such a thought might cross my mind too. But can that alone be the reason for straying into such lowly ways? Does having a knife or gun give us the license to kill people? Haven't we got our discrimination? If I go along with that animalistic side just because it is there in me, I could have stayed as a street dog. Why acquire a human life?

Sandy! He has always been someone known to do things driven by his impulses. Only that it is now working in an opposite direction, making him more and more unscrupulous.

Few weeks back, I had felt he had to face a crash in his life to get out of his present ways. Now I sent that up as a fervent prayer. *'If it is so destined, please make that guy face a terrible crash in his life soon, God – something that crushes his smug ways of life totally and brings him back to his old self.'*

To move on to the Gita, well, my old friend has slipped to a new low, and paradoxically the write-up has just entered the part on the highest state of consciousness, Para-Bakthi.

ॐ

BECOMING THE KITTEN

Sri Ramakrishna often quoted an example to explain how to have true Bakthi towards the Divine. A baby monkey always holds on tightly to its mother; otherwise it would fall. But a kitten doesn't do that. It is the mother-cat that carries it safely in its mouth all the time. The kitten happily rests in its mother's mouth. The highest form of Bakthi should be like the kitten, Sri Ramakrishna said.

God is the still, alive presence in our core, we were told. In Karma Yoga we saw how we, the little egos, can open ourselves to that presence. Dyaana Yoga was about nourishing that presence in us more and more, through getting our outer selves totally silent. Both the Yogas complement each other.

Next arrives a stage where that mighty, still presence comes to the fore and takes control of our being. A stage where the baby monkey becomes the kitten. All our efforts cease, the table turns and our little ego encounters the source of the divine light with which it felt a connection so far, and becomes embraced by that. Our little ego becomes consumed and inebriated by the bliss of Divine.

'Oh my Arunachala, when the devilishness (of ego) left me, you firmly caught hold of me like an unexorcisable Spirit, and made me mad for you,' Sri Ramana writes in one of his compositions. This is the stage where,

> **He who is always engaged in meditation**
> **One whose being is possessed by the Divine...**
> **He obtains a Supreme devotion towards me. 18.52–54**
>
> **By devotion one truly understands**
> **what and who I am in essence. 18.55**

Para-Bakthi is the name the Gita gives to this supreme devotion (Para meaning supreme). Apara-Bakthi is what we have in our hearts as beginners on the path. We hold on to a particular form of god, do our work for him, observe daily rituals like japa and meditation to strengthen our connection. Gradually, as we open ourselves more and more, we progress to Para-Bakthi.

Para-Bakthi is when we, the one-second beings, feel the embrace of Eternity. And we start living in that warmth moment to moment. It is the stage where god enters into our house, takes control of our little self, and is there to stay.

> **All know that the drop merges into the ocean;**
> **but few know that the ocean merges into the drop.**
> **Kabir**

Karma and Dyaana Yoga facilitate it. This encounter with the pure, untainted light of our True Cosmic Self in all its glory occurs entirely by the grace of the Divine. *Dhatuh prasadat* is the term used in Katha Upanishad to explain it, meaning 'through the grace of the Creator.' There is no way to predict when, or to whom, it will happen. It almost feels like an accident for the Baktha. The Zen master Baker Roshi was once asked by his student when he would become enlightened. The words the Master spoke in reply applies to the Yogic path too, 'Enlightenment is an accident. But meditation can make you accident prone.'

ॐ

HELLO GOD!

What happens to a Yogi when he reaches the other end of the divine thread? What happens when 'God,' which is a concept we believe or disbelieve, becomes a moment to moment living experience?

In the Gita, Arjuna expresses his wish to Krishna to see this form of the Divine that bakthas encounter.

> O Lord,
> I wish to see your Divine Cosmic form O Supreme Being ...
> If you think it is possible for me to see it. 11.3-4

The Lord accepts his request and replies

> You cannot see me with your physical eye.
> Therefore to see my power and glory
> Let me give you the divine eye. 11.8

'The most beautiful things of the world must be felt within the heart,' Helen Keller said. Encountering our divine self too is such a beautiful experience. It is with the *eye of the heart* that we can see the Divine who is, in Kabir's words, 'One with no face, no head, no form and who is subtler than the fragrance of the flowers.'

> Having thus spoken, Krishna, the Great Lord of Yoga,
> Showed unto Arjuna His own Supreme Easwara Form. 11.9

With the inner vision that Krishna blesses him with, Arjuna 'sees' the Lord. Once he does, the experience literally blows his mind off. It was beyond anything he had expected or imagined. All the doubts, all the uncertainties he might have had till then vanish without a trace. His reaction exemplifies the state of a baktha who encounters the Divine.

> Arjuna filled with wonder, with his hair standing on end,
> Bowed down to the God and spoke with joined palms 11.14
>
> I see all the Gods in your body, O God. 11.15
> You are the Imperishable, Supreme Being
> worthy to be known. 11.18

With a voice choked with awe and with an enlightened understanding of who the innocuous-looking charioteer before him really is, he speaks,

> O Lord of Lords, O Abode of the Universe,
> You are the Imperishable,
> That which is beyond the manifest and the unmanifest. 11.37
>
> Salutations to Thee a thousand times.
> Again salutations unto You! 11.39
>
> Whatever I have rashly said from carelessness or love,
> Addressing you as 'O Krishna, O Yadava, O friend,'
> Regarding You merely as a friend,
> not knowing the greatness of Yours,
> In whatever way I may have insulted You for fun...
> That, O Immeasurable one, I implore you to forgive. 11.41-42
>
> As a father forgives his son,
> a friend his friend, a lover his lover,
> Even so should You forgive me, O Lord. 11.44

It is not that he hadn't known before then that Krishna was an incarnation of the Divine. However, he perceived only now what that meant. And that utterly overwhelmed him.

It is no wonder then that we become deeply devoted to the Divine, 'our source, our father, mother and supporter,' the one Cosmic Being whom we are all a part of.

The sage Narada says how such Bakthi manifests in a person, 'It manifests outwardly in the baktha as suspension of breath, perspiration, horripilation, a choked voice, trembling of the body, change in complexion, shedding of tears and loss of self-consciousness.'

The new-age book *Home with God* tries and describes the inner feeling of such divine embrace this way, 'A feeble attempt (at describing it) would call it the feeling of being warmly embraced, deeply comforted, dearly cherished, profoundly appreciated, fully understood, completely forgiven, long awaited, happily welcomed, totally honoured and unconditionally loved – all at once.'[2]

That is about encountering god whose real nature is, in Sri Adhi Shankara's words, *Nitya-Suddha-Buddha-Mukta-Swabhava*, meaning that which is Eternal, Always Pure, Always Enlightened and Always Free.

ൡ

Think of the best relationship you have ever had in your life. Why do you hold it dear? Is it not because we felt loved as we are? We love the people in whose presence we feel unconditionally accepted and loved.

Imagine then the inner being of these bakthas, who, in every moment of life, were in such an exalted state of divine embrace. It is no wonder then that saints like Sri Chaitanya, when they tried to utter the first letter of the name of their lord, found their voice becoming choked in the attempt and tears starting to flow down from their eyes.

That is what it means to encounter the Divine and live in his embrace. We can speculate. But only experiencing it can tell us what it is like. 'All your talk is worthless when compared to one whisper of the Beloved,' in Jalaludeen Rumi's eloquent words.

By the way, how can we function in the world at all, once we have reached this stage of Para-Bakthi? Will we even care to come back?

Remaining in such an exalted inner state doesn't mean a baktha would forsake the world and sit idle basking in the Divine. Though he has reached full circle, though he has done what he has come here to do, he would honour the assignment the Divine has given him till the time he is here. He will come back and work in the world as a humble instrument of god. One of the attitudes described below becomes the foundation on which his inner being would rest.

ൡ

THE BHAAVAS

As the baktha experiences this oneness with the Divine, the devotion in his heart spontaneously takes the form of a particular *bhaava*, an attitude towards the Divine, depending on his inner nature. Sri Ramakrishna says it would be one among the below five.

Shaanta bhaava: A serene connection and oneness with the Divine. This baktha is not emotional. His heart is filled with restfulness. Bhishma was one such baktha of the Lord. Though he was lying on a bed of arrows in his final days during the battle of Mahabharatha, he was able to bear the pain and patiently await the auspicious moment of his union with the Divine. 'I shall bear everything, whatever the pain, however long the agony. I shall be silent until the moment comes. Take me when it dawns,' he was able to say. He was a Shanta Baktha.

Daasya bhaava: The attitude of a servant towards his Master. Sri Hanuman was one such baktha. He found great joy in being of service to Sri Rama. 'I have no desire for liberation, if I would forget that you are the Master and I am your servant,' he says in Valmiki Ramayana, such was his Bakthi.

Sakhya bhaava: A deep friendship. The devotee moves with the Lord on equal terms, as a friend. Arjuna had this bhaava towards Sri Krishna, which is quite palpable throughout the Gita.

Vaatsalya bhaava: The attitude of a mother towards her child. Not just the women with motherly love in their hearts, even many great male saints found joy in treating their beloved Divine as their child – serving, feeding and singing lullabies for Him as parents do for their children. The Divine is your pet-child in this bhaava. In temples like Guruvayoor and Udupi, the Divine is worshipped as a child.

Madhura bhaava: The attitude of a woman towards her lover. Meerabai's devotion to Krishna is a well-known example. Her love was at first private, but on occasion it overflowed into an ecstasy that led her to dance in the streets of the city. The bhaava is not limited to female devotees of God, but was seen even in the lives of Sri Chaitanya and Sri Ramakrishna.

'In whichever form people worship me, even so I bless them,' our Big Boss has already told us. For Christianity, men are sinners and Christ, the redeemer. For Islam, Allah is the Great Master. Hinduism, being a composite religion, presents us with little more choices. When one finally merges with the Divine, forsaking the last trace of his ego, all those bhaavas vanish; the dualism of you and God vanishes. Just oneness is what remains.

One can hold on to one of these bhaavas since one's initial steps along the path of yoga. It is an easy way to feel connected to the Divine, as each bhaava is after all a natural human emotion. However, the bhaava that arises in us at this stage of Para-Bakthi is called *Mahabhaava*. It arises by itself. Here the devotee eats, moves and lives every moment with his being deeply soaked in Divine consciousness.

JNAANA

I have been putting off getting married for more than two and a half years now. Since I entered PG, my Mom kept insisting on me getting married citing my age, and receding hairline.

'No way, Mom! No wedding before the wherewithal,' I had been telling her all throughout.

But seeing her on stage during Suba Aunty's daughter's wedding, somehow moved me to change my decision. Suba Aunty was my mother's elder sister, who had settled with her family in Seattle. She has two daughters and had had grandchildren at a relatively young age.

Mom was holding two-year old Akshara, Suba Aunty's second granddaughter, in her hands all through the ceremony. The cute little one had become very attached to mom.

The little girl was holding a pink Barbie doll in her hands. It was her favourite doll; she had brought it all the way from Seattle. Maybe, in the strange environment she was in, she derived some security from that doll.

I was looking at the stage. Something that happened there moved me.

The child was pulling my mom's hair, pinching her, smudging her *kumkum* and indulging in all sorts of mischief. I was looking at mom as she was doing all that. Mom's eyes were wide and glowing. There was a bounce in her steps, as she chased down the little girl, who occasionally tried to run away from her. Her face displayed a joy that I don't remember having seen for some time, not even when her Dattu Baba visited our house.

༶

We were on our way back home. My mind was still contemplating on my decision to postpone marriage.

The stories I had heard about her youth, crossed my mind. Imagine a girl brought up by an authoritarian father of a former generation; her being married at just seventeen years of age, that too to a groom almost septic with his own business concerns; who did not know the meaning of warmth or loving his family.

I calmly thought about it all. Suddenly the half-baked Swamiji, the pujas, the pilgrimages, all those that she was clinging to appeared as a confused soul's attempt to cope with things, and find some solace in an unloved and unmeaningful life. Her own version of Akshara's Barbie doll!

'Mom.'

'Mmm?' She turned towards me.

'That Bengaluru girl you mentioned, has she finished her studies?'

Mom turned and looked at me with a huge surprised frown. In a while I saw her face light up in such a way, that I felt something inside me liquefy. I myself was in disbelief for some time, that I had taken such a huge decision.

ॐ

The house bustled with activity over the next few weeks. Many relatives, distant and near, kept coming and going. The marriage had been fixed three and a half months later, in September.

I looked at myself as all that was happening around me. Was it the things I came across while preparing the write-up that inspired me to do that? Who knows? How could a person like me have given his consent for marriage, otherwise?

'Let Yajna be your way of life,' the Gita says. Yajna, in our relationships, is about putting the good of others before our own and feeling happy in their happiness – even when their wish is diametrically opposite to ours. I experienced that joy to its fullest depth the first time. The strong edifice of my ego with all its stubborn preferences had come down crashing. And I wasn't feeling sad inside, but *blissful!*

ॐ

I was sitting by the sea on the sands, watching the tiny waves breaking on the shore near my feet. Kumar was combing his hair often, looking at himself in his cell phone's screen.

'What is that new hairstyle of yours?' I asked him.

'Oh this? This is called striking streaks. Don't I look like Shahrukh in this?'

'Oh, Shahrukh! So, now you have switched to Hindi after those string of crappy films your thalaivar did!'

'Just for a change, man. Answer my question. Don't I look like Shahrukh?'

'Just like the bhaktas need their God, you need a film star to model yourself on, huh?'

He wasn't listening. 'Alright, look at me for a minute and tell the truth.' He turned his head sideways. 'Isn't there a faint resemblance with him from this angle?'

'Yeah, a Shahrukh-clone we can call you, perhaps.'

'Is it? That's nice. . . . Shahrukh-clone. Thanks, da.'

I kept gazing at him as he was munching on the groundnuts in his hands. He was staring unrelentingly at the college girls who were walking past us. This Kumar, though a to-the-core *tamasic* being, was a much more benign and harmless person compared to Sandy, I felt. I told him next that I was getting married in a few months and showed him the picture of the girl.

'Oh? That's great man. I too have always wanted to get married, you know? Right from my childhood! But that old fart in my house never takes me seriously.' Saying that, he took a look at the snap I showed him. As he did, his mouth fell open. 'This girl? This girl is going to become your wife? Man, I can't believe this.' Those were the considerate comments he made.

The girl was indeed charming, almost like a glamorous model we see in fashion shows.

'No wonder you agreed to marry all of a sudden.' Kumar's incredulous eyes were looking at my face and the photo of the girl alternately. 'Did you meet her?'

'Yes, last week. She said that her father, who is no more, was a doctor in the army. It seems I resemble him a lot.'

'Oh, lucky you! But man, imagine! When a child is born to you in the future, I wonder how he would be like. Hope he is not born like a zebra.' He guffawed saying that, before I caught hold of him to bash him up.

ಇಲ

As my days as a happy bachelor are nearing their end, so is our spiritual expedition through the Gita. 'Nothing really matters, guys,' those were some of the oft-repeated words of our Barath Sir. And that is the essence of what we are going to see in the pages that follow. So far we saw that the Gita touched upon many aspects along the spiritual path – Karma and Dyaana on a foundation of Bakthi or Jnaana and it all culminating in Para-Bakthi. The question to consider now is, is that the end of an individual's spiritual journey?

Nope. There is a realisation that occurs after such Para-Bakthi, which is the essence of Jnaana, our next topic of discussion.

The question frequently discussed in books and classes on the Gita is, what is the core message of the scripture? The Gita is a manual of the right way of action, some say. 'Do thy duty; forsake the result,' is its essential message, according to them. True, it does stress on such action, but action only as a means of self-purification.

> **The Yogis, having discarded attachment,**
> **Perform actions for self-purification. 5.11**

Some stress on bakthi. Yes, a heartfelt bakthi towards the Divine is absolutely essential in walking the Gita's path.

> **Among all Yogis, he who is full of faith,**
> **With his inner self merged in me,**
> **Worships me, is according to me, the most superior. 6.47**

However, the culmination of it all, the one thing the Gita had been preparing us for throughout, is something else. In the last chapter, after having said that through works and dyaana one comes to a point where, 'He obtains a supreme devotion to me' (18.54), our Big Boss goes on to say this next,

> **By devotion one truly understands**
> **what and who I am in essence.**
> **Having known me in essence,**
> **One forthwith merges into me. 18.55**

'Through Bakthi, he comes to *know me* in essence,' the verse says. And 'through this *knowing*, he merges into me.' This knowledge, this Wisdom Divine is the culmination the Gita has been preparing us for.* We see the same idea conveyed in Gita's tenth chapter (verses 9 to 11).

Well, the baktha has encountered god himself! What more knowledge is there to gain? That knowledge, to put it in brief, is this: Brahman is real. The world is unreal. **Brahmam Sathya. Jagath Mithya.**

Krishna gives a brief glimpse of this truth even as he starts his exposition.

> The unreal has no existence.
> And the real never ceases to exist.
> The truth of this is indeed seen by the seers of truth. 2.16

To expand on that piece of wisdom: the material world we live in, space, and time are all illusions. Dreams! You, me and all the individualities in this world are illusions! Ultimate Reality is Absolute Oneness. God alone is real. He *is* the Ultimate Reality.

The statement doesn't mean there is a separate god out there – the real thing – and we are illusions. No. Cut ourselves from all identifications, from our puny little egos, from all the boundaries of time and space we live by – 'you, me,' 'here, there,' 'now, then.' *We are that God!* Right here, right now.

Brahma-Jnaana is the stage where the pure individual ego, now unclad of all its impressions, is totally taken up by the Divine, and a Sublime Oneness alone is left. The saint-poet Kabir expresses this truth in one of his compositions in this way –

> When I was, Hari was not. Now Hari is, and I am no more.
> Him whom I went out to seek, I found just where I was.
> He now has become myself, whom before I called 'another!'

This Wisdom Divine is called the wisdom of non-dualism or **A-dvaita**, meaning *one without a second*. The Gita itself is called *'Advaita Amrita*

---

*There are differences in interpretation of Para-Bakthi and Jnaana among the Bakthi and Jnaana schools. The Bakthi schools claim Para-Bakthi as the final stage, while the Jnaana schools claim Brahma-Jnaana as the final stage. I have stuck to the way Sri Ramakrishna and Swami Vivekananda interpreted Para-Bakthi and Jnaana.

Varshini,' meaning, the scripture showering on us the nectar-like wisdom of Advaita. Advaita is the non-dual infinite truth. No trillion individualities, no you and me, no space, no time. Just One Untainted Spirit. No more 'you here – God there' duality. Just a Supreme, Sublime Oneness with nothing outside it.

Para-Bakthi was our experience when we come to encounter it. In this stage, *we become that.* Brahma-Jnaana is what we realise as truth once we become that, and the Divine alone remains. That is where it all started from. And that is the culmination of it all. In Swami Vivekananda's words, 'What does the Advaitist declare? . . . He Himself is this universe. What are you and I and all these things we see? Mere self-hypnotism; there is but one Existence. . . . It is the Atman. It is the only Reality. . . . There is neither nature, nor God, nor the universe, only that one Infinite Existence, out of which, through name and form, all these are manufactured.'[1]

Sounds improbable? Flabbergasting?

Let us keep aside the Gita and spirituality for a few pages and take a tour into the scientific world to test the truth of those declarations. All that philosophy is what an ancient esoteric text propounds. Does it make sense in the light of contemporary science?

Well, a few hundred years ago scientists would have given it all a scathing look. 'Everything is an illusion? In that case, I overpaid for my carpet,' an American comedian quipped hearing this philosophy. But after the arrival of quantum mechanics into the scene, it seems science has got no choice but to say, 'Mmm, those ancient scriptures seem to be right.'

ॐ

THE SOLID WORLD

As I take a look out of my window, I see cars, buses, bicycles and many people passing by. I perceive a world before me. It hurts when I pinch myself. The cluttered table before me, the flakes of paint coming off the wall, the new ballpoint pen I hold in my hands all appear pretty solid and real. I see and feel them. And you and I do exist separately; I write all this sitting in front of my table in my clinic right now, and you are reading it somewhere else in time and space. What is unreal in this?

Let us take the pen in my hands as the representative for our real world and analyse it in the light of modern science. The basic building block of this pen in my hand is a molecule of plastic. Or still further we can say it is the atoms that make up the molecule; those are the basic units the pen is composed of.

What is an atom? An atom, as I remember studying in early school days, is a mini solar system, with certain stuff at the centre – neutrons and protons – and certain other stuff revolving in the periphery – the electrons. It is like the planets revolving around the sun.

The nucleus is said to be one hundred thousand times smaller than the whole atom. That is, if the nucleus is taken as a cricket ball placed at the centre of a stadium, electrons are just the specks of dust floating at the farthest corner of it. All the rest is vast, free space. In other words, not 'lot of free space,' but 99.9999% of an atom is empty! That is how ghostly we are. This is the classical Newtonian view of what is inside our basic building block, the atom.

Unfortunately, this view has become obsolete long back – even before my father was a twinkle in my grandfather's eyes – when quantum mechanics arrived into the scene.

In the 1920s the independent works of Nobel prize winning physicists Heisenberg and Schrodinger showed that the particles inside an atom – the 0.0001% – don't have a definitive existence like the objects exist 'up here' in our world. They just show a tendency to exist!

What does that mean? It means what was thought of as solid particles – the electrons, protons and neutrons – are not really solid at all, but just a probability function, a 'now-it-exists-now-it-doesn't' stuff. The "solid" particles also behave as waves.

The defining characteristic of the subatomic world is, in the words of the astronomer Marcus Chown, 'Its denizens have a bizarre, schizophrenic nature. They can behave both as localised, bullet-like 'particles' and as spread-out 'waves,' much like ripples on a pond.' Then he humourously adds, 'Trying to imagine how this is possible will give you a migraine.'[2]

Physicists simply had to accept that the subatomic world is profoundly different from anything in the everyday world they had come across. That is about the atom, the basic building block of our physical existence.

So, what do I have here? The pen in my hand, which appears real to my eyes is really 99.9999% free space! And even the apparent solid part of it – the 0.0001% – is just an energy flash, a probability function. We do not really know what is beyond that, where the subatomic particles come from or where they go. The pen appears solid because this occurs at the subatomic level that our eyes cannot detect it. It is our eyes and brain that solidify and smoothen out reality.

How does it *feel* solid then? It is because of the atomic forces that hold things together in an atom. Or my fingers may go right into the pen through its apparent solidness.

❧

HERE, NOW

Let us continue this head-spinning exercise by taking up the next building block of our world: space and time. We assume that they are the fundamental fabric out of which our universe is made of. It is on this stable scaffolding of space and time, all the dramas of our lives unfold, we imagine.

However, even before Quantum theory – probably around the time my grandfather was a twinkle in my great-grandfather's eyes – Einstein proposed and proved through his papers on Relativity, that space and time are relative. When his lifelong friend Michele Besso died, Einstein wrote a letter consoling Besso's family. In that he mentions, 'Now he has departed from this strange world a little ahead of me. That means nothing. People like us, who believe in physics, know that the distinction between past, present and future is only a stubbornly persistent illusion.'[3]

Time, according to him, is not something that exists apart from the universe. It is part of the fabric of the universe. Outside the universe, time has no existence. Einstein said that massive objects – the giant stars and planets – 'bend' space-time as a bowling ball would distort a sheet supporting it.

To get a feel of the implication of that, imagine watching an entire cricket ODI live in five minutes, or crossing a 100 metre race within the first one metre.

❧

THE SUBSTRATUM

We saw on the chapter on mind, how our individuality too is like a constantly changing kaleidoscopic image which doesn't have any stable existence. So what do we have here? Space, time, the pen in my hand, and even the person holding that pen are all just changing, relative and shadowy realities. As an Upanishad verse asserts,

> **Time, space, law, chance, matter, none of these,**
> **Nor a combination of these**
> **can be the final cause of the universe.**
> **For they are all effects, and exist to serve the soul.**
> Svetasvatara Upanishad 1.12

We will take up what Vedanta says on these in a shortwhile. To continue looking at it through the eyes of science, if it is all relative and changing stuff, there should indeed be some constant entity behind it all; something that is the cause and the support of it all. Without that, it will all just collapse unto itself like an image without a screen to support it. So what is that substratum which holds together all of existence when even space and time are not constant? Recent discoveries in science throw some light on this.

In the later part of the last century (around the time my family-tree reached yours lovingly), a new theory arrived in the scientific field called *the string theory*, which tried to shed light on this substratum.

The entity called music arises out of the vibrations of the guitar string. In the same way, our solid world, which is flashing on and off as per quantum mechanics, is the result of vibrations of some sort of strings in a higher dimension, according to this theory. The dimensions from which these strings vibrate and give rise to the universe are the tenth and twenty-sixth dimensions, it proposes!*

As the adage goes, truth is indeed stranger than fiction.

Michael Talbot's acclaimed bestseller, *Holographic Universe* throws some light on 'the thing behind' from a different perspective. After presenting the arguments we saw till now in detail, Talbot asks, 'If our universe is

---

*Space-time is 26-dimensional in Bosonic string theory, while in Superstring theory it is ten-dimensional. Obviously I am simplifying it all a bit for better understanding. If you want to know more about it, you can read *The Elegant Universe* by Brian Greene.

only a pale shadow of a deeper order (of reality), what else lies hidden, enfolded in the warp and weft of our reality?'

For the answer, he quotes David Bohm, a quantum physicist and a protégé of Einstein. His theory about the seeming empty space around us holds the clue, Talbot mentions. His words, '(Mathematically) every cubic centimetre of empty space contains more energy than the total energy of all the *matter* in the universe.'[4]

Like the enormous energy hidden within atoms, there is an enormous energy lying latent in the seeming empty space around us too, is his theory. In his words, 'Most physicists ignore the existence of the enormous ocean of energy because, like fish unaware of the water in which they swim, they have been taught to focus primarily on objects embedded in the ocean, on matter.'[5]

More recent researches have confirmed the existence of a similar 'dark-energy' or 'dark-matter' as it is called. It is a mysterious force permeating space that is composed primarily of a new, not yet characterised subatomic particle, claim researchers. Some say it may be associated with a force field called Higgs Field. The *Science Magazine* called it 'The Breakthrough Discovery of the Year' in 1998 when research proved its existence.*

Well, it should be mentioned here that many of the theories we discussed above are not conclusive theories the scientific world has arrived at. They are *probabilistic theories*, presumptive working models developed around available data. They give a standing place for physicists to proceed further. They are like the light science sees at the end of the bewildering tunnel it finds itself in, as it gets into the subatomic world.

The reason these theories have been around so long is because they work well. It is the only light science sees at the end of the tunnel! Science is still in a shambles regarding what is the constant, unchanging substratum behind the universe that holds it all together. To further compound matters, recently the 'multiverse theory' has arrived into the scene, which states that our universe in just one of the enormous number of universes, with each operating by different fundamental principles. As a result of this, the quest of science to arrive at the fundamental laws

---

*Adam Riess of Johns Hopkins University shared the 2011 Nobel Prize for his researches into this 'dark matter' and his 'expanding universe theory.'

of nature seems to have taken a severe beating, as each universe seems to have different fundamental properties.

We are only reminded of Arjuna's words of wonder when he gets a grasp of who Krishna really is.

> **You are the Supreme Brahman.**
> **The Supreme Abode. The Primal God. 10.12**

> **Neither the Devas nor the demons**
> **Fully understand your manifestations. 10.14**

'Neither the scientists nor the mathematicians,' we could add.

> **O Creator and Lord of all beings,**
> **You alone know Yourself by Yourself. 10.15**

If one wants to understand God, he can't do it with his limited perceptions; with his one-second brain. He has to become God-like. He has to Self-realise.

> **He who knows the Supreme Brahman,**
> **verily becomes Brahman.**
> Mundaka Upanishad 3.2 (8–9)

༺

Swami Vivekananda declared more than a century ago in his Chicago address, 'The latest scientific discoveries are just echoes of Vedanta philosophy.' As if substantiating his words, several scientists have started to see for themselves the consistency of the pronouncements of Eastern religions with modern scientific theories on reality. Erwin Schrodinger, the Nobel Prize winning founder of Quantum mechanics says, 'The multiplicity (of the external universe) is only apparent. This is the doctrine of the Upanishads. And not of the Upanishads only. The mystical experience of the union with God regularly leads to this view, unless strong prejudices stand in the West.'[6]

Scientists are now starting to recognise that the solid world, which flashes in and out of existence, is like a dance of some sublime, transcendent reality. They see the poetic beauty in the symbolism of Siva as a dancing God. The institute of CERN (European Organisation for Nuclear Research) located on the French-Swiss border, where the largest Particle Physics laboratory of the world is situated, and where cutting edge researches are conducted to study the ultimate 'God particle,' sports in its campus the statue of Nataraja, the dancing form of Siva, that was gifted by the Indian government.

Imagine this scenario: your science-geek classmate makes a sophisticated electronic device after much hard work and comes to your home to show it proudly to your grandfather, who you both know has an inclination for electronics. He inspects it nonchalantly, puts it down, then goes in and brings back something from his old shelf for you both to see. You find that it is something he had put together in his younger years, and that it is a much more advanced and sophisticated device than what your friend has come up with. The results the scientific quest into reality has yielded is something akin to this.

ಌ

Let us end this dizzying discussion on science and Ultimate Reality with the following question: suppose science in the near future manages to precisely delineate the equations and formulas to explain the real nature of God and his power, what use is it going to be for you and me?

Aristotle emphasised that different areas of life require different modes of understanding. We don't read a poem with the reasoning-brain we use to audit a financial document. Likewise, we can't gain access to the realm of the Divine through the reductionistic tools of science. Science can satisfy an inquisitive brain. When it comes to matters of the heart, it misses the whole point. Science analyses the brain's neurochemicals and scans our heads with MRI scans to understand love. Maybe I would find what happens when a person is in love, and come up with a theory for it. But unless I experience it, how do I really understand love?

Nothing is real to you and me until you and I *experience* it; especially in matters of the heart. As the Tao Te Ching puts it, 'Look, it cannot be seen. Listen, it cannot be heard. Grasp, it cannot be held. You can't know it. But you can be it.'

We are not belittling science or its quest for the fundamental principle of the universe here. Such scientific quest itself is the manifestation of man's genuine longing to reach for the beyond. It will perhaps help clear up all the unwanted clutter accumulated around the essential truths of religion; and help what is essential emerge with greater strength.

However, the Creative Force of the universe couldn't have created our world from some special imported stuff and stayed safely outside it. It is the One that should have become many. The Creative power is ever one with the created. So, to be of any real use to the seeker, the quest for Ultimate Reality should be directed within: the place inside us where it resides.

Draupadi in the Mahabharatha prayed to Krishna when she was humiliated in Duryodhana's court. She called him first several times, 'Oh, Divine being of Dwaraka and Brindavan, help me!' She could not get a response.

Finally, she pleaded, 'Oh *Hridaya nivasa* (Resident of my heart)! Will you not come to my rescue?' Immediately, Krishna came to the fore and saved her, goes the story.

If there is a place where the Divine is seated closest to us, it is in the core of our being – our hearts. That is where man should turn in and search if he wants to really find god.

I am the Self abiding in the heart of all beings. 10.20

– our Big Boss already told us. We should recognise that the boundaries we are pushing against are not out there in the sky or within an atom, but within ourselves! 'He who sees God without seeing the Self sees only a mental image. He, who having completely lost the ego and sees the Self, he has found God,' as Sri Ramana put it.[6]

A God we see or feel outside us is still a myth. The journey ends, not when you *see God*, but **when there is no more 'you' to see God**; when you lose yourself, become one with god, and see the world as it is. And for that, it is *within* we should turn. So, even though there is nothing wrong with the external quest of science, we should be aware of the inherent limitation in such a search.

Alright. When we finally turn within, as Vedanta insists, what is that we see? What does the Gita say about Jnaana, Ultimate Wisdom?

ॐ

There wasn't a cloud in the sky when I started for Pasumaikudi from my town. The Tuticorin-heat was, as always, quite scorching. On the other hand, when I reached the village, I found the weather to be quite pleasant. It was as if nature had reserved her smiling face for this little village at all times.

Muthu welcomed me with a warm smile and a glass of buttermilk. He put a *vettiver* mat on the plastic chair that was kept outside the shop, for me to sit.

'I came by this side for a camp, Muthu. Just thought I will give you and Saradha my marriage invitation.'

'Very happy for you, Sir,' he said with genuine warmth while receiving the invitation from me. He opened the cover and looked at it with interest. 'Sir, in our tradition, they say that the bride and groom come to the altar of marriage as god and goddess in human form. The bride is considered Lakshmi, and the groom is her consort, Vishnu. May you both live like that, Sir. May your life benefit everyone it touches. I'll pray for you both,' he said.

I smiled back.

'I hardly know this boy, and the boy too hardly knows me. Still what a lovely thing to say!'

'Thanks a lot, Muthu. I really value that. By the way, is Saradha's father alright? He looked a bit sick when I went to his house. Her mother wished me well, but her father's face fell as soon as I gave him the invitation. It became a bit embarrassing for me and Saradha. Any problem?'

'Well, Sir, every father at this stage would like to see his daughter married. A couple of men did come to see our Saradhamma even a few months ago. But nothing clicked. Madam lost interest after that, and she has got all involved in her work here. Her mother is happy and supportive of her decision. But her father has become too depressed . . . particularly after the hospital expansion.'

'Oh, is it?' I felt sorry for her father.

All the time Muthu was talking to me, I noticed a tender smile on his face, as if all he related belonged to a lower plane, and they were not worth worrying too much about.

'Why, Muthu? Why don't you pray to your Goddess and make some good happen in your Saradhamma's life?' I asked him half-jokingly.

'Of course I do, Sir. I pray for Saradhamma every day. I pray to our Goddess that if there is anything bad to happen in Saradhamma's life, let it happen to me. She has done so much for this village. But what good do our hurting and worrying serve, Sir? The Mother's timing is always perfect. We just need some faith.'

'Oh? So you believe it will all turn out well, huh?'
'Surely, Sir!' he nodded.

ಞ

Krishna, when he begins his exposition of ultimate wisdom, utters the following words to Arjuna,

> I shall reveal to you, who do not disbelieve,
> The most profound secret of
> Self-knowledge and Self-realisation.
> Having known this you will be freed from
> The miseries of worldly existence. 9.1
>
> This knowledge is the king of all knowledge,
> The most secret and is very sacred.
> It can be perceived by instinct. 9.2

'It can be perceived by instinct,' he says here. 'It is incomprehensible by the mind' he said elsewhere. True. This wisdom can't be confined within the territory of language at all. Given that fact, what on earth is the Gita for? It is woven together by words, after all!

Well, both Krishna and Arjuna know it is beyond words. Yet, words are the only tools Krishna has to share this wisdom with Arjuna and us. The ideas these words stir up in our mental realm are really like mines the Gita plants inside us. Even as we contemplate on them with our mind, they help us transcend the realm of the mind. That is the aim in sharing it.

We can read them with an intellectual quest, to satisfy our theoretical doubts; nothing wrong with that. The Gita says to us that it is better than not caring for these truths at all. But the intention of the Gita in explicating the ultimate nature of God and the world is for us to realise them! It is then the very intention of sharing them is fulfilled.

Wisdom is quite a different creature from knowledge. Knowledge is a function of our brains; wisdom, our bones. Wisdom is the fulfilment of knowledge.

So how do we make knowledge, *wisdom*? Vedanta gives us a three-step method for making the dry words such an enduring realisation; a way to activate the mine, so to say, **Sravana, Manana** and **Nidityasana**.

That is the three-runged ladder through which we ascend to truth. Sravana, the first step, is about listening attentively to what is said. We read or hear and get to know the truths shared with due respect and reverence. During the next stage of manana we reflect on it in a heartfelt manner; we question and reason about what we gather from sravana. Through such profound and constant contemplation and meditation on the truth, the truth becomes part of us in the third stage of Nidityasana.

The one who has faith reflects.
The one who reflects, understands.
Chandogya Upanishad 7.19-18

Lord Ganesha is depicted as the son of god. We too are. Our intelligence too can realise that fact it has forgotten. It takes the same dynamics as the figure and the mythology of that god depict. As the son of Lord Siva literally lost his head, we too have to first lose our self-importance. Our centre has to shift from the all-knowing arrogant mind that doesn't allow the Divine into our house, to the wisdom and humility of the heart. Then as lord Ganesha's large ears, head and stomach depict, we have to hear the great spiritual truths, reflect on it and assimilate it. We have to integrate those truths into our being. If we do, then we no longer remain beings of the earth alone, but beings rooted in eternity – what the one leg of Ganesha always held folded up, signifies. And the all-important mind with its demonic tendencies is subdued and becomes our puny vehicle. Though temptations surround it – like the sweets around Ganesha's vahana, the rat – it ignores them all and always remains looking up to its Lord.

After all, what the Gita is about to share is not some esoteric, high-flying theory, but the great truths about our True Self **that are alive right now in the depths of our being**; the truths waiting for our acknowledgement and unfoldment. When read with due reverence, these verses of the Gita can touch that place, resonate with that truth and help us recognise and remember what we have forgotten. They help us *re-cognise and re-member* with that truth, literally.

The mere scholar just knows; he stops with sravana. But the one who has realised these truths has seen it all for himself. He has crossed the nidityasana stage and *become* the truth.

So far we read about the sadhanas for Karma, Dyaana and Bakthi

Yogas. Sravana, manana, and nidityasana are the threefold sadhana of Jnaana yoga. It can also be performed alongside Karma Yoga, that is, from the very beginning of our quest. When done in a heartfelt way, it is a great meditation and can tremendously help our spiritual progress.

With that in mind, let us get into what the Gita has got to say on the ultimate wisdom one arrives at.

ॐ

JNAANA IN A NUTSHELL

There are two realities. The one we are used to: the changing, ephemeral, relative world which works under the constraints of space, time, name and form. The other, is the ground it rests on: Ultimate Reality. When that is realised, the first loses its realness. A reversal of identity happens. The cell which previously was humbled by the massive intelligence of which it is a part, now realises it is not a cell at all, but the intelligence itself. It was the body's intelligence that became the liver cell to metabolise and the heart cell to pump blood. The wave realises that it is not just a part of the ocean, but it was the ocean that waved. It merges wholly with the ocean.

Further, unlike the cell or the wave, the previous identity of ours appears like a dream in our case – the truth of which can be grasped only when we move to the realm of that intelligence. Consciousness doesn't complement matter. Consciousness is the primal reality. Even without matter, it is self-existent. It is matter that complements consciousness.

Our Big Boss explains it this way in the Gita

All this world is pervaded by me in my unmanifest form.
All beings exist in me and not me in them 9.4

The first line is the truth science stumbled upon. The second line says, 'it is the world that exists in me, not the reverse.' True, it is the dream that exists in the dreamer; the reason why the chief Gods of Hinduism – Siva and Vishnu – are symbolically depicted to be in a Yogic trance.

Sounds a bit abstruse, doesn't it? Wait till you read the next verse.

Nor do beings exist in me, in reality.
Behold my Divine Yoga supporting all beings,
And yet not dwelling in them,
I am myself, the efficient cause of all beings. 9.5

'Not dwelling in them, I am myself,' says the Lord. The dreamer supports the dream. Still he himself is outside it without being affected by it.

Spiritual Masters have given various names to this Reality when they came into contact with it. Sri Adhi Shankara called it Brahman; Sri Ramana, Self; Sri Ramakrishna, the Divine Mother; Plotinus, the One; Lao Tse, Tao. For the Buddhists, it is Shunyata (Emptiness). Any word will do, as all are going to be insufficient, as those masters themselves knew.

He is incommunicable, unthinkable, and unnameable.
Mandukya Upanishad (Verse 7)

This Reality is the screen, the substratum on which all the dramas of the world unfold. In Dyaana, we get an occasional taste of it and stabilise ourselves more and more in it. In Para-Bakthi, that takes over and we live as part of it. In Jnaana *we become it!*

This Ultimate Reality is not about knowing some esoteric 'up there' thing. Realising our Self, we realise God.

I am the Self abiding in the heart of all beings. 10.20

The Gita already told us. The corollary to this: self-realisation is not just the realisation of the Self in us. When we come to realise the Self within, we also simultaneously come to know and become one with the one Self of the universe. Both are one and the same.

The Self is immanent as well as transcendent reality. 13.15

This knowledge of the Self and the world is, in the Gita's terms, the greatest secret, the most profound knowledge and the supreme purifier. When realised through experience, it promises that,

You shall be freed from all sorrows of life. 9.1

This is the culmination that the Gita was preparing us for all the way. It insists we live from this Reality because, after all, *we are that*. As the *Maha-Vakya*, the grand pronouncement, of the Upanishad declares, *Tat Tvam Asi*. Thou Art That.

This realisation of the Self is too magnificent an experience to be expressed in anyway. It is beyond words. To even say, 'I experienced it,' like one can with Para-Bakthi, is misleading. That is because, like a body of water merging in the ocean, the one who experiences it vanishes in the experience.

It is the experience of Advaita, the absolute non-dual state. There is no experiencer left in the experience. That is why the Buddhists say the final stage is the 'no-self' experience. Just the Divine with nothing outside it! Just one pure awareness, I AM ness, the only I of the universe is what remains.

> That which is comprehended not by mind,
> But by which mind is comprehended,
> know that alone to be the Brahman,
> Not this which people worship here.
> Kena Upanishad I.5

Cremating a person on the Manikarnika Ghat of the river Ganga, where the river takes a sharp turn, confers *moksha* or salvation on the soul, goes a popular Hindu belief. When we too can turn our consciousness around and take a look within, that turning is the Manikarnika Ghat within us. When we can offer our ego unrestrainedly to this inner light through shravana, manana and nidityasana, we realise our True Self and attain that moksha right here.

☙

THE SELF AND THE WORLD

Many sublime verses spread throughout the Gita, especially in its seventh, ninth and thirteenth chapters, describe the relation between this Divine Reality and the world, on how this Reality is woven into the world and manifested in it. If Jnaana is getting to know the One Self at the base of the world, this knowledge of *manifest Divinity*, the Gita calls *Vijnaana*. Vijnaana completes Jnaana. When one arrives at both, one's wisdom is perfect.

'A jnaani is like one who knows beyond a doubt that a log of wood contains fire. But a vijnaani is he who lights the log, cooks over the fire, and is nourished by the food,' explains Sri Ramakrishna.[7]

> I shall explain to you in full, this knowledge (Jnaana)
> Along with the knowledge of manifest Divinity (Vijnaana)
> Having known this nothing more remains to be known. 7.2

Lot of 'I am' statements our Big Boss is going to make here. All those are not a separate God out there speaking about his glory to us; *these are the words of our True Self at the core of our being.* To quote Swami Vivekananda, 'Krishna spoke the Gita, establishing Himself in the Atman. Those passages of the Gita where He speaks with the word 'I,' invariably indicate the Atman. This knowledge of the Atman is the highest aim of the Gita.'[8]

With that introduction, we shall now start reading the Lord's words.

> **I am the sapidity in the water,**
> **and the radiance in the sun and the moon...**
> **I am the manhood in men. 7.8**
>
> **I am the heat in the fire, the life in all living beings. 7.9**
>
> **I am the intelligence of the intelligent,**
> **the brilliance of the brilliant. 7.10**

The clay from earth is what a pot is made of. The clay, without having become the pot, can't hold water. And the pot can't exist at all without the clay. In the same way, it is the one power of the universe that expresses itself as the sun and the moon and water and fire, and as all the various powers in nature and also in men.

> **I am the strength of the strong, devoid of lust and attachment.**
> **7.11**

When lust and attachment enter into the house, the human forgets his divine nature.

> **Know that the three gunas, sattwa, rajas and tamas**
> **emanate from me. 7.12**
>
> **I am the supporter of the universe,**
> **the father, the mother, and the grandfather. 9.17**

Grandfather? He is called grandfather because the creative principle Brahma has come forth from him.

> **I am the object of knowledge, the purifier,**
> **The sacred syllable Om,**
> **And also the Rig, the Yajur, and the Sama Vedas. 9.17**

> I am the goal, supporter, lord, witness, abode, refuge, friend,
> Origin, dissolution, foundation,
> Substratum and the imperishable seed. 9.18

As 'earthen wares are made of clay, remain in clay and at last merge into clay' in Swami Ramsukhdas's words.[9] It is from him we originate. It is in him we all live. And it is into him we finally merge.

> I give heat, I send forth the rain.
> I am immortality as well as death, O Arjuna. 9.19

As Swami Vivekananda put it, 'When nature shines, upon what depends the shining? Upon God and not upon the sun.... He is the colouring in the wings of the butterfly, and the blossoming of the rose-bud. Out of His fire comes life, and the direst death is also His power.'[10]

> There is nothing whatsoever higher than me.
> All creation is strung on me
> like jewels on a thread of necklace. 7.7

It is to signify this that the outer symbol of a sacred thread is worn. To summarise,

> When one perceives the diverse variety of beings
> Resting in the one and spreading out from that alone,
> Then one attains Brahman. 13.30

> O Arjuna, just as one sun illuminates this entire world,
> The creator illumines the entire creation. 13.33

☙

Though all that wisdom might sound too lofty at first read, the truth is indeed quite simple. In the Chandogya Upanishad (6.12.1–3) a self-realised Rishi teaches his son Svethaketu, this essential knowledge about the universe in this amusing way:

'Bring me a fruit of that banyan tree,' he tells his son.
'Here it is, Sir.'
'Break it,' he orders.
'It is broken, Sir.'
'What do you see there?'

'The seeds, exceedingly small.'
'Break one of those, my son.'
'It is broken, Sir.'
'What do you see there?'
'Nothing at all, Sir.'

The Rishi tells his son finally, 'That subtle essence my dear, which you do not perceive there – in that is the whole of this great banyan tree. And believe me my son, in that have all things their existence. That is the Self, Svethakethu. Thou Art That.'

༺

When I took my usual break in between preparation, in this chapter alone I saw myself caught in some strange sublime inner state. Even driving to the clinic took almost twenty minutes compared to the usual ten.

Sandy's brother Saravana was waiting for me when I entered the OP room that day.

'Thanks, Anna, for all your help,' he started the conversation.

'Hey, what happened?'

'Father and I are leaving Tuticorin and moving to Chennai. I have got a job there in a software concern.'

'Oh, is it? That is great, Saravana. Congrats. I am very happy for you. So, Sandy will stay alone here, then?'

He smiled wryly as I said that. He must have come to know that we are not on talking terms.

'If he were a child, my father would have thrashed him and brought him to his senses,' he said. 'What can we do at all, Anna, now that he is twenty-eight?'

Saying that, he let out a deep sigh looking away from me. I was looking neutrally at him, as there was a moment of brief silence.

'Appa had high fever last week. Lab tests diagnosed it to be malaria. He asked me not to tell Sandy, and consulted Dr Prakash, the one opposite your clinic. He gave drugs and tests that cost some 4,000 rupees. When Sandy heard the news and came to see him, Appa turned his face away and didn't speak to him. He set aside the drugs Sandy brought.

'No use fighting with his ways anymore, Anna. Sandy has become someone else. We came to know what he did in Mars Hospital. And Kumar Anna told me what happened between you two. What you did was right. No use, Anna, no use trying anything with that guy hereafter. He knows that we are going to leave in a week. And still all he does after coming home from his bar is to sit, smoke and watch TV in his newly air-conditioned room. Let his life go where he wants for it to. Father has asked us not to share our Chennai address with him.'

Saravana bid goodbye and left in some time saying, 'Do give us a call when you come to Chennai, Anna.'

'Sure, Saravana.'

I wondered what was going to happen to Sandy once his family left. He had brought much disgrace to everyone connected to him. I had turned down two references in Mars Hospital last week, not wanting to face the two girls there. Now his family too is leaving him. I wondered what was going to change him now.

Like passing clouds, our school days crossed my memory . . .

'Hey what's that bandage on your leg?' I asked Santosh, looking at the gauze tied above his right ankle. He was walking with a minor limp too, holding Kumar's shoulders for support. It was New Year time and we were all returning to school from our half-yearly holidays.

'Oh that? Nothing. Got hit by the bat during a match.'

'Don't lie. Let me guess. . . . When I was away, you took part in that stupid Green Sanskriti project of our headmaster during our vacation, right?'

He looked away from me with a sly smile. I learnt from Kumar that Sandy had come to school during the holidays and taken care of the plants newly planted in the school premises, as our headmaster had requested students to do. He injured his legs when digging the sand with the shovel.

'Hmm, so despite my warning to not help our HM, you went? Don't you see that it's all to save on paid labour?'

'Oh, come on, Piggy,' said Santosh, 'See that neem sapling over there under my maintenance. How nice it feels you know, to do something like this instead of just spending our time playing! Stupid Piggy!'

He ran away limping, while Kumar grabbed me to stop me from chasing him.

ॐ

I leaned back on my chair, closing my eyes. A pang of remorse shot through me as I mused about the part my thoughtless actions had played in his life. Had those things not happened, he might have been an altogether different person now.

I looked at the Gita on my table. With the serene smile etched on his face, Lord Krishna seemed to be looking at me in a reassuring way.

'Dear God, I give up on this.'

Closing my eyes, I prayed in all sincerity that day. 'All my attempts at appealing to his goodness through your words and redeeming myself have failed. Other than praying to you, I don't know what to do. Do something God, do something.'

It pained me to see where Santosh was heading.

ॐ

'After a long haul in Pisces, Sani Bhagavan is finally moving to the male fixed sign of Aries. Dramatic changes await you in the next months,' the astrology section of the newspaper declared under my zodiac sign. Almost all the signs had a similar tagline, 'Dramatic changes await you.'

'So Sani Bhagavan, it was you who made me accept marriage, huh,' I mused.

My mom served morning coffee with a happy face for a change, as father and I were seated in the drawing hall. Father was looking through the long list he had in his hands. It was something to do with the wedding, I supposed.

'What Venki? You were refusing marriage so sternly, and now this! What happened suddenly?' my mother asked me, a mocking smile etched on her face.

'Anything for my Mom!'

'Uh...hmm? That doesn't seem like a plausible reason. You know what? I knew you would agree soon. You had no other choice, da,' she grinned.

'I had no other choice!'

Dad gave me the list in his hands he was reading so far. 'PARAMAHAMSA NITHYA SRI SRI DATTU BABA'S SATYA KENDRA' – it was printed on top in glossy orange and green. It was the letter pad of Dattu's organisation.

'Coconuts, ghee, almonds, three cushioned chairs, two air-coolers...' the list went on. It was a few pages long.

'What is this?' I asked Dad.

'These are the requirements her Swamiji has given us for the puja. He is going to conduct that on your marriage,' Dad said removing his glasses.

'Your mother said it was only after she promised to do this special puja her Swamiji had insisted on, that you agreed to marriage. Otherwise you wouldn't have.'

Saying so, he revealed the total budget of the puja, from the middle of the last page. I, whose mouth had already fallen open, felt dizzy when I saw the amount printed on that page.

ॐ

Reaching my clinic, I sat down on the chair and took a few deep breaths. I contemplated on all that was happening around me.

There is a verse in the Gita,

> All beings follow their nature.
> Even the wise act according to their own nature.
> What can repression accomplish? 3.34

How true it is! People will always be people; flawed and unpredictable. Why blame them and feel exasperated? Let them all travel in the direction their vasanas take them. They will turn around when they have plumbed the depths, found the bottom and seen for themselves where their ways have led them, as Sri Aurobindo tells us. Let my peace and dependence be on what I can do alone; my duty, and nothing outside that.

'Shall I send the patient in, Sir?' the attender asked, opening the cabin door.

'Yes, please do,' I replied.

ॐ

To return to the Gita, when we first come across this sublime wisdom of Advaita that the Gita puts forward, certain questions are bound to arise inevitably. 'If Advaita is the final truth, what happens to all the forms and images of God we worship?' one might ask.

Advaita doesn't negate the dualistic relation between man and god. The great Carnatic music maestro Sri Muthuswami Dikshitar was an Advaitin whose chosen deity was Lord Muruga. Sri Ramakrishna too was an Advaitin whose chosen deity was the Divine Mother Kaali. Advaita is simply the fulfilment of dualism.

All the external images and symbols we use to worship the Divine represent a particular aspect of the Divine Self. They exist only to give us a hold to keep our mind focused, until we experience true oneness with the Divine. When that purpose is served, all idols, statues and forms of God are finally to be dissolved in the great formless Cosmic Sea of Existence!

A student asks a self-realised Rishi in the Maitri Upanishad on which form of God to meditate, the Rishi answers the question this way,

> Brahma, Rudra, Vishnu –
> some meditate upon one, some upon another.

The Rishi then goes on to make a profound and rather intriguing statement,

> These foremost forms let one meditate upon,
> praise, and then deny
> as one moves to deeper understanding.
> In that final universal dissolution
> He attains unity with the Divine.
> Maitri Upanishad 4.5–6

ॐ

People who have excessive stress in their lives may wonder, 'Anyway it is all an illusion. Why worry about acting, purifying ourselves, realising

God and all such spiritual drudgery? Why not sit idle and just shrug it all off?' Arjuna had a similar doubt initially.

> If you consider that (this) Jnaana is higher than works
> Then why do you want me to engage in this war, O Krishna.
> You seem to confuse me by apparently conflicting words. 3.1

In reply, Krishna makes this categorical statement to Arjuna,

> One does not attain freedom from the bondage of karma
> By merely abstaining from work.
> Nor by renunciation alone can one attain perfection. 3.4

Advaita is about arriving at the realm of peace and stillness at the other end of action. Shunning and withdrawing from the world can at best lead us to obesity; not the realisation of our divinity. It is through right performance of our actions do we gradually disentangle ourselves from the ties of the world and progress to the next stage in this game. However, knowing these Advaitic truths beforehand can give us the perspective to play the game better.

Minds coming across Advaita can get caught in all those traps quite easily and can stay stuck there without progress for ages. Hence the Advaita philosophy is not overtly preached to everyone. '(Advaita) is too abstruse, too elevated to be the religion of the masses,' warned Swami Vivekananda.

ॐ

Another question that might arise in our mind: 'Doesn't advaita make human love meaningless?'

'Individuality is just an illusion we are holding onto!' Advaita tells us. Won't that philosophy make the love you have towards your mother, your lover or your child, illusive and hollow? They are all just a bundle of vasanas and gunas standing upon a false sense of individuality, and they have no real existence it seems to tell us.

It seems so. And the people who misunderstand Advaita sometimes use this philosophy to coldly shun all worldly relations as illusive, stating the above logic.

However, when we give it a considered thought, we would come to see that Advaita doesn't negate genuine human relationships. It indeed takes human love to its highest fulfilment. It says your mother, your lover or your child are not separate beings at all, but are ever one with you – totally, inseparably. There is no two-ness. It is one soul that is playing a game with itself by becoming two separate souls. By becoming seven billion separate souls!

ॐ

Shelley, the English poet of Romanticism writes in one of his poems, 'Of suns, and worlds, and men, and beasts, and flowers... is but a vision... bubbles and dreams. The Future and the Past are idle shadows of thought's eternal flight – they have no being. Nought is, but that which feels itself to be.'

'That which feels itself to be' is the truth. Everything else – the sun, the worlds, past, future – are just dreams. He saw in his most sublime moments, a reality that was timeless, unchanging and perfect, of which our physical world was but a broken reflection.

The Christian non-dual work *A Course in Miracles* tells us, 'Nothing real can be threatened. Nothing unreal exists. Herein lies the peace of God.'

The words of Jalaludeen Rumi go, 'The lamps are different, but the Light is the same. It comes from Beyond. If thou keep looking at the lamp, thou art lost, for thence arises the appearance of number and plurality. Fix thy gaze upon the Light, and thou art divested from the dualism inherent in the finite body.'[11]

The magnificence of Advaitic realisation transcends all religions and sects. As Rumi put it, 'I am neither Christian, nor Jew... nor Muslim. I am not of the East, nor the West, nor the land, nor the sea... I have put duality away, I have seen that the two worlds are one; One I seek, One I know, One I see, One I call.'[12]

When you have become God, what do you care what label people give you?

Swami Vivekananda sums it all up for us this way, 'Thus man, after this vain search after various Gods outside himself, completes the circle, and comes back to the point from which he started — the human soul, and he finds that the God whom he was searching in hill and dale... in every temple, in churches and heavens, is his own Self. I am He, and He is I. None but I was God, and this little I never existed.'[13]

ॐ

PLAY O HERO

So then, where are we now at the end of it all? The world is an illusion. Space and time don't exist. You and I are just the figures in the great cosmic dream. Great. What happens when we arrive at this grand realisation? Does our journey end there?

Here comes a twist in the tale. Self-realisation isn't the end of the story, but a new beginning to the exciting next episode. A self-realised person becomes even more sincere towards his duties in the world!

How come?

The Gita told us that as one attains Jnaana, he also attains Vijnaana, knowledge of how the Divine is manifested in the world. The essence of Vijnaana is this: **All this world is God**. In the Gita's words, *Vasudevah Sarvam Iti*.

Life is a reflection, a mirage. True, but it is a divine reflection and mirage. It is an illusion with a purpose and whose laws are to be obeyed as long as we are within it. In order to illustrate this, Sri Krishna said

I am both the real and the unreal, O Arjuna. 9.19

Though you have seen through the reflection, though you know in your bones that it is an illusion, you respect it still; for it is a divine illusion. It is with a purpose it was created.

Our spiritual journey has to progress that way always. Only after we come to realise the divine self at our core can we come back to the world, see it all as divine and start acting in it from that foundation. 'Without knowing Brahman, how will you find his all-pervasiveness?' asks Sri Ramana. 'To say the world is God, don't we have to know God first?'[14]

In the Ramayana, Guru Sri Vashista shared these great truths of Existence with the young Rama. He said,

> 'You have known the Truth which is at the heart of all kinds of appearances. Without ever turning away from that Reality, released from all bonds of attachment and with equanimity of mind, Play in the world, O Hero, as if in love with it.'

That is what we too would do. We would continue acting along our Swabhava and do our Dharma as a Yajna. We would take up our work with even greater zeal and with a fresh spirit of freedom, an universal perspective lighting up our mind. 'Life and its works not only remain still acceptable,' Sri Aurobindo tells us, 'but reach up and out to their widest spiritual completeness and assume a grand ascending significance.'[15] 'The Eternal is fulfilled in the individual spirit and individual nature; the individual spirit is exalted from birth in time to the infinitudes of the Eternal.'[16]

Karma Yoga continues, but no longer as a *means* to God realisation. One continues to work respecting the world, which is a realm of action. One's actions are not motivated by anticipated results, or the love of the process even. Like the eyes see, and the ears hear, you let your ego do its job. The ego *'egos,'* as a philosopher put it. Like a flower expressing its inner fragrance, your work stands as a natural expression of your inner attainment. That is the pinnacle of Karma Yoga.

A Zen monk expresses this in a rather cheeky way, 'Before enlightenment chop wood, carry water. After enlightenment chop wood, carry water.'

The Gita places special emphasis on this final aspect: *You should act.*

> **For the one who is content in the Self, satisfied in the Self,**
> **And who is pleased only in the Self,**
> **For him there is no further work to be done. 3.17**

> **For him there is nothing more to gain**
> **by his acting (in the world),**
> **Nor does he lose anything if he doesn't act.**
> **He has no need to depend for any reason**
> **on anything (outside). 3.18**

Even without possessing any stuff on the outside which people think they need for happiness, such a person remains on the summit of bliss. Having completed the full circle, a self-realised person has no 'need' to act.

> **Yet he should continue to act, O Bharatha.**
> **As the ignorant man acts from attachment to action,**
> **So should the wise man act without attachment**
> **Wishing the welfare of the world. 3.25**

> **Because whatever (such) a great man does,**
> **The other men emulate.**
> **Whatever he sets up as the standard,**
> **that the world follows. 3.21**

That is the reason why the spiritually mature among us should be all the more sincere in our actions. The world longs for clarity. Look around yourself. Look at the daily news in TV channels and newspapers. Why do you think there is so much violence and brutality, so much noise and confusion in the world? Aren't all those just the external forms taken by this perpetual unrest in the core of man?

'All struggles and competitions in animal life, plant life, and everywhere else, all social struggles and wars are but expressions of that eternal struggle to get back to that equilibrium,' said Swami Vivekananda.[17]

Just like the body needs food, man's heart longs for truth. It wilts when it can't find it. When you have realised it, it behoves you to show through your life and your actions, the right way to live and act in the world.

> **Let no wise man unsettle the minds of ignorant people**
> **attached to the fruits of action.**
> **He should inspire them**
> **by himself performing all works with devotion. 3.26**

So continue doing your duty with composure and perspective. The peace and wisdom at the core of your being that percolates into your actions, your job and your creations are bound to touch and inspire another's being. Your actions would speak to and awaken a deeper and dormant part in them. All said and done, it is your inner being that has the power to touch another's inner being.

In the words of American mythologist Joseph Campbell, 'Preachers err by trying to talk people into belief; better they reveal the radiance of their own discovery.'

This is how a self-realised being would keep acting in the world. His inner being is like a flower whose roots are in Eternity. Having centred his being in his Cosmic Self, he would happily keep sacrificing his little self with all its possessions for the good of the world – like Lord Ganesha broke his very tusk to help write the scripture that would guide humanity.

How long shall this continue? Well, till the momentum of our old karmas takes our life. When its time comes, the flower heartily gives itself into the hands of Existence to be absorbed into the soil of time, and to be reconstituted for the next season. A self-realised man's life is thus an unending yajna he performs to heaven and earth.

JNAANI

What would it be like to take on the world rooted deeply in our True Cosmic Self? How different will such a self-realised person be from us?

I wanted to find the answer to those questions as I finished the chapter on Jnaana. Arjuna puts forward the same questions to Krishna in the Gita,

> **O Kesava, what is the mark of a person**
> **Whose inner being is stabilised in wisdom?**
> **How does he speak, sit and walk? 2.54**

That is, how does such a person act in the world? What is his demeanour? In answer, the Gita paints a detailed picture of such a self-realised person. That is the topic we will take up in this chapter.

○○

Life has the habit of making certain things happen at exactly the right time. Whether we call it coincidence or divine intervention, these just happen. It happened in that teenager Muthu's life, and in Saradha's life. And now I saw it happen in Santosh's life. I had prayed to God some time back to make him self-aware of his immoral ways. God did help by making him face a crash, but not in the way I had expected.

It was the month of August. Incidentally the day was Gokulashtami, the day of Lord Krishna's birth.

I saw off the few evening patients waiting in the OP room, and started reading the final draft of the write-up that lay on the table. For me, all the work I had done in the past year was undoubtedly a tremendously illuminating experience. Next, I had started working on making a gist of it to so it could be used as an annexure to the school magazine. Finally I was on the verge of fulfilling the promise I had made in my heart long back to Barath Sir.

The Santosh of our school days crossed my mind. I felt sorry for his father and Saravana. I looked at the date. It was the weekend they were about to leave Tuticorin.

The door screeched open and the attender came in. 'A staff-nurse is waiting outside to see you, Sir,' he said.

I called her in.

It was Sister Indhra from Mars hospital, Manisha's friend.

'Good evening, Sir. Where is Dr Santosh? His clinic is closed,' she enquired as she came in.

'Closed? I don't know. Why? Any problem, Sister?' I asked, wondering what the fellow had done now.

'No, Sir . . . Santosh Sir has solved every problem himself,' she said and took a letter out of her shoulder-bag and handed it to me to read.

I opened it intrigued. *'Dear Manisha,'* the letter started in Sandy's messy handwriting.

> *'As I write these words, the dreary hot spell our town went through this summer has just come to an end. Along with our town, what has undergone a sea change is your doctor's heart too.*
> *How wonderful of you to have such respect and reverence for this field of medicine, Manisha! It is you who should have been a doctor, not me.*
> *However, is being a staff nurse any less a profession than that? The doctor always prescribes, speaks a few words to the patient and goes off. It is you who spend time with the patient, who take personal care of him/her and help in a patient's recovery even more than we do. If the joy of medicine is about helping a co-human heal, it is you sisters who experience that joy thoroughly.*
> *In that way you'll make a wonderful nurse. Shift the respect you have for doctors like me, towards the field. We doctors are flawed human beings, just like everyone else, who have acquired some knowledge in medicine.*
> *Enough of you being fooled by me! Let me confess here . . . the intentions I had while hanging out with you had been dishonourable from the beginning. I feel embarrassed, in fact, terrible and disgusted, thinking about it now. However, I can't change the past. All I can do now is this, convey my heartfelt apology.*

Sorry, Manisha for what I had been, for trying to use in bad ways the respect you have for my profession. I shall from now on try to be at least half as worthy of the respect you had for me.

Thanks for giving me this gift. I wish you a future of contribution and real happiness.

Sincerely,
Santosh.'

Well, I was startled and my eyes were almost wet reading it. *'My goodness! The old sentimental psycho I know is back.'*

This is what I had been searching for, for a long time. How come the fellow changed so suddenly? What happened during the past month?

'I don't know where he is sister, but . . . but thanks for bringing me this letter. You don't know how happy it has made me. I will inform you once I find him. How is Manisha?' I was stumbling over the words.

'Well, she was totally upset already but still was holding on to some hope about Santosh Sir. Now she is devastated. How else will she be? Poor creature. But it is okay, Sir. I'll console her. It's far better to face the truth than hold onto some lie that is sweet and reassuring.' Saying so, she left.

I took my phone and speed-dialled Sandy's number immediately. His phone was switched off. I tried his number several times that day, but to no avail. His clinic was closed the next morning too. *'Where have you gone Sandy?'*

I went to his house after the morning OP Saravana said to me he had left the house two days ago. And Santosh had told him when leaving, that he would be back in a few days.

'Santosh was very quiet the previous day, Anna,' Saravana said. 'He didn't sleep in his new air-conditioned bedroom, but came and lay down with me and dad in the verandah. On the morning he left, he took his old cycle and went to your school. I asked him what happened. He didn't reply. Any problem in his clinic, anna?'

' . . .'

'Anna'

'Mmm? I have no idea, Saravana.'

'O Santosh! You went to our school again? What happened to you suddenly? Where are you now?'

ॐ

'So, how's your father? Is he alright?' I asked Saradha. She had called me that evening to discuss about the skin exfoliation patient she had referred.

'Ah, don't bother. He gets upset. Then in a couple of days he forgets about whatever is bothering him, and becomes normal. Funny old man!'

'How is Muthu doing?'

'Muthu? Well, as usual, in his own inner world... not bothered about things,' she said.

I told her next that Sandy had gone missing for a few days.

'Is it?'

'I am a bit concerned about what happened to him, Saradha. He is such a... person, you know.'

Saradha thought for a moment, and then said in reply, 'Don't worry, Venki. I remember how he used to be in college days – a loner and a sort of oddball with regular boozing habits. I have seen the photos of all his antics too in the tour photos you had put up online. But you know what? Despite all that, I have always felt he has a good core in him untouched by it all. Don't worry. Nothing would have happened to him. He will come back soon.'

Oh, the photos I put up on the net have become so famous? Hope the nasty comments below the pictures, about all that he was doing in his practice didn't catch her eyes.

It was then something struck me. *'Could it be that?'*

I drove straight to Santosh's house after the OP.

'What, anna? You heard from him?' Saravana asked as he opened the gate. He looked a bit anxious.

'Not yet, Saravana. Is his room open?'

'Yes, anna.'

'Let me ask you something,' I said, as we opened the

door and entered his bedroom. 'You know how to hack into an e-mail account?'

'Hack his account? Anna . . . '

'Come on Saravana,' I said sitting before Sandy's system and removing its dust cover, 'If we have to find out where he has gone, I see this as our only chance. And Sandy has told me about your skill in computers. Aren't you a PhD holder in computer science?'

'Well, we don't exactly learn these things in PhD. But no problem, I can do it.'

After much struggle, we opened his inbox.

There, finally, we got an answer to our query.

It was Gayatri! Our school-time buddy and Sandy's only true love interest. The girl who was forced into marrying an NRI more than a decade back, and was sent to UK. Her mail to him lay in his inbox below a dozen unread ones.

'Should we read it, anna?'

'Saravana, our interest is not in what is in that email. We have to find where our Santosh is. That mail can give us a clue. Come on, open it.'

Saravana moved the cursor and clicked on the name Gayatri in Sandy's inbox. The mail opened over Sandy's customised background theme.

'Hi Santosh,

Gayu here. Your old batchmate in school. Remember? Well, that question is superfluous, I know in my heart. Santosh, I am seeing and hearing things about you which are very unlike you. I therefore felt I should communicate and share a few things with you.
Let me bring you up to date about my life first. I now work as an accountant in a trading concern here in London. I am well-settled now. (Six digit monthly income, imagine!) I have two children, Saran and Chandini. Both are with me now. Yes, I got divorced few years ago. The Sri Rama my father got me married to turned out to be a Raavana! There was another woman in his life, and even during

the brief period I was with him, I was only abused and tortured physically and emotionally.

Ah, let me not go into those things. Too painful for a rehash, and useless too! I have no plans to remarry either. I have crossed that stage. Both my children are quite grown up.

I need to tell you something Santosh. When I got divorced a few years ago, the whole world, especially all the men in it appeared so evil to me. Be it my father, my husband or the people I happened to meet through him, all were just unbearable, to say the least. My father should have enquired well instead of doing things in haste. But leave all that aside! I have started to believe that there is a predestined way for things to happen.

As I came out to face the world by myself, a BCom degree was all I had – which I had done in correspondence after marriage! And I had two children with me. I had no interest in going to court and all that. I didn't want to go back home either. I had nothing with me . . . the resources, strength or willingness to carry on with life.

Many of my school friends had just finished their engineering degree and got posted in good companies. But here I was, out of a bad marriage, in a strange land, with two kids. I wondered if I should carry on at all. It was such a gloomy period! The patriarchal world before me seemed dreadful. But you know what gave me the strength at those times? It was you, Santosh. Your memories!

The consideration you have always shown for others, you going out of your way to help people in need, your honest core – a simple plagiarism in an inconsequential project giving you sleepless nights, the whole attitude you had towards life at that young age. . . . I trained my then-pessimistic mind to keep all those in the forefront. I kept constantly contemplating only that. The faith in God and in life I had acquired as a child too helped. But more than that, it was you who helped me a lot at those times, Santosh. . . . Your presence I felt in my heart! Maybe it is God who comes like that in each of our lives.

And you know what? I got through it! I got through such a tough time of life. I owe a big, belated thanks to you for that.

As per the belief I trained myself in, I met many good men at my new job. After all, not all the world is bad. It is only that the bad things make more noise, I think. What is the use in focussing our mind on that?

I saw in my new office that there are people in the world who take the path of morality and goodness despite all odds; people who value love and honesty more than material things. Santosh, there are people like you all over the world. Not a day passes without me thinking of you with gratitude, you know.

You have become a renowned doctor now, huh? Very happy to hear it. God has given a wonderful talent to the right person. Use it well, Santosh. Let people be happy that you are there for them.

All the best for your career, Doctor Sir! I shall pray that you get a princess soon as your bride. Will meet you and your wife when I come to India sometime.

Take care,

Bye,
Gayatri'

As I reached those final words in that mail I was startled, to say the least. I closed my eyes for some time. *'Dear Big Boss, you have heard me, huh?'*

Our school days . . . Gayatri and Santosh in their uniforms . . . all their long chats on the bus and on the way back from tuitions . . . with me walking a few feet behind them munching on peas, feeling a tinge of jealousy, so much wafted into my mind. What I had been struggling to do over a long period of time, was done in one stroke thanks to Gayatri's email.

I looked at Saravana. He had tears in his eyes.

I finished my dinner and lay down in the bed that night. I felt light and relieved thinking of Santosh. I even felt a bit funny about myself! Though I was introducing him to the Gita, inwardly I was only fighting with the darkness in him, with all his faults and shortcomings. It was those things that I was trying to set right. But Gayatri had seen the light in him. And through her words and conviction she had given strength to that light. This brushed away all the darkness in him; the darkness I had been condemning, cursing and fighting with all these years. I thanked God in my heart.

> **Divine qualities lead to nirvana,**
> **The demonic (qualities) are said to be for bondage.**
> **Do not grieve, O Arjuna. You are born with divine qualities. 16.5**

Krishna consoles the grieving Arjuna with the above words in the Gita. Sandy too is one such soul, it dawned on me. Behind all his skewed opinions of the world, I saw for the first time a willingness to live well and do good for people; a genuine concern for the world. It struck me then that it was that, that had gone awry in him. But this man has divine qualities in him. It can never be cast adrift permanently, even if he tilts grossly to his demonic side. Maybe that is the truth about every soul on earth?

I lay on the bed embraced by a blissful serenity that night. I slept peacefully after a long time.

ॐ

THE JIVAN MUKTHA

There are many teachers who teach the Gita and help remove the darkness in our hearts. What if there is one who – like Gayatri saw in Santosh – sees the untainted truth in us? One who sees us not as puny egos imprisoned inside the mind, but as Pristine, Eternal souls never touched by worldly dirt? What effect would such a person have on us?

A Jivan Muktha, the man who has realised his Self and attained mukthi even while in the body, is one such being. It is such a self-realised person that Vedanta refers to as Guru.

Kabir eulogised Gurus in one of his verses the following way, 'If all the land were turned to paper, all the seas turned to ink, all the forests into pens to write with, they would still not suffice to describe the greatness of the Guru.'

In our country's spiritual tradition, great importance is given to the Guru, a Jivan muktha. The Gita says of the self-realised person and his role in the aspirant's life,

> All actions in their entirety culminate in Jnaana. . . .
> Acquire this Jnaana
> by humble reverence, sincere inquiry and service.
> The wise who have realised the truth will teach you. 4.33–34

Guru is God. 'The perfect among the sages is identical with me. There is absolutely no difference between us,' proclaimed the Divine in the Advaitic scripture *Tripura Rahasya*.

And the words of a Guru are scriptures itself. One look, one word from him is enough for an earnest soul to experience the truth within itself. Even the silence of a Guru is eloquent.

'There is nothing higher and holier than the knowledge which comes to the soul transmitted by a spiritual teacher,' said Swami Vivekananda. He stresses on the significance of a guru this way, 'You may go and knock your head against the four corners of the world, seek in the Himalayas, or the bottom of the sea, but it will not come until you find a teacher. Find the teacher . . . open your heart to his influence, see in him God manifested. . . . As the power of attention concentrates there, the picture of the teacher as man will melt away; the frame will vanish, and the real God will be left there.'[1]

CR

A GURU'S INNER WORLD

What is such a man's inner being like? A *jivan muktha* is a man of utmost composure. His being is rooted in the bedrock of Ultimate Reality, in the Self.

> The man stabilised in wisdom casts aside
> All the desires and agitations of the mind
> And is contently seated in the Self. 2.55

Most men of the world live caught up in the superficialities of life. And then there are people who, amidst all those superficialities the world pulls them towards, live their lives with some depth. They are the people who live close to the essence of life. A jivan muktha is the culmination of living life in such a manner. His is the highest possible way of existence. His being is not just close to the essence of life, it is taken up by that essence! It is life that lives itself through him.

The Gita calls a jivan muktha, 'twice born' (1. 7). A self-realised man has died to his little self and is born in God. What words can capture his inner being? As Sri Adhi Shankara put it, 'One may be in the company of yogis or materialists. He may be with people, or above them. But he whose mind is always revelling in Brahman, he rejoices, rejoices and keeps rejoicing.'

We saw that being egoless is not possible till we are in our world, and that ego is necessary for performing our actions. What about the jivan muktha? Does he have an ego? A Jivan muktha does have an ego. However, his is a very mature ego, a totally different creature compared to the rigid, inflexible ego of worldly men.

Sri Ramana compares the ego of a self-realised person to the moon after sunrise. It is still there, but it is the sun that is shining through now. In Vedantic language, such an ego is like *a burnt rope*. It can't tie the jiva anymore to the world. The light of the Self has totally burnt his ego of its harmful tendencies. It exists merely as a channel for the Divine to shower his grace on the world.

In Gurus like Ramana Maharishi, the great Vaishnava saint Nammalwar or Jada Baratha of Bhagavatha, even this 'moon ego' rarely arose at all. The sun was all that shined through them, with the moon very rarely becoming apparent. A complete absorption in the divine self was ever their state. A total and eloquent silence was their being all the time. When it arises at all, a jivan muktha's ego is in a state of Para-Bakthi, an intense oneness with the Divine.

ॐ

A GURU'S LOVE

Ramana Maharishi's only teaching to his disciples was self-enquiry. 'Turn within and look who you really are,' was all he preached. Compared to sects that taught love and compassion, it seemed strange and dry to many. A visitor once wanted to know what Sri Ramana thought of the ideologies of love and compassion that many other spiritual masters taught.

'Maharishi, how are we to treat others?' the man asked the sage.

The sage calmly replied, 'There are no others!'

That is what happens when one realises the Self. A baktha sees all beings as his spiritual brethren, as children of one God. The self-realised goes a step further, he sees them as himself.

> **By this knowledge you shall behold the entire creation in your own Self, and also in me. 4.35**

When our centre is our ego, we treat others narcissistically. An ardent patriot treats all his countrymen as his brethren. When our identity has expanded to infinity, we hold the whole world in our embrace. When you self-realise, you don't feel separated or superior to people or other beings. You feel closer to them. In fact, you see them as you see your hands or feet, as part of you. Everything in the world is a manifestation of your own Self. It is not, 'You love me because you like me,' but because, 'I am part of your Self.'

> **An enlightened person, by perceiving God in all**
> **Looks at a learned person, an outcast,**
> **Even a cow, an elephant, or a dog with an equal eye. 5.18**

As light shining from the sun, a motiveless compassion shines forth from a self-realised person. It is this truth that is behind Swami Vivekananda's stirring proclamation, 'All the world is my country, the whole universe is mine, because I have clothed myself with it as my body.'[2]

What greater foundation for universal love and compassion has ever been given to man?

ॐ

A GURU'S VISION

'*Vasudevah sarvam iti* – All this world is God,' we have already read in the Gita. That is how a self-realised man sees the world. He doesn't see a physical world before him, but a world of spirit, a world soaked in divine consciousness. What appears inanimate to us, blazes with an intense and intimate aliveness to him. Matter and the phenomenal world appear only as a faint shadow in this vision. The Gita describes this vision in a beautiful metaphorical language,

> **What is night to every being,**
> **in that the Self-mastering sage is awake.**
> **Where all beings are awake,**
> **that is the night for him who truly sees. 2.69**

What is the 'night' referred to in the verse? Not being able to see the spiritual behind the material and basking in the material plane alone! That is the 'dark night of the soul,' according to the Gita.

When we are able to perceive the spiritual behind the material, then what happens?

> **He is neither shaken in adversity**
> **nor does he hanker after pleasures.**
> **He is free from attachment, fear and anger. 2.56**

Life doesn't appear grim or serious to him anymore. He is like an actor who loves his role in the illusive play with all its twists and turns; knowing that the perfect writer has written the script.

> **This is the Brahmic state. Attaining this, none is deluded.**
> **Being established in it even at the end of life,**
> **One attains to oneness with Brahman. 2.72**

ॐ

HIS ACTIONS

When he acts, there is no personal will directing his actions. He steps out and lets the universe unfold its plans through him. He knows that the potential given to him will be adapted to the result decreed.

> **All these (men) have already been slain by me.**
> **Be merely an apparent cause, O Arjuna 11.33**

said Krishna exhorting Arjuna to participate in war. A Jivan muktha's will is not his personal will, but the drive of the divine Sakthi in him towards a preconceived aim. He doesn't create, just conveys. Like a leaf floating through air, he lets the wind take him where it would.

> I continually support the entire universe
> By a small fraction of my energy. 10.42

says the Lord. The Self-realised man too operates the same way.

To put it even more clearly, a Jivan muktha doesn't act at all! He reaches what the Gita calls the *Nishkarmya sthithi*, the state of inner 'actionlessness' even amidst action.

> The person whose mind is always free from attachment,
> Who has subdued the mind and senses,
> and who is free from desires,
> Attains the supreme state of inaction in action. 18.49

That is the way a Self-realised person acts. There is not only no strain or effort, but no 'doing' at all as far he is concerned. He has let go of his identification with the body and mind, and calmly abides in the Self.

> He who recognises (such) inaction in action
> And action in inaction, he is wise among men.
> He is a Yogi and a true performer of all actions. 4.18

When our actions are performed as an Yajna for the world in such a way, then

> Brahman is the oblation. Brahman is the clarified butter.
> The oblation is poured by Brahman into the fire of Brahman.
> Brahman shall be realised by the one
> Who considers everything as an act of Brahman. 4.24

The verse has a direct meaning, regarding the oblative fire ceremony. But it metaphorically means, 'The action you do is Divine. The means to do it, Divine. You, the doer, are Divine. Where it is offered is the world of the Divine. All there is, is the Divine. Nothing but the Divine.'

Every single form and entity of the world, the tears and the laughter, the child snuggling close to its mother for warmth, the policeman beating up a convict, water drops falling on the roof on a rainy day, stars exploding as supernova, penguins migrating to inland for nesting, sand dunes in the desert shifting shapes – it is all the One Self dancing a duet with itself. The sound of one-hand-clapping, as the Zen Masters put it.

The Self-realised is still and lets the game unfold. Every little action of such a person demonstrates the truth of his inner being. The fragrance of his inner truth is released in every action, every word of his. His life itself is a great teaching. It is such Self-realised beings who are the real doctors of the human condition.

Self-realisation isn't the end, but the beginning of a new kind of life. We know that the karmic baggage that got us here in the first place, should be done away with. We would let the universal harmony play itself out through us. We would live our life more lightly. It would become an impersonal life. It is not you living life; but life living itself through you. From being a dreary drag life becomes a dance. And you dance without touching the ground!

> **Other people are excited; I alone don't care.**
> **Other people have a purpose; I drift like a wave on an ocean.**
> Lao Tse (Tao Te Ching. Verse 20)

The presence of such a guru towards whom we have respect and openness greatly helps our spiritual unfolding. A guru is Bhagavad Gita in flesh and bones.

ॐ

RESORT GURUS AND REAL GURUS

A pertinent question: there are so many commercial gurus in our times; gurus who seem intent on breaking our legs today, and promise us a wing tomorrow, if we follow what their organisation teaches. So, how do we identify a real guru among them?

India is a country blessed with so many Jivan mukthas. Commercialisation and popularity alone can't be the criteria to either consider or ignore a spiritual master. There really might be a true self-realised guru among them. And a guru being unknown, is no guarantee that he will be true. Then, what is the criterion?

Sri Ramana advises us, 'The world contains many great men. Look upon him as your guru with whom your mind gets attuned. The one in whom you have faith is your guru.'[3] That is the criterion; our mind becoming attuned and still!

In the *Guru Gita*, the scripture that recites the glory of a Guru, five signs of a Supreme Guru are mentioned: 'By whose mere *darshan*, one attains calmness and cheerfulness, peace and steadfastness, such a one is Param Guru.'

So learn to go by what your heart says, not what a propagator promises. And not all of us are lucky enough to find a live guru in our lifetime. However, this could be advantageous in a way. We stay away from the chance of getting attached to the physical form of the Guru – which many of the disciples were caught up in. We can ever stay in a heartfelt connection with him. Be it Krishna or Ramana or Buddha, the truth about them is not the physical form they came in, as we discussed before. Remember the words of Sri Ramana,'The real Guru is in your heart as the true Self.'

Reading about a Guru's life, contemplating on his words, even constant remembrance of him, all are ways to stay attuned with the truth that is the guru. This is the authentic bond we can develop with a Guru.

ॐ

Every time I crossed Sandy's clinic, I saw it was shut down. *'Where has the fellow gone?'* I kept wondering.

I tried calling him often. His cell phone was switched off. Just once during a Monday morning, I heard it ringing. He didn't pick it up.

Two weeks had gone by. And three months since we had that bitter quarrel. Then Sandy called me on a Saturday.

I was in the morning OP session. Arumai Selvan, that caste-obsessed guy who visited me before, had brought his wife for consultation. The cell phone in his pocket rang incessantly as I was examining his wife's skin lesions. The man too didn't mind picking it up every time and speaking in his booming voice in the middle of the consultation.

'Oh, please don't thank me. I consider it my responsibility. Any such problem you face in your constituency in the future, know that Arumai Selvan is always ready to help.'

After waiting patiently for some time, I kept the torch down and started staring at him, waiting for him to finish his call.

In a few minutes the man sensed that the room was silent except for him, saw me looking straight at him and finally said, 'Okay, I am in a clinic now. Will call you later.'

'Ah, at last!' I sighed and switched on the torch again.

It was then that I saw my phone ringing. It was Sandy!

Keeping the torch down immediately, and turning away from the patient, I picked it up and asked, 'Hey Sandy, where are you? What happened? We have been searching for....'

'Coming to Raja's?'

'Raja's canteen?' It was the place we used to go to during school times.

'Okay fine. Where did you...'

'Evening, six.'

With that terse reply, he hung up.

'What is this? Is he back from acting in some Mani Ratnam movie or what?'

He only spoke five words. But from the solemn calmness in his tone, I could feel quite strongly that the Sandy who talked to me was not the one I broke ties with, but the old Santosh I knew.

Switching on the torch, I started re-examining the middle-aged lady before me again, ignoring the ridiculing smile on that Arumai Selvan's face.

ॐ

I was approaching the canteen in my bike where Sandy had asked me to meet him. From a distance I could see him standing there waiting for me.

'Hey Sandy, what is this?' I asked as I neared him.

He had shaved his head! His eyes were sunken, and he was looking leaner since I had last met him.

'Hey, what's up, man? Shaven head, become a bit thin too...'

'Come, let us go in,' he said, paying no heed to my words.

The canteen was exactly the same as it was during our school times, including the rickety chair I was sitting on. We were waiting for our tea. Sandy hadn't yet answered any of the questions I had asked.

'Two teas, two plate bajjis,' was all that he had said.

I was looking around, trying to think of something to say. Finally, I came up with, 'Quite sultry today, huh?'

'Yeah. Too humid.'

'Too much oily the bajji is, isn't it?'
'Yes.'

We were merely exchanging formal words. I looked furtively at him now and again. He was looking at the road with a grim face.

'Maaps, you really are looking like a Tamil cinema villain, you know,' I mumbled to myself having my bajji.

ॐ

We had gone to the beach on my bike. The beach was bustling with activity – children busy building sandcastles, teenagers playing cricket and many men and women sitting on the sand in clusters and chatting.

We were walking along the shore. Sandy was munching on groundnuts; quietly watching the waves that were breaking on his legs. We had covered quite some distance walking and had arrived at a relatively calm section of the beach.

'So, you broke into my mail account, huh?' Sandy asked all of sudden, without lifting his head from the packet of groundnuts.

I looked slyly at him.

'Well, you should have told someone where you were going,' I said.

'But that's okay.'

A few more minutes of uncomfortable silence passed.

I got impatient. I gathered up some of my old candour with him and said, 'Look at the world. A friend painstakingly prepares and tells someone all these days, the wisdom of an ancient scripture. The guy brushes it all off just like that. His old love comes at last and says, "You are a good man." And voila! In one moment he is transformed altogether.'

He turned his head and gave a long, pensive look at me as I said that, and turned back to his packet of groundnuts. I wondered if I had said something inappropriate.

'What did you expect?' Sandy next asked, 'You thought your patronising advice would transform him?'

I turned and looked at him. He too looked at me. And we broke into a loud laughter. We laughed heartily for a minute.

After a long walk, we plopped ourselves down in the sand under the shade of a fishing boat.

'Okay, boss. How about going for a trip to Kumbavuruti this weekend?' Sandy asked.

'This weekend? Er . . . '

'See, I have decided, and anyway need your dad's car. Whether you come along with it is your choice.'

'Psycho!' I exclaimed, and laughed heartily again.

☙

When I dropped him at the bike-park near the canteen, a housefly came and sat on the packet of groundnuts Sandy was still holding in his hands. He was watching it curiously, without driving it off.

'What? Never seen a housefly before? Have forgotten your past to that extent, huh?'

'I have almost been like this housefly, haven't I . . . ? Feeding on crap so far!' he said still looking at it.

Well, well! This is the Sakshi bhaava that Vedanta told us about at the start.

'Don't debase the housefly like that Sandy,' I replied.

As I waved goodbye to him that night, I realised there was a wide grin etched on my face, evidence of a joy I couldn't contain.

Entering my room, the Gita caught my eyes. 'Strange are your ways, Boss!' I said looking at the picture of Lord Krishna on the cover.

☙

THE GITA'S ASSURANCE

The Gita offered us a pretty interesting path: Karma and Dyaana – Para-Bakthi – Jnaana. Aligning our active parts with the truth in us, nourishing that truth in our being, surrendering to it, attaining a oneness with that truth, and finally losing our self-identity in it totally, that the truth alone shines through us – that, in a nutshell, is the Yogic path of the Gita.

Yoga is the way of truth in our hearts. It is the path we all would take if we are true to it. With the words of the Gita, we walk it with awareness.

After knowing it all, a natural doubt could arise, 'Suppose we take this Yogic path. All begins well. But then we get distracted somehow. What happens then?'

Or in the words of our inquisitive friend, Arjuna,

> O Krishna, a man, though he has faith, is lax in his striving
> And whose mind deviates from yoga,
> and fails to attain perfection in it,
> What end does he meet?
> Does he not perish like a dispersing cloud? 6.37-38

In reply to Arjuna's question, the Gita gives some amazing reassurances for people who take the Yogic path.

> The striver in the Yogic path never comes to grief.
> There is no (permanent) fall for him
> Either here or hereafter, my friend. 6.40

Nowhere else in the Gita do we find the words of endearment Krishna uses here. Such is his loving assurance. Through those words, Krishna assures us that real shraddha in the Divine, once germinated, can never be wiped out.

> The fallen Yogi attains heaven.
> And he is reborn in the house of the pious and prosperous. 6.41

The above takes place when one's yet-unconquered materialistic impulses have made one fall. But if one has developed some dispassion in oneself, then

> Such a person is born in a family of enlightened Yogis.
> This kind of birth is indeed very difficult to obtain. 6.42

Only few people in the world are fortunate enough to obtain the company of great souls. A yogi is born in such a family of great souls in his subsequent birth, assures the Gita.

> He is instinctively carried towards Brahman
> By virtue of his past latent impressions of Yogic practice. 6.44

If we have trust in those words of the Lord, how assuredly and securely can we take the path!

For many, being 'spiritual' means a forced renouncement of worldly affairs and going in search of truth. For some it is about becoming a scholar of all the theoretical knowledge of our ancient scriptures; and for others it is performing regular elaborate rituals for god. But the Gita emphatically asserts

> **The Yogi is superior to the ascetics.**
> **The Yogi is superior to the mere scholars.**
> **The Yogi is superior to the ritualists.**
> **Therefore, O Arjuna, be a Yogi. 6.46**

Saranagathi

WORLD II

There was no interesting program on TV at 11 in the morning. I was dog-tired, so I went back to bed. The tour program we had planned for the weekend had to be put off because of the acute diarrhoea I was affected with.

Santosh's father and brother had postponed moving out of Tuticorin. Saravana had gone to Chennai to complete the joining formalities in the software firm.

As I lay down, my tired eyes kept looking at my reading table in the corner of the room.

'Bhagavad Gita! How I had once looked to escape when Barath Sir had requested us to read it! Is it true that I have come to terms with the philosophy that has guided people like Gandhi and Tilak and Emerson? And have I really finished preparing the write-up that our Sir asked us to, all my failings notwithstanding? Not bad, Venki!'

Leafing through the papers in the file in my hands, I felt a warm wave of joyous satisfaction. There was also a feeling of anticipation as I had to give the brief write-up I had prepared for our school to our headmaster. At last I had done that too.

The spiritual masters say that no human mind, even after a lifetime of study, can arrive at the full depth of understanding of the thoughts shared in the Gita. They call the Gita a fathomless ocean of wisdom. It is true that only so much of an eternal philosophy can be brought in within our mind's confines. I recognize that just one verse of the Gita discussed thoroughly with all its imports could have taken up a good part of this write-up. I have only barely touched the surface of many significant verses of the book. But at least I have gotten a good start. Now I have a lifetime to contemplate and live by them.

I remember how Sandy and I used to ask for one or two extra days every time Barath Sir gave us an assignment. 'Grace time again? Too slow, these two guys are,' he would say to the other boys. Only that the grace period has extended a little bit too long this time – extra twelve years!

But imagine! I have completed our Sir's last assignment. And when we start walking the Gita sincerely, this life of ours too could become the last assignment on our planet.

I drank the ORS solution in the bottle kept by the bed. That parotta boy Muthu from Pasumaikudi came to mind again. How can I thank him enough? But for his timely inspiration, I doubt whether I could have got through the book at all, especially the second half.

I wondered about Muthu and Saradha. Saradha had called me some time ago.

'Venkat, Is there any good pulmonologist in Tuticorin?' she asked.

'For whom, Saro?'

'Our Muthu.'

'Muthu? Why? What happened?'

'I don't know what strange connection he shares with his grove. Some businessman has bought the land adjacent to his Alangadu, it seems. Many agricultural lands here are getting converted to plots . . . the paddy field near his grove met with the same fate. They are going to build a resort on it. An old neem tree in the grove which had grown enormously, crossing the compound wall, was blocking the frontage of the resort, I believe. So he has got permission from the elders of the village in charge of the grove, and has cut it down, leaving only the stump behind. Muthu went for his Friday worship, saw the tree chopped off, and guess what? His asthma worsens.'

'Oh? . . . Strange!'

'He only inhales the forest's oxygen, it seems. And his asthma is not responding well to routine bronchodilators. That's why I thought of getting an expert opinion.'

'Well, don't worry, Saradha. Pulmonologist Abdul is a good friend of mine. I will consult him and tell you,' I reassured her before ending the call.

'A tree is cut and the boy's bronchioles get constricted? Unusual!'

'The mind can cause every disease in the body and cure it too,' Rajagopal Sir's words came to mind. Maybe there is more to the boy and his relation with the grove; something we can't comprehend with our minds. Whatever it is, everything about the boy is pretty interesting.

The phone's screen flashed again in about ten minutes' time. It was a call from Pasumaikudi.

'Vanakkam, Sir!' said the young male voice at the other end.

'Muthu, is that you? Good to hear from you. How are you?'

'Fine, Sir. How are you?'

'How am I? Well, unlike you, still wondering and wandering around a bit, I guess,' I replied, laughing.

'You know what happened over here?' he asked me.

'Yes, Saradha told me. Don't worry. Your grove will be safe and your asthma too will be alright soon. Early onset asthma usually responds well to treatment.'

'Oh, that's nothing, Sir. Madam didn't tell you about her father?'

'Father?'

Muthu went on to tell me what had happened. Saradha's father had suffered from acute chest pain two days ago. The old staff-nurse in the hospital had told Muthu that it was the early stage of a heart attack.

'Saradhamma doesn't want to bother anyone. Her father isn't willing to move out of the village and go to a hospital in the city, Sir. He keeps saying that whatever happens, he would like for it to happen within the village. He is not even eating well. I called you up thinking that you might make some good heart specialist come over here and see him.'

'Oh? Don't worry, Muthu. Everything will be alright soon.'

I was a bit confused as I put the phone down. These two people didn't even consider their problem important enough to share or seek help. Saradha tells me about his disease and he, about his Saradhamma's concerns.

I took my phone and searched for Abdul's number.

The first few papers of the write-up on my table fluttered

as I heard the ringing tone. My eyes fell on the words of Sri Adhi Shankara that I had quoted in the initial chapters.

ೲ

THE GITA – ITS BRILLIANCE, ITS IMPORTANCE

Let us take another look at those words of Sri Adhi Shankara on the Gita, 'Human beings must bathe in water every day to get rid of the dirt of the body. But bathing in the water of the Gita once is enough to get rid of the dirt of the cycle of birth and death.'

The Gita is a book that has withstood many thousand years of history. That it is highly held by the Hindus is no surprise. However, outside India too, the book is universally acknowledged by every sincere spiritual seeker as a great gift to mankind.

'(it is) one of the clearest and most comprehensive summaries of the Perennial Philosophy ever to have been made. Hence its enduring value, not only for Indians, but for all mankind,' said the English writer Aldous Huxley.[1]

Henry David Thoreau described the book this way, 'In the morning I bathe my intellect in the stupendous cosmological philosophy of the Bhagavad Gita, in comparison with which our modern world and its literature seem puny and trivial.'[2]

Several Nobel laureates, acclaimed philosophers, scientists and humanists around the world hold the book in high regard. What is it that is so great about this book and its message?

First of all, the Gita can't be considered a Hindu scripture alone. Its sublime message is universal and non-sectarian. The Gita's ultimate aim is not to assert that Lord Krishna is superior among gods or that worshipping him helps one attain enlightenment. The Gita says, 'The form in which you see God is not important. Your shraddha is what matters.' And according to it, religion's essence is not belief in an external dogma or subordination to a particular form of God, but **the realisation of our inner divinity**! What sectarianism can hold within itself such a powerful message?

Second, it stresses on making spirituality a practical affair. '(The) gospel of works which it enunciates with an emphasis and force, we do not find in other Indian Scriptures,' Sri Aurobindo pointed out.[3]

The Gita reconciles high spiritual truths with the outer life of man. It takes the lofty philosophy of the Upanishads and makes it a day-to-day and practical affair.

The third aspect is its relation to Hinduism. Hinduism is 'a mighty banyan tree with infinite ramifications' said Swami Vivekananda. The Gita, a relatively short poem of 700 verses, manages to capture the very kernel of entire Hindu thought.

The Gita takes the essence of each Yoga – Karma, Dyaana, Bakthi and Jnaana – and integrates them into one holistic path. What the Gita puts forward is not a single philosophy, but a compilation of all the good things in ancient Indian thought. In Swami Vivekananda's words, 'Wherein lies the originality of the Gita?... It is this: Though before its advent, Yoga, Jnaana, Bakthi etc. had each its strong adherents, they all quarrelled among themselves... no one ever tried to seek for reconciliation among these different paths. It was the author of the Gita who for the first time tried to harmonise these. He took the best from all the sects... and threaded them into the Gita.'[4] There is a place for everything in its scheme.

What problems can result when we stick to one alone ignoring the others? If we get into serving the world without knowledge about the ultimate truths behind it or without holding on to a higher source of wisdom, then the world would overwhelm us and bog us down in no time. 'Get your foundation right. You can do your service even better,' insists the Gita.

To be a Baktha and depend on God shunning self-responsibility and initiative makes one dull, indolent and fatalistic. 'Trust in God, but tie your camel when asleep,' goes an Arabic proverb. And, Bakthi without a base of Jnaana, not knowing who God is or what our relationship is to him, not realising all Gods are various facets of that one reality, would make us blind, insecure and fanatic. Instead of realising 'We all belong to God,' we would start believing 'God belongs to us alone.' People belonging to other faiths would make us edgy.

Jnaana yoga without Bakthi and Karma Yoga, would make us dry intellectual vedantins. We would start deriving pleasure in talking spirituality, arguing and doing all kinds of intellectual gymnastics, but in truth remain as stuck as the spiritually ignorant. An Upanishad makes a striking statement in this regard.

> Into blinding darkness enter those who worship ignorance;
> And into a greater darkness than that enter
> Those who are (thus) devoted to knowledge.
> Brihadaranyaka Upanishad 4.4.10

And Dyaana yoga alone, without Bakthi or Jnaana would make us insecure creatures seeking after states of consciousness and experiences.

To walk the Gita's path is to embrace all four Yogas. Each of the four Yogas has its place in our life. Each Yoga appeals to an aspect of our being. The Karma Yoga path is for our outer active being; Jnaana is for our contemplative and intuitive part; Bakthi appeals to our emotional nature. And Dyaana is the sadhana we do to strengthen our bond with the Divine, whether we feel it through Jnaana or Bakthi. All are needed to take us humans to our destination.

ॐ

'Oh, that's nothing. Just mild angina. The old man is quite all right now,' Saradha was quick to brush off my questions regarding her father's health. She asked me next, 'Know the news about our Muthu's grove, Venkat?'

'What news?' I asked, wondering what astonishing thing I was going to hear next about the boy.

'They are going to destroy Alangadu totally, along with the temple.'

'What?'

'Big bulldozers and electric saws are being brought in. It seems the construction company that is building the resort, liked the area and has decided to expand on its plan bringing in the neighbouring land too. Those people have political connections, it seems. There is a lot of agitation going on in the village day in and day out. The people of the village are protesting, but the company is still determined to carry on with it.'

'How come, Saro? Doesn't the land belong to the temple? Unthinkable.'

'True, but the construction company has greased the palms of five out of seven elders of the village who are in charge of it. A pretty big amount has been exchanged, they say. Only two from that lot are protesting along with the villagers.'

'But how come? Aren't there documents?'

'Yes, but they don't seem to care. We have it in our hands... an old hand-written document by the owner of the land who had bequeathed it exclusively to the temple, a few decades back. However, the people who are building the resort and the resort proprietor... it seems they would go to any extent to acquire it.'

'Is it? Who is it?'

'Sheik Mohideen, a big shot in Tuticorin who has just returned from Middle-East.'

'Sheik Uncle?'

'Saro, you know what? He is our family friend and my father's best buddy. He is a bit business-minded, but not that bad a man. Tell Muthu not to worry. Give me the documents. Maybe the construction company people are misrepresenting facts to him. I am sure he doesn't know how much the grove and the temple mean to the villagers. I will talk to my father about it. I think I can help here.'

'Really? If you can do it, it would be great Venkat.'

ॐ

When I opened the door to his room, Dad was surfing channels on his personal forty-inch LED TV that he had bought recently. In his other hand was his cell phone, its hands-free plugged into his ears.

'What, dear boy? My son is coming into my room? Now, that's unusual,' he said, keeping his phone down.

'Appa, I have come to discuss something important with you.'

I put forward the documents Saro had sent me through her assistant, told him about the construction company, and what they had been doing in the village.

'Is it?' he asked with concern. 'Sheik was telling about the resort he is going to build, but he doesn't know about such a problem, I am sure. The company people are hiding all this from him, probably.'

He took a careful look at the documents and then dialed a number from his phone.

'Zab, that resort project Sheik is up to . . . yeah . . . no, Zab. We have to stop it immediately.'

'Don't worry, Venkat,' he said turning towards me. The music channel on the TV started airing a high-pitched song. Dad raised the remote to lower its volume. 'I will certainly look into it and inform Sheik about the problem.'

'Thanks, appa. It would be a great relief to the villagers if we can do it.'

'Don't worry, my boy. We can do business, but not at the expense of others. I will take care.'

For the first time, I noticed a warmth in his voice as he was talking to me.

'*Not bad*!' I mused, sitting on the terrace that night. In a strange way, the Gita had brought me closer to my confused mother. Now the same is happening with me and Dad too. 'It will all turn out well,' the words of Big B came to mind.

※

THE GITA AND THE WORLD

A popular verse in an Upanishad goes

> **Truth alone triumphs, never falsehood.**
> Mundaka Upanishad 3.1.6

That is, 'It will all turn out well.' However, when we take a look at the real world, at all the violence and wickedness and brutality among men today, by any stretch of the imagination, do we feel like saying that? I am reminded of a question, a dry-witted medicine professor of ours asked his students often. 'First there were single-celled amoebae . . . little later, monkeys. Then man came. What next?'

As we look at him puzzled, he would, with relish, spell out the punch line of his great joke, 'What else? The same amoeba!'

If we look at the present times, it seems no joke at all, though. It appears as if we as a race are heading towards that. The world really looks like a vehicle running out of control towards the cliff, as Sandy told me once in the bar. Why is there so much 'noise' in the world – to the extent of jarring our ears? Why is mankind in the state it is?

When will 'truth finally triumph,' as the Mundaka Upanishad promises us?

Sri Aurobindo puts forward a pretty radical idea to explain this. He says that man is not a finished product. He is the intermediate stage of something greater, something waiting to come next. 'Man is a transitional being. He is not final,' he writes.[5]

We feel proud about the remarkable progress mankind has made in science and technology, and the improved quality of life we enjoy through that. We think that it puts us modern men in a higher place than our predecessors. However, if we give it a moment's thought, we would see all those are but progresses in the external and utilitarian aspects of life. Because we have in our hands a smartphone or a tablet or PC or because we can cure many previously fatal diseases, it doesn't mean we are superior than our ancestors. We are still undergoing the same struggles and fighting the same wars, though with advanced instruments. We have not progressed at all, according to Sri Aurobindo.

The developmental stage waiting to unfold next is, **the man who has become self-aware of who he really is, and who lives his life rooted in the deepest truths of his existence.** The same evolutionary currents that gave rise to human life from a primordial life form are waiting to produce Jivan mukthas out of us human beings. This growth to fullness is, 'apparently uncertain but secretly inevitable,' as Sri Aurobindo puts it. It is bound to happen one day or the other because that is who we are!

However, there is a difference between the previous evolution and this. So far the evolutionary process was on the physical plane. Hence it proceeded without hiccup. The next evolution by which the universal cycles reach their completion is an inner one! Because there is this entity called mind with its free will that is central to the human organism, this evolution too calls for our conscious endeavour. This evolution is not a matter of chance, but *a matter of choice.* It calls for our conscious decisions!

So as we walk the Gita, it is worth remembering that it is not our destiny alone we work towards. In our destiny lies the world's destiny too. As we evolve, the world too evolves with us.

Unless we end all the violence and brutality inside us, how can fighting with a perceived brutality on the outside do any good? Darkness needs light; not another darkness to fight against. The world can be restored to peace only by people who are peaceful!

And until man addresses the original gnawing incompleteness inherent in him, until he is able to establish a connection with his true roots, whatever peace he experiences on the outside will only be a fleeting, temporary state of mind.

The one who has gained knowledge attains supreme peace. 4.39

**By practising Yoga (with the Divine) one gains contentment.
Crossing the dualities of the world, he attains tranquility.**
Maitri Upanishad 3.29

So, if looking at the world with all its violence and brutality sickens us, it should motivate us to be even more sincere in our spiritual path. We owe it to the world. You and I walking the path of truth is no longer a luxury, but a necessity. The world might be a vehicle running out-of-control towards the edge of a cliff. However, Vedanta says to agitated souls, 'You are not the passengers in this vehicle, but the crew! It is you who are responsible for setting it right.' The world's condition isn't an excuse for cynical resignation, but a call for our more responsible participation.

In the information age we are living in, the world's brain has united. The advances in telecommunication have made the earth one large global village. Next should arrive a stage where the world's heart unites. Man should be able to feel from his heart that the whole earth is his home and every human being here is his spiritual brethren. We have seen economic revolutions, political revolutions and technological revolutions. What is needed now is a more fundamental spiritual revolution – a change in the very way we view ourselves, the world and God. When that occurs in the minds of majority of people, all the problems torturing the world would disappear like darkness before the sun.

'Give me a place to stand, and I will move the earth,' declared Archimedes. The abode of the divine in our hearts is that place from which it can be done.

ॐ

My phone rang as I was reading the morning paper while chatting with my dad. It was Rajagopal Sir.

'Hello, Sir, I was about to call you. I have sent you my marriage invitation . . .'

'Oh, yes. I heard from Dany. Sorry to hear the news, Venkat. Sometimes such things happen. We should learn to accept and move on, you know,' he said in his usual frivolous way.

'Well, Sir, wait till I see madam next.'

'Why bother? I tell her that daily. Jokes apart, Venkat, you know something? They are going to expand our clinical wards considerably. Each of them is going to become triple the size it is now. We are moving to a new block too.'

'Oh? Dany never told me. That's great, Sir.'

'Great? No, Venki, not really. These people should first improve the infrastructure and then go for such expansion. Do you know how they are getting their MCI recognition? By bringing in temporary doctors and pretending to the MCI, that they work here. God bless them. What happens when they leave? What will happen now with this expansion? Some extra post-graduates for the college and extra money for the administration from its management quota! However, the expanded set up is going to function with the same amount of medical and support staff as the old. What is the use?'

'True, Sir,' I said, thinking over what he said. I was looking at my father's PA, Zab, who was parking his bike at the gate. Father got up and went inside as Zab opened the gate.

Coming near, Zab asked me, 'Sir, where is father?'

I signalled to say that he was inside. He took out a list from his pocket and gave it to me. It was the list of lodge rooms booked under my name for the marriage.

'By the way, Gopal Sir, no excuses this time. You are surely coming for the marriage. I have booked rooms for your family already.'

'Oh, I forgot that totally. I actually called you to confirm that. You know something? As soon as Daniel told me, even before I got your invitation, I had booked my train tickets. I was only waiting for an outing. Akil will kill me if I don't take him out during his quarterly leave atleast. I have planned to go to Kutrallam while I come there. I will surely come, Venkat!' he promised.

As I hung up, I wondered about the news Sir had shared, the clinical departments of CIIMER getting expanded to triple its present size.

'Thank God, Sandy is not getting transferred there now,' I thought, relieved. 'The psychiatry set-up with its inept chief is maddening enough already, that too with just twenty-five beds. Two PG's who had been classmates of Sandy were taking psychiatric drugs, unable to deal with the stress of working there, Sandy had once told me. Imagine the set up becoming thrice its size!'

Sandy called me as I was thinking about him. 'All set to go to our Kumbavuruti this weekend. How is your leaky butt?'

'Leakage fixed. We can go.'

ॐ

Sandy again made me regret the decision to give the write-up to him. It was only a week ago. While I was in bed with the stomach flu, he had finished reading it at one go! After reading, he again did what he does best, put forward some pretty difficult questions for me to answer. He had fired several missiles till now, but the question he put forward that day was an atom bomb!

He entered my bedroom and placed the bulky file containing the write-up on my table.

'So that is it about the Gita, huh?' he asked reclining in the chair.

'Yup.'

'In a way, the Gita's Yoga is like your Muthu making his parottas, you know?'

'And how is that?' I asked, frowning.

'Well, like him kneading his flour well and frying it in oil, we subdue our egos and surrender it to the Divine in us. Isn't it all about this?'

'I don't know if you are saying so sarcastically, but there is a poem composed by Ramana where he compares the recipe for making pappads to the spiritual path, in a similar vein.'

'Oh? Not bad man. See, I am starting to think like the great sages.'

He browsed through the papers for some time and said, 'Things happening through us. We just having to remain still.... Nice things to know. Happen, non-doing ... I can use it next time my father finds me with a cigar in my hand. 'Dad, I wasn't doing anything. It just happened through me.' Imagine his reaction to that.'

I gave him a stony stare. He laughed. 'Just joking boss, but you know what? All the things the Gita told me are fine. One thing alone doesn't gel in its entire philosophy.'

'Well, errr ... '

'If there are no others at all and we are all parts of one extended body, and correcting ourselves is the greatest good we do to the world, how on earth can Krishna ask Arjuna to kill those bad men in the war?'

I kept looking at him. He had not yet lifted his eyes out of the file.

'You know something, Sandy?'

'What?' he asked, raising his head.

'I really wish we had stayed fighting. How peaceful it was to prepare the write-up without your damn questions and comments! Hmm ... '

I did prepare an answer to that in the next three days and gave it to him. Looking at him read it all patiently, our combined-study times in school crossed my mind.

'Oh, so that's about it, huh? Not only Gandhiji, but Bhagat Singh too, in a way, walked the way of the Gita you say? Interesting. Though Gandhiji had a problem accepting this call of the Gita, our Holy Book doesn't see a contradiction in that, huh?'

'Yes. And it would have smiled at Gandhiji's difficulty and seen it too as his swabhava expressing itself.'

'Oh? Even then something doesn't gel for me. If the Gita says ... '

'Sandy!'

'Yes?'

'Let it remain un-gelled this time. I need a break.'

We left for the Kumbavuruti Falls that weekend.

WAR AND PEACE

How can a scripture that gives such a profound foundation for human love, exhort a soldier to kill someone in a war? Once we have become one with the intelligence that orchestrates the universe, how can we cause harm to a portion of ourselves? Will a body's intelligence ever harm its component cell?

Some commentators interpret the whole battle scene of the Gita to be an allegory of our inner life. Even the entire Mahabharatha is interpreted in a similar way. However, this according to Sri Aurobindo, is a 'laborious and puerile mystification' and 'wresting it to the service of our fancy.'[7] The war in the Gita is very much a real one and when Krishna says 'Kill,' he does mean 'Kill.'

Now then, how can the Avatar who said 'See and love all beings as your own Self' also say –

**A war fought for Dharma
is like an open gate to heaven for a Kshatriya. 2.32**

We saw that it is the words of the one Universal Intelligence that is recorded in the scriptures of the world through various Spiritual Masters. Let us take a look at what each of them have to say about war.

'Military arms are tools for misfortune, not for good will; (they are) to be used under absolute necessity, without satisfaction,' it is said in the *Tao Te Ching* (Verse 31).

'Go and completely destroy those wicked people, the Amalekites; make war on them until you have wiped them out,' enjoins the Bible (Samuel 15:18). It is the same Bible which also tells us, 'Thou shalt not kill.'

The Quran says, 'You reach agreements with them, but they violate their agreements every time; they are not righteous. . . . Therefore, if you encounter them in war, you shall set them up as a deterrent example for those who come after them, that they may take heed.'(Sura 8.56–57)

Astonishing, huh?

To return to what Sandy asked, 'Will the body's intelligence ever destroy its own component cell?' The surprising answer to that is, yes, it does on occasion! Through a biological process called *apoptosis*, the cells that show harmful tendencies are eliminated from our body from time to time. The body's intelligence induces such cell death through its immune cells. Defective apoptotic processes lead to a variety of debilitating diseases including cancer.

Kshatriyas are the immune cells of the macroscopic world, so to speak.

In the *Artha Shastra*, which is the Indian treatise on political science, there are four ways prescribed to approach a contending party: *sama, dama, bheda* and *danda*. We do not fight with an enemy at once, even if we despise his immoral ways totally. We always try to pacify, calm, and plead for proper sense to prevail in the mind of the enemy, insisting that it is not good to have war; neither for them, nor for us; it would end in mutual destruction.

This is what the Pandavas did in the Mahabharatha, mediated by Krishna himself. It is only when all measures failed, was war resorted to.

War is bad. It is to be avoided. However, sometimes the only way to keep the 'demonic' among men from doing great harm to the world is through war. As long as free will is there in humans, there is bound to be such wanton extremism and extremists. And such rampantly running free will of certain men can cause much damage to the harmony of the world, if truth always chooses to be patient with them.

Non-violence is indeed a wonderful philosophy. The Ahimsa movement of Gandhiji is a supremely courageous movement that he led against the British. That he inspired millions to do the same was breathtaking. But how can one practise such non-violence with a man who coldly quips, 'One death is a tragedy. A million deaths is just a statistic?' Isn't it a travesty? Imagine how many more would have been killed if Hitler was not defeated in World War II? Or if a Mussoulini and Idi Amin were not deposed? The role of war in our world 'can only be denied by the fanatics of pacifism,' in Sri Aurobindo's striking words.

War is a part of earth. It is never a good thing, but given the nature of our world, it is sometimes a necessary thing. *War is necessary for peace at times!* The Gita acknowledges this truth of our world.

The Gita tells us when talking about Varna that certain souls are born with an inherent warrior tendency in them. They are the Kshatriyas of the world. According to the Gita, the natural qualities of a Kshatriya are

Heroic attitude, courage, fortitude, skill, readiness to fight, Generosity and godly attitude. 18.43

It is in cleansing the society of its bad influences, the swabhava of these souls finds its highest natural fulfilment. For such a soul, it is a warrior's life that serves as the right field for the disciplined flowering of its inherent qualities.

'By being subjected to high ethical ideals ... the function of war was obliged to help in ennobling and elevating instead of brutalizing those who performed it,' said Sri Aurobindo.[8]

It is interesting to note that, be it the Samurai of Japan, the martial arts like the Kungfu, Karate and Judo, our own Kalari pattu of Kerala or Silambam of Tamil Nadu, it is the Eastern countries which were the home of ancient spiritual traditions, that also had such parallel martial art traditions.

Vedanta respects the warrior spirit and its predominance in some men. It gives a natural outlet to channelise that and ennoble man through that. It lays a way to subordinate it to higher principles, or it might go wayward and end up in disastrous consequences.

Look around at our society. There are rogue elements in it which brutalise children for earning money, brazenly immoral men who push innocent girls into illicit businesses, terrorists who don't mind killing innocent families for their personal beliefs. When you choose to be forbearing and patient with them, much damage can be caused by them to the integrity of the world. Hence, Dharma too shouldn't flinch from resorting to force at times. It is hence Gita calls for a 'heroic attitude and a readiness to fight' in its Kshatriya.

However, apart from that it also insists that a Kshatriya needs to have 'generosity and godly attitude.' That needs to be expanded upon.

We saw that darkness can't drive away darkness. To get into war against a perceived enemy with a view to avenge oneself, is easy. However, that is not what the Gita advises. Doing it in the right spirit is the scripture's emphasis. **As per the Gita it should be compassion – not hatred or vengeance – that should motivate a Kshatriya into war!**

You know that everyday life can be a hard battle for some. It is by facing the huge, mad, confusing world before him, that a deluded soul has become so. Hence, defeat such a person, not with anger and vengeance, but with compassion! It is your love for Hitler that should kill Hitler if need be! It is a radically different kind of love that the Gita calls for in a Kshatriya.

'There is a divine compassion which descends to us from on high,' tells Sri Aurobindo. 'In the saint and philanthropist it may cast itself into the mould of a plenitude of love or charity; in the thinker and hero it assumes the force of a helpful wisdom.' But in a Kshatriya it is the same compassion that, 'smites down the strong tyrant and the confident oppressor,' he adds.

A Kshatriya of the Gita gets into a war not in wrath and hatred, but with love for the world and its well-being in his mind, '(and) with as much love and compassion for the strong Titan erring by his strength and slain for his sins, as for the sufferer and the oppressed who have to be saved from his violence and injustice,' in Sri Aurobindo's striking words.[9]

Sri Aurobindo puts the entire exhortation of Lord Krishna to Arjuna this way: 'Look not at thy own pleasure and gain...but around at this world of battle and trial in which good and evil...are locked in stern conflict. Destroy when by destruction the world must advance, but hate not that which thou destroyest. Do thy work with a calm, strong and equal spirit; fight and fall nobly or conquer mightily. For this is the work that God and thy nature have given to thee to accomplish.'[10]

When we take a look at the early chapters of the Gita, we see Arjuna telling Krishna

> O Lord, stop my chariot between the two armies 1.21
> Until I behold those who stand here eager for battle
> And with whom I must engage in this act of war. 1.22
>
> I wish to see those who are willing to serve
> The evil-minded son of Dhritaraashtra
> By assembling here to fight the battle. 1.23

It was personal enmity and vanity that drove Arjuna in the beginning. The Kauravas had refused to give the Pandavas what was rightfully theirs. Arjuna wanted to teach them a lesson.

The Lord knew that this vanity and pride of his beloved friend and disciple has to be done away with before he got into the great war, and that he had to win the war in the right spirit, if it is to do him good. So he placed the chariot right between the two armies in the place where Arjuna's beloved grandfathers, teachers, maternal uncles, brothers, sons, grandsons, and comrades standing ready for war, would catch his eyes.

Arjuna's being was bewildered as he saw them all. With a dramatic reversal of his state of mind, he said to Krishna,

> O Krishna, seeing my kinsmen standing with a desire to fight,
> My limbs fail and my mouth becomes dry...
> My body quivers and my hairs stand on end. 1.28-29

> Alas, we are ready to commit a great sin
> of slaying our kinsmen
> Because of greed for the pleasures of the kingdom. 1.45
>
> It would be far better for me if the sons of Dhritarashtra
> Kill me with their weapons
> while I am unarmed and unresisting. 1.46

Hatred and attachment are both children of vanity. No wonder, the first changed into second in one stroke. This fundamental flaw in Arjuna's viewpoint is what Krishna sets out to correct through his exposition.

A personal enmity can never be the motivation for a Kshatriya to get into war. And secondly, Arjuna said, 'let the Kauravas rule the kingdom.' That too can never be the right attitude for any man.

If we are to prevent our world from becoming a world of amoebas again, then Dharma should stand up against adharma by all means. If you are a Kshatriya by nature, fight adharma with the strength of your arms, like Bhagat Singh did. If your swabhava makes you believe in soul power, stand up against it through ahimsa. Be the light that enlightens that darkness, as Mahatma Gandhi did. But stand up you must!

'The horrors which we have seen, and the still greater horrors we shall presently see, are not signs that rebels, insubordinate, untameable people are increasing in number throughout the world, but rather that there is a constant increase in the number of obedient, docile people,' the French author George Bernanos very rightly said.

All it requires for evil to triumph, is the good among men doing nothing! Hence does Krishna insist,

> **Do not become a coward, O Arjuna. It does not befit you.**
> **Shake off this weakness of your heart and get up. 2.3**

For Duryodana, the archvillain in the Mahabharatha, it was vanity that drove him. He saw no evil in the destruction of the family, and no sin in being treacherous to friends. His conceited words as he gets into the battle are,

> **Our army, commanded by Bheeshma, is invincible.**
> **While their army, protected by Bheema, is easy to conquer 1. 10**

For Arjuna, first his motive was, 'I am going to seek my vengeance and get our kingdom back.' However, after the Lord expounded his teaching, it became 'I am just an instrument of the Lord to establish Dharma in the world. It is Dharma that is going to establish itself through me.'

He saw the truth in the Lord's words,

> All these (men) have already been slain by me.
> Be merely an apparent cause. 11.33

Arjuna participated in the war as a mere instrument of the Divine, and with a spirit that saw the opposition without hatred. That is the entire point of the Gita.

Thus for the Gita, its exhortation 'See all beings in yourself,' doesn't really contradict its words, 'You must conquer these men in war.'

The deluded are free to stay deluded if it is their life alone they are ruining. However, if their action is a threat to the integrity of society, then they sure have to be brought down. And, it should be our love – love for the world, and love for the deluded as well - that brings them down.

The spirit of a warrior who gets into war should be, 'I detest having to fight with you, and kill you, if need be. But to establish Dharma in the world, do it I must, fully knowing that I can never hurt or kill the real you. God bless you.'

'When two opponents meet, the one without an enemy will triumph,' it is said in the Tao Te Ching (Verse 69).

Jalaludeen Rumi tells the intriguing tale from the life of Ali ibn Abi Talib, the first Imam of Shia Islam, which emphasises the same point.

Once when Ali was about to defeat an opponent in battle, the opponent spat on his face!

Ali put his sword down at once, and insisted on continuing the battle the next day. The explanation he gave for his action was, 'I am God's Lion, not the lion of passion. I have no longing except for the One. When a wind of personal reaction comes, I do not go along with it.'[11]

That is, 'When my personal like and dislike dictate it, I won't do it!' That is the spirit in which Arjuna too finally gets into war.

> Destroyed is my delusion,
> And I have gained knowledge through Your grace.
> My confusion is dispelled. I am firm. I will do what you said 18.73

are his humble words. He lost himself to find himself. He lost his lower vengeance-filled self to find his Higher Self.

An important and necessary digression: isn't all that we discussed till now a dangerous philosophy to preach to fanatics out there in every religion, who commit heinous crimes in the name of faith? Would they not take to their swords and pistols with a new gusto, thinking that their god has given them the nod to do it?

The truth all such people should understand when coming across this scriptural injunction to war is, when the holy scriptures of the world exhort us to fight adharma, it is not against common people who lead a peaceful daily existence, loving and caring for their families. It is against the people who stand up for adharma; the men whose existence is a threat to the integrity of the world. It is them the Gita, Quran or the Bible exhorts us to fight. And that too should be done in the right way, respecting the laws of the world.

If yours is a kshatriya swabhava, join the police force; or the army. Become a constructive social activist; or a truthful and conscientious journalist. There are so many ways a kshatriya swabhava can be rightly channelized. Unlawful and intentional killing of common men in the name of religion is cold-blooded murder, and not war for Dharma. It is this that the Bible refers to when it says, 'Thou shalt not kill.' The Quran too says something similar, 'And if they incline to peace, so shall you, and trust in Allah.' (Sura. 8.61)

No religion would sanction such brazen violence and murders performed in the name of its god. Even after we have self-realised and gone beyond all the laws of the world, the Gita constantly exhorts us to function here respecting the laws of the world. Then how can violence committed in the name of religion be considered a part of Hindu Dharma?

If we think about it, it is the repressed societal anger and deviant streak in some men that drives them toward such self-righteous violence. Religion is just a convenient alibi for them. Take that away, and it would come up with something else.

When a terrorist who was arrested for planting a bomb in a public place and killing numerous lives was asked whether he would have planted the bomb if his mother were there in that place, he answered coldly to the questioner: 'I shall even kill my mother for my God.' That is how perverted an interpretation we make of the words of scriptures!

'Men never do evil so completely and cheerfully as when they do it from religious conviction,' the philosopher Pascal rightly observed.

Hindu fundamentalists who take the law into their own hands and commit horrendous crimes against people belonging to other religions, should remember that their action not only shows an utter disregard for the laws of the world, but a blithe disregard for the Lord's words in the Gita too. Such unlawful violence in the name of Hinduism is an open attack on, more than anything, the ideology of open heartedness that is unique to this religion. Swami Vivekananda spoke the following words in the Parliament of Religions, 'I am proud to belong to a religion which has taught the world both tolerance and universal acceptance. We believe not only in universal toleration, but we accept all religions as true.

'Sectarianism, bigotry, and its horrible descendant, fanaticism, have long possessed this beautiful earth. They have filled the earth with violence, drenched it often and often with human blood....

'I fervently hope that the bell that tolled this morning in honor of this convention may be the death-knell of all fanaticism....'

True. The Earth has seen enough bloodshed in the name of religion.

ॐ

The weather was quite pleasant and the surroundings, lush green. I doubted whether we were at the good old Kumbavuruti Falls, or in some dreamland. Thank God, Kumar was not with us this time. When Sandy said we would go without him, I was only too happy to agree.

I had assumed Sandy giving that letter to Manisha was the culmination of his return to his older self. However, it was in Kumbavuruti that I came to know that the fellow had decided on quite a few other things already.

'So, boss, now that you have finished with your write-up on the Gita, what's your next plan?' Sandy asked me.

'Well, I will try and live by its wisdom for the rest of my life. What else? And you know what? I feel some strange relationship with that parotta boy Muthu and his grove since the day I visited that place. Somehow he reminds me of our Barath Sir. I plan to visit him and the place often from now on.'

'Oh?'

'More than words, a person living it in flesh and blood is a much greater inspiration, you see. Whatever I hear about him impresses me. Saradha told me what happened when his asthma worsened a few weeks ago. He got admitted with a pretty acute and severe exacerbation. Yet, during his treatment it was he who was calmly reassuring the hospital staff. Our chest physician Abdul who went there for a visit was quite amazed as well, Saradha said. The boy is pretty interesting, and that place Alangadu . . . what a great natural altar it is!'

'Whoa! Hope you don't leave your profession and become a parotta master.'

The queue was moving rather slowly. It was pretty long that day despite it being off-season. I was looking at Sandy waiting in front of me in the line with his newly shaven head. *'Good that he declined his transfer to CIIMER,'* I mused, *'The awful living conditions of the patients there, the inhuman things that happen in the ward . . . Had he accepted the transfer, he might have easily gone back into his pessimistic world again. Thank God he rejected it. Let the guy stabilise himself here for some time.'*

'You know something, Venki?' Santosh said, turning towards me. 'I am getting . . . '

'What?' I asked loudly. He was barely audible above the sound of the falls and I was not sure if I had heard him right.

'I am getting transferred to C-I-I-M-E-R – our parent institute!' he said at the top of his voice.

'What? Are you serious?'

'We'll talk later. Now take a bath.'

Our turn had come. He plunged into the falling water and bathed with great joy, paying no heed to the astounded look on my face.

Not a simple decision to take at all – getting a transfer there. The words he spoke about the place in a bar a year back, still rang in my ears. This was a crazy decision.

ॐ

We had come out of the falls.

'The weather is damn good,' he beamed.

'Sandy, can you please repeat what you said before getting in?'

'You heard it right, maaps,' he said as he took his clothes out from the bag in the storage area. 'I don't know whether I am following your Gita and all that, Venki boss. I contemplated on where to go next in life. And this is the choice that felt right.

'I can't change the whole world, but when I go there with the advantage of, you know, a post like this, I can try doing something for those poor souls there. With people suffering and me having such a chance now and not even giving it a try . . . something didn't seem right.'

'Maaps, it is true we have to stand up against such things. However, we should know our limitations too. The people in authority there will overpower and dispose you off in no time you know, if a mere lecturer tries such adventurous things . . . like changing the entire system . . . . And by the way, do you know something about CIIMER?'

'It is getting triple its present size, right? So what? . . . Complete the sentence if you have heard it before, "When we have faith in our hearts . . . "'

I kept looking at him without answering.

'Come on, maapi . . . we are the all-powerful Hanumans, right? We will fight and fall nobly, or conquer mightily, Venki boss. Mine is kshatriya blood,' he said showing me his flexed arm.

His flabby muscles were hanging loose from his arm. 'You know what this is? The arms of god! I am god's helping hands for those souls.'

'Hey, wait a minute! Didn't you already pay a huge amount for getting a re-transfer here?'

'Oh yes. They said they can't give it back . . .'

'So you mean you spent another few lakhs to get this again, huh? Maaps, let me tell you, you are mad. Absolutely mad. But . . .'

'Venki!' he interrupted, 'Enough with your but! Too leaky it is still!' he grinned.

'Quite nice isn't it, the weather today? I thought we should have one last trip to the Falls before I leave. By the month-end I am leaving Tuticorin along with dad and Saravana. So can you please stop your questioning now? Let's go for a walk in the woods one last time.'

I expressed my reservation when he told about his decision. However, when he walked out of the dressing room crossing me, I felt proud within.

I looked at the waterfall again. The water seemed to be flowing with great zest. Nature had created it to be a magnificent waterfall and it is being so, joyfully! But for us humans, how many mistakes, how much muddling around before we align ourselves with our calling in life, all caused by this curious entity called mind.

I looked at Sandy's face as we were strolling around the woods. I could feel that he had finally found his calling; his Dharma.

ଊ

My phone started to ring as I got up from bed the next morning. It was from Pasumaikudi.

'Hello, Muthu?'

'How are you, Sir?'

'Fine.'

'Do you know what happened a few days back?'

'Don't worry, Muthu,' I consoled him. 'Saro told me. Nothing will happen to your Alangadu. I have told my father about it . . .'

'Oh, it's not about that, Sir. Saradhamma didn't tell you about her father this time either, did she?'

'Father? What happened now?'

'He suffered from a bigger heart attack this week.'

'Oh, is it?'

'A second attack? That too within a month's time? This doesn't sound good at all.'

SURRENDER

Krishna, after elucidating at length the various nuances of walking the spiritual path, goes on to say something quite interesting at the end of his exposition.

> Now hear my supreme teaching, the most secret of all
> You are very dear to me.
> Hence I shall tell you this for your benefit. 18.64

He says he is going to speak of something he hasn't touched upon yet, something he has reserved for the last. When he utters those words to Arjuna, Sri Aurobindo explains, '(we can feel) it was this for which the soul of the disciple was being prepared all the time. (All) the rest was only an enlightening and enabling discipline and doctrine.'[1]

Once we have got a taste of our Real Self and developed shraddha in it, once we have established an authentic connection with our divine roots, there is a path that we can take which is higher than all that was shared till now. It is –

> Setting aside all Dharma, surrender completely to me.
> I shall liberate you from all sins. Do not grieve. 18.66

A whole-hearted self-surrender to the Divine! That is what the Gita calls its highest teaching. The scripture hinted about this at several places. In its last chapter, the Gita puts the teaching before us emphatically. In surrender, we don't court the Divine, but kneel before him and offer ourselves to him. 'Take me, dear Big Boss. I am yours,' we say.

If we can do that, the divine presence in our hearts will take care of all concerns in our journey, the spiritual and material. We let our lives be taken over and be used by a higher power for its purpose. We would see ourselves blossoming into a greater person than we could have ever envisaged. Such surrender will make us yogis. Surrender will take us to complete union with the Lord. That is the teaching the Gita reserves for its last.

It has been more than a year since I went up to the terrace on a cold night with the Bhagavad Gita in my hands. Despite reading it and trying to follow its teachings, despite feeling a connection with my roots in the heart, somewhere within me, my ego was viewing it all like a guest in the house. My heart hadn't yet embraced the wisdom completely, I often felt. Having seen someone like Muthu and having seen the completely surrendered state he was living his life in, at that young age, my habitually-anxious mind couldn't help wondering at times, 'When will I reach such a surrendered state?'

'Don't be in such a haste, dude. It is the journey that is important,' I told myself at those times.

However, life had decided to grant my wish soon.

ॐ

Revising the last section of the write-up, I looked at the phone on the table ringing incessantly. It was Zab.

'Hello, Zab, what's up?' I asked picking it up.

Zab shared the news. And I, as I heard it, found my grip on the phone loosen and the phone about to fall out of my hands.

It happened a few months back. Someone had once said that life is made up of years that mean nothing and moments that mean everything. How true that is! In the mundane routine of everyday life, we sometimes come across certain moments, certain unforeseen, heart-rending moments. They sneak into our life rather innocuously. We have no idea how deep or tremendous their impact on our life is going to be, when they happen.

That moment, that day when Zab told me over the phone that Alangadu was destroyed, was one such moment.

'What? Come on, Zab. You can't be . . . I . . . Father . . .' I stuttered.

Zab was silent.

I still remember my visit to Alangadu. My lungs can still feel the cool, crisp air of that place. The chirping of birds, the chittering of squirrels, the butterflies that fluttered by me . . . it was like entering into a large cohesive family in nature. I could see how valuable and sacred the grove was for the boy and the villagers. I had hence requested, in fact, pleaded with my father a few months back to avert its destruction.

And on the last Tuesday of that month it was destroyed recklessly, except a few well-trimmed trees that were spared for the sake of creating an ambience. The construction of the resort had begun full swing in that place.

'I . . . I . . . But didn't father agree to . . .'

Zab was still silent.

It was what I had said that had given the man a business cue. He took the documents I gave him, to his friend. They sought the help of the politician Arumai Selvan. He mediated and brought in the eldest man in charge of the place, and the three had set up a deceased old man in the village with the same name as in the document, as the owner of the place and shown legally that they had bought the land from his heir. They had achieved this quite easily, and with a measly amount, I learnt from Zab. In those first few minutes of what felt like heartless betrayal, I berated the messenger.

'Come on, Zab. Open your damn mouth and speak. How the f*** could you do it? How did the village people allow such a thing to happen? How could you. . . .'

I controlled myself from using further foul language. I felt as though I had been pushed down into an abyss by my father. I was teeming with sheer disbelief.

'Calm down, Venki Sir, please,' Zab began speaking in a firm voice.

'True, it could have become quite problematic. The village people protested a lot despite the solid documentation in our hands. But our Sir handled it deftly. Arumai Selvan helped our Sir a lot. He saw that the issue didn't gain media attention . . .

'Venki Sir, don't mistake me when I say this. We can do no business and build nothing new if we worry for such things. You know what? Sheik Sir has agreed to include our Sir too as a 30% shareholder for the favour he did,' he said with a sense of accomplishment seeping through his solemn tone of voice.

'Don't worry about the trees, Sir. Anyhow they wouldn't have survived the sulphur in the air with the new smelting plant starting to function nearby. And with so many such industrial projects on the pipeline, resorts are the next big thing in our town. There is not even an issue of resettlement here. The village people are unnecessarily making a big issue out of it. Just a few trees, Venki Sir.'

'Just a few trees!'
Months have gone by since it happened. Who could have expected that the boy Muthu's life and mine would cross in such a fateful way through my father?

There are some moments in life that are very hard for the heart to bear; where crossing the stage of disbelief seems very difficult. We just do not know what to do or how to respond.

However, it is such moments that call for giving up all our old ways of tackling things and surrendering our lives in the hands of Existence, in the hands of god.

ଔ

The rising sun in the eastern sky greets my eyes. With the chirping of birds, the slowly ascending noise of traffic, the customary devotional song rising noisily in a distant temple, another day is about to present itself in the world's hands. It has been quite a few months since I started getting up before sunrise. I think of my father and the shocking thing he did few months ago. Amazingly, it is gratitude that wells up in my heart!

Sorrows, frustrations, disappointments - how much we despise them! However, the Mahabharatha mentions a unique prayer Kunti Devi, the mother of Pandavas, placed before the Lord. She pleads for such things to be a constant part of her life, 'O Preceptor of the Universe, I pray you to give us bad luck all the time. Let danger surround us always. For it is only when peril threatens us from all sides that we feel your divine presence.'

'Bless me with sorrow,' what a prayer that is!

During such times of distress, no doubt we can fill ourselves with denial and anger and frustration, contracting within ourselves. It happened to me too when I came to know what my father had done with the documents he had got from me. A stranger on the road or a new friend doing such a thing to us, is hard enough to bear. But when someone close to us does something like that, let me tell you, it is a dreadful thing to undergo.

So far my attitude towards my father had been neutral. My anger and frustration towards him for all the childhood pains and emotional neglect I have experienced from him had all been pushed to the back of my mind, once Barath Sir came into my life. However, that night, it was angst, unbearable angst that welled up in my heart towards him.

My father sheepishly justified himself saying, 'Dear boy, you are just entering the real world. You will learn these with time.' I was not able to sleep a wink or even close my eyes for a minute as I lay down that day. My whole body trembled with the question, 'How could my father do such a thing? Has he always been such a man?' The thought of Muthu tortured me. I did not have the courage to speak to Muthu or Saradha for a while after that.

This Venki, in his erstwhile reading of the Gita, thought he was simultaneously trying to apply the great scripture's principles alongside. But nothing in the Gita came to his rescue that day. Not one word could he remember from the book that he considered a great blessing for fumbling humans like him. Anger and frustration at that heartless man, his father, was all his being was filled with. He just didn't know how to handle all the painful emotions that arose within him.

ॐ

After fidgeting around in my room, not knowing what to do, I lastly looked at my table. Krishna with his beatific smile on the cover of the Bhagavad Gita caught my eyes. Strangely, an indescribable anger welled up inside me towards the God in the picture.

'What type of sadistic being are you?' I yelled. 'Creating us all in this f*****g world and letting everyone play their games according to their whims, with you not interfering whatever happens. . . . What type of system is this? No. . . . Come on, tell us all the truth . . . that you don't care the least for us here . . . that you have gone off leaving the world to its own fate. The Gita, the Self-realised Masters, you helping your devotees in need – I seriously doubt if they are all true! No . . . all are empty talk! Plain humbug! Come on . . . spell it out to the world you heartless God . . . that you don't give a f***ing s*** about us or this world.'

It shocks me when I think about it now. In a fit of extreme anger, I took the book in my hand and flung it to the ground.

The Gita fell on the floor with a thud. I fidgeted around in the room. Then coming out, I fidgeted around on the terrace. I hadn't the faintest idea how to react to what had happened, or what I should do next. Then when I again entered the room that day . . .

My eyes fell on the Gita that lay on the floor . . . with Krishna on its cover still smiling at me.

I walked slowly towards it, sat calmly next to it, and opened the book.

Till that time I had been reading, trying to understand, and in bits follow, what the Gita was saying. However, that night when I opened the Gita and started to read its verses, well, it felt as if it was the first time I was reading them!

It was not the book I opened that day. It felt like I was opening myself to the book . . . totally and unrestrainedly for the first time.

> My heart is overpowered by weakness.
> My mind is confused about Dharma.
> I'm Your disciple and I have taken refuge in You.
> Teach me what's good for me. 2.7

Those weren't the words of a warrior in ancient times. Those were my words!

> Lord Krishna, as if smiling,
> Spoke these words to the despondent Arjuna,
> in the midst of both the armies. 2.10

> While speaking learned words,
> You are mourning for what is not worthy of grief.
> Those who are wise lament neither for the living nor the dead. 2.11

I closed the book and looked at Krishna's sublime smile on the cover of the Gita. The painting seemed divinely inspired. I realised that with my little mind, I can't fathom this being in the book's cover. When one's mind is rooted at the level of Jnaana that the Gita calls us towards, there is indeed nothing worth grieving for in this illusive world of ours. The avatar who is the very embodiment of Jnaana will only smile at *ajnaana* grieving before him with all its concerns. It struck me that day, the man portrayed on it was not just Krishna. He was something else. He was Lord Krishna.

༄

I lay down near the book closing my eyes – the wisdom of the Gita I had prepared for the past year reverberating within me.

'When our boat capsizes totally, if we can let go of all our preconceived expectations and ideas of how things should be, and let go of the resultant struggle, if we can calmly surrender to existence and let the river take us where it will . . .'

**The calm person who is not afflicted by these feelings
And who is steady in pain and pleasure
Becomes fit for realising his immortal self, O Arjuna. 2.15**

The turbid waters of my mind started clearing slowly. There is a great ocean of awareness in which the happenings of every moment take place. There is a great silence at the base of all the noise of the world. I had read about it before. I felt it for myself that day. I thought of the incidents of the morning again. It all seemed distant at that moment.

It is impossible to express here what I felt that day. I couldn't even understand it fully. I felt myself like the calm bird of the Upanishad seated at the top of the tree that was watching its own partner at a distance. That day as I walked out of the room again and stood on the terrace at night, I experienced what it is to surrender completely to the Still, Silent Divine presence in us. *I felt what it is to be embraced by God.*

༄

So that was it: the man who had so far developed some expertise in reading the map, had genuinely stepped into the territory at last.

Spirituality, meditation, the various forms of Gods with hundred rituals for each! We get confused and fed up with our routine way of living, try various such stuff to see if something works. However, at last it all comes down to something simple: whether we can unrestrainedly surrender to Existence or not. That is what our life is all about; an exercise in surrender. That is why the Gita, after enumerating to us several aspects of the spiritual path, goes on to give this last as its 'supreme teaching.'

Surrender means, of many things, we embrace life in its totality, with all its highs and lows, without letting our confused concepts and interpretations intervene. That is how the exalted inner attitude of surrender meets our daily life. Difficult to accept though it may seem, pain and suffering are not there in reality, as I realise now, but only in those interpretations of ours.

I don't understand how or why, but as I look back on that day and all that happened, the inevitability of it strikes me. I don't see any other way it could have happened. Nothing was out of place. Nothing was imperfect.

> **All is perfect, so perfectly perfect!**
> **At every level from atom to galaxy**
> **It is all absolutely perfect and in its place.**
> **Isa Upanishad.***

If we can get at this place, and stay there, there is nothing more left for us to experience in life, but unceasing gratitude and wonder. And we would have etched on our face a big, broad smile.

Such surrender doesn't mean we become docile and doormat-like. We still take the appropriate action a situation calls for. I took an important decision in my life that day, as it all winded down. However, we do it not reactively, or in rebellion, but from our serenity!

Let me come to that later and move on now to a heart-warming moment I came across. It happened about a fortnight after the one I just described, a day before Sandy left for CIIMER.

'Do your Dharma and contribute to the world. I will take care of your concerns,' our Big Boss promised us. It seems a difficult promise to trust. Many don't believe it, hence. However, let me tell you, He sure does take care!

❃

I had been planning to visit Saradha's father since the time Muthu told me he had suffered a second episode of chest pain.

'Boss, are you coming?' I asked Santosh over the phone on

---

*A free-style poetic trancreation by Alan Jacobs, from his book *The Principal Upanishads*, New Age Books, 2005 a Saturday morning. I knew he was leaving the following day and it would be difficult for him, and thus I expected him to reply in the negative.

However, after thinking it over for a moment he said, 'Okay, I will come if we can return before evening, Venki. I have got quite a lot of packing left to do.'

'Sure, boss.'

When I entered his house after lunch, Sandy was cleaning up his room's topmost cupboard. His father was standing nearby holding the stool he was standing on. Saravana was packing Sandy's shoes, raincoat and the other stuff from the bottom shelves.

Coming out of the room, Saravana whispered in my ears, 'Anna, the changes at home seem very difficult to believe. Has this guy really changed or are we in some trance?'

I stopped myself from expressing the first response that came to my mind, 'Both are true, Saravana.'

'Enough with your packing, Sandy. Let's go. We will return before it gets dark.'

ஃ

It was three-thirty noon. We were at Saradha's house standing near her father, who lay on his cot quietly. There was a thick band of sacred ash on his forehead. Saradha hadn't come for lunch yet. She had got busy with a ward-patient, her mom told us. The lunch Muthu's mother had sent was waiting in a tiffin-carrier kept on the bedside table.

Saradha's father gestured us to sit, after he saw us standing for some time. I could hear his lungs crepitating even as he breathed. He was in quite some strain.

'How are you feeling now, Uncle?' Sandy asked.

He smiled weakly and nodded at Sandy. We didn't feel like talking any more to him.

'We'll wait outside, Uncle. Let Saradha come,' I said looking at the clock. 'Too sincere our doctor is, when it comes to her duty,' I added while opening the room's door to go outside.

My intention in saying that was only to break the ice a bit.

However, it evoked an unexpected reaction from the old man.

'Yes, yes. Too sincere, she is. Too sincere . . .' he repeated after me like a child, his voice breaking. Even those words came out with much strain.

Then he broke into tears, unexpectedly!

Sandy and I were standing there not knowing what to do or say. We were looking at him intently. He started to sob like a child.

He gestured, 'It's okay. You both go,' wiping his eyes with a handkerchief

'Maaps, did I say anything wrong?' I whispered into Sandy's ears.

Sandy wasn't listening. He was looking pensively at the old man's face.

In a minute or so, we stepped outside the room to let the man be at ease. Saradha's mother was sitting in the hall outside with an old-age walker near her. She too had a small band of sacred ash on her forehead.

'What? The man cried to you too?' she asked, looking at my face.

'Er, we can understand, aunty.'

'What is the big deal? Is life all about getting married, giving birth to children, and all that? God has given some people a different type of life! The man can never accept that. All the boys who come to see her and then become hesitant only confirm that for me . . . that Saradha is born to do the work she is doing here. Do you see how many people in the village are well and happy because of her? He never thinks of it this way.' Saradha's mother told me all that in a rather angry way.

I smiled with slight astonishment at her words. Then I turned and looked back at Sandy. He wasn't standing next to me. He was back to the entrance of the bedroom and was gazing pensively at Saradha's father again. I sensed something was about to happen.

'Hello,' we heard a sudden knock at the door of the hall.

It was Saradha. She entered the hall waving her hands at me and Sandy. She looked tired and dishevelled.

'When did you guys come? The staff never told me. . . . ' As Sandy made way for her, she entered her father's room. 'Got busy with a delivery case,' she added.

I was watching through the open door, as she went towards her father and opened the tiffin-carrier by the bedside. Pausing for a moment, she looked at her father with a frown.

'Oh, the old man cried to you people too?' she asked looking at Sandy standing at the door.

'My dear dad, marriage, children, family . . . all those are not the only things to live for. How many times do we tell you? Come on, take this plate.'

As Saradha served food to him, I found Santosh still staring hard at both of them.

Then he began saying something that shocked me.

'Saradha,' he called gently.

She turned and looked at him.

'I don't know if what I am going to ask you is right . . . ' he started. ' . . . I have meandered aimlessly for a long time in my life. You too must have known all that. It is only now I realise it . . . and I am looking to correct it.'

Saradha's mother and I were listening inquisitively to his words that seemed to come from a place of calm self-assurance.

'Someday after I settle well in my life,' he continued, 'I would certainly think of marrying, bringing in a woman into my house and have a family for myself, to give and receive love. All those I have never had the fortune to have when I was a child, you know? The curse of a motherless home! I'll do it surely someday. But this minute as I see you, I think how great it would be if I have someone like you as my wife. I ask this after giving it enough thought. . . . Will you marry me, Saradha? I have not been a good person till now. But I will never go back to those ways again, I promise. I will feel blessed if you say yes. I can't get a better life partner than you.'

Saradha, her father, and her mother remained in a stunned silence for a while.

After he asked that question, we were there for about two or three minutes. Not many words were spoken by anyone in that span. Saradha's face turned a beetroot red. I could see that what Santosh had asked her had made her very angry. She turned her gaze swiftly away from him, towards her father. Saradha's mother was looking at Santosh with surprise. Then she turned and smiled at me in a somewhat mischievous way.

Santosh, after a brief moment of silence, again opened his mouth and said, 'Saradha.' She turned and looked at him. I too did the same.

I wondered what he might say next.

'Give it a thought and let me know. I will wait,' he continued

Saying that, he walked up to me and asked softly, 'Shall we move, maaps?'

As we got out of the house, and I started the bike, I looked at Saradha's terrace garden. The roses in it were in full bloom.

ଓ

'By the way, maapi,' I asked Sandy as we were returning, 'when are you planning to leave this darned impulsiveness and behave like other normal human beings?'

'What do I do, boss? Each one acts from his own nature, isn't it? What was that? *Swabhavastha pravasthe*, right?'

Not exactly. It is *Swabhavasthu pravarthathe*. However, I don't think Saradha could have ever got a better life-partner than Santosh. Such is the goodness of the man. I have seen it up close right since my early childhood, and it is all reawakened now and raring to go and touch the world. The Gita said, *You have the right over your duty alone*. The results, our well-being, are all the concerns of the Divine Self from which we all have emerged. We think that we humans going through the journey of life, doing our stuff, succeeding, growing spiritually and so on is what the story is all about. It holds true too as long as we lead our lives from our egos. However, from an universal perspective, that is really a myopic point of view. As a plant blossoms, as the ocean has waves, it is the One Divine Self that has become you and me. It is that which has 'peopled' as a philosopher put it.[2] Then won't that power which sustains the sun and the moon and the galaxies know how to take care of our little lives?

For those ever in Yoga (with me),
I take care of their Yogakshema. 9.22

If at all we have the minutest trust that there is a god, and that we have come forth from him, let us surrender to him and let him play the game through us. Just as a flower is the responsibility of the plant and the cell is the responsibility of the body's intelligence, we can relax into that presence and rest assured that, our Big Boss will take care of our concerns.

CR

I was with Sandy as he was vacating his clinic that evening. The workers were bringing down the signboard of his clinic.

'One thing amazes me, Venki boss,' Sandy said. 'It seems every religion ultimately points towards the same truth and a similar way of life centered in god. However, how drastically different the external forms are! One religion insists that women dress in a certain way, another says something else. One says Sunday is holy. Another says Friday. It is perplexing when we look at it, isn't it?'

'Well, there have been Masters and Avatars in every era, and they presented these truths and gave us a way of life as it applies to the particular time period. We should just be aware that we don't get too attached to the form and are able to discern the essential truth behind it all.'

'Not many people do that, huh? By the way, did you see Manisha after that?' he asked me next. 'How is she?'

'Manisha? Er . . .' I hesitated.

'Come on, boss. I know you visit the hospital regularly.'

'She is becoming stronger mentally, I believe. She has enrolled for a job in Abu Dhabi. 'Why should I feel sad for some stupid person's wrongdoing?' she had asked Indhra. She is quite angry with you too, I think,' I replied matter-of-factly.

He smiled with a calmness hearing my words and replied, 'I am happy for her.'

Though it all felt good, within me, I was not totally happy with Santosh. After some internal deliberation, I decided to express that to him.

'I have to tell you maaps, I still have a gripe within even as I see you like this.'

He turned and looked at me, surprised.

'One whole year a friend has been trying to bring you to your old self. You pay no heed to it and brush it all off. Now your old girl comes into the scene, and immediately, you decide to go to CIIMER and change it, propose to Saro ... do all such things. Then what's the use of all that I shared with you?'

'So what? You thought the condescending advice you offered will transform people?'

'Get lost,' I snapped and began to walk away.

'Hey, relax, boss. What you said was ... '

'Shut up.'

'Hey guys, how are you both?' I heard a sudden loud voice from behind. It was Kumar. He had come by to see Sandy.

'You guys heard the news? My thalaivar has announced his next film.'

We both turned towards him, and he got a glimpse of us. His mouth fell open as he did. His wide-eyed stare kept alternating between us both. I had a band of sacred ash on my forehead and Sandy sported his shaved head and stubble. Puzzled, he approached Sandy slowly.

'Maapis, what happened to you both? And what is this new Ghajini hairstyle?' he asked stroking Sandy's scalp. 'You are looking like a diseased broiler hen, darling. I heard you are getting transfer to CIIMER? Are you okay?'

'Perfectly okay, Kumar,' Sandy said, patting his shoulders. There was a brief moment of silence as Kumar was still looking bemused.

'Kumar,' I then said, 'How long shall we keep doing our usual, petty stuff? We can have some high aspirations in life for a change, and try fulfilling it.'

Hearing me say that, Kumar paused for a moment, and then gave me a funny look. 'Well, Venki boss, thank you for your advice. Whatever that means,' he replied, looking at Sandy with a smirk on his face.

'You don't understand that?' asked Sandy without smiling.

'So what? You understand that? Okay, I aspire to be the husband of Sunny Leone. Is that high enough? Stupid idiots, as if all these lectures are practical in such darned times!'

Sandy and I turned and looked at each other. Sandy winked at me.

'Dei, maaps,' I started, 'don't belittle yourself by blaming our times. Our darned times will always be darned till we decide to do something about it.'

'First, you acknowledge this is as a world of Kaali da' said Sandy.

'Therefore, we should derive our happiness not from what we accumulate or enjoy here,' said I, next.

'But from what we become inside as a person,' continued Sandy.

'That is the more permanent one,' I piped up.

'That was our Big B's last message for us too. Remember?' finished Sandy.

Kumar was looking at Sandy, shocked.

'We should follow our swabhava and do our dharma in the world, Kumar. We should live life as a yajna in every way,' I said.

'In short, *"Yogastha Kuru Karmani,"* Kumar,' said Sandy to him at last, with his deadpan expression.

Kumar, who had already got on his bike, turned it around swiftly and started riding away from us. As he did that, he stamped upon the tail of a skinny street dog that was sleeping on the pavement. The dog got up and began chasing his bike in a state of frenzy.

'Hey Sharukh-clone, your heroine is coming after you. Wait for her.'

'Go to hell, Piggy.'

'The fellow is hardly a shade lighter than you. But look what pleasure he derives in calling you Piggy,' said Sandy. He was laughing watching Kumar speed away from us with all his might.

Sandy turned and asked me next, 'After I leave, why don't you try sharing the Gita with this Kumar fellow and see, Venki?'

'Kumar? I would share it with that dog, instead.'

We were both watching as the glass panel in Sandy's clinic was being uninstalled next.

'By the way Sandy, do you think Saradha will accept your

dramatic proposal?' I asked him.

'Maaps, you know what? It is all under our control only till we act,' replied Sandy.

'Oh! I never knew that.'

☙

Lord Siva's vehicle is the bull called Nandi. The bull is considered the symbol of the uncontrollable energies of the mind. The Nandi in every Siva temple is seated facing Siva. It is hence that he is called Nandi at all, meaning 'the happy one'. The animal is a symbol which teaches us an important truth concerning surrender.

Spiritual surrender means, in a moment of earnestness, our attention power has got released from the cramped room of our mind and tasted the great peace that lies outside. It has got a taste of its own divine origin. However, not everybody is a Buddha or Ramana to stay in such a state for the rest of their lives. The attention power does return to its usual state as it re-enters daily life. It gets caught in the mind and its melodramas quite often.

Therefore, for surrender to be fruitful, it should also be a moment to moment affair. It is not just an act to be done once and be satisfied with. It is also an attitude of our mind to be cultivated day by day; the attitude that should colour our inner being every moment. Like the Nandi of Siva, we need to keep the frittering energies of the mind turned towards the Divine Self by effort, if we are not to get lost in our own mind games. Hence does Lord Krishna say in the Gita,

> **Fix your mind on me. Be devoted to me. Offer service to me.**
> **Bow down to me. And you shall certainly reach me.**
> **I promise you, because you are very dear to me. 18.65**

That is the practical translation of surrender. That is why the Gita shares it just before telling us about its supreme secret of surrender. As long as we are of the mind, as long as we have strong worldly impulses in our mind which we have not yet conquered fully, all that is required of us is to keep the mind turned towards its source: the Divine. That is the essence of a surrendered life. That is the reason behind the sacred ashes, vermillion bands, holy threads, long white robes, *taqiyas*, the turbans and so on – the various external symbols we see among spiritual people. For them, all those are external expressions of their subordination to the essence of life. Through all those, they reaffirm to themselves their commitment to the deeper aspect of life they are subordinate to.

So, returning to that sacred ash thing Kumar made fun of, on seeing me; these days, when I sometimes look with a neutral eye at how things have changed, I can't stop wondering at myself. I do all the things that I used to view with suspicion, when my grandfather did them. I get up before six, tell myself a morning prayer of perspective. Finishing my morning chores, I perform pranayama and my daily meditation. I apply a band of sacred ash with kumkum in the middle, as Muthu did, before I get into the day's work. My diet too has become predominantly Sattwic. At least one hour a day I stay silent and remain in the stillness I feel within. Whenever the gross ego with its strong whims and fancies looks to take over, I keep reminding it, 'Why don't you behave responsibly, dude? Don't you realise the game is not about you?'

When it grumbles back, I smile. I have learnt not to make much of the mind and its ways. I see now that just by a small change of attitude and our inner atmosphere, what a blissful life of peace and connection is available to all of us.

Such surrender doesn't mean we have done away with the world, once and for all. We still enjoy the pleasures the world has to offer. However, we do it not to escape, but with perspective. They are like 'sceneries we come across on the shore,' we know even as we enjoy them. And we know in our bones that what is important in this ride is what we are inside, as a person. In that alone is our focus.

ॐ

By the way, when I say all that, if it appears as though yours lovingly has reached some kind of culmination point in his spiritual journey, well, sorry! The world we live in is a world of divine maya. Never underestimate its power. It would sure prove its mettle over us many times.

Take a look at the words Gandhiji once used to describe himself, 'I claim to be a simple individual liable to err like any other fellow mortal. I own, however, that I have humility enough to confess my errors and to retrace my steps.'[3]

It is the world that delighted in calling him a Mahatma and put him up on a pedestal. However, the man saw himself as a simple human liable to err, and who had the honesty to correct himself.

That is a crucial point for us to grasp as we walk the spiritual path. Rest assured, that even when we feel the power and presence of the Divine in us, we will get caught in the world's melodramas quite often.

However, there is one thing we would notice, the time taken for our return keeps decreasing every time as we keep walking the path. We won't be possessed by the mind. We wouldn't sweep our weaknesses under the rug. Rather, we would learn to laugh at them.

To facilitate ourselves in such a quick return, it requires that we maintain the Gita inspiration tangibly in the background. That brings me to the most important ritual I adopt to maintain my little ego in a surrendered state; my daily reading of Gita.

These days as I get up in the morning I look forward to reading the Gita. My intellectual quest with it has been done away with, thanks to my father. Some days I get up from bed a bit confused. Rather than looking to anaesthetise the discomfort by diverting my mind to something else, I witness calmly what exactly is happening inside me, go to the Gita and read a relevant verse to clarify my thoughts. I calmly meditate on the meaning of the verse I have read and try to get in alignment with its truth. I feel the Gita embracing me like a loving teacher at those times. When I close the book, I feel renewed. The world around me seems renewed.

Some days, there is an alive connection in my heart as I wake up. At those times I go to the Gita as I go to a friend.

The clarity contained in the verses is enthralling. I almost look at it all and wonder sometimes, *'How did I live without it all these days?'* Maybe it wasn't living at all.

☙

Sanjaya, who recites the entire Gita to the blind king Dhritarashtra, says at the end of his recitation

> Wherever is Krishna, the Lord of Yoga,
> And wherever is Arjuna, the archer,
> There will be everlasting prosperity, victory,
> Happiness, and morality. This is my conviction. **18.78**

'*Gita is my abode,*' Lord Vishnu proclaims in the Varaha purana, '*I ever dwell in the place where it is read, heard, taught and contemplated upon!*'

'*All the sacred centres of pilgrimage dwell in that place where the Gita is kept, and where the Gita is read,*' the Purana adds. [4]

Thus, blessed people are we! Scarcely few people have ever had any contact with these sublime truths of our existence. After having gone after ill-guided materialistic pursuits all their lives, they have discovered its hollowness only at the end of it all. Having got acquainted to it now, we need to take time to assimilate it, re-awaken the wisdom within us, and slowly start aligning ourselves with it.

The spiritual path ends, they say, when a person is truly awake to his original identity. Then the human is said to have 'awakened' or 'enlightened.' However, it is not we separate humans who awaken. It is the Divine Presence that awakens in us. There is no human self to whom it happens or belongs. An interesting and rather shocking Upanishadic verse comes to mind here.

> **He to whom the Brahmanas and Kshatriyas are both food**
> **And death itself a condiment**
> **That Self – who can know where he really is.**
> Katha Upanishad 2.25

I await the day when this happens, when my ego is devoured totally by the Divine; the day when I die even when alive. However, I am not agitated in anticipation. To know that I am walking along the right path gives me so much peace. Travelling along this path is in itself blissful.

There is another truth we need to remember in this context. The Atharvana Veda explains the law of Karma this way –

> **There is no flaw in this law of Karma, no reservation.**
> **It is an exact and accurate regulation of action and its result.**
> **Man eats what he cooks. He reaps what he sows.**
> Atharva Veda 12.3.48

Surrender doesn't alter the karmic laws operating on us – the incidents that we are destined to face in our lives. However, while an ordinary mind gets caught up in the clamour and feels lost, a surrendered attitude gives us the inner space to view it all in a detached manner. We would be able to smile at the drama of our own miseries.

I saw Santosh and Saradha again on the day before my wedding.

My engagement function and reception were taking place together that evening. I was standing on the stage with the girl – my, ahem, would-be-wife. She was indeed looking like an elegant model who had just walked in from a fashion show on TV. There was a rare exuberance in her smile.

The cameras in the front kept flashing their blinding lights on us.

'Oh, my God! I think I am going to match her complexion only on the photo's negative,' I said to myself.

However, she appeared quite cordial and friendly. 'How is she going to react when I tell her about the decision I had taken few months back?' I wondered.

Santosh and Saradha were seated in the front row. Saradha was having a friendly and animated chat with Saravana, I noticed. They all came up together when I called. Saradha has not yet accepted his proposal, Sandy had told me over the phone.

When Saradha walked up to congratulate me, I told her on an impulse, 'Please don't say yes to that fellow. You will have to suffer a lot.'

The next moment I felt that I had blurted out something inappropriate in my excitement. But I saw her smiling calmly at Santosh. Santosh was standing next to me; Saradha was next to my fiancé. As we posed for the photo together, I took a quick, furtive look at Santosh and Saradha again. *'What a couple they will make,'* my thoughts went. And I felt the same tinge of jealousy as in our school times.

And this time, I was very happy to experience that tinge of jealousy for that fellow again.

ɞ

It was the morning of my wedding. Dattu Baba's BMW entered the parking lot as the watchman drove away the blind woman who had been begging near the entrance.

It was my mom's sincere belief that I was about to take sannyasa and it was the yajna she promised to perform for me to Dattu, that got me to agree to marriage.

The grand yajna was performed in the first floor of the marriage hall. Along with that a Chatru Samhara Yajna had also been organised which Dattu Baba had advised father to perform for warding off the evil influences that could result from destroying Alangadu.

The devotees were sitting in circles around Dattu Baba as the puja progressed in the marriage hall. Father too was standing there with folded hands near his new Guruji – with a large band of sacred ash on his forehead. Perhaps something bothered him about destroying the grove along with the temple, but maybe not strongly enough for him to abandon the project and let go of the profit from it.

Zab told me two days ago that a broad swimming pool had been constructed in the place where Muthu's temple had been. It seemed that the construction of individual suites was underway in the place of the grove and it was progressing quite well.

All those words and all that which happened along with my wedding could have been utterly repulsive for me. But they weren't. I had released those energy congestions into the inner silence I had discovered within me on the fateful day that Zab first told me about it.

I looked at my father as we posed together on the stage for a photograph. It surprised me to see what was happening inside me: it was compassion, unfathomable compassion that welled up in my heart towards him.

What a sad way to go through life he has chosen for himself! What ignorance he is wallowing in! If I were a village citizen affected by him, or a soldier in ancient times like Arjuna and he were on the opposing side, I might have resorted to something different, perhaps. But here I am, born as his son. All that matters is me being sincere in my Dharma towards him.

'I leave it to you dear Big Boss, I leave it to you! Take care of it all.'

That was all that I thought that day. And I have to add that there is no way that the ego that is me – with all its stubborn preferences and ideas – could have felt that. When the ego is kept subdued and surrendered to the Divine, it is the Divine presence in our heart that expresses itself as an immense compassion towards everyone it comes across.

> The Divine doesn't consider the demerits and merits of any.
> Knowledge is enveloped by ignorance,
> Thereby beings are deluded. 5.15

In the midst of it all, I couldn't help thinking often, 'Barath Sir, how can I thank you enough? Where would I have been without your Gita under such circumstances?'

ॐ

After a long lapse, fourteen years to be exact, I went to my old school last month. It felt like opening an old album after a long time. The memories of Santosh and me going to the school for one last time, meeting Barath Sir, the request he had made; all those wafted through the mind as I stepped inside the campus. I had finally fulfilled the vow that I had made to him in my heart during the last days of college.

I gave the large box with all the booklets I had gotten printed, to our headmaster. The man had become quite lean now. He no longer wore his trademark moustache. The coarse wrinkles on his face announced impending retirement. Well, I was seeing him after fourteen years, after all. I smiled within, as the nickname we had kept for him came to mind – Gorilla. He didn't recognize me and at first viewed me and the booklets I gave him with suspicion. Quite a few Hindu religious organisations often try to persuade the students of our school to join them that way.

'Give me a sample. Let me read and see,' he said.

I gave him a booklet from the box. He took out the thin reading glass from his shirt pocket, wore it and started reading it.

'Sir, let me take a walk around the school while you read it,' I said, and stepped out to give him some space.

I was strolling about in the school premises.

The ground where we played football and had fights with seniors, the corridor where we spent time as 'outstanding students,' the classes we took, with Barath Sir sitting among us students, all those scenes passed in front of my mind's eye.

I saw quite a few children and adolescents in trousers standing outside the classrooms with naughty smiles etched on their faces. Looking at them, it felt like looking at myself and Sandy.

'Got caught eating a burger in the middle of the class, boss,' one of them volunteered with a chuckle.

I smiled in reply. My phone rang as I was walking around. It was Rajagopal Sir.

'Sir, I am very angry with you,' I said, as soon as I pressed the call-answer button. Despite his promise, he hadn't come for the wedding.

'Sorry, Venkat, at the very last minute a patient with severe exfoliation got admitted in the hospital. A very young girl. I could have left her to my assistants and come, but I felt that I should be with her. Unfortunately, I couldn't save her. In a fit of anger, her attenders smashed the windows of the hospital and injured a staff-nurse, as they left. It is very saddening seeing the mindset many people approach doctors with, these days. However, I definitely couldn't have left her like that and come for the wedding.'

'Oh? Sorry, Sir.'

'Okay, someday I'll try coming to your town with my wife and Akil, for sure. So Venkat, it has been a year since you finished your PG. What did you learn in your butterfly period?'

'Well, quite a lot, Sir.'

The Gita's philosophy came to mind as he asked me that, and the reason he gave me for not coming, 'A young girl Venkat. I felt I should be with her.' Saradha's mother's words next echoed in my mind, 'Is life all about family and children? Let her continue with her practice. Look at how many people are happy because of her.'

As I was mulling over it, my eyes fell on the outline of the country embossed next to the words 'Sanskriti Hindu School for Boys' on the school gate. Within the outline was written, 'India – my pride'

'India – my pride!'

That's when it dawned on me, 'It is individualism and liberty that has always been the defining characteristic of the Western nations. However, when it comes to this country, it is this sense of duty towards others, putting other's welfare before ours and deriving happiness from it, that has defined it always. What Gita or Vedanta have these people read? The philosophy is in their blood already!'

'The world is in a running order because of such people and the yajna-spirit still alive in them,' the words from my write-up crossed my mind.

'What, Venkat? Such a long silence!'

'Nothing, Sir. I was lost in my thoughts.'

'Yes. Yes, I understand. This darned married life! We will have to get used to it with time.'

I laughed at his words. 'Okay, Sir. When you are done with your devotion to duty, take a break and do come over here someday. At least do it for your wife and son's sake,' I told him before I ended the call.

India – my pride. I was still turning those words around in my mind; as I put my smartphone back in my pocket.

India! It is in this country, the men of yore – rather than just looking to improve the utilitarian and external aspects of life – dug deep into themselves and discovered the sublime truths behind our human existence. They understood that a man's first requirement was that he should know himself and his universal roots. They realised that there would be no real peace or happiness for him, otherwise. Having discovered those truths of our origin and our life, they presented it to the entire despairing world to benefit from. How much pride should every Indian take in that! Swami Vivekananda had rightly observed, 'The more the Hindus study the past, the more glorious will be their future.'

'Sir,' the man who came out of the headmaster's office, called me. 'Are you Doctor Venkat? Sir has called you in.'

'I took a glimpse at it young man. You have prepared it quite nicely. It'll definitely bring some light and clarity to our students' minds . . . they never show any interest in such things these days, you know?' he said. There was a mild tremor in his hands and his voice. 'I will make arrangements to give it to all of them. What prompted you to do such a work, by the way?'

I told him about Barath Sir and the promise I had made to him. I knew he wasn't very comfortable having our Big B as assistant headmaster. Barath Sir's proactiveness used to put a lot of pressure on him. Therefore, I was slightly cautious when saying that.

However, I sensed he was a different man when he began speaking next.

'Barathan?' his voice conveyed surprise. He removed his glasses, put it on the table and started speaking contemplatively. 'Your name, doctor?'

'Venkat Duraisingam, Sir.'

'Doctor Venkat,' he said taking a deep breath and reclining in his chair, ' . . . there is a saying that a teacher can never know where his influence ends. A teacher affects eternity, they say. I have been quite skeptical about all that . . . and about this profession even! I used to believe that students only mock us when they leave school.'

I was listening silently as he proceeded in a solemn way.

'It is that man Barathan who taught me how true that saying is. And see . . . he continues to teach me even to this day. Just a brief tenure, some seven years or so, I think, he was in our school. But see how far its effect is still echoing? Quite a man he was, isn't it?'

'Well yes, Sir.'

'Teachers come and go out of our school but that man . . . he has done much more than people like me sitting in this chair for fifteen, twenty years haven't,' he said with a wry smile.

He then went on to tell me something quite astonishing about Barath Sir I hadn't known till then.

'You know something? His daughter, who was working in Chennai, passed away a few years before his retirement.'

'Is it, Sir?' I was startled. 'We never knew!'

'He told no one except me when he asked for leave. The man had so much love for her . . . his only daughter. She had some congenital lung disease I believe, but she was coping well with that. That is why he accepted the transfer, he told me. Yet, in a twist of fate, she succumbed to sudden heart failure! It was quite a difficult time in his life. He requested me to not tell people. He came back to school the very next day. When I enquired about it, he said, "Sir, it is sad that I lost one of my children, but don't I have hundreds more here?"'

I was dumbstruck.

'I couldn't contain my surprise,' he continued. 'It was that day I realised I was with someone special. Instead of engaging in petty politics with him, I should give him the respect that is due. He was someone whom the gods had sent here for this profession, Doctor Venkat. Even his tragic passing away in the last month of his job only proves that. He was born for this. It is only natural I respected him. I will surely give this write-up to all the students of Sanskriti, Venkat. I see it being orchestrated for our students by that man from the heavens, perhaps.'

I stepped out of his room in a while.

My eyes fell on the gold-plated wooden board with the list of all the past headmaster and assistant headmasters of the school – Sri Kannan 1982–1989, Sri Chidambaram Pillai 1989–1992, Sri Barathan 1992–1999.

I stood there unable to take my eyes off that last name.

'I have a daughter working in Chennai. She becomes unsettled and calls me every time she faces a crisis,' the words he spoke during our farewell crossed my mind.

'What a man you are, Sir! This was the crisis you mentioned nonchalantly in that speech?'

ॐ

The sun rises in the eastern sky. The entire town in front of me is shining with the golden orange hue cast by it. What our headmaster shared that day about Barath Sir still lingers strongly inside me.

'But I understand you now, Barath Sir. You were a person who got the truth of our world. That is why you could smile at it all. Anyone who gets a grasp of it would only do that. He would be able to do that even during a seemingly momentous event like death as you did. Who really dies after all?'

I felt that truth intensely on a Friday evening a few months back... when Muthu passed away. His asthma worsened when a tree in his grove was cut down. How would he bear the whole beloved grove of his, being destroyed? He passed away three days after that heartless demolition took place.

We saw that surrender can free us of our mental judgements and help us perceive people with compassion. We also saw that surrender lets us give ourselves into the hands of Existence and allow it do what it will with our lives. Surrender can also help us do one more thing. When our time comes, it lets us embrace our end with calmness and composure.

The Gita gives great importance to one's state of mind during the time of death.

He, who at the time of death quits his body meditating on me,
Doubtless attains to my being. Of this there is no doubt. 8.5

'If birth is a becoming, death too is a becoming,' declares Sri Aurobindo. That is the time we can't fake it. What is the deepest truth we have lived our life by, where our shraddha is truly fixed on, that alone comes to the fore and shapes the further journey of our soul. 'What the thought, the inner regard, the faith, settles itself upon with a complete and definite insistence, into that our inner being tends to change,' tells us Sri Aurobindo.[5] That is the decisive force in our soul's further journey.

Intent on me, departing thus from his body,
He attains the Goal Supreme. 8.13

In Dyaana, we cease to exist and let our real self shine through. In death too, pretty much the same thing happens. However, we do it once and for all. Seen that way, isn't death too a type of meditation?

ॐ

Muthu was suffering from status asthmaticus, a very acute and severe exacerbation of his asthma. All the hydrocortisones and aminophyllines were, surprisingly, of no use in Muthu's case, Saradha told me. My colleague Abdul who had checked

Muthu, told me that the boy's body had some strange resistance to all the drugs.

Saradha said to me that there wasn't any despair or grief in him since he heard that his grove was destroyed. Esakki, the caretaker of the grove, and many of the ardent devotees of the Goddess in that holy place were shell-shocked by what had happened right in front of their eyes.

However, in Muthu, none of those reactions were to be seen. He remained silent for a day, and the next morning he got admitted in the hospital with severe exacerbation of his asthma. It was as if he decided, *'Is it destroyed? So be it. I have no more work here. With that ends this game.'*

When I entered the ICU ward he was in, he was lying on the cot with an oxygen mask on his face and IV fluid flowing into his veins. His body was very weak, I noticed. All his chest muscles were retracted. I could see he was in great agony – his face contorted in pain even if he had to move a hand. His mother was standing by his side holding her son's hands. Her saree was drenched in tears. It must have been a very difficult load for her to bear; first she lost her husband and then her child was in such a state. Muthu's brother and his wife, Saradha and her father, were all standing in the corner of the room.

'How are you feeling, child?' the aged staff nurse in Saradha's hospital asked him in a voice suffused with compassion. She was trying to comfort the boy as she was injecting the final vial of hydrocortisone into his cannula.

However, the staff was taken aback when the boy turned towards her slowly, smiled and forced a nod as if saying, 'I am perfectly alright.' The peace that permeated his face was unmistakable.

None of us felt like talking after that. A peace radiated from him and in some unknowable way connected to the core of us all standing there. It seemed as though the boy was giving solace to us all.

I sat near him and held his hands as the nurse went out. They were rather cold. His breathing was shallow and strained. It seemed that it was not the disease which affected him. Muthu appeared to have taken a decision to leave, perhaps to a more real and eternal Alangadu after his death.

I lowered my head to his ears and said, 'Muthu, the work I told you I was into, it is over now. I really feel like coming over here often and spending more time with you. And see, Saradha, your mother and all of us here. How can you do this Muthu? Don't cheat us all.'

He lifted his right hand that was over his chest slightly as I told that, and gestured with difficulty as if saying, 'No, Sir, it is not possible.'

At around eleven, his breathing got shorter. It came in short gasps. The boy was nearing his end.

I held his hands and asked him, 'What happened, Muthu? How are you feeling?'

In all the strain, his eyes turned towards me and he smiled. That smile would become etched in my memory forever. What did it mean? Did it mean that he was peaceful, or blissful, even? You can say that. However, I felt there was no 'I' at all. Just that peace. His being was hollow. Like a flute. It always had been.

I left the room as his gasping got worse. I didn't want the lifeless body of the boy to get registered in my mind.

I was walking down the stairs. I heard his mother break into a loud cry. I could hear Saradha crying too. I walked out silently.

The birds were chirping in the tree nearby. A gentle drizzle had begun. Without telling anyone, I came out of the hospital and started my bike.

My journey into the Gita had begun more than a year back with the death of another pious boy. I remember seeing the same peace and the same serenity in his face, and in the face of all his family members when I saw them last. I had been confused, and startled with that reaction. But when I walked out of the ICU in Muthu's last moments, it surprised me to find that there wasn't any grief in my heart, either. I was feeling an immense calm.

I was riding back amid fallow fields. The sun was setting over the horizon. I didn't turn to look at the site of the grove on the way. Like Muthu, may that sublime grove remain in my memory as I saw it last.

I never got the chance to get to know Muthu as well as I would have liked. The same is true regarding Barath Sir. They were people who lived in an exalted inner state, and deeply nourished the core of people who were fortunate enough to cross their lives – just like the sun nourishes all living beings on earth. In a strange way, I felt lucky to have been there with the boy during his last moments; to be a witness to such a happening.

'Thanks Muthu. Meet you again someday.'

ॐ

My profession has made me come across many deaths – deaths of the high and the low. The eyes of a person on the brink of death are indeed powerful and unmistakable conveyors of their inner insecurities and incompleteness; all that they kept swept under rugs throughout their life. I could foresee the same emptiness waiting to greet all the men – including my father – involved in the destruction of that grove.

However, the perfect serenity and bliss I saw on Sameer and Muthu's face as they embraced death was something else. Paradoxically, I have never seen healthier or happier souls than those all my life!

> **May my breath return to the all-pervading Prana.**
> **May this body be burned to ashes.**
> **O mind, remember, at the point of death**
> **to remain fixed on the Divine.**
> **Remember at the point of death**
> **to remain fixed on the Divine.**
> Isa Upanishad. Verse. 17*

ॐ

Saradha said that it drizzled when Muthu's body was cremated the next morning. I went to his house in the evening. His

---

*An exact translation goes 'O mind, remember Brahman. O mind, remember thy past deeds.' 'The Vedic term term *kratu* means sometimes the action itself, sometimes the effective power behind action,' explains Sri Aurobindo. I have gone by the second meaning.

brother informed me that he and his family were going to stay along with his mom in Muthu's shop, and keep running it.

'You have taken a good decision,' I said. 'Hasn't the owner of the shop come for the funeral?' I asked him.

'No, Sir.'

I looked at the hotel and the twelve cent land it was situated in, and then at the words 'Prop: Francis Arockiam' below the Mother Mary drawing on the signboard of the hotel. The squabbles between Muthu and his mother came to mind.

'That owner, Francis, he has earned so much thanks to Muthu. He hasn't come for the funeral. But at least he can write off his share that Muthu is still sending from the shop, no?' I asked Saradha who was sitting next to me. 'Quite a few people are going to be dependent on the shop now. After all, the land is always going to be in Francis's name, right?'

'Sir,' responded his brother, 'Francis Ayya called me this afternoon. He said he was too ill to come to the funeral. When he prayed for Muthu, he said that his Lord Jesus ordained him to give the shop and the land to our family. He has decided to bequeath it all to my mother. His son has agreed to it too. He will come here for the registration in two weeks.'

'Oh!'

❦

It has been a few months since Muthu passed away. I wonder whether people will even believe if I tell them about such a boy who existed in our times, the remarkable bond he shared with a grove and a new kind of spirituality he had created and was following. And, like the rainbow vanishing as the clouds disperse, that he passed away when his grove was destroyed.

My father and his action crossed my mind. It was he who was the cause of the boy's death, in a way. I should be feeling angry and disgusted with him. And I should be feeling sorry for Muthu. However, I wasn't feeling either.

Who should I be feeling sorry for? I thought of Sameer's death that started it all; Barath Sir's demise at the age of fifty-eight, and the death of this boy, Muthu. *Is death really a tragedy?*

No matter who we are, no matter how much name and fame and wealth we may have acquired, one day, in a moment as real as I am writing this and you are reading it, we too are going to get old, weary, and face our end.

Death is certain for the one who is born,
And birth is certain for the one who dies.
Therefore, you should not lament over the inevitable. 2.27

There was never a time I, you, or these kings did not exist.
Nor shall we ever cease to exist in the future. 2.12

People who fought against mighty odds in their lives, like Rani Lakshmibai and Helen Keller; people who inspired a nation with their vision like Gandhiji and Subash Chandra Bose; people who caused powerful spiritual revolutions in the minds of men like Swami Vivekananda and Sri Aurobindo; the saints who lived at the pinnacle of consciousness like Sri Ramana and Sri Ramakrishna – they all met their ends one day. Would we call those deaths a tragedy?

Standing on the terrace I look at the brightening town in front. In each moment, how many joys and sorrows, how many ups and downs, how many dramas get enacted in this world before me!

The words of Swami Vivekananda comes to mind, 'This human body is the greatest body in the universe, and a human being the greatest being. Even the Devas will have to come down again and attain to salvation through a human body.'

It is this we should term as a tragedy, if there was ever one: squandering such a rare privilege called human life bestowed on us, scampering through it with half-baked convictions, wasting it for ill-guided materialistic pursuits, damaging others, and ourselves terribly in the process, and arriving at the end of it all with a painful weariness. That is indeed the real tragedy in life.

A distant temple bell rang.

Our Barath Sir, those two boys Sameer and Muthu, that old man who wrote his shop and the entire land for Muthu's family, all crossed my mind again.

How does it matter what name you call your God? How does it matter which place you go to worship him? Or what rituals you adopt to keep your mind reminded of him?

Does that make you a good human being? Does that help you face the inexplicable side of life and the world with the right perspective and composure? Does that drive you to lend a helping hand to other beings in need? Then indeed you are a religious man; the yogi, the Gita insists men to be, no matter which religion or sect you belong to.

> One is considered the perfect Yogi O Arjuna
> Who regards every being like oneself,
> And who can feel the pain and pleasures of others
> As one's own. 6.32

ॐ

Today is the day I had planned to tell my wife about a decision I had made a few months ago. I kept wondering how she would take it.

When mom was serving me breakfast, I asked her, 'Amma, did you watch the "Sri Ragavendra" serial yesterday?'

'No, da. Why?'

'They showed him becoming a monk after marriage, that too after he has a child.'

After standing in a stunned silence for a brief period, she dropped the spatula and left the room as the sambhar spilled onto my shirt. This made my wife look at me rather suspiciously. The Gita and many other spiritual books that lay scattered on my study table only added to her doubt. I had promised to take her out for dinner to explain what was happening in the house.

The day went by quickly.

I was gazing at my watch pensively. It was 9:30 pm. A soft melodious piano-piece was playing from the speaker over us in the dimly lit hotel room.

'One American chopsuey and vanilla milk shake for me, and a masala dosa for him. Can you make it a bit fast?' my wife asked the waiter with a smile while placing the order.

'Sure, ma'am,' he replied and went into the kitchen.

'Man, I am feeling damn hungry. So, after evening practice you come home and have food by this time, huh?' she turned and asked me, looking at her watch. Quite a chatterbox she was!

'Yes,' I nodded, as I kept wondering how she would take what I was about to share with her.

'And Venkat, I noticed when we were coming to the hotel. You were staring quite intently at the board of a CD shop near the signal.'

'Ah, that? A friend of mine had his clinic there.'

'Oh? His name is Santosh, right?'

'Yes,' I said.

'I remember seeing him at our marriage. I know a bit about him . . . from all the snaps you had put up on the net. Quite a naughty guy he is, huh?' she asked curiously.

'I should remove those snaps soon,' I told myself as she asked that. 'They have more than served their purpose.'

'Naughty? No, that is not the word, dear. He is one annoying and seriously sick freak,' I said as his farewell came to my mind, his infuriating farewell from Tuticorin a month back when he stretched my patience beyond its utmost limit.

ꧏ

The year's monsoon had begun. Among the days drenched in massive downpours, it was the only morning when it didn't rain very heavily. Sandy called just as I was about to end the morning session of my OP. He was leaving the town that evening.

'What Sandy? When is your train?'

'8:30, boss. I can't imagine that I am going to permanently leave our town, you know? I am going to miss it terribly I think. By the way, before leaving, I want to do one thing.'

'Dei, you have lately made me undergo too many mushy moments. I am still wrapping my head around your histrionics yesterday at Saradha's house. What else are you planning to do?'

'Don't worry. No more mushiness. We will enjoy our town's parottas together, one last time, before I go.'

'Deal!'

ꧏ

Sandy's train was in an hour's time, and we were still waiting at the parotta shop for our seats. It was me who was a bit anxious and was looking at the clock frequently. He seemed pretty relaxed.

His father and brother had gone to give the house-key to the owner and to meet a relative before leaving.

'Good things come only to those who wait. If you wait patiently, in five minutes you will taste our shop's parottas,' a waiter was giving his sarcastic solace to the overflowing crowd waiting outside even as he was busy serving. The crowd too didn't seem to mind waiting. The humour lightened the situation.

I smiled within to find another person relishing his work. I took a look at the time again, forty minutes to departure.

'Sandy, we will take a parcel and go. It might get late,' I said as we got our seats.

'Relax, boss.'

I looked at the table we were sitting at. We had been sitting here a year ago when I told Sandy how I would start reading the Gita. It was exactly the same place. Sandy noticed it too.

'Life goes in circles, huh?' said Sandy. 'You know what I think, boss?' he asked me as the waiter placed the water-glasses before us. 'I feel it is not the Venki I knew who has done the job our Big B gave us. It is as if some power has taken control of you and got you to do this write-up.'

'Well, thank you, Sandy.'

'Thank you? I didn't mean that as a compliment!'

I glared. Sandy was placing the order, unconcerned, 'Two parotta sets. One regular and one special gravy, boss.'

'Travel, you know? I am not willing to risk my stomach with that special gravy. By the way, what happened to the write-up you gave to our school? Any news?' he asked.

'Well, it's been just a few weeks back. But I saw one guy in a school uniform in the temple last week... must be in ninth or tenth. It wasn't our uniform, but Aanand Vidyalaya. He was holding the xeroxed copy of the write-up I had given to our school.'

'Oh? That is not bad!'

'Yeah, I too felt so happy as I saw that. Every one of us has these questions about life, Sandy. Everyone wants to know what we are doing here. If we are taught all these at a young age, it would make a huge difference to our lives and to the world. These things are not retirement-plans after all, as many people think. In that way I am happy it is of use to a few people.'

'Whoa!' he exclaimed.

It was then that I noticed that Sandy's eyes were bloodshot! They would be like this only when he was drunk. I noticed something else too as he sat close to me, he reeked of alcohol! I looked at him in disbelief. He too had sensed from my look that I had found out.

'Sandy, you have resorted to the bottle again?' I asked looking incredulously at him, 'Didn't you say just yesterday to Saradha that you will never turn to your old ways again?'

'Oooh! Our dermatologist has made his diagnosis in one look, as usual,' he laughed sheepishly looking down. 'Well boss, you said so many things from the Gita in the last one year. But I don't remember it telling us anywhere not to booze. Come on, man, just an occasional drink to ease ourselves a bit?'

Well, his words may have sounded reasonable, but the manner in which he said that didn't give me any hope. From the way he was slurring and his head was swaying, I sensed that he wasn't just drunk, but roaring drunk.

'I can't believe you are doing this, Sandy. You ignored the Gita I shared with you, alright. But, after all that you underwent, you are doing this again? And aren't your father and brother too coming with you? What would they feel if they see you like this?'

'Father, brother!' he chuckled. 'Don't worry. Those two dull-wits won't find out. I will go to sleep as soon as I get into the train.'

Our order had come. Turning away from him, I started eating the parottas that were on the plate before me. The meal could not end fast enough. I was simmering within. The food too wasn't up to the mark that day. The parottas were a bit hard and rubbery.

'Look at this parotta,' Sandy spoke with a mock-disdain holding one in his hand, 'Just like our rigid ego. They should have kneaded it a little further and made it soft, isn't it Venki? Just like we subdue our hard ego to the Divine in our hearts and make it soft.'

Well, that infuriated me and only added more fuel to the already seething anger. Again the Gita and all its words had gone out of my mind.

I took a few deep breaths and I told myself that I had done my best to redeem myself for a few mistakes I had committed with the guy, that pushed him into such wanton ways in the first place. I had tried to my utmost, but this person seems to be some special case whose roots run deeper than I could imagine. Why take it all on my shoulders? Doesn't God know? It would all happen as it is destined. Maybe he has to see a darker abyss before coming back. That thought pacified me somewhat. I ate without saying another word to him. I didn't even look in his direction, except when asking him to eat faster once.

'What composure, maaps! As Kumar once said, our Piggy has really become a Piggy Baba now, isn't it? Great maaps, great! *Samatwam Yoga uchathe.* . . . Am I right?' Sandy chuckled.

In a while we reached the station and were waiting in the bike-park. Sandy was seated on the bike's seat and I was standing a few feet away from him. We saw Saravana at a distance coming into the station premise with the luggage – a large suitcase in his one hand and a yellow polythene cover in another. The cover had a gift-paper-wrapped parcel in it. Sandy went and got hold of the suitcase from him.

'No, Anna. I have kept everything else in our cabin. Just this one thing is left. You talk to Venki anna and come.'

'Dear brother, when your elder one asks you for something, learn to obey it, okay? You go and help father climb the stairs. The train is on the third platform,' ordered Sandy.

It was nice to see Sandy talking to his brother with some warmth. Still, I didn't feel like talking to Sandy.

ॐ

We were standing outside his compartment as the train waited for the green light. It seemed like it would start raining anytime.

I had still not spoken to Sandy and was looking away from him.

'You know what? It feels strange, but looking at the train I am unable to control my laughter. Why is that, Venki?'

The train's whistle blew in the middle of his prattle.

'Hear that, Boss? Doesn't it remind you of the conch that our Big Boss Krishna blew before the war of Kurukshetra? That which is mentioned in the starting of the Gita? Booooo! Maybe it is telling me to get ready for the tough time I will face there,' Sandy was blabbering with his body swaying unsteadily.

I controlled my temper, else I would have given him a tight slap for his intoxicated chatter. I took a deep breath, turned towards him and said finally, 'Okay, Sandy. It is your life. Take care. I will leave now. Tell Uncle and Saravana.'

A mild drizzle had started already, accompanied by a strong, cold breeze. Sandy got in and was standing near the steps of the compartment holding the side bar – his body still swaying uncontrollably.

'Hey, you will fall down. Go inside.'

'Fall down? I have just returned from an abyss, Boss. Do you think I can fall any deeper?'

'Sandy. Go inside!' I yelled.

'Ooh, anger man! Okay, Boss, take this parcel with you. I have something for you.'

'What the hell is in this?'

'Go home and open it. You will know,' he said.

Before the drizzle gathered momentum, I reached home on my bike with the parcel he gave to me, in my hands.

After drying my hair and changing into my *lungi*, I went to the terrace with the parcel. There had been a wide grin on Sandy's face when he gave it to me. Sitting on the chair under the sunshade I looked at the sky. It was a full-moon night. The weather was kind to me. The gentle drizzle hadn't gained momentum.

I opened the parcel wrapped in gift-paper. Inside it, there was a letter and another smaller parcel. I was pleasantly and totally shocked as I unfolded and started reading the two-page-long letter that Sandy had written in his characteristic messy handwriting.

'Hi Venki Boss,

I know your brain which becomes stiff in anger would have believed me when I said I drank again.

You know what? For the last year or so, I am seeing a new, serious, philosophical tinge in your face. I felt like seeing that cute, old piggy face of our school times one last time before I leave.

Let me tell you now, I didn't drink!

Bloodshot eyes, smell of alcohol – where did they all come from, you wonder? Well, if something is worth doing, it is worth doing well too, you see. I saw a new unopened bottle of TASMAC whisky in my room as I was cleaning it this morning. Kumar had given it to me some time back. Then I saw my eyes in the mirror. They were bloodshot due to lack of sleep. (Two whole days I have been packing things non-stop. And it was you who spoiled my afternoon nap yesterday taking me to see Saradha.)

Then I got this idea – I could sprinkle a few drops over myself and put up a drama. My father and Saravana too knew it. How was my acting? Pretty real, isn't it? (Seething with anger? Wish you could pound me to the pulp right now? Ha, intention fulfilled! Mm, how I wish I could see your face as you read this!)

Coming back to why I resorted to this letter business. For this too you are responsible, Venki. I had planned to tell you something important before leaving. It was you who asked me not to get mushy. And telling it in a letter is more comfortable too, I realise as I write.

Let me switch over to mushy mode one last time with your permission. Ready? Here I go.

I look at myself now, Venki. It is as if I am seeing the old school-time Santosh again. I feel pure, I feel overhauled. You think Gayatri's mail was the only thing responsible for it? No, Boss, you are wrong.

My father going to another doctor and spending a huge amount and him setting aside the medicines I gave him – that incident had already shaken my world to its core. After all, it was that man, who brought up both of us with great difficulty after our mom passed away.

He even refused to marry a second time, that he could have easily agreed to, as he was bothered about his two children. I respect him greatly. When he ignores me like that, how can I be unaffected, Venki boss? Then, at exactly the same time, Gayatri's mail arrived in my inbox. Maybe as you said, it is a mysterious force behind it all that orchestrates things like this.

I didn't tell you where I went, isn't it? Let me tell you now. I went to Kodaikanal. Why Kodaikanal? Well, I didn't plan it. I walked into the bus-stand. That was the first bus I saw, boarded, and reached there.

Having got there, I spent most of the time at Coaker's Walk — that tourist spot Kumar's friends and I visited and had fun during last year's puja holidays. Sitting in that spot, I contemplated calmly on my life, on how, without holding on to anything, I had let certain unfortunate incidents cast me adrift over the last ten years or so.

The memorable school days, the guidance of our ever-smiling Barath Sir all came to mind. Then I looked at myself . . . at the person I had become. It felt utterly disgusting. Do you remember Anbu? The old guy who used to come to our surgery O. P. during our internship with a massive soft-tissue tumour over his back? I felt exactly like that as I looked at myself.

I wished it were all a dream and would just vanish right then. The 'me' I had let myself become felt so repulsive to be with. It was quite a painful thing to experience, Venki boss. Maybe in a moment of madness that I am known for, I might have resorted to something stupid in that place. You know what stopped me?

Your astute brain should have guessed by now. It was the wisdom of the Gita you shared, Boss.

I had a dream as I slept on a bench there. In that, our Barath Sir appeared before me. He looked as vibrant and energetic as he was when he joined our school. Approaching me from somewhere, he asked me like he used to in his class, 'Did you understand what I taught you so far, Santosh?'

It was the Gita he was asking about. I, who was sitting before him as a teenage-boy in our school uniform, said, 'Yes.'

'Really well?' he asked next.

'Yes,' I said again.

You know what he did next? He sat near me on the bench and asked quite firmly, 'Dear boy, if you really understood it that well, what makes you think you can squander your life any further? Come on, get up, you have so much to do...' He shook me hard as he said that.

I got up. What you shared with me over the last one year came to mind. All that knowledge came to the fore as if it were mine. Particularly a verse, what was that (?), 'Don't yield to unmanliness.' The words of Vivekananda you quoted along with that rang in my ears, 'Shake off the delusion that you are sheep and arise O lions.' That just rocks, Boss! Those words possessed me.

So this lion finally got up, caught a bus straight to Chennai to reapply for the transfer to CIIMER it had declined. I felt it was a golden opportunity to redeem myself that had come in search of me. No way could I ignore it.

See the irony? I joked to you once about shaving the hair when you shared this part of the write-up with me. That day before I returned I did exactly that. I just felt like doing it.

I was wondering as I travelled, 'What happened to me during the time you shared the book's teachings?'

I was indeed inspired to change myself many times during the last year, I should say, as you were sharing our Sir's Gita. Why did I keep going further and further down? What happened to all the respect and gratitude I had for our Sir?

I guess this is what happened. As I kept hearing stuff from the Gita, my inner demons grew stronger and stronger to combat its wisdom. They pulled me lower in defense. At last, Truth, through the impetus given by Gayatri, found a way to conquer it and emerge the victor. See, my psychiatric brain diagnoses it all only now. As the adage goes, doctors are indeed poor patients, Boss.

What a life many people like me live, Venki boss! Eating like pigs, boozing regularly, the fantasisings, the unthinking desire cravings that push us to do various stupid things... we have no choice, but to keep going that way blindly till we get a real, strong taste of the truth in us. Very sticky stuff all are,

I see now. One brings in all into our house.

Remember one thing though, Venki. If we are lucky, there comes a moment of truth in our life . . . when the entire edifice we have built on a false base comes crashing down spectacularly. When it does, at least knowing what it is all about will help, right? For that I owe a big thanks to you, for having faith in me and sharing the Gita despite all that I was doing.

I have work to do now. The tumour is there on my back even now. Rest of the days, all I plan to do is compensate for the time I have wasted so far. That is why I took up this work. When the psychiatry department in CIIMER gets rid of all its scum, I will consider that the scum over me too has cleared.

Will someday come to your little town again when I find time, to taste its parottas. Mmm, that is what I am going to miss most.

Go on and open the gift-parcel now if you haven't yet.

Love,
Sandy.'

'You crazy fellow!' Saying that, I unwrapped the gift keeping the letter aside. It was a pair of wristwatches, one each for me and my fiancé. There was a slip inside the parcel with a handwritten note, 'Thanks Piggy Baba,' it said.

I called him up immediately.

'Was expecting your call, maaps. You took so long to read that two-page letter, huh? Pretty old you have become, I guess.'

'You psycho! You acted drunk to see my cute piggy face? Wait till I catch you.'

I could hear his brother giggling in the background. '*Oh my God! You too Saravana?*'

'Regarding the gift, Venki, I wanted to give it to you for your marriage. But then I felt I should give it to you before I leave,' Sandy said.

'Stupid, why spend so much again for a pair of watches?' I asked him.

'Pair of watches?' he said, 'look again at yours.'

I looked. I saw that it was the same watch he had given me after plus two – the one I had smashed into pieces a few months back in his clinic.

'Sorry, maaps,' I told him holding the watch in my hands with remorse. 'Sometimes we do things in haste, you know?'

'Well, don't be. You only saved me a few bucks. Didn't take much for renewing the nickel polish and its strap.'

'You are one crazy freak, Sandy.'

I heard the loud whistle of his train as he said before ending the call, 'Alright boss, bye for now. Meet you again someday.'

ॐ

**Lord Krishna and Arjuna seated in the grand chariot
Yoked with white horses, blew their celestial conches. 1.14**

**The tumultuous uproar,
Resounding through heaven and earth,
Tore the hearts of the Kauravas. 1.19**

What Sandy said in the station was true in a way. The train's whistle, as I heard it on the phone, indeed reminded me of the sound of the conch mentioned in the Gita as the war of Kurukshetra begins.

If all the modern-day youngsters who have a sense of Dharma still alive in them, realise who they are and their responsibility towards the world like Santosh has, and surrender their lives to their Dharma, it might indeed be the death-roar of the clueless Kauravas spoiling our world.

Santosh! The guy's Dharma was never in medicine or the field of psychiatry. It is to help people – the deprived, underprivileged souls out there; to bring light into their lives. And at last he has grasped the opportunity to do it, which presented itself before him. He was blaming God and our times so far for the world being in pain. For the first time he had realised, 'It is *my* world out there which is in pain.' All his goodness that was lying dormant for a long time is raring to go and embrace the world. Things will turn out right, I am sure.

'It will all turn out well,' the final words I had heard Barath Sir speak crossed my mind. And now I could see that that had come to pass.

I went and lay down on the bed. I was smiling. I thought of the night I read that mail from Gayatri a few weeks back. That had been the most peaceful of nights for me, in a long time. But this night as I lay down and closed my eyes... the peace I felt in my heart... well, it felt sublime, incomparable to anything I have experienced.

That darned dream that was disturbing me for over a decade; I sensed it would never return again.

ଔ

'Hey Venki, what happened?' my wife asked. Our order had come and she was midway through her American chopsuey.

'Oh, sorry! Was lost in thoughts. You were asking about Santosh, right?'

'He has got a transfer from this place to Chennai, huh? Lucky guy,' she sighed.

I looked at her as she said that.

'Oh, don't get me wrong. I like this town. Despite the scorching heat, it has a nice relaxed atmosphere, none of the hustle and bustle we see in Bangalore is here. The beaches too are quite nice. But it feels a bit sad inside too, you know? I have to go without my weekly stuffed-crust pizzas and multiplex movies,' she said sporting a self-mocking smile. 'The dosa they give here in the name of pizza, hmm!'

I smiled back at her. And I realised that the time had come to tell her about my decision.

'Yes, dear, I too have decided on it. We are shifting out of Tuticorin in a few months' time.'

'Oh? That is great Venki,' she said swiftly, and with obvious excitement. 'I was really hoping you would say that.' She put the fork down with the chopsuey in it and asked, 'Where? To Chennai, like your friend Sandy? Bangalore too would be a good choice. My uncle can help you settle there. Your branch has very good opportunity there, you know?'

'It would be nice if we could shift to those places, dear. But I have some unfinished duty here. The place we are moving to is a village near Tuticorin, called Pasumaikudi.'

The pleasure on her face became perplexity and a big incredulous, 'What?' slipped out of her mouth as she heard my reply.

ଔ

That's it boys and girls! The story of Venki coming to terms with the Gita, him teaching it to that filthy Sandy and the irrevocable ways their lives ended up being altered by their study. And here I am again – the guy who introduced you to Venki at the start – back to wrap things up. A punchy ending serves a book well you see – just as its bizarre opening got your attention.

And if you haven't guessed yet, this is the same filthy Sandy speaking.

To be honest, sorry, I don't feel that the name suits me anymore. I, these days, have started feeling like the Santosh of school times once again. Playing in the rain with Venki, our combined studies and we helping each other do well in academics, I feel as though all those belong to the present.

I am married to Saradha now. Saradha, with her father and mother, has moved to Chennai. The people of Pasumaikudi gave her such an emotional farewell when she bid goodbye to her hospital. (Hmm, Tuticorin too bid farewell to a great psychiatrist a few months back. I wonder if anyone even noticed! Mad fellows!)

Saradha! It feels fascinating to be with the girl. Her whole internal mechanism seems to operate in quite a distinctive way. She hardly thinks about herself. She often expresses her wish to start her practice in Chennai soon. However, I have told her firmly, 'Dear madam, let us have a child first, and then you can continue with your life of service.' Saradha is five-months pregnant now. It is a boy-child, we saw on the scan. She has already selected a name for our son, Muthu Kumar.

Venki has moved to Pasumaikudi with his wife, and is living the relaxed, restful country life that he often wished for. He is the one looking after Saradha's hospital now. He is finally earning his keep and has stopped living off his father. However, he accepts whatever money his father gives him. He is using that to set up another grove and temple on the outskirts of the village, with the village people's help, he told me. He goes to his house in Tuticorin once a week to see his parents. Also, he comes to Chennai once in a month or so – to give his wife her due of stuffed crust pizza!

After seeing the response his write-up had among the students, Venki is now planning to publish it as a book. He told me a few days back that he has sent a sample chapter to a popular publisher.

'That's great, man. What's the title?' I asked him.

'Haven't decided yet. Something like "Living by the Gita in today's world,"' he replied.

'Maaps,' I said to him, 'if there is such a title in the bookstore, I swear I will stay at a safe distance. Please change it. Give it a weird title, maapi, something that makes people notice it. Let me think . . . "Butterflies, Parottas and the Bhagavad Gita," how's that for a title?'

'What?' he asked incredulously, as if I asked him to change his sex.

'Alright, we'll make it *parathas*. That'll have a pan-Indian appeal. Is it okay for you now?'

He didn't reply. Obviously, he was a bit miffed.

'Ha ha, was just kidding man. But do send me the final manuscript before you send it to the publisher . . . will add some spice to the work. The reader should not fall asleep in the middle of all your verbose philosophising, you see.'

'Mm, okay. But don't touch the title.'

'Come on, boss. You can trust me on that. Now that I know you don't like it, why would I do it?'

He thought for a moment before agreeing to my request.

Rest assured, Venki boss. The first thing I will do when you send it to me is change that dull, drowsy title. Who will buy such a book, Living by the Gita in Today's World? Eeeww!!! I will hack your mail with Saravana's help to keep you unaware. It is my chance to avenge myself. 'It's all a big Cosmic play of God,' didn't you say in your write-up? Try practising it too, dude. What will you do when you find out? Bash me up? You can't, dear friend. I am in CIIMER now. In Chennai. Far away from you. Mmm, how I wish I could see your face as you receive the first copy of your book!

And, how's my work at CIIMER, you ask? Absolutely mad, of course. Coping with the set-up is hard enough. Imagine trying to change it! All that the management here cares for is getting longer prescriptions and meatier investigations from doctors. The one who tries bringing in some change is viewed as a bug worth squashing under the foot. To their bad luck, they can't transfer me, as I came in through a government posting.

'Why are you making your everyday life a hell by opposing the system here, Dr Santosh? Do you think you can singlehandedly bring any change here?' some of my co-lecturers ask me. I smile in return. And those people also say that I look remarkably composed for the enormous tension and stress I undergo in my work.

I wish I could tell them that it is a book that lies on my reading table I owe my composure to: *The Bhagavad Gita*.

The Gita has taught me to not take myself or the game I am playing here, seriously. It has taught that it is not me who is running the show; I am just an instrument, a channel of entry! How can tension or stress creep in when that is now etched strongly in my mind? As Venki said in his write-up, there is only a sense of calm responsibility and a sort of joyful emptiness that I feel as I do my job.

These days, depending on what my mind seeks, I read a verse or two from the Gita daily before starting the day. Whatever I come across in day to day life – the joyful stuff and the mean and menacing ones – I accommodate it with a mind and heart in touch with the Gita.

Can I singlehandedly overhaul the entire set-up here? Such a question seldom crosses my mind. I feel this to be my duty and I am doing it. That alone matters for me. I don't allow the huge, mad, chaotic world before me to overwhelm or stress me anymore.

I sleep well. I see that my lips are always turned up. It feels blissful to be just living and it feels blissful to do the work I am doing. It has taken me a long time to arrive at this place within myself. But I can say that my days of being bewildered by the complexities of life, the frustrations and exhaustions, and the resultant escapist and despicable ways I was resorting to unthinkingly, all those have come to an absolute end. I feel safe and secure. I follow the Gita.

I have a strange dream these days. Venki and I are pushed off a huge, towering cliff. First he pushes me off. After a brief gap, he too is pushed down. We are both hurtling down. Our eyes fall on the great, bottomless abyss before us. We look at each other, and smile. We do not experience even a tinge of anxiety or fear.

Why should we? We were both flying.

APPENDIX

THE FOUR-FOLD VARNAS

The four Varnas are the fourfold way an individual Swabhava fits into the society. 'Each Jiva possesses in his spiritual nature these four sides. (He) is a soul of knowledge, a soul of strength and of power, a soul of mutuality and interchange, (or) a soul of works and service, but one side or other predominates in the action and expressive spirit,' in Sri Aurobindo's words.[1]

As long as we lived as hunter-gatherers, our social structure was egalitarian. However, once we progressed to live in complex societies, people started to specialise in various fields of work. Depending on the need and importance people attached to each work, some kind of hierarchy became inevitable in every complex society. The feudal system of medieval Europe was a way of division based on birth, wealth and possessions. In modern times, the division is predominantly based on one's wealth, education and social status. Gita gives us a division that is more rooted in one's individual Swabhava, rather than such external standards.

Let us briefly discuss what each of those four Varnas are about.

Brahmanas are the spiritually evolved people, the exemplars of the right way of life. They are the thinkers who are 'moved to find the law and truth and the guiding rule of the whole matter.'[1] Studying, teaching and guiding the world intellectually, morally and spiritually is their duty. They are the guiding conscience of the world.

True Brahminism isn't decided by birth. In the Mahabharatha, Bhishma in his last moments describes the true meaning of Brahminhood this way, 'Acts alone determine who is a Brahmana and who is not. Performing all rituals and sacrifices does not make a Brahmana. He who is free from the bondage of desire is a Brahmana. He who restrains his senses, who is constantly in Samadhi is a Brahmana.' According to the Gita, the inherent qualities of this group of people are

> Serenity, self-restraint, austerity,
> Purity, forgiveness, uprightness,
> Knowledge, realisation, belief in God. 18.42

It is the men with such Brahmana temperament who serve as the conscience and the exemplars in every field, who take their individual fields – and the world – forward in the right direction. It is such men Vedanta refers to when it says,

> **Whichever Brahmanas are superior among us,**
> **Should be received by you with reverence!**
> **Give your offerings to them with reverence and humility!**
> Taittiriya Upanishad 1.11

Kshatriyas are people with a kingly warrior spirit in them. 'Governance, politics, administration, and war' is what they are cut out for. To govern and to protect people is their natural function.

Vaishyas are traders and business people. They produce or procure all objects necessary for daily living – the objects varying with time.

The function of the last group is 'to execute the duty given to them' (18. 44). The Gita calls them **Shudras**. It refers to the people who belong to the working class who are employed for wages by the other three.

This group's function demands some elaboration. Citing the reason that they belong to a 'lower' caste, legions of human right abuses have been inflicted on these people in our country over centuries.

Certain truths need to be grasped about this group and their role in the society. Yes, Shudra refers to the labourers who don't have any of the previous three qualities predominant in them, and who know only to execute the duty given to them. Let me share a popular joke in this context. A teacher asked his students, 'Who built the Taj Mahal?' and the students replied, 'Masons'!

However, when we think about it, where is the joke in this? Isn't it the truth? One who designs the Taj may be an intellectual, but without the real executors, where would the Taj have been, or anything else, for that matter? The function of the working class is similar to the legs we stand upon. 'It is the members of this caste who ably bear all the burdens of the earth by helping those born in the other caste,' declares an ancient inscription on them.[2] So it behoves people to have a thankful attitude towards this group and uplift them as much as they can.

Secondly, it is not about those doing manual work alone. It can also refer to people in medicine, software, art, law or any other branch, who are good at 'executing the duty given to them' rather than working on their own initiative. That too in a way comes under this classification. After all, the Gita doesn't talk about their external jobs, but only the inner disposition in the verse. It doesn't matter whether our work is white-collared, blue-collared or no-collared. As long as we are executors with none of the above three qualities dominant in us, we belong here.

And there's no shame in being such a labourer anymore than the legs feel shame for being what they are. There are no menial jobs in the world, only menial attitudes, as a wise man said. The most innovative business model and the solid, well thought-out strategy to implement it are nothing without the people who really carry out that implementation at the grass-root level. They are the support on which any organisation stands.

This Varna system was a fluid system when it was conceived. If not, many saints our nation adores greatly like Kabir, Valmiki or Namdev couldn't have done the work they did, having born in the last group. Sadly, over the centuries, it became birth-based and rigid due to the opportunistic interpretation of a group of people. The Gita reinstates this original truth behind it.

And it should also be remembered that one can adopt any Varna to any field of work. There have been Kshatriyas even among spiritual Gurus. Swami Vivekananda was one. With his warrior spirit the monk in his short span of life single-handedly shattered the widespread misconceptions the western world had towards Hinduism.

Those according to the Gita, are the four inner dispositions of man. If mine is an undeveloped mind which can't nurture thoughts larger than my own survival and the survival of people close to me, then I am a Shudra. If mine is a mind and a temperament that is naturally inclined towards supplying the daily needs of the society and helping in its smooth functioning, then I am a Vaishya. If I am inclined towards protecting my society and governing it in the right way, I am a Kshatriya. If the quest for a higher truth defines me, then I am a Brahmana. Think about it. Is there any other way an individual swabhava can fit into the society?

ॐ

GROWING IN SATTWA

The Gita gives a set of internal principles and external aids to adopt for us to grow in the noble guna of sattwa.

A sattwic man does his actions with only one motivation

Because it ought to be done as one's duty. 18.9

The Yajnas he does are

**The Yajnas enjoined by the scriptures,
Performed with a firm belief that it is a duty,
and without the desire for the fruit. 17.11**

'The more impersonal the motive of action the more sattwic is its nature,' says Sri Aurobindo.[3]

A sattwic is dictated to act by the just rhythm and law of his works, we discussed about before. It is his sense of righteousness that drives him; not just the fruits of his work.

Thus, he does his Swadharma, contributes to the world through that, all because it is his duty here. He is a pure, joyous instrument of Dharma.

In the same lines **sattwic charity** is

**The charity that is given as a matter of duty,
to a deserving candidate at the right time,
and in which no return is expected. 17.20**

Next, a few words on **sattwic austerities**. Austerities are the limits we set on ourselves. The spiritual path becomes easier with the observance of certain austerities. They are like the fences we put around our plant till it grows fully.

I am the austerity in the ascetics. 7.9

says the Lord in the Gita. Austerities need not mean injunctions which we have to follow in a stoic, impassive way. That is imprisonment. We should develop a genuine taste for anything we try to incorporate in our life, and relish doing it. It is then it can benefit us and help in our journey. The Gita talks about the various austerities we can abide by and about the sattwic way of practising those.

**The worship of Devas, Brahmana, Guru, and the wise;
Purity, honesty, celibacy and nonviolence –
these are said to be the austerity of deed. 17.14**

> Speech that is not offensive, truthful, pleasant,
> beneficial and is used for the regular reading of scriptures
> is called the austerity of word. 17.15
>
> The serenity of mind, gentleness, silence, self-restraint
> and the purity of mind are called the austerity of thought. 17.16
>
> (These) threefold austerities practised by Yogis
> with supreme faith, without a desire for the fruit
> is sattwic austerity. 17.17

The mind assumes the shape of the 'mould of thoughts' we constantly subject it to. Thus, the above are wonderful principles to read regularly, assimilate and abide by.

The same austerities can be followed in a pretentious and extravagant way as well, without really relishing their essence. Then it becomes a rajasic austerity. 'Austerity practised to gain respect, honour and worship, and with ostentation is rajasic. It is unstable, and transitory,' (7.18) says the Gita.

The Gita also speaks of a **sattwic diet.**

> **The foods that promote longevity, virtue,**
> **Strength, health, happiness, and joy**
> **Foods that are juicy, smooth, substantial**
> **and agreeable to the stomach,**
> **Such foods are dear to the sattwic persons. 17.8**

We know that food has quite a concrete effect on the body. It has a profound effect on the mind too, declare our scriptures. The Chandogya Upanishad (6.5.1) explains how food influences the mind.

> Food when eaten becomes threefold.
> What is coarsest in it becomes the excreta.
> What is medium becomes flesh.
> And what is subtlest becomes mind.

'Mind consists of food' (6:5:5) according to it.

Sattwic foods include most vegetables and fruits, water, cereals, beans, nuts, grains, honey, milk and milk products. On the other hand, the spicy, salty, bitter, and sour foods are termed rajasic. The stale, preserved foods like pizzas, burgers, colas and other canned foods are tamasic.

A sattwic diet promotes sattwa guna in the mind, calms down the body and promotes strength and longevity.

> **When the food is pure, the mind becomes pure.**
> Chandogya Upanishad 7.26.2

A good practice along the Yogic path is simply to observe the effect of each food we consume on the body and mind. At first we can, as an experiment, stick to such a sattwic diet for a brief period, say a fortnight or so. If we do, research shows that our now-detoxified body will become more sensitive and aversive to non-sattwic foods. We will start craving healthy food, as the changes become ingrained in us. Then we can begin to make gradual changes in our regular food habits through the yardstick of our own experience and awareness.

Moving on to **sattwic knowledge** . . .

> **That by which one sees**
> **the one indestructible reality in all beings,**
> **Undivided in the divided, know that knowledge as sattwic. 18.20**

A sattwic person sees behind all beings an inseparable oneness.

> Sattwic discrimination is
> **That which understands**
> **what should and what shouldn't be done,**
> **What leads to bondage and what leads to liberation,**
> **That understanding is sattwic. 18.30**

That is quite an important practical message for us when we look to walk the Gita's path. Our Big Boss insists, 'Dear boys and girls, during any action you do, with a keen discrimination, observe if you are becoming furthermore gross materialistic beings, or light spiritual beings. Discern if you are taken into custody by your mind or released into the freedom of your heart. Do it with your every action.'

When we start walking the spiritual path, it is a *moment to moment Kursukshetra* in a way. The world and our abetting mind is always waiting at every turn to tempt us into its clutches and pull us down. When it does, we should be aware enough to sense that happening inside us, so we can combat it. Hence developing this subtle sensitivity is crucial in walking the spiritual path.

About **sattwic determination** the Gita says,

> **The unwavering fortitude by which through Yoga,**
> **the functions of the mind, the prana and the senses**
> **are restrained, that fortitude is sattwic. 18.33**

The Gita not only talks about meditation here, but about training the mind puppy and the sensual horses as much as possible, and keeping them under our control.

'Don't let the puppy take you for a walk, with that sniffing its way towards every post and pillar, with you getting dragged behind,' it urges.

REFERENCES

ABBREVIATIONS

CW–The Complete Works of Swami Vivekananda. (From www.ramakrishnavivekananda.info)

EOG–Essays on the Gita; Sri Aurobindo. (Sri Aurobindo Ashram, Pondicherry: Ninth edition. 1997 reprint)

Gosp–The Gospel of Sri Ramakrishna translated by Swami Nikhilananda. (Sri Ramakrishna Math, Chennai)

SS–Srimad Bhagavadgita Sadhaka-Sanjvani; Swami Ramsukhdas. Vol. 2. (Gita Press, Gorakhpur.)

TWR–Talks with Ramana Maharishi. (Sri Ramanasramam, Tiruvannamalai: 2010)

SCRIPTURE

1. Gosp. p. 423
2. CW. Vol. 1, Raja yoga. Introductory.
3. EOG. p. 10
4. Gosp. p. 476
5. EOG. p. 88

LIFE

1. The Synthesis of Yoga. Sri Aurobindo. (Sri Aurobindo Ashram, Pondicherry) p. 6
2. CW. Vol. 3, Lectures from Colombo to Almora. The Vedanta in all its phases.
3. CW. Vol. 5, Notes from Lectures and Discourses. On the Vedanta philosophy.
4. Gosp. p. 273
5. The Synthesis of Yoga. Sri Aurobindo. (Sri Aurobindo Ashram, Pondicherry) p. 20, 21
6. CW. Vol. 5, Notes from Lectures and Discourses. Law and Freedom.
7. That whole explanation is borrowed from: The Book: On the taboo against knowing who you are. Alan Watts. (Vintage books; 1989)

The principle behind Kaali is from Swami Sithbavananda's *'Sakthi thathvam'* (Sri Ramakrishna Tabovan, Thiparaithurai)

MIND

1. Freedom from the known. J Krishnamurthi. Chapter 2. (From www.jiddu-krishnamurti.net/en/freedom-from-the-known)
2. EOG. p. 534
3. Towards a psychology of being. Abraham Maslow. (Wiley; 3rd edition, 1998)
4. CW. Vol. 8. Notes of class talks and lectures. Hindus and Christians.
5. As quoted in *Rumi and His Sufi Path of Love*. M Fatih Citlak and Huseyin Bingul. (Tughra books; 2007)
6. CW. Vol. 1. Addresses at the parliament of religions. Paper on Hinduism.

KARMA

1. Motivation and Personality. Maslow, A H (Harper and Row, New York; 3rd ed, 1987) p. 22
2. EOG. p. 372
3. EOG. p. 519
4. CW. Vol. 1. Raja Yoga. Prat-yahara and Dharana.
5. The Making of an Expert. Ericsson, Anders K. ; Prietula, Michael J; Cokely, Edward T. Harvard Business Review (July– August 2007)
6. EOG. p. 517
7. EOG. p. 520
8. Paths to God - Living the Gita. Ramdass. (Three Rivers Press; 2005) p. 60
9. http://www. rdasia.com/the-generous-vegetable-seller/
10. As quoted in www. arunachala-ramana.org/forum/index.php?topic=5698.0
11. CW. Vol. 5. Conversations and dialogues.
12. EOG. p. 486
13. EOG. p. 514–523
14. A General Theory of Love. Thomas Lewis, Fari Amini, Richard Lannon. (Vintage; 2001) p. 216
15. EOG. p. 171
16. CW. Vol. 4. Lectures and Discourses. Thoughts on the Gita.
17. EOG. p. 469

KARMA II

1. A striking example:
   www.colin-andrews.net/UFO-EdgarMitchell-X-Conf. html
2. Sermons, Meister Eckart. (Cosimo classics; 2007) The Angel's greeting.
3. CW. Vol. 1. Lectures and Disc-ourses. The Gita III
4. Integral Yoga. Sri Aurobindo's Teaching and Method of Practice. (Sri Aurobindo Ashram, Pondicherry) p. 159
5. EOG. p. 345
6. Gosp. p. 819
7. Gosp. 782
8. Gosp. 825
9. CW. Vol. 4. Lectures and Discourses. Thoughts on the Gita.
10. CW. Vol. 7. Inspired talks. Recorded by Miss SE Waldo, a disciple.
11. The Synthesis of Yoga. Sri Aurobindo. (Sri Aurobindo Ashram, Pondicherry) p. 47
12. CW. Vol. 2. Bakthi.
13. CW. Vol. 1. Karma Yoga. Chapter VII Freedom.
14. One Taste. Ken Wilber. (Shambala publications; 2000) p. 171
15. CW. Vol. 5. Notes from Lectures and Discourses. Law and Freedom.
16. CW. Vol. 3. Lectures from Colombo to Almora. Vedantism.
17. EOG. p. 191
18. EOG. p. 497
19. CW. Vol. 5. Questions and Ans-Wers.
20. EOG. p. 126
21. EOG. p. 547
    The line about 'Hands of God' is a paraphrasing of a quote from Rabbi Lawrence Kushner.

DYAANA

1. CW. Vol. 2. Jnaana Yoga. The Atman: its bondage and freedom
2. CW. Vol. 2. Jnaana Yoga. The Atman.
3. Gosp. p. 605
4. TWR. Talk. 406
5. CW. Vol. 1. Raja Yoga. Pratyahara and Dharana.
6. The Four Yogas. Swami Adiswarananda. (Advaita Ashrama; 2007)
7. www. kathamrita. org/kathamrita4/k4SectionVII. html
8. CW. Vol. 4. Lectures and Discourses. Meditation

9. CW. Vol. 1. Raja Yoga. The Control of psychic prana
10. CW. Vol. 1. Karma Yoga. Chapter VII Freedom.
11. Day by Day with Bhagavan. *Devaraja Mudaliar* (Sri Ramanasramam, Tiruvannamali.) 1-12-45
12. CW. Vol. 7. Conversations and Dialogues. XXXI
13. TWR. Talk. 371

BAKTHI

1. EOG. p. 474
2. Home with God. Neale Donald Walsch. (Atria books; 2007)

JNAANA

1. CW. Vol. 2. *Jnaana Yoga*. The Atman.
2. www. telegraph. co. uk › Science › Science News
3. As quoted in physics. info/space-time
4. The Holographic universe. Michael Talbot. (Harper Perennial; 2011) p. 51
5. What is life? Erwin Schrodinger. (Cambridge University Press; 1992) p. 129
6. Forty verses on Reality. Verse 20
7. Gosp. p. 476
8. CW. Vol. 7. Conversations and Dialogues. From the diary of a disciple. XV
9. SS. p. 1083
10. CW. Vol. 1. Lectures and Discourses. What is religion?
11. Mysticism and the mystical experience: East and West. Donald H. Bishop. (Susquehanna University Press; 1995) p. 36
12. Selected poems from the Divani Shamsi Tabriz. Reyno Nicholson, Reynold A. Nicholson. (Routledge; 1999) p. 125–7
13. CW. Vol. 2. Jnaana Yoga. The Atman.
14. Reflections on Talks with Sri Ramana Maharishi. S. S. Cohen. (Sri Ramanasramam, Tiruvannamali.) p. 55
15. EOG. p. 546
16. EOG. p. 354
17. CW. Vol. 2. Jnaana Yoga. The Atman: its bondage and freedom.

JNAANI

1. CW. Vol. 4. Addresses on Bhakti Yoga. The Teacher of Spirituality.
2. CW. Vol. 2. Jnaana Yoga. The real and apparent man.
3. From bhagavan-ramana. org/ramana_maharshi/books/letters/letter 099. Html

WORLD II

1. In his introduction to Bhagavad Gita – The Song of God. Swami Prabhavananda and Christopher Isherwood (Sigent classics; 2002)
2. Walden. Henry David Thoreau. (Arc Manor LLC; 2007) p. 279
3. EOG. p. 19
4. CW. Vol. 4. Lectures and Discourses. Thoughts on the Gita
5. As quoted in *World union* Vol. 21. p. 36
6. EOG. p. 519
7. EOG. p. 21
8. EOG . p. 52
9. EOG. p. 59
10. EOG. p. 67
11. From Rumi's poem: Ali in battle. From wikiquote. org/wiki/rumi
12. CW. Vol. 1. Addresses at the parliament of religions. Paper on Hinduism.

SURRENDER

1. EOG. p. 555–556
2. Borrowed from: The Book: On the taboo against knowing who you are; Alan Watts. (Vintage books; 1989)
3. From www.mkgandhi. org/momgandhi/chap01.htm
4. www.gita-society.com/section1/1_graceX8ofgita.htm
5. EOG. p. 294–295

APPENDIX

1. EOG. p. 514–523
2. 'Akkalapundi grant of Singaya-Nayaka: Saka-Samvat 1290' *Epigraphica Indica*, Vol. XIII. Sastri, K. Rama (Archaeological Survey of India. 1982). p. 259
3. EOG. p. 487

FURTHER READING

If you plan to start reading the Gita verse by verse, I would recommend starting with a simple, heartfelt commentary: the one by Swami Sithbavananda (Sri Ramakrishna Tabovan, Thiparaithurai) is my personal favourite, and is ideal for beginners.

Bhagavad Gita and its Message (Sri Aurobindo Ashram, Pondicherry) is another beautiful work which presents the Gita in a verse by verse manner along with notes compiled from Sri Aurobindo's elaborate work, *Essays on the Gita*. If you wish for a more in-depth study, I would full-heartedly recommend going for 'Essays on the Gita,' though his writing style can be a bit dense for starters.

Swami Ramsukdas's *Sadhak Sanjivani* (Gita press, Gorakhpur) is another elaborate devotion-filled explication of the Gita.

Swami Chinmayananda's book which presents many concepts of the Gita in a modern context too was useful for this preparation. (There are quite a few wonderful commentaries on the Gita. I am mentioning here only the ones that have helped me the most.)

If you would like to study Vedanta and its application to our daily life, go to Swami Vivekananda's writings. And also Sri Aurobindo's *Synthesis of Yoga*. Then there are many valuable books written by the monks of Sri Ramakrishna order, *The Four Yogas* by Swami Adiswarananda, my personal favourite. The topic-wise compilations of Sri Aurobindo's writings by Sri A S Dalal are handy and highly valuable for seekers.

The website www.swami-krishnananda.org has many fine articles and discourses on various Vedantic concepts by Swami Krishnananda, a disciple of Swami Sivananda. For knowing more on Advaita Vedanta, there are many works of the great saint-teacher Sri Adhi Shankara – his *Vivekachudamani*, being the prominent one.

And a few good books from the West for those who wish a general introduction to the subject of spirituality:

Seat of the Soul by Gary Zukav, *Conversations with God – Book 1* by Neale Donald Walsch, *A New Earth* by Eckhart Tolle, *No Boundary* by Ken Wilber and *The Book: On the Taboo Against Knowing Who You Are* by Alan watts (which is based on the teachings of Vedanta).

For people particularly interested in Sri Ramana's way, start with

Sadhu Om's beautiful explication of his philosophy, *The Path of Sri Ramana*, especially the first two volumes of it. Then the discourses of Nochur Sri Venkatraman. It is through them both, this writer got a grasp of the great sage's wisdom. Sri Nisargadatta Maharaj's *I am That* is another wonderful elucidation of Advaita that has helped many.

Further reading on Para-Bakthi: *Gospel of Sri Ramakrishna*, hands down. It is a work that paints a beautiful and inspiring picture of a man who lived in the supreme state of Para Bakthi in his daily life. You can feel such bakthi pulsate through every page in the book.

Further reading on symbolism in Hinduism:
- Many of Swami Sitbavananda's books – compilations of his questions and answers, especially (*Sri Ramakrishna Tabovan, Thiparaithurai*).
- *Symbolism in Hinduism* (Central Chinmaya Mission Trust; 2007)
- *The Symbolism of Hindu Gods and Rituals.* Swami Parthasarathy (Vedanta Life Institute; 2001)

Though many books have been mentioned, I should also add here that one should be careful to not get caught in the trap of intellectual knowledge while reading those spiritual books. When you read those, if any principle in any of the books strikes you as truth or resonates deeply within you, then that is the cue to close the book and go away! If you read for five minutes, remember to reflect for fifty-five minutes.

AUTHORISED WEBSITES

The chief works of the great Gurus of India based on which this book was written, you can find put up in the websites of the respective ashram. But for those, and the ease of accessibility it provided, I couldn't have put together this work. Let me take this opportunity to express my gratitude to all those ashrams for their generosity and for the service they are doing to humanity. Those sites for you:

www.ramakrishnavivekananda.info
www.sriaurobindoashram.org/ashram/sriauro/writings.php
www.sriramanamaharshi.org

Let me conclude this work with a heartfelt thanks to all the teachers of humanity who have, since time immemorial, guided people in leading their lives with the right perspective and wisdom. Along with the Gita, this book is a tribute to them all. So many Barath Sirs the world is blessed with. And has blessed us with.

ABOUT THE AUTHOR

S. Hari Haran is a 1977 born dermatologist practising in Coimbatore, and a sadhak belonging to Sri Ramananda Ashram, Palakad. A former editor-in-chief of his college magazine and an avid reader of books on spiritual wisdom, this is Hari's first book. He wrote it after a decade-long study of Vedantic teachings, with the intention of making the Gita's wisdom accessible and interesting to a general reader.

For comments and speaking engagements, the author can be contacted at hariharan.author@gmail.com.

Visit the FB page of the book for more details: facebook.com/bhagavadgitaandthebutterflies/

(Note: If you are a spiritually inclined person hailing from Tamil Nadu (preferably Coimbatore), with good fiction-writing skills, and you wish to collaborate with the author in his future works, you may send your resume to the above email address.)